I0612755

SHEM FLEENOR

SEVEN DAYS IN A
MAGIC CITY OF SIN

1848 Publishing Company

New York City

ISBN: 9781951231-07-1

TABLE OF CONTENTS

CHAPTER ONE

Monday, October 27, 1919

Orit Abrahams sat bundled in a gray wool overcoat over a modest purple dress made of cotton. Her black leather ankle high boots were tied tight. A red scarf was wrapped loosely around her neck. She woke suddenly as if startled and pushed her graying bangs from her weary but determined brown eyes, which took a quick inventory of the other seemingly morose commuters packed onto the subway car. Nothing, however, seemed too terribly amiss. "Fourteenth Street Union Square," a deep and muffled voice crackled from the newly installed intercom system overhead.

"Was I dreaming?" she wondered silently while scanning the horde of rush-hour commuters pushing their way from the car towards a packed and narrow staircase ascending towards the grey morning light above. One of the other passengers navigating his way off the car glowered at Orit. "Did I scream in my sleep?" she silently wondered, worried that she had perhaps spooked some of the other commuters on the car. She then took a deep and composed breath, straightened her overcoat and scarf and then tucked her leather briefcase tightly under her arm and finally forced herself from the car just before the double doors clanked shut behind her. She trudged down a darkened tunnel and then hurried up the staircase leading out onto Union Square, which was bathed in a gray mist.

An unseasonably cold wind ripped from west to east along Fourteenth Street. She tightened and then tucked her red scarf behind the top button of her overcoat in order to brave the gusty trek north across the square to the offices of *The New York Call*, the fledgling muckraking daily where she worked as an investigative reporter. She braced herself a moment with another deep breath while worriedly scanning a melee unfolding towards her right. Hundreds of women bundled in black hats, coats, and scarves had gathered in front of the George Washington war memorial near the center of the square. Many of the protesters held signs and placards with slogans scrawled in red and black bold print that read, "The War Would Have Been Lost Without Us: Justice Demands Women's Suffrage." Some of the women engaged in protest on Union Square that chilly and grey Autumn morning were bludgeoned black, blue and bloody by shiny and oaken batons wielded by some of New York City's most happily misogynist cops. Several of the women were also accosted by some dark-hearted vigilantes who used the protesters' own placards as weapons against them as the manhandled women were being dragged kicking and screaming by their hair, arms, legs, and scarves towards a long row of shiny midnight-blue police vans idling on the north side of Fourteenth Street. The police, of course, made no effort to apprehend the vigilantes who had assaulted the suffragettes.

Orit's fit and nimble body quickly bobbed, weaved, and waded through the carnage on the square, until finally arriving at *The New York Call* office, which was a very modest and nondescript brownstone. Orit hurried up the steps to the second-floor offices, fixed herself a quick, though sludgy, cup of black coffee, then sat dutifully at her tiny desk, which overlooked the riot unfolding on Union Square. Her morose eyes stared out the window a while with the cool studiousness of an anthropologist or sociologist studying a subject or cultural event. Her face, however, winced slightly upon taking her first cautious sip of hot and especially bitter coffee.

"Orit?" a deep yet somewhat effeminate voice sounded from an office down the hall. "I need to see you a moment please."

Orit managed to swallow the mouthful of acrid coffee while plucking her briefcase back up from the desk and making her way down the hallway.

Nicholas Rabinowitz, the managing editor of *The New York Call*, was nearly as diminutive as Orit. "Crazy, huh?" he asked dejectedly as he sat down in the modest wooden chair behind his modest wooden desk. "All this because some women want a human right that rightfully belongs to them."

"I guess President Wilson was mistaken when he said it was imperative that the Yanks join the allies to save democracy," Orit sighed snidely as she plopped down in the chair in front of his desk.

"They could have never sent all those boys that had been drafted over to France had it not been for the women doing their civic duty here," Nicholas lamented the hypocrisy. "It's such a travesty these women even have to demand the vote, never mind be brutalized because of it."

"Sometimes I feel like this city is giving me the cancer," Orit confided while slightly placing her cup of coffee at the edge of the desk.

"I know what you mean," Nicholas said while gently rubbing his sternum with the palm of his hand. "Fending off bankruptcy on a daily basis is giving me such an ulcer. I can't sleep any more, not ever." His weary eyes stared disconsolately at Orit.

"I need a vacation," Orit huffed.

"I'm glad you said that," the editor chuckled somewhat timidly while digging into the top drawer of his desk for a manila folder stuffed full of documents. "Perhaps you'll be a bit more receptive to your new assignment than I had imagined."

"New assignment?" she dreaded.

"Yeah," he retorted. "I need you to get down to Miami, Florida, as soon as you can." He slid a manila folder containing secondary research, a train ticket, and information about a hotel reservation across the top of his meticulously uncluttered desk.

"What in the hell is in Miami?" Orit wondered.

"Beaches, golf course, women in skimpy bathing suits," he grinned somewhat queasily.

"Okay," Orit replied as if pained, "what the hell is there for me to do in Miami then?"

"There is rampant corruption," his eyes grew wide, trying to get Orit excited at the prospects of an adventure, "and tons of it."

"Political corruption?" Orit asked, her interest was nearly piqued. She slid eagerly to the edge of her seat and leaned forward to inspect the ticket, reservations, and secondary research inside the envelope atop the desk.

"I'm quite sure there is," he admitted. "There have been some rumors of wild speculation in land deals down there. A former worker over at the Domino Sugar factory in Williamsburg went down there after buying land he saw advertised in *The New York Times*. Turns out, the land was three feet under marsh. When the fella went to the realtor who sold him the parcel in order to get his money back, he was told to suck a lemon. The fella refused to leave the firm that robbed him until they provided satisfaction, so the cops down there, who are apparently in cahoots with these crooked brokers and bookbinders, locked him up for three months and gave him a few savage beatings before turning him loose. The man is, as you can imagine, completely shattered. He lives on a bench in Tompkins

Square now. The poor bastard couldn't even get his job on the line at Domino back," Nicholas lamented. "He says some Irishman took it the second he left for Miami. His wife took their son and left him last month. They went back to Poland."

"What exactly am I expected to find in Miami?" Orit sighed, somewhat daunted. Then, sliding the ticket and itinerary off the top of the desk, she stood suddenly and, as if deep in thought, made her way back towards the narrow hallway leading towards her cramped and cluttered office. Nicholas followed her.

"I need you to get to the bottom of what's happening in the real estate market down there," he explained. "How deep does the corruption go? If there is widespread exploitation of workers who've been sold on the Miami Dream of living like a king and never having to work again only to be sold a bill of goods, it is our duty to expose that corruption and to inform and protect workers of the world, especially those who hail from our own backyard. If there is a relationship between corruption in the real estate market and local politics, we might also be able to sell enough copies to keep the paper afloat for another few months, at least."

"I see," Orit exhaled deeply. She then popped open her briefcase and shoved the envelope inside.

"Look," Nicholas, who could sense Orit's trepidation, said as soothingly as he could, "take the rest of the day off. Go home, pack your suitcase, and relax a bit. And Orit," he added as she made her way towards the staircase, "just a kindly word of caution; they do things a bit different down south, so be especially careful, mind your Ps and Qs."

"What?" she said sarcastically while plodding glumly down the steps with her briefcase tucked tight under her arm, "they don't love leftist women who speak Hebrew south of the Mason-Dixon? How's that too terribly different than up North?"

"Orit," the editor called out after the reporter. She paused, slightly rolled her eyes in annoyance, then turned back around and looked up at him. "Seriously," he cautioned, "be extra careful down there. As bad as things are up here, it is a different world down there." She slightly nodded, somewhat appreciative of his attentive concern, and then hurried down the steps towards the violent travesty unfolding on windswept Union Square.

Nearly a thousand miles south of Lower Manhattan, in a sleepy cow town called Brunswick, Georgia, the Homecoming Queen's dead body was found by peach pickers one dewy Monday morning in a secluded and otherwise beautiful grove. The seventeen-year-old victim, Kelly Lee, was dressed in her white Sunday school best, which was covered in dry crimson, almost black, blood that crackled when the coroner cut her clothes from her fast decaying body. She had been brutally strangled to death while being raped; her face had been bludgeoned into mush. Her *King James Bible* was found nearby.

Kelly's parents agonized while waiting for their daughter to come home for Sunday supper. Her favorite meal, spaghetti and meatballs, however had gone cold and untouched because she never arrived. By morning, her mother knew something was terribly wrong. She could sense it in her marrow. "Kelly would never think of missin' school," her momma said repeatedly throughout the wee hours of the morning and afternoon while pleading with Mr. Lee to call the law.

Brunswick was a tiny two-mule town just north of the Florida border. Word spread fast in those parts. The local Sheriff, Jim Bob Cooter, a lanky man older than sixty with thinning gray hair atop his sun spotted head, thus hoped that perhaps word of Kelly's brutal murder had already found its way to her parents' modest one-story and three bedroom home before he could get there so that he might dodge having to be the one to shatter the parents' already aching hearts. Cooter was, however, out of luck this hot and humid Monday morning.

It was nearly sunset by the time the Sheriff finally arrived at the Lee residence. Though the parents intuitively knew something heinous had happened to their daughter the moment they saw the Sheriff through the screen door of the porch, nothing could quite prepare them for the raw, blunt, and unvarnished blow of being told their only child had been killed in the most diabolical manner imaginable.

Cooter's nervous hands wrung his sweat stained cap as he took a deep breath in the hope of preparing himself to do a dreaded task he was never taught to do while at the police academy. His sun-spotted head hung like a scolded dog's as Mr. Lee pushed open the porch door.

"Why Sheriff Cooter," the reservedly worried Mr. Lee said through a thick South Georgian accent, "Any word yet on Kelly's whereabouts?"

"Where is she, Sheriff?" Mrs. Lee demanded while looking past the lawmen into the far-off distance.

"I'm afraid I got some awful news to tell ya about Kelly," Cooter's emotions were getting the best of him, as evidenced by the wavering anguish in his voice and quivering of his upper lip. "I'm so very sorry to be the one to tell y'all," his voice cracked, "but I'm gonna need y'all to come down to the morgue and identify Kelly's body."

"Identify?" the bewildered father asked. "What in God's name do you mean?"

"Ah hell," Cooter, who had five adult-aged daughters of his own, began to sob, "Kelly is with the Lord now. Y'all understand? You need to come downtown to identify her remains."

Mrs. Lee's legs quaked as her head swooned. Her knees dropped out from under her like a trap door and smashed atop the warm hardwood porch floor. She trembled hysterically. Mr. Lee, a normally stoic man of few words, cast a thousand-yard stare past the disconsolate Sheriff. A single bulbous tear slid down Mr. Lee's cheek and collected in a bit of sawdust on the porch.

"But," the disbelieving and shocked father said matter-of-factly, "Kelly just won Homecoming Queen last week. She can't be dead."

"She was such a beautiful girl," the anguished Sheriff's voice shook as he struggled mightily to force words of consolation from his aching soul.

"How'd she die, Sheriff?" Mrs. Lee's sorrowful sapphire eyes stared desperately up at the lawman.

"Some monster killed her," Cooter forced the words out.

"Who in the hell would do this to my little girl?" the sobbing mother demanded as Mr. Lee helped drag her up onto her feet and steady her in his reluctant but loving embrace.

"I'm afraid I haven't a clue," Cooter shamefacedly confessed. "God help me, I can't even begin to imagine the mad dog that could have committed such unholiness."

"You gonna find the man that killed Kelly, ain't cha Sheriff?" Mr. Lee pleaded.

"I sure as hell hope so," Cooter sobbed while slightly shrugging his shoulders. He, however, was woefully devoid of any confidence or optimism. "I just hope I can find the man that did this," he added, "before the Klan hangs every nigger or itinerant in the county."

CHAPTER TWO

Tuesday, October 28, 1919

Jasper Jackson, a light-skinned African American horn virtuoso, sat at the end of a wooden bench not too far from a steam engine that seemed to hum, hiss, and spit as it readied to haul hundreds of passengers down the east coast of the United States. Jasper, however, did not notice the train at all as he lovingly polished the bright brass trumpet, which seemed as much his appendage as his thumbs, held tenderly in his hands. "Now boarding," a muffled voice sounded over the intercom system, "Florida East Coast #7 to Miami, Florida."

The lean yet muscular twenty-year-old horn player sported a crisp black suit, houndstooth newsboy cap, and white surgical mask he hoped might protect him from the influenza outbreak. He gazed at his reflection in the brass a moment. His attention was then commandeered by the harrowing sight of Emory Ingram, a man with a straggly beard and unkempt hair who donned a green, sleek, clean, crisp and elegant American Expeditionary Force uniform that did not fit the sleeping paraplegic sloppily slumped forward in the wheelchair wearing it.

Emory woke suddenly as if frightened by some terribly unspeakable nightmare. He appeared confused to have woken near a steaming and screeching locomotive deep in the caverns of Penn Station and surrounded by a throng of passengers wearing white masks climbing aboard the train. Emory then looked down where his lower extremities once were. He seemed to have momentarily forgotten that they had been amputated. The heartrending spectacle tugged at the horn player's heartstrings.

Jasper gently placed, closed, and then locked his horn into its case. He then plucked a worn leather satchel up from atop the shiny marble floor and began to trudge towards the train. He passed Emory, who was still somewhat out of sorts. Dozens of passengers hurried past on their way onto the train, but none stopped to assist the clearly distressed and disheveled war veteran.

Jasper likewise thought better of disturbing the ailing vet and began to board the last car of the train. He, however, glanced back at Emory once more as he ascended the second step onto the car, and then intently watched the soldier a while. Jasper, his baggage still in hand, felt oddly compelled to hurry back off the train.

He quickly made his way back towards Emory, dropped his bags atop the cold and slick marble floor, and placed his hand gently on Emory's shoulder. "Hey there, soldier, this here train is fixin' to leave. You need to get on it?"

Emory's glazed and exhausted eyes stared confusedly up at Jasper, who flashed an awkward and pained grin. "Sorry to bother you," Jasper said softly, "I just didn't want you to miss your train. Is this your train, the FEC #7 to Miami?"

"Do I know you?" Emory's garbled words tumbled from his mouth.

"No sir," Jasper said politely while looking at the insignia on Emory's lapel, "but I was a Doughboy in France too, so you might say we'z brothers in arms, I reckon."

"Last call for FEC #7 to Miami; One stop in Charleston, South Carolina," the muffled voice blared through the intercom speakers overhead.

"Is your train the FEC #7 to Miami?" Jasper asked again.

"I'm going to Miami," Emory had trouble putting the words together into a coherent sentence. "My dad is in Miami. He's picking me up at the station."

"Well then," Jasper graciously asked, "can I give a soldier a hand gettin' onto the car?"

Emory stared shamefacedly down at his thighs a moment. He then gazed helplessly up at Jasper. "I suppose I probably could use a hand," he was loath to admit.

"Okay, no trouble at all, boss," Jasper smiled kindly. He then took a deep and composed breath and heaved Emory out of the wheelchair and up onto his shoulder. He struggled to hoist Emory's lanky torso up the three steps onto the train car, but finally managed to situate Emory in a nice window seat close to the front of the car. Some of the other passengers in the first-class car seemed awfully put out.

Jasper then hurried from the car in order to retrieve Emory's wheelchair and luggage, which he piled into the undercarriage. He then plucked his horn case and satchel up from the marble platform and hurried back onto the first-class car audaciously hoping he might be able to stay a while. He sat down one seat away from Emory and offered his hand, "Jasper Jackson," he said kindly while smiling charmingly.

"Emory Ingram," the ailing soldier said solemnly as his clammy hand reluctantly latched onto to Jasper's dry and calloused hand.

"Ingram?" Jasper queried. "You don't by chance know anyone who works at the Royal Palm Hotel in Miami, do ya?"

"My father, James Ingram, runs the place," Emory said matter-of-factly while wheezing a bit.

"Hot damn," Jasper said excitedly." Ain't this a small world. Your daddy hired me for a season-long residency at the hotel." He looked eagerly over at Emory, who was nauseous. "Say there, Emory, you alright? You look white as a ghost."

"I'm not feeling well at all," Emory admitted. "The bastards at the veteran's hospital got me hooked on morphine but didn't give me any when they discharged me. I think the orderlies, those crooked swine, keep it for themselves."

One of the train attendants, a pug-nosed Irishman with rosy cheeks in his late-fifties had been alerted by another passenger, a patrician white woman in her early sixties wearing a black bonnet, that Jasper was occupying a seat on a car in which he was by custom barred. The surly attendant waddled down the aisle towards Jasper, who noticed that the man reeked of rye whiskey. "Hey buddy," the attendant slurred. "This train is bound for the New South; Miami. The colored car is the last in the back. I suggest you either find your way to it or to a jail cell at the local precinct. Catch my drift?"

"I was just talkin' to this fellow Doughboy, a war hero," Jasper seethed. "He, like me, went to France to save democracy for the rest of y'all."

"You watch that tone, coon," the attendant sneered. "You just try and flip that lip down South. Just wait and see what happens."

"I'm from New Orleans," Jasper explained while stepping into the aisle, "ain't gotta tell me which way the wind blows down South." Jasper surreptitiously dug down deep into his satchel and soon produced a shaving kit, which he deftly handed to Emory. "Here," he said softly to the ailing war vet. "A taste of this'll fix you up right as rain until you get home. Just make sure you get it back to me when we stop in Charleston. I'll come fetch you then so you can get a whiff of fresh air and stretch your legs a bit." He smiled oddly, realizing he put his foot in his mouth. "You know what I mean," he shrugged embarrassedly.

Jasper then hurried down the aisle towards the exit of the car with the impatient attendant close behind. The patrician snitch appeared pleased that the black man with the temerity to momentarily occupy the same public space was headed to the back car, "where he belongs," she silently exalted as Jasper raced past her window towards the last car on the track.

Emory, meanwhile, eagerly, though cautiously, opened the shaving kit and peered inside to find at least an ounce of chalky brown heroin wrapped neatly in butcher's paper along with a few pipes covered in residue, a few unused syringes, and a stainless-steel butane lighter next to a silver spoon.

Jasper darted past Orit just as her longtime boyfriend, Moses, had dropped to a knee and presented her with a modest gold ring. Moses was a pale man with orange freckles all over his tense face. He had a glorious head full of wavy red hair with a royal-blue kippah pinned atop it. Tiny bifocals rested precariously at the tip of his nose, which was covered by a white mask meant to ward off influenza.

"We've been together since our second semester at City College," his voice betrayed the fact that he was unnerved. "I love you and would like it very much if you were to give me children, especially a son."

"All aboard!" The pug-nosed attendant who had been so rude to Jasper hollered as the hissing train began to ease away from the station.

"I'm sorry, Moses," Orit said softly while gently caressing a stray stand of hair atop his head. "I do love you. But I can't marry you."

"Well," he said dejectedly while climbing to his feet and gazing deeply into her sympathetic brown eyes, "why in the world not?"

"I do love you very much," she confessed. "Please believe me when I say that. You are the kindest and sweetest man I have ever met, and the very best friend I could ever ask for, but I just don't love you like that and you don't love me like that either."

"What in the world do you mean?" he bewilderedly demanded. "How can you know how I do or do not love you?" His beady eyes welled with tears.

"I'm sorry," she said while gently kissing and caressing the side of his white surgical mask, which covered his cheek. "I do love you very much and hope you can find a way to understand that my refusal of your proposal comes from a place of love and care for you. You deserve so much better than me."

She then raced after the train and summoned all the power in her slight but toned frame to climb up and onto the bottom step of the colored car, as it were. She plopped down in a window seat near the front of the car and cast a long, loving, and apologetic gaze at Moses as she waved goodbye. Moses's felt his heart cave into anguished despair as the train sunk into the black abyss under New York City.

CHAPTER THREE

Friday, December 31, 1895, Lower Manhattan

The cold wet hooves of Clydesdales lugging tuxedoed pipe and cigar smokers who were bundled in black wool coats and sheltered in covered, but by no means warm, chauffeured carriages clanked hollow atop the slick and salty cobblestone before halting in front of the large plate-glass glass outside of Delmonico's butchery and restaurant on Beaver Street. The newly canyons of commerce and capitalism of Wall Street seemed to glower over the high-end eatery.

The New Year's Eve gathering, which was hosted by the New England Society of New York, was attended by some of Gilded Age America's most revered and moneyed men, including Henry Flagler, the man who within a year would be known as the "Father of Miami." Flagler was a renowned taskmaster at Standard Oil, the world's biggest and most powerful corporation at a moment in the nation's history when Thomas Nast and other cartoonists commonly lampooned J.D. Rockefeller and Andrew Carnegie. Rockefeller, who was also in attendance, was the country's largest creditor and was thus oft depicted to be the emperor of the United States. Even William Tecumseh Sherman had ventured out to Delmonico's that cold and dreary night to hear a yarn spun by Henry Grady, an infamous and somewhat disreputable yawp from Atlanta, Georgia. Grady jibed that Sherman, the Union General who had burned the booster's beloved hometown to the ground during the Northern Army's destructive march to the sea in 1864, was "a careless man about fire," which stoked the laugher of all in attendance, save Sherman, who was the architect of the total war strategy that ultimately laid waste to Atlanta.

But the part of Grady's boisterous boosterism that particularly caught the attention of the moneyed men in attendance at the gathering on the final night of 1895 was his assertion that, "The New South's soul" had been "stirred with the breath of a new life," and that "the light of a grander day" was "falling fair on her face." Grady then declared that the South was "thrilling with the consciousness of growing power and prosperity."

Flagler, like so many of the other well-to-do white men in attendance at Delmonico's that dreary final night of 1895, was already heavily invested in industrializing and modernizing the Deep South. Flagler, for example, had built a string of coastal resorts along his railroad, which stretched through the Carolinas, South Georgia, and into the section of Florida southeast of Lake Okeechobee as far south as Palm Beach.

Wherever Flagler's railroad and resorts were built, business and commerce – general stores, post offices and newspapers selling ads for this or that plot of land along the rail-line – altogether fostered the rise of real estate markets and urbanity all through the American South during the Gilded Age and Progressive Era in American history. Flagler was, in short, as these men often referred to themselves in tripe memoirs, a master of the universe.

But South Florida remained unexploited and thus a kind of golden apple these men were eager to bite into, if only they could figure out how to do so without losing money in the process. South Florida was an especially difficult well to tap. In 1889, for example, a newspaper editor in Cleveland, Ohio, described South Florida as "a region mysterious, unknown, beautiful — a terra incognita — of which as little is known as the center of the Dark Continent." A year later, adventurer James Davidson published his "Guide for Florida Tourists and Settlers," in which he likewise described South Florida as a place where "there can be nothing but insects, vermin, mud, malaria, Indians, desolation, abomination, discomfort, disease, black death and poverty where nothing will grow but comptie and mangroves, and where nobody lives anyway." That same year, the Unites States census recorded fewer than 400,000 residents in all of Florida and no more than 2,400 on the peninsula south of Lake Okeechobee. As late as 1895 – just a year prior to Miami's incorporation – a tourist guide described Dade County as a "wild and uninhabitable district, in the main inaccessible to the ordinary tourist and unopened to the average settler."

Part of South Florida's incessant depiction in the popular press as an ignominious site for investors to lose money was its history of being impenetrable to even the Union Army, which had given up on trying to track the renegade American Indians who had fled deep into the dark hearted swamps of South Florida during the 1830s and 1840s in order to escape Andrew Jackson's genocidal Indian removal policies, most notably the forced march of Native Americans from the Deep South to the godforsaken and desolate Oklahoma territory, which may have well been the dark side of the moon.

After Grady's longwinded speech had finally subsided, the tuxedoed men in attendance massaged cigars with their chapped lips and the tips of their tongues as they sipped bottles of brandy older than the empire itself. Many of these tipsy and money-drunk men also gladly regaled each other with prideful stories about their capitalist ventures south of the Mason-Dixon Line, including Cuba and parts even further south, namely Panama.

Grady, who was a former newspaperman at *The Atlanta Constitution*, introduced Flagler to his young protégé, Everett Sewell – a dashing and ambitious Harvard graduate and advertising pioneer who originally hailed from Savannah, Georgia. Sewell's groundbreaking use of fear and desire in advertising and propaganda was greatly exploited by Grady, who used the principles pioneered by Sewell to sell the New South to

Brahmin of American business such as Flagler, Carnegie, Rockefeller and Cornelius Vanderbilt. Sewell's cutting-edge techniques were later exploited to even greater effect by the likes of Sigmund Freud's enterprising young nephew, Edward Bernays, who was often erroneously credited in the twentieth century for inventing the idea that "sex sells," although Sewell and many others on both sides of the Atlantic had taken to exploiting that particular tactic to sell consumers on the idea of visiting cities as heavily industrialized as Birmingham, Alabama and Johannesburg, South Africa while Bernays was still wearing short pants and fiddling with his dick while in Vienna.

"Rumor has it that you might be considering extending the Florida East Coast Railway south of Palm Beach," Sewell eagerly and hopefully asked the ever-magisterial Flagler, whose cotton-white hair and handlebar moustache made him appear to be ten years older than he actually was, especially in contrast to the clean shaven and baby-faced Sewell, who had a head full of slick black hair combed back atop his head.

"I'm not quite so sure how accurate your information is, m'boy," Flagler grinned coyly but politely as he exhaled a deep and soothing lungful of Cuban red tobacco smoke towards the oaken rafters overhead, "business at the Royal Poinciana Resort in West Palm Beach is booming, as are real estate values surrounding the new golf course that has only recently been completed. I see no great reason to build south of it just now."

"But what of all that land in the Everglades?" Sewell eagerly asked. "I spoke recently to a scientist – a Progressive, in fact, – E.O. Wilson. He seems certain that once the swamps are drained that the soil will be the most fertile the world has ever known – black gold."

"I am familiar with Dr. Wilson's report," Flagler huffed somewhat gruffly, as if he were hoping the report would remain a trade secret. "But you see, Mr. Sewell," Flagler explained while setting his hand gently on the young man's shoulder, "the problem with modernizing South Florida is that it has no deep-water port, so one – in this case me – would be tasked with building a port before a single steamship could ever actually bring building supplies, patrons, and the like to the region. Either that, or I extend the railroad, which presents incredible problems of its own. Some of the land south of Okeechobee has been surveyed and graded by one of my best men, Mr. Ingram, but the deeper south surveyors go, the denser the swamps and jungles become, which makes extending the FEC line exceedingly difficult and expensive. As of now, the cost of extending the line outweighs the benefit. But I'd be very glad to ride the coattails of some other venture capitalist daring enough to make the effort."

"I see," Sewell said in flat and monotone voice, as though his hopes for getting rich quick had been dashed by Flagler's quashing of the rumor. "It is a terrible shame, to be sure," Sewell lamented. "South Florida is the last frontier we enterprising Protestant white men have left to conquer in the New World. Conquering such a terra incognita seems as though it is nothing short of our American destiny. From all I've been fortunate enough to read about you in the newspapers of late," Sewell pandered, "you seem like just the man with the right amount of grit, determination and vision to make the dream of modernizing America's last frontier into one of the most marvelous real estate ventures the world has ever known."

"If settling South Florida proves to be the will of God almighty," Flagler grinned as he plugged his cigar into his mouth as he set his other arm gently around Sewell's broad shoulders while steering the young man towards the bar at the back of the smoke-filled, dank and musty restaurant, "then nothing, not even the greatest evil imaginable, can prevent it from occurring."

"When that blessed day does finally occur, sir," Sewell brimmed with optimism, "I hope to write the words and create the images that seduce leisure seekers and investors to what I'm sure will be a glorious venture and endeavor."

"That's a fine vision, m'boy," Flagler grinned as he guided Sewell through the horde of tuxedoed white men huddled together under a dense cloud of cigar and pipe smoke as they boisterously regaled each other with anecdotes and tales of what many referred to as "civilizational conquest," rather than using the more common euphemism of imperialism. "But tonight is New Year's Eve, Mr. Sewell," Flagler hollered above the din of the horde huddled around the bar at the back of the restaurant, "so don't fret over what may or may not be; leave the big picture in the purview of the almighty for a while, if only for the night."

Sewell forced a cordial, but toothless and somewhat dejected grin as he compliantly nodded his head.

CHAPTER FOUR

Saturday, January 1, 1896, Midtown Manhattan

A hollow and resonant bell reverberated throughout Henry Flagler's luxurious townhouse on Park Avenue. A young woman with skin as pale as sour cream and a head full of wavy red hair wearing nothing but a skimpy purple silk negligee and gray wool knickers hiked up to her knees lounged atop a velvet chaise in the corner of Mr. Flagler's massive and oak trimmed office. Her eyes, which were as green as bluegrass, gazed drowsily at an advertisement in the January edition of *Scribner's Magazine* depicting an aborigine in some far-flung tropical frontier merrily using a Singer sewing machine. Dolly's pouting mouth was wrapped tightly around the white stick of the cherry Dum Dum lollypop resting gently atop her pink tongue. She then carefully turned the page and gazed longingly at a finely crafted drawing of men and women of Henry Flagler's ilk engaged in idle luxury in Newport, Rhode Island, which Flagler had made into a popular vacation destination for his friends and neighbors who lived along Park Avenue and around Central Park to gladly escape to during the summers, when the heat, humidity, and lower classes out drinking and carousing at the wee hours of the night became just a bit too much for the Brahmin to bear.

Though the stately beauty on the chaise could hear Mr. Flagler incessantly ringing a golden bell as well the somewhat muffled dispute raging behind the closed door made of Ghanaian mahogany in the room adjacent to the one she occupied, she paid the dinging and odd conflict little mind, as she calmly set the magazine down on the end table next to the Tiffany lamp. She then serenely glided over to the frost-covered window and gazed at the tightly bundled pedestrians and carriage drivers navigating Park Avenue as the snow grew thicker and fluffier. She huffed a bit of hot breath on the glass and wrote "Dolly and Hanky Poo 4-Ever" in the condensation on the window. She finished her message by drawing a heart around the words. She stepped away from the window and smiled brightly, very pleased with her craftsmanship.

Down the hall from where Dolly was comfy and cloistered, Henry Flagler's wife, Mary, savagely quarreled with her husband, who was wearing the same finely tailored three-piece tuxedo as the one he had the prior evening at Delmonico's, albeit a bit more mussed. He was somewhat tired, disheveled, and frightened and thus a modest shell of the swaggering master of the universe he had appeared to be while conversing with Mr. Sewell the previous night. Flagler's bewildered shrinking this New Year's morning was also in stark contrast to his wife's rage.

Mary was in her late forties, which made her twice the age of Dolly, Flagler's mistress down the hall. Although Mary was still a decade younger than her husband, she, due to a long bout with mental illness that she developed only gradually after marrying the tycoon, seemed four times the age of the serene beauty empty-headedly gazing out at the snow falling on Park Avenue.

Mary seethed while demanding a divorce from her increasingly cold and distant husband because, as she explained, the King of Prussia had fallen madly in love with her. She insisted that Sigismund of Prussia and she had, in Flagler's absence, become soul mates. Mary further explained to her frustrated and frightened husband that Sigismund had promised to either make her the empress or disavow his throne to be with her.

Mr. Flagler was far more adept at quelling labor dissidence (thanks to hired goons such as the Pinkertons) than he was quelling his wife's angst. But he tried in vain to reason with Mary by saying, "Now alright dear, you've only ever met

Sigismund once, and that was more than three years ago at the Astor's gala."

Mary then shrieked wildly, which caused Dolly and some of the domestic workers plying their trade throughout the house to pause and ponder, "What is the matter?" Mary then raced over to the fireplace, which was roaring, and smashed the antiques and picture frames atop the mantle, taking special umbrage with the wedding portrait of she and Flagler, which she stomped on. Blood seeped through her house slipper due to deep cuts on her foot that she did not seem to feel. She then saw Sigismund's finely goateed face raging in the blaze and began to scurry on her hands and knees towards his magisterial scowl roiling in the fire.

Flagler dropped the bell he had been ringing in a desperate attempt to summon Mrs. Flagler's nurse. He managed to drag his wife away from the fire and pinned her atop a rug made from the hide of giant polar bear. "There now, Mary," Flagler urged his momentarily exhausted and panting wife. Beads of her sweat and sobbing tears soaked into his tuxedo. "All is well, just please calm down and take a breath until your nurse arrives," he huffed and pleaded.

"I don't need any god damned nurse, you stumbling want wit!" Mary insisted as she tearfully glared into the flickering flames, where she again detected the Nicholas's visage scowling back at her, beckoning her. "There he is! Can't you see? Now and forever more I can be with him," she squealed as she fought with all her might to free herself from her husband's tenuous grasp. She finally dug her nails deep into his neck and bit his arm as hard as she could. She then wriggled free from his grip, raced across the room, and dove face first into the burning logs, scalding stone, and flitting flames.

Flagler managed to drag his wife from the fireplace by her ankles. He was frantic while dousing her head and shoulders in his plush velvet burgundy-colored smoking jacket, which was hanging in the closet. He cradled and rocked her in his arms for a moment before Mrs. Flagler's portly, short, disheveled and sleep-deprived British nurse, followed by the statuesque and handsome James Ingram, Flagler's personal assistant and fixer, rushed in to aid their employer and his wife through her horrifying and debilitating ordeal.

Ingram and the nurse helped Mrs. Flagler, who was trembling as if hypothermic, into the wheelchair the twenty-something nurse, Alice, had lugged up from the basement, which was parked next to the egress of the third-floor drawing room. The overworked nurse exhaled a deep and anguished sigh as she escorted Mrs. Flagler into the long hallway towards the elevator. "There now, dear," the nurse whispered into Mary's scorched and blistered ear, "everything's going to be just fine in no time. I've got a fix of morphine and laudanum in my quarters."

"What in God's name took you so long, Alice?" Flagler aimed his ire at the nurse. "I rang the bell for nearly five minutes. My favorite smoking jacket has been ruined, which is coming out of your pay."

"I'm very sorry, sir," Alice said. "The misses gave me New Year's evening and morning off to spend with my sister. I'm afraid I was late to respond because I had yet to wake."

"Please Alice," Mary sternly corrected the nurse, "do refrain from referring to me as 'the misses.'"

"As you wish, your majesty," Alice blurted as she hurried Mrs. Flagler down the long and dimly lit hallway and then onto the rickety wooden elevator.

Mr. Flagler sighed, deeply anguished as the elevator doors slid shut. He lumbered into the drawing room and flipped open an eleven-by-eight-inch pine box resting atop the end table near the bay window overlooking the garden. He then plucked a cigar from the box and, wedging it into his somewhat chapped lips, gazed disconsolately at the snow falling outside the window. "We've done all we can for the woman," he professed to Mr. Ingram while lighting his cigar with a long wooden matchstick.

"Indeed, you have, sir," Mr. Ingram, the thirty-nine-year-old tower of a man said in a thick Welsh accent.

Ingram first immigrated to the United States when he was nineteen years old, not long after his mother had succumbed to tuberculosis. He never knew his father, who had abandoned the family before Ingram was born. Though Ingram first landed in Boston in 1876, during the nation's centennial, he discovered little opportunity for employment or social advancement in the city on the hill, so he rode the rails west as far as Cleveland, where he was robbed by a gang of young Irish toughs and unceremoniously separated from what little money he had. His assailants were, however, illiterate, so they permitted the young lad to keep possession of a tattered edition of *Risen from the Ranks* written by Horatio Alger that had been gifted to him by his priest not long before he left Cardiff for America. The book ended up profoundly shaping Ingram's view of himself and the rapidly industrializing world he inhabited.

Despite the early setback, Cleveland proved to be fortuitous for young James, an enterprising young lad full of graft and ambition. Within a week of arriving along the shores of the Cuyahoga River, he had lucked into a job laying tracks for the Baltimore and Ohio railroad, which was a subsidiary of Standard Oil, a corporation in which Flagler had already distinguished himself as a brilliant and ruthless negotiator and taskmaster. Within a decade, Ingram had also proved himself to be indispensable to the B&O's shareholders, which helped pave his path into middle-management at Standard Oil, then eventually as Flagler's right-hand man in New York. Though Flagler was not too terribly warm or inviting to any of the men in his employ, Ingram had always thirsted for a father figure, and Flagler's aloofness quenched the younger man's pangs in odd ways that not even he could explain. Flagler intuitively sensed this power over Ingram and took advantage of it whenever it served his immediate interests, often with dire consequences.

"Though it pains me beyond the effable," Flagler said as he exited the drawing room, "it is perhaps in Mary's best interest to have her committed to that institution in Ithaca at long last."

"From the research her physician performed," Mr. Ingram said timidly as he followed Flagler out of the room, "the sanitorium seems very therapeutic. It's certainly much nicer than most of the other asylums she could be sent to in the city. Perhaps they could even fix her once and for all up in Ithaca."

"I'm quite afraid my wife is beyond repair," Flagler sighed as he swung the door to his office open. "Hell, you saw how mad she is."

Flagler and Ingram's sudden entrance into the office startled Dolly a bit, who tried to palliate the awkwardness with a timid and slightly deferential giggle. Neither Ingram nor Flagler, however, paid her any mind. "Is everything alright," her mousy and soft voice softly squeaked as she rubbed her dainty hands together to warm them by the fireplace.

"It is certainly nothing for you to be concerned with, mi amor," Flagler not-so-suavely assured his mistress as he gently patted her pert fanny and kissed the nape of her soft and sweetly scented neck.

Ingram, who was both a teetotaler and unwaveringly faithful to his wife, tried to act nonchalant but was clearly made uneasy by his employer's unveiled affection towards his mistress just moments after deciding to institutionalize his wife. Dolly, who would not have been bothered by Ingram's uneasiness even if she had noticed, seemed unfazed by any of the morning's turmoil as she plopped back down atop the chaise and resumed flipping through *Scribner's*.

Flagler, meanwhile, exhaled a lungful of bluish tobacco smoke as he hunkered down in a large leather chair behind a massive, hand-carved desk forged from a California Redwood. He then excitedly shoved the morning edition of *The New York Times* across the top of the finely polished desk. He jabbed his index finger at a headline that read, "Massive Cold Snap Devastates Florida's Farms."

Ingram's intense eyes soaked in the headline. He then looked hard at Flagler, who was grinning gleefully up at his subordinate. Flagler excitedly produced a map of Florida from the top-right drawer of his desk and splayed it open next to the newspaper. He explained to Ingram that, "tens of millions of dollars' worth of crops have been rendered worthless due to the deep freeze the last three nights of 1895." He then dragged his finely manicured index finger from a nondescript dot on the map labeled "Melbourne" down to a dot that read "Fort Dallas," which was at the southeastern most end of the peninsula. "Everything north of Melbourne was destroyed," Flagler beamed. "Isn't it wonderful?"

"I'm sorry if I seem somewhat confused, sir," Ingram loathed to admit. "But aren't all of those farmers who depend on those crops going to be ruined?"

Flagler slightly rolled his eyes, annoyed as he scowled up at Ingram. "Perhaps in the short run of things," he grunted,

"But you have to look at the big picture in times of crisis," Flagler pejoratively educated his underling on the tenets of disaster capitalism. "The farmers will take a hit, to be sure," Flagler admitted, "but in the long run, our intervention will open untold avenues of success and social advancement for the farmers throttled by the freeze and millions of others. You understand, James?" Ingram slightly nodded his head and exhale a calming breath while resisting the urge to offer his employer a moral lesson. Flagler then guided his hand didactically over the map atop the desk. "West Palm, thank God," he said, "survived the freeze. That will cause the property values around the FEC lines south of Melbourne, especially our hotels and land ventures, to double overnight. And, you see James," Flagler had difficulty concealing his enthusiasm, "this seems to be a glorious and ordained sign that it is finally time to extend the FEC line as far south as we can. This deep freeze means the iron is very hot indeed. Call it serendipity, but I spoke to a very enterprising advertising expert from Atlanta just last night who is very keen on us extending the line south of Palm Beach," he dragged his finger south on the map a tad, "all the way here, to Fort Dallas," he added. "This lad seemed quite certain that the real money to be had was all the way south and east. And, considering that none of this land froze, I'd say this young ad man might be onto something after all."

"I don't disagree entirely with you, sir," Mr. Ingram attempted to play Devil's advocate, "it's just that..."

"Just what, god damn it?" Flagler cut his underling off as he banged his fist atop the map, which startled Dolly and Ingram a bit.

"It's just, you see, sir," Mr. Ingram proceeded with extreme caution, "as you know, the shallow waters surrounding the bottom half of the peninsula create some very expensive challenges for us to overcome in order to make the region into a center of quick and easy profit. It could be decades before we got our money back out of the venture, if ever."

"To hell with money," Flagler blurted. Mr. Ingram momentarily wondered if his employer had gone quite mad and might also need to be institutionalized along with Mary. "I'll always have more money than I can spend," Mr. Flagler qualified. "Besides, making a deep-water port is a small price to pay for opening such fertile soil for those poor and unfortunate yeomen who lost their farms in the freeze, never mind civilizing a region that has for so long been considered impenetrable and uninhabitable to all but a few breach-clothed savages. Just think of all those wiped out farmers desperate to buy land south of the freeze zone. When it is all said and done, James," Flagler gazed proudly out the bay window at the snow falling over Park Avenue, "civilizing South Florida will be my greatest achievement, legacy, and gift to humanity."

Flagler then excitedly revealed another map from the middle drawer of his desk and spread it open for Ingram to peruse. "Here is where the line is to end, Flagler said as he poked his index finger into a large body of water labeled "Biscayne Bay." He grinned at Ingram as he dragged his finger around the edge of the bay. "We will turn this area into the greatest resort town the world has ever known and make it a playground for the world's aristocracy," he enthused. "This will be some of the most prized real estate in the entire world, equal in value to Park Avenue." Mr. Ingram again wondered if Mr. Flagler had gone mad. "The hinterlands," Flagler continued, "can be sold off to farmers. Once the Everglades are drained, the soil will be the richest in the world. But the city will be a haven for the world's aristocracy."

"It is certainly a marvelous vision of the future, sir," Ingram conceded somewhat timidly, "but…"

"But what?" Flagler's gleeful grin transformed suddenly into pained frustration. Dolly's emerald eyes glanced up from the magazine and settled on Flagler.

"You see, sir," Ingram continued, "we inquired about the property adjacent to Fort Dallas last year; it is owned by the Tuttle clan of Cleveland. The boy is prone to illness, so the family spends the winters on the bay. They've owned that land for quite a few years now and don't seem to harbor any interest at all in selling it."

"Well," Flagler sneered determinedly, "I suppose you're going to have to do a better job of convincing the Tuttle clan that selling is not only in their best interest, but in the best interest of civilizational progress. Besides," Flagler added, "my man in Cleveland, Mr. Madison, has informed me just this morning that Mr. Tuttle has fallen quite ill indeed this winter, and the family has decided to weather the winter in Cleveland, rather than risk the arduous trip by rail to Palm Beach, and schooner the rest of the route to Biscayne Bay with the father Tuttle in such a precarious state of ailment. That said, considering Mr. Tuttle's failing health, I can't help but wonder if he might not be more motivated than he has been in times past to relinquish the property, if the price were to his liking, of course. Always remember, James," Mr. Flagler offered a somewhat condescending lesson in business ethics, "where there is crisis there is opportunity."

"I agree, sir," Mr. Ingram masked his frustration, "but do you have any specific ideas on how I might proceed to accomplish the task of prying the land from the family?" Ingram asked.

"Come now, James," Flagler said arrogantly as he squinted and exhaled a plume of tobacco smoke. I pay you the ungodly salary I do to figure out those details. Now, I need you on the next train to Cleveland. Get the deed to Tuttle's land on Biscayne Bay back on my desk as quick as you can. We need to strike while the iron is hot," he explained. "Plus, once word gets out that South Florida survived the freeze, there's going to be a run on the land. We need to get as much of it as quick as we can, if you catch my drift."

"But sir," Mr. Ingram's nervous eyes darted towards the wooden floor and priceless Egyptian rug under foot, "Sigrid has not been feeling very well and she has been especially fearful of having another miscarriage. She'll be hopping mad if I leave for Cleveland while she is feeling so poorly."

"Mr. Ingram!" Flagler snapped. "You know damn well I have a very strict policy about permitting your home life to interfere with your duties for me and the company. Now, if you feel you are incapable of completing this very modest task that I have asked of you, I'm sure I can find another man who will gladly comply without this infernal hullabaloo about his wife's wants, fears, desires, and the like. Your wife, in short, is not my business or concern, Mr. Ingram."

Flagler then glanced past Ingram over at Dolly, who was giggling a bit at her lover's haranguing of his underling while taking off one of her wool socks. Her foot was clammy.

"You're right, sir," Ingram's weary eyes stared at the maps atop Flagler's desk. "Please forget I mentioned it," he said while turning on the heel of his cold and wet wingtip. "I will be back from Cleveland as quick as can be. You can count on me, sir."

Dolly then wiggled her toes, smiled seductively, and winked at Flagler. "Good man," Flagler eagerly said to Ingram while standing up from the leather chair parked behind his desk. "I know you will come through, as you always do," Flagler said as he draped his arm around Mr. Ingram's shoulders and led him towards the exit of the office. "Stop by my secretary on your way to Penn Station. She will furnish you will all the pertinent details and travel arrangements. Now," Flagler concluded while ushering his underling into the dimly lit hall leading towards the elevator and staircase, "if you'll excuse us, I have some other urgent matters to tend to. Oh, and James," Flagler added, "do give my best to Ingrid when you get back."

"Yes sir," Ingram resisted the urge to tell his employer that his wife's name was Sigrid.

Flagler swung the door shut while eagerly loosening his tie. Ingram stood in the hallway with the palm of his hand pressed against the wall while his eyes adjusted to the darkness of the hallway.

CHAPTER FIVE

Sunday, January 2, 1896, Cleveland, Ohio

By nightfall next, Mr. Ingram was in Cleveland, which was plagued by lake-effect snow and terrible industrial pollution that made the city reek of wet tar and burnt compost all winter long. He dutifully met with Flagler's top man in Cleveland, Mr. Madison, at the train station, a magnificent neoclassical building comparable to Penn Station. Madison was an odd and portly fellow with a crooked nose that had made looking at him difficult ever since the time he was kicked in the face by an alpaca on an otherwise successful gold venture in the Yucatan when he was a young man.

Madison escorted Mr. Ingram, who was wearing the same musty set of clothes he had the previous day during his meeting with Mr. Flagler, via streetcar from Brookpark Station to the Tuttle's grounds, a stately and gorgeous Victorian mansion and garden located in the suburb of Medina, which was right around the corner from William McKinley's family home, which was an even greater treasure than the Tuttle's.

Ingram was more aggrieved than usual. For one, he was unable to sleep on the train, which reeked of coal and sundry other fumes. Secondly, not only had Flagler sent him to pry land away from a man who had never showed any interest in relinquishing it, but he had arrived just two days after Mr. Tuttle had succumbed to pneumonia and died. Ingram, thus, especially rued intruding into a wake attended by mourning family, friends, and esteemed business associates. He felt as though Mr. Flagler had insisted on him going in such haste in order to not merely impose, but to prey on Mrs. Tuttle in her time of travail. Ingram, however, detested the idea of the haranguing and possible dismissal from duty he might receive from Mr. Flagler if he dared to return to Manhattan without acquiring the parcels of land his employer had demanded.

Ingram waited somewhat impatiently at the back edge of the dimly lit parlor where Mr. Tuttle's body could be viewed as the mourners gradually filtered out of the wake and into the driving snowstorm. He finally approached Mrs. Tuttle whilst she was on her knees at the edge of the casket praying. "Excuse me, Mrs. Tuttle," Ingram softly interjected as he approached the rapidly ageing woman who was only in her late-50s, but looked much older. She was dressed in all black Victorian garb, including veil and bustle. Her weary and beady eyes stared somewhat morosely into her husband's open casket, as if she did not immediately notice that Mr. Ingram had addressed her.

Mr. Tuttle's pink and bloated appearance looked as though hard plastic had been powdered with flour. Judging from the slight and very fleeting tremor in Mr. Ingram's face, Mr. Tuttle's macabre appearance made the former a tad queasy. Tuttle's rather homely twenty-eight-year-old daughter, Margaret, and her impish twenty-four-year-old brother, Charlie, who was perpetually sickly and disheveled, politely nodded at Ingram before silently excusing themselves from the parlor.

Ingram's head was aching due to immense stress and lack of sleep. But as tied in knots as he was by Flagler's demand to wrench away Mrs. Tuttle's land during her husband's funeral services, he was even more aggrieved that he did not have time to go home to inform his wife that the ticket purchased by Mr. Flagler's secretary did not provide Mr. Ingram time to go home for a change of clothes, bath, and chance to break the news to his extremely pregnant wife that he was being sent away at Mr. Flagler's behest once more. Though he perhaps wisely sent a telegram from Penn Station, he knew a justifiable reckoning awaited him upon arrival back at their very modest flat on Spring Street.

Ingram rubbed his throbbing forehead ever so gently as he occupied the empty seat to the left of Mrs. Tuttle, who stared at her husband's casket for an extended period of time. She finally looked upon Mr. Ingram with very heavy and somber eyes, as if dazed or half-drunk on sorrow. "My name is James Ingram," he said as pleasantly as he could with a headache that made the room seem to jitter and gyrate. "I work for Mr. Flagler in New York City and his Florida East Coast Railway."

"Ah," Mrs. Tuttle said flatly, "I know exactly who you are. You and that carpetbagger, Mr. Flagler, have been buying up the entire New South of late, it seems."

"Yes ma'am," Ingram chortled while smiling somewhat wryly. "I really am terribly sorry for the awful timing of this visit, what with Mr. Tuttle having passed along so recently. But Mr. Flagler is, as you may have already been apprised, a terribly impatient and insistent man and, you see, he is wholly determined to make you a very rich woman, richer even than Mr. Tuttle, God rest his soul, ever dared dreamed of being."

"Oh," Mrs. Tuttle chortled, wholly unimpressed, "and how exactly does the benevolent Mr. Flagler intend to do that?"

"As is," Ingram's mood changed suddenly from kindly and sympathetic to focused and determined on closing the deal and getting home to his pregnant wife as quickly as possible, "your land on Biscayne Bay, stunning and remote as it may be, is essentially worthless without the railroad connecting the bay to markets along the East Coast, such as Jacksonville, Savannah, Charleston, and parts north."

"It's quite all right by me if the bay is wholly sequestered from your so called 'markets,'" Mrs. Tuttle defied. "If the railroad were to connect Biscayne with the rest of the world, it would surely only be a matter of time before the area was as rife with pollution, whorehouses, crime of every stripe, foreigners, and Negroes, just like any other godforsaken city north or south of the Mason-Dixon line." Her anger spiked suddenly as she added, "You, Mr. Flagler, and that godforsaken machine that spews coal dust and steam will despoil one of God almighty's last bastions on earth over my dead body. Tell Mr. Flagler to keep his contraption away from that blessed bay. There will be nothing worth visiting if you bring that infernal machine to what is presently a bastion." She smirked and stared deep into Mr. Ingram's weary and bloodshot eyes. She delighted in his exhaustion and pangs. "I appreciate your predicament, sir," she continued. "Truly I do. But you can tell Mr. Flagler that I will not sell; not in this lifetime or the next. Do you hear?"

"I hear you loud and clear, ma'am," Ingram's head pounded. "But you see, Mrs. Tuttle," he apprised her, "you don't actually have much more say in the matter than Mr. Flagler decides you do or do not. It is a plight that I can assure you I am sympathetic to myself, believe me, ma'am. I certainly do not want to seem as though I am condescending you in any way, especially during such a trying time as this." He motioned towards the casket. "I simply mean to enlighten you to the ways of this brave new world we are all victims of in one way or another," he continued. "But you see, Mrs. Tuttle, the harsh reality we both need to better grapple with is that Mr. Flagler is wholly devoted to the idea of building a line to Biscayne Bay. More importantly, he plans to develop all the real estate around the line into value to exploit. Furthermore, I do understand your admiration and compassion for the natural wonders of the world, believe me, I do. I've read John Muir's essays and admire his notions as much as any conservationist can. I also very much sympathize with taking the utmost discretion when dealing with God's natural wonders. But South Florida is no Yosemite or Grand Teton, ma'am. The swamps that comprise South Florida are a godforsaken hellscape rife with mosquitoes the size of hummingbirds, dozens of varieties of venomous vipers, Jurassic reptiles, and illiterate savages who might like nothing more than to cut your throat in the night. Truth be told, Mrs. Tuttle, I do not myself personally think it wise to expend the capital nor manpower required to civilize South Florida at this juncture in time. But Mr. Flagler is a man of vision and incredible resources. He is a pitbull with a bone, ma'am. And one way or another, as surely as day follows night, Mr. Flagler will develop the region sooner rather than later, and with your blessing or without it. But you have my word, ma'am, on the souls of my wife and unborn children, Mr. Flagler has no wild ideas about turning South Florida into another Cleveland, Manchester, Liverpool, or what have you. He intends to make the region into one of the most renowned resorts and playgrounds of American aristocracy. There will be modest industrialization of the region, to be sure, but not the kind with factories and smokestacks. The FEC will be sure to preserve all that you hold dear of Biscayne Bay. But in the name of progress, we will eradicate anything which stands in the way of civilizational progress and economic development, including you, if need be, ma'am. Man's dominion over earth and all her glorious resources is the very will of God almighty. Surely you have read the *Book of Genesis*?"

"Is this some kind of threat or sermon? I'm not quite certain by your tone." Tuttle snarled as she stood suddenly and glared hard into Ingram's exhausted eyes, which glanced nervously towards Mr. Tuttle's corpse.

"No ma'am," Ingram said matter-of-factly while standing and clutching his derby tightly in his hands. He towered over Tuttle, but she somehow seemed more formidable. "The FEC is not in the business of making threats to widows or anyone else. We are in the business of propagating civilizational progress. We venture to transform South Florida into a respite from the grime, crime, filth, and social degradation associated with cities such as this godforsaken accident on Lake Erie." The wind suddenly howled outside the house, as though Cleveland had taken offense at the slight. "You can either be part of the progress we are making and become one of the richest women in the world in the process, or you can stand idly by and end up firmly on the wrong side of history." He then offered her his hand as a cordial gesture. She declined to shake it. "You do have my greatest condolences in regards the loss of your husband," Ingram added as if rehearsed as he placed his derby atop his head. "Mr. Tuttle was a titan of American industry and the city of Cleveland will not soon forget all that he did for what I'm certain must be a grateful community. I do hope that someday people will remember you in a similar light – as the Mother of Biscayne Bay." He forced a gracious smile, bowed his head politely, and then hurried towards the front door of the Victorian mansion where Mr. Madison waited rather impatiently, and then out into the moaning wind and blinding white blizzard.

Mrs. Tuttle sighed slightly while kneeling once more next to her husband's casket. The subconscious easing of tension via the sigh was partly due to grief and frustration, but also because she realized far sooner than Mr. Ingram the mettle she was made of, and that her new adversary had been sent on a fool's errand by Mr. Flagler, whom she had long perceived to be a terribly greedy, arrogant, pompous and recklessly irresponsible man.

CHAPTER SIX

Monday, January 10, 1896, Biscayne Bay, Florida

The Miccosukee emerged in a process of ethnogenesis from various Native American groups such as the Muscogee, Creek and Cherokee who had intermarried with runaway slaves and settled in Florida in the nineteenth century. During Andrew Jackson's Trail of Tears in the 1830s, most American Indians who hailed from the southeast headed west on harrowing and godforsaken forced marches to the Oklahoma territory. Some Miccosukee, however, escaped and went south into the dark heart of the Florida peninsula. President Jackson dispatched the Federal Army to the most southern reaches of the territory, near what later became Miami, to exterminate the escaped Miccosukee with extreme prejudice, which he hoped might serve as a warning to any other renegade band that dared to defy even the most arbitrary of orders handed down by the United States Federal Government. The U.S. Army built Fort Dallas, a supply station near Biscayne Bay, for the primary purpose of eradicating these rebels. But the Everglades proved to be too impenetrable and indominable for even the U.S. Army, which eventually abandoned the fort entirely after the Civil War. The fort was then later happily reoccupied by the descendants of the Miccosukee renegades who had defied the long arm of what they sneeringly referred to as "American justice."

Fort Dallas had, by 1896, become a kind of spiritual epicenter and citadel around which numerous shacks, huts, and cabins had grown into a modest community dependent on small farms, fishing, and hunting for protein-rich meat such as those provided by reptiles.

Many of the Miccosukee who lived in the Everglades had met, or at least seen, the Tuttle family during the Clevelanders' annual sojourns to Biscayne Bay. At first, the

Tuttle's were greeted with great skepticism and caution, but over time, the mostly reclusive family began to give the children in the village candied treats, trinkets and clothes, which broke the ice and thawed the inherent tension that had long existed. Eventually, some of the adult Miccosukee began to trade handmade wares and handicrafts with the Tuttle family, who provided things in return, such as pots, pans, and Coca-Cola, which the Miccosukee elders were especially impressed with, and not just because the soft drink was laced with cocaine, which made life in a steamy and mosquito infested swamp a tad more bearable. The Tuttle family also gladly displayed and gifted Miccosukee handicrafts to enthusiastic and admiring patrician Anglo-Americans back in Ohio who fetishized them as exotic treasures from a backward and peasant people who seemed a relic of a preindustrial past. Mrs. Tuttle and her daughter also offered lessons in the English language to any Miccosukee willing to learn to read and write.

Although their sparse and intermittent interactions had, thanks mostly to the Tuttles, been mostly benign or positive with white folks in the decades since the U.S. Army left the region, the villagers seemed terribly worried when they noticed the Tuttle's skiff pilot, who was donning his faded and worn straw hat and mud stained denim overalls, slowly approach in his boat with a burly white man dressed in all white linen suit and a safari pith helmet atop his head like he were a British colonial overlord landing on the shores of India.

The villagers gradually trickled out of their dwellings to observe the striking figure slowly drift down the tributary towards them. It suddenly occurred to Ingram that he, dressed in all white and toting his trusty Winchester rifle, might have the same effect that Hernán Cortés and the Spanish had on the Aztec when the conquistador first arrived in Aztlán. Ingram's fear of the unknown thus naively turned to hope that he might be happily received as a deity or liberator from darkness amongst what he assumed to be not fully civilized people. The first time he laid eyes on a Miccosukee, many months earlier while grading rail lines near the Everglades, he was struck by how dark skinned most of them were and that most were, and thanks to clothes provided by the Tuttles, dressed more like cowboys out west he had seen depicted in magazines and Karl May books.

The skiff pilot finally slid the boat to a halt at the edge of the tributary a few hundred yards from Fort Dallas. He white knuckled his rifle as a bead of sweat dripped from the bridge of his nose and settled on his faded and worn denim overalls; his hands trembled and he refused to leave the vessel for fear of being scalped.

Ingram and the pilot, however, were both somewhat relieved that none of the few dozen Miccosukee seemed to be concealing any firearms or blades. "I'll cover you," the pilot's voice quivered in a deep French accent that Ingram could barely comprehend. Ingram then slung his rifle strap over his shoulder to secure it and cautiously climbed over side of the boat. His knee-high black boots were soaked from the ankle down. With each step closer he crept up the embankment and towards the villagers, they cautiously inched away from the intruder dressed in white, as though they believed him to be, like Hernán Cortés ended up being, infected with some kind of disease that might prove catastrophic.

Ingram wisely made a point of aiming the double-barrel of his Winchester towards the verdant green grass and sticky brown mud underneath his slick-black boots in an effort to elucidate that he meant the villagers no harm. "I say," he bellowed so that the most cautious Miccosukee gathered in the back of the gathering could hear him clearly, "which of you men is the head honcho of the clan?" Some of the Miccosukee men exchanged quick and cautious glances, but nobody stepped forward to shoulder that burden.

Ingram, who was sweaty, covered in stinging mosquito bites, and by now beyond exhausted after a week straight of grueling travel, was especially ill tempered upon arriving at Fort Dallas. "Come now," he huffed gruffly, "surely one of you men must be in charge of this clan." But no one assumed the position.

"Why have you come here?" a young man no older than the age of seventeen and no taller than five-feet and five-inches tall, though he cast a long shadow, finally asked suspiciously. Ingram, assuming that the young man with the temerity to speak up must have been in charge, or at least ought to be if he was not already, tucked his rifle under his left arm and walked sternly towards the younger with his right hand extended cordially.

"My name is James Ingram. I have been sent by a man named Henry Flagler to make you the richest Indian band in all of the Americas."

The young Miccosukee man, who Ingram would later learn was named Garnet Reynolds, shared a quick and nervous handshake with Ingram while glancing side-eyed at a lovely young woman who was standing towards the left flank of the denizens that had gathered to examine the peculiar man in white. Her name was Goldie. She was a year older than Garnet. Her eyes were brilliant, black, and penetrating; her sleek black hair was tied back in a braid that extended the length of her spine. She had perfectly symmetrical facial features and stood nearly five feet tall. Her dark almond shaped eyes penetrated Garnet's soul. She had also taken to English better than anyone else in the village, and had even begun to instruct some of the younger children to read a handful of the books they had acquired from the Tuttles the previous winter. *20,000 Leagues Under the Sea* was her favorite. She slightly and cautiously shook her head to warn Garnet against being lured into a trap by this man who she had a hunch was an intruder who, whether realizing it or not, portended harm.

"Please," Goldie worked up the courage to address Ingram, "we don't want any trouble. Just get back on the boat and leave us be."

"I can surely understand your caution and trepidation," Ingram replied as gracious as his pangs of exhausted impatience would allow. "Things have gone very poorly for your people since my kind arrived on this great continent many hundreds of years ago, to say the least. But I assure you that I have come only to help your kind make progress and to become fully civilized participants in the American economic system – capitalism. I think that if you would just listen a moment with an open mind to my very simple proposition that I have for you that you will see that I am making an incredibly generous offer that even the most boorish of savage could understand is in its best interest."

"History taught us," Goldie was emboldened by Ingram's insistence, "that when white men arrive beyond the horizon promising to civilize and uplift us with offers that seem too good to be true, that it is actually too good to be true. Besides, if you give us ten dollars, it is because you are making a million."

Ingram took a few steps back towards the skiff and waved his hand at the pilot, who cautiously tossed a stuffed leather satchel up the embankment towards his employer. Ingram quickly unzipped the bag and held it open for the villagers to see. "Do you know what this is?" His voice boomed. "This is cold, hard U.S. currency," he answered his own question. "Do you know what money is? Money is power. Money is security. Money is progress and civilization. With this, you could tear down these primitive abodes and this dilapidated old fort and build a proper community. One day, after the railroad arrives, you could even have electricity and indoor plumbing."

"What do we have to do for the money?" Garnet asked, determined to get down to business. His nervous eyes, however, stayed fastened on the cash and avoided contact with Ingram.

"You know the family that lives adjacent to the bay – the Tuttles?" Ingram asked.

"We know the Tuttles," Goldie said. "They are fine folks."

"The Tuttles stand in the way of progress and your own uplift," Ingram declared, "and they need to be removed by any means necessary."

Goldie looked ominously upon Garnet and slightly, though determinedly, shook her head to warn him against doing business with the man dressed in white.

"So," Garnet said as he defied Goldie and inched a step towards Ingram and the bag full of cash, "how much money is actually in there?"

"Feel free to count it yourself, if you are able to count," Ingram said, not even realizing he was being condescending.

CHAPTER SEVEN

Monday, January 17, 1896, Biscayne Bay, Florida

One week after Ingram's visit to the Miccosukee lands at the edge of the Everglades, the skiff pilot was spotted on the horizon by Garnet as the sun was high in the midday sky. Garnet was shirtless and sans shoes as he sat atop the second-story roof of the Tuttle's modest winter home, which was nestled at the western edge of Biscayne Bay. Garnet noticed Mrs. Tuttle fanning herself as the vessel slowly approached. And, due to the fact that she was still in mourning, Mrs. Tuttle was, perhaps unwisely, wearing a Victorian dress made of black satin and lace, and sitting under a blue umbrella next to her son, sickly Charlie, who was, despite the heat and humidity, and thus bundled in a gray woolen blanket. Margaret, Mrs. Tuttle's eldest child, sat at the other end of the skiff where she was, despite the ravenous mosquitos devouring her flesh, is absorbed in Henry James's *The Figure in the Carpet*. As the boat drew nearer to land, Mrs. Tuttle noticed Garnet atop the roof of her home as if a shotgun-gripping gargoyle atop some ancient European cathedral.

"What in God's name is the meaning of this, young man?" she demanded of Garnet as the skiff slid onto shore.

The reclusive skiff pilot was a distant descendent of the Huguenots who had escaped religious intolerance in France for the desolate isolation of Florida in the 1560s. He had very little contact with other people and thus spoke very little English. The little English he did speak was thus garbled and hard to decipher. He, however, could rightly decipher Tuttle's frantic question, to which he forced a reply, "a Monsieur in the employ of the train pay da natives da money."

"Those damned diabolical bastards," Mrs. Tuttle seethed. It was the first and last time Charlie and Margaret had ever heard their mother swear. Their tired eyes widened and their jaws fell open as they glanced disbelievingly at each other. Garnet, meanwhile, slid down a ladder and began to walk across a sprawling field towards the embankment.

"I say, Garnet," Mrs. Tuttle demanded as she waded into the water, "what in Heaven's sake is the meaning of you climbing atop my roof like you were some kind of chimpanzee?"

"I have been waiting for you for ages," he said aggrievedly. "We need to have us a talk."

"I really don't have time to chat just now, young man," she snapped. "Charlie is as ill as the day is long and I need to draw him a warm bath immediately."

"It shouldn't take long," Garnet explained, "I just need you to sign a contract, then we both can go about our business."

"A contract?" she said while smirking haughtily and glaring arrogantly at him as though he were fast and foolishly approaching an intellectual depth to which he was woefully unable to navigate or inhabit. "What in the bloody hell do you know about a contract?" she seethed. "I suppose you have become a barrister since last we met, is that it?"

"No ma'am," he said while pulling a folded document from the pocket of his mud-and-sweat stained denim overalls, "I've just been hired to do a job. That's all."

"A job?" Tuttle scoffed, equally amused and bemused. "I've never seen any one of you goddamn idling Injuns lift a finger to do any bit of work in the time I have inhabited these parts. All you ever do is whittle, hunt, fish, and smoke whatever in God's name it is that you smoke all the time." She was referring to the marijuana that grew wild on Miccosukee land.

"Yeah, well," he said impatiently and a bit offended, "hopefully I can go back into retirement after you sign this contract. Look," he added, "We've been paid very handsomely to get you to sign this here contract by any means necessary. That's what I aim to do. Now, we can do it the easy way or the hard way. But one thing's for certain as the sun rising tomorrow."

"Oh," Tuttle smirked haughtily while interjecting, "please enlighten me, lad."

"You see," he informed her, "you are outnumbered 40-to-1 in the middle of nowhere, and I can assure you that you ain't gonna get a moment of peace from us 'crazed savages' until your name is right here," he jabbed the end of the ballpoint pen given to him by Mr. Ingram into the dotted line at the bottom of the contract that he held aloft for her to see.

Mrs. Tuttle's haughty smirk turned to ire. "You fool," she seethed. "Do you have any idea what will happen to this territory if I sell my land to the FEC? The same thing that happened to your people out west as a result of the railroad – urbanization, pollution, disease, death and destruction of your people. Do you want there to be another Wounded Knee here, boy?"

"Ain't no Miccosukee out west that I know of, ma'am," Garnet explained as he glanced down at his leg, wondering what Mrs. Tuttle meant by 'wounded knee.'

"Neither Mr. Flagler, Mr. Ingram, you, or God almighty has the right to coerce me to sell land that I legally own. My husband has died. His foundry has been sold. I intend to live here all year round; it is what is best for my dear boy, Charlie." Garnet looked past Mrs. Tuttle. The skiff pilot was helping the sickly twenty-four-year-old man to navigate the shallows and then shakily up onto the embankment leading from the bay up to the Tuttle's property.

"I am rightly sympathetic to your plight, ma'am," Garnet conceded. "You have tried to treat us as kindly as you know how to. But this ain't your land and never has been, no matter what your piece of paper might say. You have always been a guest here, whether you thought so or not. My ancestors settled these lands and made them habitable for you and your family when even the full force of the U.S. Army could not manage the task. Without us, there'd be no way in hell you could have ever survived here. Whether you sign this contract or not, this land has never and will never really be yours. We allowed you to stay. We have the right to decide if and when you leave."

"You fool," Tuttle snarled, "allowing the FEC to come here will prove to be suicidal to you and your people. Can't you understand that?"

"Mr. Ingram promised to make us the wealthiest tribe in the Americas," he explained.

"Even if that were true, you will all surely be wiped out. You and your people will go down as the wealthiest tribe of natives to be wiped out by the white man in world history. Is that the ignominy you dream of, you foolish and naïve boy?"

"Maybe you'll be right," he said while shrugging his trim but broad shoulders, "but at least we'll get some comfort and enjoyment from this miserable existence before your kind destroys this land."

"You silly and ignorant little boy," she chuckled in an attempt to protect her psyche from what she perceived to be the harsh reality of his negligible stupidity. "Do you really think wealth can insulate you from the misery part and parcel of human existence? If you think your pathetic little life is miserable now, just you wait until this region is turned into a city rife with factories, air pollution, water pollution, human waste, whorehouses, foreigners and Negroes of every stripe. Just you wait and see what becomes of you and your people then. The saddest part is, little man, you think you are being quite clever by playing Mr. Flagler's game. The hard truth is, you could not possibly be any dafter."

"That's easy for a rich white lady to say of a red man in rags, I reckon," he tried to keep his cool as he glared into her soul. "Try living in abject poverty and suffering weeks on end of intense hunger and deprivation, then you can offer lessons on what is or is not clever."

Charlie, thanks to the steady aid of the skiff pilot, finally managed to climb up the embankment. Mrs. Tuttle wrapped her arm lovingly around her son's slight and shivering shoulders as she led him across a sprawling and verdant lawn towards the front porch of the house. "I will never sign that piece of paper," she assured Garnet as she passed, "so I suggest you get back in your sad little canoe and find your way back to your sad little ruinous village." Garnet smiled somewhat awkwardly and apologetically at Margaret, who he had always got along very well with, as she passed by on her way towards the porch behind her mother and brother. She did not return any of Garnet's warmth of sentiment.

Mrs. Tuttle was further appalled upon entering the house to find dozens of Miccosukee occupying it. Some were sleeping in Mrs. Tuttle's and her children's beds, while others were drinking whisky and playing cards. Some of them were wearing the Tuttles' clothing. Goldie, the young and lovely Miccosukee girl who had earlier expressed such grave misgivings about Garnet doing business with Mr. Ingram, was enjoying a relaxing bubble bath in the clawfoot tub in the water closet.

"You've finally come back," Goldie said to Mrs. Tuttle while smiling brightly. Goldie's hair, having been washed with shampoo for the first time in her life, flowed over her shoulders. She adored the mint and lavender botanicals, which she had never before smelled. Charlie, who had never seen a naked woman before, was somewhat revived from his illness, as if Goldie's nude body and glistening skin was just the tonic he needed. His mother, however, clenched her hand over her son's delighted eyes and he seemed sickly again.

"How dare you, child," Mrs. Tuttle said dejectedly. "After all I've done for you. Why, you'd have never learned to read or even heard of Coca-Cola, let alone tasted it, if not for my largesse and generosity. And this is how you repay me?" Mrs. Tuttle shook her head ominously as though a great sin had been committed against her by an impudent heretic. "And don't think I can't smell that you've also pilfered the luxurious shampoo my dearly beloved and belated husband so graciously gifted me the last time we were in Paris." Mrs. Tuttle began to weep and swoon theatrically; her face contorted. "I had, foolishly I now concede, naïvely convinced myself that you were a brand apart from these other savages, something perhaps a bit more promising and special than the rest of these oafs. I foolishly believed that you were perhaps even able to be a fully civilized young lady who could comport with a fine gentleman of industry and means in Cleveland. But now I see all too well that you are just a common Injun like the rest of these scalawags."

"Would you mind fetching me the towel from off the sill, Charlie?" Goldie said while smiling wryly and gazing down at the palms of her hands. "My hands are startin' to prune."

Mrs. Tuttle was aghast and sweating profusely by the time she and her children had made it back down the embankment of the bay to the skiff. The fifty-mile ride to Palm Beach took more than two hot and arduous days up the

Intercoastal Waterway. By then, Charlie had fallen far more ill. Palm Beach was home to a rail line and a luxury resort hotel, the Royal Poinciana, which was owned by Flagler. But the town was home to no hospital. Mrs. Tuttle obstinately refused to stay even one night at Flagler's hotel, even though Margaret, fearing for her brother's life, pleaded with her mother to drop her grudge, if only for a few hours of respite. Mrs. Tuttle's pride was, however, so provoked that she was willing to further risk her son's health by waiting in a gazebo out front of the train station through the night until the 9:15 a.m. locomotive to Jacksonville mercifully arrived. The journey by train from Palm Beach to Jacksonville was a bumpy, hot, and grueling ten-hour odyssey over swamps and through dense pine forests. Charlie's temperature was 103.6 degrees by the time he arrived at Jefferson and Lee Memorial hospital in Jacksonville. By then, Mrs. Tuttle's will had been broken and she was finally ready to concede to Flagler's and Ingram's demands to sell the land.

"It's not worth losing Charlie over," she confided in Margaret soon after sunrise the morning after her son's fever finally broke.

CHAPTER EIGHT

Monday, January 24, 1896, Midtown Manhattan

Fluffy white billows of snow fell in sheets to the salt doused pavement of the sidewalk beneath Mr. Ingram's black scuffed Oxfords as he hurried north on Park Avenue. He soon arrived at the front gate and steps of Mr. Flagler's townhouse. A young and not entirely unattractive maid wearing a light blue uniform hurriedly hung his overcoat and derby on a hook in the foyer and then escorted Ingram upstairs and down the long and dimly lit hallway to Mr. Flagler's office.

Flagler seemed to Ingram to be in much better spirits than normal as his employer was standing at the window gazing at the snow falling while enjoying a cigar hand rolled in Ybor City by a master craftsman from Santiago, Cuba, and indulging in a nip of brandy, which, considering that he had never known his boss to drink spirits before lunch, came as a surprise.

"I'm sorry to interrupt sir," Ingram's interjection disrupted the splendor and serenity of the moment, "but I'm very pleased to report that the contract has been signed, sealed, and delivered via courier this morning."

"Wonderful," Flagler exclaimed while shoving his bifocals onto the tip of his nose and hurrying over to his desk to inspect the document being laid atop it by Ingram. "Any sticky wickets thrown into the mix by the widow Tuttle?"

"Just one," Ingram sighed. "She insisted on an addendum to the contract," Ingram's suddenly sheepish voice dropped an octave. Flagler's lighthearted mien grew suddenly heavier than a black led balloon.

"An addendum?" Flagler demanded flatly as his eyes glared deep into Ingram's. "What in God's name for?"

"Tuttle demands that the Negroes not be permitted to live or work outside of the confines of this section of the city between the two FEC lines you added to the original map," Ingram explained as he jabbed his index finger into a rough sketch of a map of the proposed city that Tuttle had added to the contract, which Flagler decided to name "Miami" due to his admiration for the American Indians who hailed from the Ohio River Valley. Ingram set his finger atop the phrase "Colored Town," which was scrawled atop a small section of the map and fenced in by rail lines. Flagler sat down into the plush leather chair behind his desk and then spun around gleefully while exhaling a lungful of tobacco smoke. Flagler began to laugh merrily once the chair ceased spinning, which caught the somewhat confused Ingram a bit off guard.

"That is exactly what I had planned all along," Flagler guffawed as he scribbled his signature with a ballpoint pen made of twenty-four-karat gold along the dotted line at the bottom of the legally binding document. He then cheerfully tossed the pen atop the contract and gazed giddily up at Ingram. "James, m'boy, you've done it again. I don't know where I'd be without you."

"It was nothing, sir," Mr. Ingram kindly lied as his mind flashed back to the trip to Cleveland during a blinding Blizzard, and then reminisced about his arduous trek into the dark heart of the Everglades to employ Garnet and the rest of the Miccosukee he had hired to coerce Tuttle into relinquishing her land. Despite the turmoil and travail of it all, the fleeting admiration from the gruff and slow to praise father figure made each moment of agony, in that fleeting moment, worth it.

"And what of Mrs. Tuttle?" Flagler asked cautiously. "How are the widow's spirits after becoming one the richest women in the country?"

"I get the sense that she is more resentful than she is glad, sir," Ingram admitted. "But once her new villa on the south side of the bay is complete and the finest ilk of American society start wintering there and playing bridge with her, I believe she will warm to our endeavor a bit more readily. If not, to hell with her."

"Indeed," Flagler belly-laughed like Santa Claus as he reached into the cabinet of his desk and revealed a hardly-touched bottle of scotch. "This calls for a celebratory sip of small batch single malt from the mother country, m'boy."

"Thank you, sir," Ingram politely declined, "but I really must get home to Sigrid."

"Of course, Sigrid," Flagler said as if suddenly remembering she existed. "And how is the soon-to-be mother enduring her ordeal?"

"Fine sir, thank you," Ingram said, "as you can imagine she is a bit miffed that I have spent so much of her pregnancy away from home. She was more amendable to it in the early stages, but is getting terribly weary of me riding the rails the closer she arrives at the due date."

"I see," Flagler sighed. "Well, please tell the wife that it simply could not be prevented. It was for the sake of human progress. Explain to her what a conquistador you are. More importantly, explain to her how rich you will soon be. She'll come around in no time, mark my words. I know, I've been married for twenty-five years now." The fact that Flagler's wife was now institutionalized in Ithaca seemed lost on the tycoon, but not on Ingram, who was more desperate to get home to his wife with each second that was squandered chit-chatting with a man he knew did not give a cold gray damn about his wife.

"Yes sir, I most certainly will," Ingram said somewhat impatiently and emboldened by Flagler's reluctant praise. "And since I was able to accomplish this seemingly impossible task and my absence from the process is sure to put me in the frying pan with the wife, would you be at all amenable to the idea of me staying here in the city with Sigrid until after she has given birth?"

"I'm sorry, James," all the splendid joviality in Flagler's face seemed to instantly fall away to be replaced by unbending consternation. "You know as well as I that your presence in Miami at this trying time in the endeavor is beyond imperative. I can afford you a few days, if it appeases the wife. But I need you there by the end of this week, come hell or high water. There's simply too much riding on the grading and planting of the golden spike to outsource the management of the project until after your children are born. If things were to go sour while the tracks were being graded and laid, it could cost us months, not to mention millions of dollars. Bad publicity could also put us behind the eight-ball in terms of our ability to set the price of land surrounding the tracks."

"I figured that your man in Cleveland – Madison," Ingram pleaded, "might be able to hold the fort down in Miami until after Sigrid delivers."

"I'm quite sorry, lad," Flagler levied the blow, "but you simply have to be there until the job is done right, which could, depending on weather and sundry other factors, take months. Please do explain to the wife that you will be sure to be there for the birth of your next child, and the next, and the next," he smiled, trying to console his dejected underling. "Most of all, tell her that you need to be in Miami for the sake of all of humanity."

"Yes, sir, I've given her the line about 'civilizational progress' and all that in times prior, believe me," Ingram said disappointedly, "but she does not seem to buy it."

"Well then," Flagler said as he gnawed as if a bit unnerved at the end of his cigar, "do a better job of selling her on it."

"Yes sir," Ingram's voice oozed consternation, "I've tried my damnedest, but she does not seem too terribly amenable to the idea of me traveling again until after the twins have been born. She is, as you might imagine, terrified that something will go wrong with me a thousand miles away from her."

"That's to be expected the first go around, I suppose," Flagler admitted, "but your wife is of Swedish stock and thus as hearty as an ox. She'll be quite all right, I'm sure. Those Scandinavian lasses are experts at giving birth, which is partly why they are such a superior race of people."

"Please sir," Ingram said as a tense sigh escaped his chest, "I beg you to reconsider. Sigrid's youngest brother, you see, died during childbirth. Sigrid still has nightmares. I'm afraid Sigrid simply cannot abide by me not being by her side during the birth of our children."

"Goddamn it, James." Mr. Flagler fumed. "I've told you time and time again to not mingle your personal and business affairs. If you find that the two are not compatible, I suggest you find a new line of work."

"I've always put you first, sir," Ingram's voice hollowed. "I've helped you make a fortune many times over, and I will do so again, sir. But all I'm asking you for is a wee bit of understanding and compassion."

"I tell you what, James," Flagler feigned magnanimity while exhaling a plume of cigar smoke towards the finely crafted crown molded oaken ceiling overhead, "I'll pay for your wife and a physician to travel to Miami to be with you. That way you can be with your wife while she gives birth, concomitant to you overseeing the birth of Miami."

"But sir," Mr. Ingram interjected, "Miami is but a frontier. There's not even a post office or saloon as of yet, never mind a hospital or running water."

"Hospital?" Flagler scoffed. "Women gave birth for thousands of years before there was ever any hospital. Why, my mother herself gave birth to me in a wheat field in the morning and still did her bit to bring in the harvest by sundown. Giving birth in a hospital amongst millions of microbes and germs is a much greater threat to the health of your children compared to the clean air and sunshine of the frontier. Why, have you heard anything at all about the discovery of germs, James?" Flagler added ominously.

"Yes sir," Ingram reluctantly explained, "I've read that many cities in the New South have passed ordinances against Negro nannies taking white children into the darky sections of town due to fear of exposing white children to the black maladies and germs that crawl all over colored sections of cities."

"Exactly James," Flagler leaned forward in his chair. "We're going to pass a similar ordinance in Miami during the first election, mark my words. Now," Flagler continued, "if mostly sick people go to hospitals, where they take their germs, is that really the most responsible place for a father to want his children to be born? Do you really want to risk it, James?"

"No sir," Ingram conceded, "I suppose there's merit in your point."

"Good then," Flagler smiled gladly. "Consider the matter settled. I'll have Mrs. Blankenship," his geriatric secretary, "make all the arrangements for Ingrid and her physician."

Ingram's eyes betrayed grave frustration and anger, but he remained as cool, calm, and collected as he could under such immense stress. "As you wish, sir," Ingram exhaled frustrated as he started hard towards the exit of the office.

"One more thing," Flagler added. "I've hired Everett Sewell, a Harvard grad from Atlanta, to do publicity for Miami. He will meet you as soon as he can provide proper notice to whatever newspaper currently employs him. See to it that he gets all he needs."

"Yes sir," Ingram's voice was monotone. "Is there anything else?"

"No, not just now," Flagler smiled contentedly while pouring a bit of scotch into a snifter. "Just be sure to give my best to Ingrid, and of course, keep me posted as to how things are going in terms of progress being made on the laying of the tracks and construction of the hotel on Biscayne."

"As you wish," Ingram said as he trudged from Flagler's office towards the dimly lit hallway. His jaw tightened as his back teeth grinded together. "One more thing, sir," Ingram, whose anger had emboldened him, added before exiting the office, "my wife's name is not Ingrid. Her name is Sigrid."

Flagler was, however, completely oblivious or disinterested in his underling's consternation. He smiled and nodded nonchalantly while licking a bit of scotch from his thick white moustache. "Of course, it is," he chortled, which seemed to mindfuck Mr. Ingram.

CHAPTER NINE

Tuesday, January 25, 1896, Cleveland, Ohio

Once settled back into the bridge and gin circuit, with Charlie somewhat recovered from his illness, Mrs. Tuttle made a point of telling any maid or marm who would listen, including Governor McKinley's wife, about Flagler's diabolical scheme to destroy what she affectionately referred to as "God's last bastion on earth." She also unabashedly expressed her acrimony towards Flagler himself. Unbeknownst to Tuttle, however, she often unwittingly made matters worse for herself by informing eager investors that they had the opportunity to get in on the ground floor of the commodification of a new frontier in real estate development in South Florida.

But Tuttle's longtime friend, Mrs. Applebee, who had attended Wellesley with her many years prior, quietly informed her sorority sister of an old Polish matron rumored to be older than one-hundred-and-fifteen years old who resided in the Old Brooklyn section of Cleveland. The centenarian Polish mystic was infamous for effectively cursing people for the right price. Her services, however, were exorbitantly expensive, which was an effect of her renowned reputation as a purveyor of the Dark Arts. Whether it was simply very easy for a tragedy to befall even the most privileged in industrial cities at the turn of the century or whether the sorcerer actually had some kind of mystical power cannot be verified. But "her curse," Mrs. Applebee ominously assured Mrs. Tuttle as her nervous and glazed eyes looked deep into her friend's tired and angry eyes, "cannot be undone after it has been cast."

"Really?" Mrs. Tuttle's slightly revived eyes widened. "Her curses last forever?"

"Yes," Mrs. Applebee grinned mischievously while nodding her head slowly and theatrically. "Do you remember the

Palmer's nasty little pooch, that little sprat that used to bark all through the night?"

"Yes," Mrs. Tuttle said as she looked ponderously into the distance as the memory of the yappy corgi flashed in her mind's eye.

"You don't hear him bark anymore," Mrs. Applebee smiled wryly as her over-plucked eyebrow heightened inquisitively, "do you?"

"No," Mrs. Tuttle was impressed, "I don't."

"That is because the little bastard was run over by a streetcar two days after I visited Klavdiya."

"You don't think it was just some kind of coincidence?" Tuttle checked her optimism.

"Klavdiya said the dog would experience an unfortunate tragedy within a week," Mrs. Applebee whispered secretively. "At first I dreaded the idea of the poor pooch being killed. But after it happened, I could once again sleep all through the night undisturbed." She smiled proudly. "Do you know how important sleep is to one's mental and spiritual health? I could not abide by some damned dog robbing me of my quality of life, could I?"

"No, I don't suppose you could, or for that matter should," Mrs. Tuttle admitted. "It sure was a cute little dog, though. Margaret adored it. It's a shame it was not better mannered. Come to think of it, I blame the Palmer's for the dog's death more so than you. They had a responsibility to properly train it so that it would not bark all through the night."

"Thank you, Julia," Mrs. Applebee was relieved to have her friend's support, "that's kind of you to say."

"Tis a shame though," Mrs. Tuttle, who was still mourning her husband, lamented, "it was a very cute pooch indeed."

"Well," Mrs. Applebee was desperate to change the subject, "what's done is done and that is that."

"Can you take me to see this sorcerer in Old Brooklyn?" Mrs. Tuttle hoped.

"Of course," Mrs. Applebee said while glaring into the distance. "Klavdiya is always very grateful for new clients. She told me she will provide a free curse for every new referral I send her way."

"Oh, how wonderful," Mrs. Tuttle replied.

Mrs. Tuttle and Applebee, who would never think of riding with the rabble on a streetcar, were chauffeured in a horse-drawn carriage three neighborhoods away. But traffic was mostly clear due to it being midday and terribly cold. The ladies had thus made their way to Old Brooklyn by teatime. They, however, had to wait nearly two hours in line to meet with Klavdiya, who was, due to a global economic downturn, flush with clientele desperate for revenge on the people they believed had effectively made the quality of their life worse of late. Many recently laid off workers from Poland who had labored dutifully at the textile plant along the Cuyahoga River were especially eager to cast spells on factory managers. It was thus nearly dark by the time Mrs. Tuttle and Mrs. Applebee were provided an audience with Klavdiya in her macabre and candlelit parlor, the walls of which were painted a deep shade of purple. The windows of the parlor were covered by flowing red velvet curtains that seemed to pulsate. The interior of the room was mostly bare, except for a round wooden table and four chairs surrounding it, and a bookshelf rife with leather-bound texts that created a collection of some of the seminal texts in both western and eastern philosophy, everything from *Torah* to the *I Ching*.

Mrs. Tuttle had terrible difficulty bottling her animus as she explained to the sorcerer how Flagler had coerced and threatened her into selling her land along Biscayne Bay, and about the underhanded occupation of her beloved vacation home by "savages in Flagler's employ," who she had previously "treated so kindly" and "tried her very best to civilize."

"Who or what exactly do you want accursed?" Klavdiya, who originally hailed from Olsztyn, slurred in broken English.

"I don't know if Jesus could forgive me for wishing the death of another person, though I am terribly tempted to curse both Mr. Flagler and his wantwit lackey, Mr. Ingram," Tuttle's angered voice quivered. "I also know in my heart of hearts that God almighty would not abide by the desecration of Biscayne Bay. Mr. Flagler's railroad is sure to destroy one of the last untouched corners of God's green and gracious earth."

"What is it I am to curse?" Klavdiya asked, fast approaching impatience.

"I want Mr. Flagler's entire enterprise cursed so that his resort city, Miami, knows nothing but misery, peril, and woe."

"You have all the money for such a curse?" Klavdiya hoped.

"Of course, I do, yes," Mrs. Tuttle replied, somewhat offended at a veiled insinuation as she snapped open her pocketbook, which was stuffed full of billfolds wrapped into a bunch by a thick and sturdy rubber band. Klavdiya snatched the entire wad of cash from Tuttle's arthritic and crooked fingers and then leaned under the table, unzipped her scuffed black boot, and shoved the wad down next to her calf, which was laced with varicose veins.

"The curse will be done," Klavdiya assured, "now go."

"What curse?" Mrs. Tuttle was certain that she was being ripped off.

"This man – Mr. Flagler," Klavdiya grunted, "his enterprise will be cursed," she promised.

Mrs. Tuttle glanced over at Mrs. Applebee to ask, "is that it?" Applebee slightly and nervously nodded her head to reassure her friend. She then motioned with her head for Mrs. Tuttle to quietly leave the room.

"How can I help you today, Mrs. Applebee," Klavdiya asked as Mrs. Tuttle awkwardly absconded from the small wooden table in the parlor and made her way towards the foyer, where many others anxiously waited to patronize the sorcerer.

"My eldest son, Monroe, he has a new debutante he is courting," Applebee explained to Klavdiya, "but I do not care for her at all. Perhaps there is something you can do to help?"

Mrs. Tuttle then wandered out of the house and onto the porch. A cold wind whipped up from Lake Erie, so she bundled her gray wool scarf around her neck and gazed up at the full moon shining down on her, then silently whispered a prayer to the God of Abraham that the curse she had just spent a small fortune on would soon come to pass.

CHAPTER TEN

Monday, February 14, 1896, Miami, Florida

Though he had warned his wife of how bumpy, arduous and debilitating the journey by train from Pennsylvania Station in Midtown Manhattan to Palm Beach would surely be, his description of the train trip paled in comparison to the day-and-a-half long drift down the lazy lagoon known as the Intercoastal Waterway from Palm Beach to Biscayne Bay in the days before the FEC's lines had been extended all the way south to Miami. Even in the winter season, the mosquitoes along the river could be ravenous.

It was the second week of February when Sigrid arrived in the region. The weather was thus still very hot and humid in frontier South Florida as she and her foggy-bespectacled physician, Doctor Heinz Schivelbush, M.D., slowly drifted south at what seemed to be less than mile per hour. The mosquitoes were relentless. The nets meant to protect the pregnant woman, physician, and skiff pilot, who was far more immune to the vexation inducing stings of the bloodthirsty insects, were ripped in several sections, and thus provided very little relief from either the heat or mosquitos.

Sigrid, whose parents had migrated to Akron, Ohio, from Kiruna, Sweden, a generation earlier, had distinctly Scandinavian features – a long jawline, broad forehead, and full lips. Standing at five-feet and eleven-inches, she was nearly as tall as her husband. She had a head full of wavy, shining and pristine blond hair and eyes that shined and sparkled like sapphire. She was normally very poised, powerful, prim and lovely. But that vision of Mr. Ingram's wife that had served him so well on the cocktail party set amongst Manhattan society types in the preceding seasons was the antithesis of the angry and disheveled mess about to burst with two human lives that finally arrived in Miami at high noon on a particularly steamy and stinky day.

Poor Sigrid was eight-and-a-half months pregnant by the time she had decided to reject her husband's pleas to stay in the city to deliver. She was rather insistent on joining him in what was days away from officially being incorporated as the city of Miami. She had been a feast for insects too many to count for nearly a day by the time she arrived at Biscayne Bay. Some mosquitoes got so drunk on her blood they died from over-intoxication. Her long, slender and pale arms, legs, and face were covered in swollen pink and bleeding bites she had been feverishly digging her fingernails into for masochistic relief.

By the time the skiff mercifully slid ashore after more than ten hours of drifting under the baking South Florida sun, Sigrid felt as though she had lost a decade from her life. The skiff pilot clumsily guided her over the side of the boat and then into the shallows of the bay, but she, due to her huge belly and weakened legs, lost her footing on a rock and fell hard, drenching her in slimy muck. The skiff pilot was terribly embarrassed, but Sigrid was as gracious as her exhaustion and anger would permit her to be. Her normally long and slender feet had swelled to the size of tennis rackets. The two children growing inside Sigrid's massively protruding belly were such a strain on her lower back, that she was forced to hunch forward, which put a terrible strain on her neck and shoulders. Her body did not merely ache, it throbbed as though her entire being was but a haggard collection of raw, ragged, and exposed nerves, as if her entire presence was the wound left by a tooth that had been torn out with pliers sans anesthetic. Even the fleeting thought of her favorite foods, none of which were within three-hundred miles of frontier South Florida by the time she had finally arrived, made her want to vomit her entire lower intestine over the side of the skiff. And though the river so tepid, the boat was very small, and Sigrid thus suffered terrible bouts of motion sickness and intermittent moments of vertigo along the harrowing journey south from Palm Beach.

The physical pain she endured, however, paled in comparison to her anxiety and fear at the thought of losing one, or perhaps even both, of her not-yet-born children as a result of the tragicomic epic poem she had endured from Manhattan to the frontier where Mr. Flagler expected her to sanguinely bring two children into what she increasingly perceived to be a godforsaken modern world.

Her husband had pleaded with her to stay behind in Manhattan to rest and prepare to give birth to the first two of what Mr. Ingram prayed would be nine children, "a baseball team," he often joked at cocktail parties amongst New York High Society types, who politely feigned interested amusement. Both members of this young and up-and-coming couple dreamed of one day being fully included amongst Flagler's ilk and fantasized about their own sons going to the finest and best-respected prep schools in New England, and then onto the Ivy League, and ultimately as productive and respected members of American aristocracy.

Mr. Ingram had promised and then reminded his wife on several occasions in the preceding months, including the day before he left to oversee the laying of the FEC line from Palm Beach to Biscayne Bay, that he would do all in his power to drive the rail workers hired to do the job as doggedly as possible in order to attend to his wife while she was in labor.

But by two weeks from Sigrid's due date, the rail line was still another week to fortnight from being completed. When she read her husband's letter to her in which he communicated that he was "terribly sorry and regretful" to inform her that he would be unable to return the city before her due date, her heart ached with pangs of anger and despair. She also feared that the words in his letter would prove to be portentous. He pleaded once more with her in the postscript of the letter to stay in the city due to how risky it would be to travel to Biscayne Bay, and promised to never again miss the birth of one of their children. But Sigrid, who had come to see her husband as having abandoned his sense of reason in order to appease Mr. Flagler, did not believe her husband could be trusted to put the needs of her children above the whims of his employer. She also simply could not abide the idea of not having her partner by her side during the birth of any one of their children, least of all their first. Against her husband's wishes and her own instincts, she went to Miami to be with her husband during the birth of what both parents hoped would prove to be a brood.

Doctor Schivelbush, who was not actually Sigrid's normal physician, was a stout man with a head full of slick-backed gray and white hair and a bushy handlebar moustache over his pouting mouth. The doctor who had been with Sigrid all along during the pregnancy had other patients to attend to and was thus unable to make the journey. Schivelbush, Flagler's personal physician and by no means an OBGYN, was only slightly older than sixty years of age, but the heat and humidity seemed to add ten more to his disheveled mien, especially considering his pudgy body was dressed in a black three-piece suit that especially soaked in the sun's already intense and penetrating rays. The bedraggled physician's dark attire was in stark contrast to the white, though somewhat dusty and sweat-stained, linen suit donned by Mr. Ingram as he received his wife and her doctor near the furthest end of track that had been laid near the bay.

Schivelbush, due to how slick the bottom of his worn Oxfords were, struggled mightily to navigate his way up the embankment of the bay. His beady and sleep-deprived eyes scanned the desolate and sun-soaked landscape that seemed to stretch beyond the horizon. He was horrified at the conditions under which he was expected to perform the miracle of childbirth, which he had never before done in his long and illustrious career. He was even more mortified upon first inspection of the so-called infirmary, which was but a canvas tent erected next to a vast orange grove that seemed to glow under the resplendent late-afternoon Florida sun. The infirmary was also frequently occupied by FEC workers suffering from heat exhaustion, the flu, typhus, water moccasin or spider bites, and an array of other maladies which were part and parcel of transforming a subtropical environment into one of the world's most renowned real estate markets. There was also no running water within fifty miles of Biscayne Bay. The natural water in Florida was in deep aquifers, but difficult to tap into. Many of the more dehydrated and thus desperate workers were therefore made terribly ill by digging a few feet into the soil and drinking spoiled groundwater that was full of microbes and bacteria and thus horribly unsafe to ingest. The water shipped into the region by rail was also often contaminated with noxious fluids or bugs that had defecated and died in the wooden barrels that transported the water, which ultimately turned into poison.

"It's going to be like giving birth in a goddamn Confederate infirmary," Schivelbush inadvertently blurted the first time he stepped foot into the infirmary tent rife with ailing laborers. His ominous words stirred even more anguish, stress, and fear in the deepest recesses of Sigrid's weary soul.

Mr. Ingram tried to console his terrified wife by saying, "this is what it takes to climb the social ladder in New York City, my love. Once the track has been laid and the special election has passed, Mr. Flagler will surely not be able to ignore my value and our right to be included more often in social engagements. Why," he added a bit timidly, "the successful completion of just such a monumental endeavor as this might even get us invited to the Astor's New Year's Eve gala," he said.

"I don't give a tinker's cuss about the Astor's gala just now, James," Sigrid fumed.

Garnet peaked into the opening of the infirmary tent. "I'm sorry to interrupt, Mr. Ingram," he said somewhat sheepishly. "But a Mr. Sewell has requested an audience with you."

"Ah yes," Ingram said, suddenly remembering he had an appointment. "Please tell Mr. Sewell I'll be with him in just a moment and offer my apologies for making him wait so long for the audience." Mr. Ingram then turned his attention back to his wife, who he kissed gently on her mosquito bitten, sweaty, and sun stroked cheek. She did not reciprocate his hurried and half-distracted attempt at affection. "Please, my dear," Mr. Ingram pleaded with his bedraggled wife, "I beg you and Dr. Schivelbush to try and get some rest and relaxation. I believe you'll find that the bay has an irrepressible and rather ineffable beauty and charm at twilight. I'll have Garnet bring you both a Mint Julep and draw you a warm bath." Mr. Ingram then hurried from the infirmary and made his way across a vast expanse of verdant land towards the canvas tent that served as his field office.

Sewell was a sweaty, lanky, disheveled and awkward, though still quite dashing, man, as he shook Ingram's hand for the first time. He was dressed in an all-white linen three-piece suit and had a large leather portfolio full of his designs for advertisements he had crafted tucked lovingly under his arm. Ingram, who was dressed nearly identically, motioned for Sewell to sit at the makeshift desk towards the back of the tent. Sewell obliged while blotting a bit of perspiration from his forehead with his handkerchief.

"Can I fetch you gentleman anything?" Garnet asked graciously. "Iced tea, a Mint Julep, perhaps?"

"Ah, thank you for reminding me, Garnet – good man," Mr. Ingram said as he sat in the canvas and wood director's chair behind the card-table he used as a makeshift desk. "Please fetch my wife and her physician Mint Juleps and draw them warm baths at once. And Garnet, don't be stingy with the bourbon. Sigrid has had a rough go of it." Ingram, who was relieved Sigrid had finally arrived, smiled.

"Yes sir," Garnet nodded compliantly. "And you, sir?" Garnet directed the question at Mr. Sewell.

"Well," Mr. Sewell huffed through a deep north Georgian accent, "I suppose it's never too early in the afternoon for a refreshing Mint Julep. Hell, make it a double."

"Very good, sir," Garnet said as he slightly bowed deferentially and then hurried from the tent.

"I'm terribly sorry, Mr. Sewell, that it has taken me more than a day since you arrived to formally sit down and look over your work," Mr. Ingram said graciously. "It's just all this business with the work stoppage this week due to the water crisis, now my wife arriving, it's all been a bit much, even by the FEC's standards."

"Ah yes, and a hearty congratulations on the soon-to-be expansion of your family," Sewell forced a cordial smile before adding, "there is nothin' in this big wide world more important than family."

"Do you have children of your own?" Mr. Ingram inquired.

"Not just now," Mr. Sewell smiled a tad more genuinely, "I'm havin' too much fun still to settle down just yet," he confessed.

"No shame in enjoying all that youth has to offer, I suppose," Ingram said, "so long as you can keep business at the center of things." He looked across the table to gauge Sewell's response. Sewell glanced over his shoulder out the egress of the tent hoping to see Garnet donning pristine white gloves and fast returning to the hot and steamy tent with a glittering and icy Mint Julep atop a sterling silver tray. But Garnet was nowhere to be seen. "How are you finding our clime here in the sunshine and swamps so far, Mr. Sewell?" Ingram inquired.

"Truthfully," Sewell lamented as he blotted sweat from his forehead with his handkerchief, "this place must be like what living in the Stone Age was like. I feel as though I've lost a fortnight of my life in the two nights I've spent here. The mosquitoes and heat are maddening. My canvas tent provides no relief from the insufferable heat and humidity."

"I admit," Mr. Ingram reluctantly concurred, "it has been an especially hot winter, as it were. But just you wait until next January. This place will be a veritable heaven on earth compared to anywhere north of the Mason-Dixon Line, mark my words, sir. In the interim, I suggest a steady diet of Garnet's magical Mint Juleps to ease your suffering."

"I say," Sewell said while glancing over his shoulder towards the tent's egress and slightly smacking his lips in great anticipation of his refreshing beverage, "I do hope I'm not being too forward, but I am as red-blooded as any other American man, if you catch my drift. I don't suppose there is anywhere to acquire the accompaniment of a female kind in these presently abysmal climes?"

"As you may have heard, I am a teetotaling man who only has eyes for his lovely and cherished wife," Mr. Ingram said as he cast a long and searching glance towards the egress of the tent in order to assure that no would-be intruder might overhear, "but Garnet confided in me that he was more than a bit bothered that one of the abodes on the Miccosukee's lands has recently been appropriated as a kind of brothel, as it were, that is popularly frequented by some of the white workers laying down the FEC line. I think the workers have taken to calling the establishment the 'Noble Savage,' or some such other unfortunate moniker. Despite his consternation of the establishment having come into existence, I'm sure he might abide, albeit reluctantly, to the notion of apprising you of the brothel's specific whereabouts, if the price of that information was quite to his liking. If you prefer to ask one of the white men, they might also be able to apprise you."

"Very good, sir," Mr. Sewell said while slightly licking his sun chapped lips as his bloodshot and sleep deprived eyes glanced at the ray of sunlight shining into the tent. "Where in God's name do you suppose that little red fella with that Julep is, anyway?"

"He'll be by directly," Mr. Ingram said flatly assured, eager to get to the matter at hand, "let's talk a bit of shop, shall we? Your man in Atlanta, Mr. Grady, seems to have convinced Mr. Flagler that you are just the man to market Miami to the world beyond Biscayne Bay."

"I sure do hope so," Sewell sighed as if under immense pressure. "I drew some sketches of prospective ads for the space Mr. Flagler purchased in *The New York Times* and *Chicago Tribune*." Sewell walked around to the other side of the card table Ingram used as a makeshift desk and plopped his leather-bound portfolio atop and quickly flipped the pages toward the back of the book. He finally came upon a dozen or so glitzy and lusciously produced ads for Miami that seemed to glow like it was ordained by a higher power. One of the ads vibrantly depicted South Florida being drenched in gloriously shimmering pastel sunrays with a caption that read, "Miami: Paradise Regained." Another ad gorgeously depicted a steaming locomotive that seemed to hover above a swamp as it raced by a picturesque beachscape in which dozens of women were sunbathing in one-piece bathing suits. A few ads also depicted wealthy white folks engaged in idle luxury while being attended to by black servants oddly dressed in white uniforms as though they were servants of the British Raj in India. One thing each ad had in common was the sensual depiction of Miami as a utopian "Magic City" of splendor that was free of the supposedly endemic crime, grime, filth, social despair, competition and soulless technocratic Taylorist mechanization associated with cities north of the Mason-Dixon Line at the turn of the twentieth century.

"These are marvelous, simply wonderful," Mr. Ingram gushed as he adoringly ran the tips of his fingers over the glossy finish of the ad depicting wealthy white folks engaged in idle and suburban luxury overlooking the Atlantic Ocean in the foreground and glorious skyline in the background. "They make Miami seem like the antithesis of the hellscape it actually is. They are also what every white man in America dreams of having and being."

Sewell chuckled and smiled proudly while patting Mr. Ingram heartily on the back. "One day soon, we'll have us a city worthy of these ads," he said. "Just you wait and see what these babies look like when you open your newspaper in a snowy armpit such as Cleveland or Newark. Every white man in America is going to be seduced into coming to Miami. You mark my words, Mr. Ingram. These pictures have magical powers. Just you wait and see."

Garnet rushed into the tent. "It's time, Mr. Ingram," he blurted, nearly out of breath, "it's finally time."

"Sigrid is in labor?" Mr. Ingram asked franticly, his dreamy visions of the future of Miami were suddenly shattered by the weight and stress of his wife's ordeal.

"No sir," Garnet smiled ever so slightly, trying to conceal some misplaced embarrassment, "it's time to plant the golden spike."

"Hot damn," Mr. Ingram cooed as he hopped up from the director's chair behind the card table. "Follow me, Mr. Sewell," Ingram, who was beaming with excited pride, exalted, "we're about to make history." Ingram then rushed from the tent, followed closely by Garnet, who was trailed less enthusiastically by Mr. Sewell.

"Say there, boy," Sewell griped to Garnet, "what's the status on that Mint Julep?"

Ingram stepped onto a small makeshift wooden stage at the very end of a rail line that stretched all the way to the north end of Biscayne Bay, just a half mile from Fort Dallas and less than a tenth-of-mile from what was formerly the Tuttle's respite from Cleveland. The line linked the bay all the way to Palm Beach, then Melbourne, then Jacksonville, and eventually to Pennsylvania Station, in midtown Manhattan, and all points in between. Though Miami, what Mr. Sewell coined as "the Magic City" in sundry ephemera and ads designed to seduce consumers to South Florida, was still but an outlandish dream, Flagler's vision was finally, albeit haltingly, taking shape and becoming a reality as Ingram held a glimmering and golden spike over his wide-brimmed hat like a trophy as he addressed Sewell and dozens of rail workers who donned dirty and stained light blue or brown overalls, almost half of whom were African American men. All of them had assembled around the small stage where they cheered wildly as Ingram hammered the final spike into the last plank of wood at the southernmost point of the line. Ingram then cheerfully handed the hammer to one of the laborers – the foreman, who was a gruff and middle-aged white man from South Boston – and then brushed the palms of his hands together, straightened his waistcoat, then waved the open palms of his hands towards the horde of cheering men in order to bring them back to order.

"Now," he declared after the fervid crowd had finally simmered down a bit, "with the laying of this golden spike, we, especially all you men, have made history here today." The men again cheered wildly; some waved their sweat-soaked hats high above their heads. Ingram again fanned his hands at them until order was finally restored. "What we have done these past weeks in these dismal and infernal swamps and pine forests has been nothing short of monumental, comparable to the building of the Great Pyramids of Giza or the Great Wall of China. We have endured insects and reptilians of every pernicious stripe. We have braved horrendous heat, humidity, and tropical storms. But in spite of all the pain, sacrifice, sickness, and travail that you men confronted day and night, you would not be bowed by the elements. God was on our side and so history is on our side. And we have made the world a better place for time immemorial. We have together carved out a piece of what will one day soon become a glorious utopia where there was once only a vast wasteland. We will, God willing, exploit these resources to the best of abilities and harvest wealth and riches that others had only ever dreamed of. We, you men especially, have opened America's last frontier to the bosom of civilizational progress. There is a special place in heaven for men like us, mark my words, lads."

Most of the workers, particularly the black men in the audience, again cheered enthusiastically, but many of the white men shared curious and quizzical glances, bothered by the notion of being in heaven with black men. Ingram again brought the cheering men back to order. "Now," he continued while pulling a list of names scrawled on a notecard from the pocket of his sweat-stained coat, "we will be conducting a special and historic municipal election tomorrow at noon. You men have the morning to rest and relax. But it is imperative that you all meet dutifully in front of the saloon in order to vote for the following." Ingram then read off a list of names and the positions they were running for. "You men will each be given a five-dollar bill note and a pint of Bahamian rum for voting for the FEC's slate of candidates. This election will give the FEC political control over the course and shape of the city's development and identity, which is of utmost importance at this very critical and inchoate stage in the city's existence. There are some natives to the state of Florida, including its governor, Napoleon Bonaparte Broward, who might like to destroy our endeavor and hard work. They are backed by a wealthy benefactor named Mrs. Tuttle. We must defeat these oppositional candidates by any means necessary, lest all of the sacrifice and hard work we have endured these many months to make human history be for naught. Therefore, many of you men will need to be shaven after your first vote in order to vote again. You will be given another five-dollar bill note and pint of Bahamian rum for performing this civic duty to the company."

The majority of the white men assembled around the makeshift stage seemed suddenly confounded by Ingram's pronouncements. Sewell was also especially concerned at the notion of the black workers being enfranchised. "Now," Ingram concluded, "you men are free to take the rest of the day to relax at camp, play your merry songs and instruments, bathe in the bay, or what have you. Just be sure to not hit the bottle too terribly hard this evening so that you can attend church services before meeting at the polling place in front of the saloon and across from the general store on the corner of Flagler Avenue and Main Street at noon tomorrow, sharp." He then dismissed the men for the evening.

The workers began to make their away from the stage towards their racially segregated camps, both of which were comprised of numerous canvas tents and communal canteens where things such as Coca-Cola, candy, cigarettes, and soap could be purchased. It was a kind of racially segregated company town that was not yet a town.

Some single-story structures made of wood, including a post office, general store, and saloon had been haphazardly erected a few hundred yards from where Ingram had laid the golden spike. But none of the streets had yet been paved, nor was there any type of running water, or sewage, nor electrical systems to speak of. Miami thus seemed like one of the many frontier towns that dotted the Wild West in the latter half of the nineteenth century. Certainly law, order, and justice were as bereft from Miami as it was from those Old West towns that were so often mythologized in American popular culture.

One of the white workers, a surly and gruff Cajun who hailed from Baton Rouge, Louisiana, had lagged behind the other men in order to converse with Mr. Sewell, who was desperate for a Mint Julep. The Louisianan who approached Sewell was especially perplexed as he whispered vehemently into the ad man's ear. Sewell sympathized with the Louisianan's plight. The aggrieved Cajun then begrudgingly caught up to the horde of white workers plodding towards their tent city. Sewell, meanwhile, hustled across the verdant field to catch up to Mr. Ingram, who was making his way towards the infirmary.

"Excuse me, sir," Mr. Sewell, who was terribly disheveled and worried, hollered as he approached Mr. Ingram.

"Why, whatever is the matter, Mr. Sewell?" Ingram said, confounded by the distress causing the ad man's face to contort so sourly. "You look as though you've seen a ghost."

"Yes, well," Sewell's southern accent was hushed but horrified. He struggled to find the right words with which to broach such a touch subject. "Was I correct in understanding that these men are being paid to vote tomorrow?"

"Of course," Ingram said matter-of-factly. "You don't think Mr. Flagler is going to leave the election to chance, do you? There is too much riding on it to let these hicks and environmentalists have any political power in this city."

"Yes sir," Sewell was concerned, "but you can't let the darkies vote, can you, sir? I mean, think of the precedent." His brow furrowed and his eyes glanced at the black workers trudging tiredly towards their tent city. "This is the South, sir. Darkies votin'? It just ain't done. It's a slippery slope, you see. I know you are from, what is it, Wales? I know you don't have niggers over there; God bless you. But the last time the niggers had a vote down here, they turned the whole world upside down. If we let the niggers vote, it's only a matter of time before it's us – the brainworkers – that's layin' these tracks in the goddamn jungle. I don't even want to tell you what would become of the white women."

"I understand your concern, Mr. Sewell," Ingram said softly as he placed his arm gently around the ad man's shoulders in an attempt to calm the latter's jangled nerves. "The FEC needs to consolidate its political power in the city so that we can control the shape, growth and development of this region. We need to have the absolute power to decide where the farms are built, where the hotels are built, where the Negroes can and can't live, and ultimately who can build near Flagler's resort and who cannot. Once political power and control of the real estate industry is consolidated, it'll be status quo antebellum, you have my word." He patted Sewell heartily on the back and led him towards his tent.

"But sir," Sewell fretted, "how in the hell do you put the genie back in the bottle once it's out?"

Ingram pondered the question deeply a moment, as if calculating. His eyes stared as the lush green grass between his scuffed boots. "Well," he finally said while nonchalantly shrugging his shoulders, "I suppose by employing the same measures your forefathers did in Atlanta, if necessary." Ingram then suddenly stopped walking and turned very serious as he looked hard at the anxious ad man. "Look, Mr. Sewell," he explained in low tones. "We just made history. Tomorrow we're going to make even more history. After that, we are going to build one of the bonniest cities the world has ever seen. And do you know what else, Mr. Sewell? We're going to get filthy rich too. We are going to be American aristocrats, m'boy, barons of Miami. Stop worrying and relax a while. Everything is just as it is meant to be. I suggest you take the evening to rest, relax, and have a cold Julep, because you're going to be a very busy man in the near future."

"I sure could use that damned Mint Julep," Sewell confessed. "Where in the hell is that little red boy, anyway?"

Sewell and Ingram glanced across the field in the hopes of flagging Garnet down. Ingram's heart, however, suddenly skipped a beat as he noticed his wife's physician frantically hurrying across the open field from the infirmary. Ingram instinctively ran as fast as he could towards the bedraggled and mortified physician.

"It's Sigrid, sir," Schivelbush blurted through heavy breaths and a thick German accent. "Please," he pleaded with all his might, "you must come quickly."

Ingram sprinted as hard and fast as his tired and lanky legs could carry him, as though his very life depended on getting to Sigrid as quickly as he could. But by the time he arrived at the tent, it was too late to do anything but begin grieving her. His wife, whose lower half was soaked in more blood than Ingram knew could be contained in a human body, had suffered a sudden and devastating hemorrhage. The doctor was, however, ill-equipped to adequately address the emergency. Penelope, the unborn baby girl growing inside Sigrid, was dead even before the hemorrhage.

Mr. Ingram wilted when Schivelbush informed him that he was miraculously able to save the boy's life, but that saving the mother and daughter were beyond the ken of his abilities under such abysmal circumstances and conditions. "I'm not God," the physician explained in response to Ingram asking, "What can you do to save my wife?"

Mr. Ingram spent very little time in the denial stage of grief, which was partly the result of being confronted with the harsh and stark reality of his wife's half-nude, blood soaked, and rapidly bluing corpse next to the fast rotting unborn fetus plopped haphazardly atop an army cot near the egress of the tent. Ingram thus jumped straight through denial into soul ravaged rage. That assessment is based largely on the fact that Ingram savagely attacked the impish and unguarded physician, whose humidity-fogged glasses shattered from the first blow that connected with his fevered and pink face. Sewell, who had entered the tent just in time to see Ingram plant his fist in the physician's face, soiled his linen suit with grass, mud, and Schivelbush's blood while putting all his might into prying Mr. Ingram from atop the doctor's listless and unconscious body.

Hours later, just after sunset, Garnet was stark naked and covered in a film of sweat as he sat atop the straw mat he used as a bed that lay on the dirt floor inside his shabby, candlelit wooden shack somewhere on a particularly secluded section of the Miccosukee reservation. His primary focus appeared to be rolling a cigarette mixed with marijuana and tobacco. His shoulders were hunched abnormally forward and the contortion of his usually serene face betrayed him as a man suffering incredible emotional and psychological turmoil.

He pleaded with his lover, Goldie, to stay. "I got a bad feeling," Garnet said in a low and ominous tone. His sweaty brown skin glistened in the light emanating from the white candle dripping wax onto the dirt nearby the mat. "Please, I'm begging you," he pleaded, "just stay here tonight."

"You know I can't," she said annoyedly. "All the rail workers will be gone soon enough now that the golden spike has been laid. I need to earn as much cash as fast as I can before they've all gone."

"Well," he seethed, "do you gotta dress like a goddamn minstrel performer?" He rued her donning traditional Miccosukee dress rather than the Anglo-styled clothes provided by the Tuttles that they had grown accustomed to wearing.

"I told you a thousand fuckin' times," she growled, "this is what the customers want, so this is what I have to give them boys, or they'll just pay one of the other Miccosukee girls who dresses like this. I mean holy hell, Garnet, do we have to go through this every goddamn night? It's hard enough doin' this shit without you bellyachin' over it every goddamn time I'm headin' out the door."

"Please," he begged, "I'll pay you the wages you'd have lost."

"And how in the hell are you goin' to afford to do that?" she chortled as if her man had gone mad. "You've only been workin' on that construction crew at the Royal Palm a week now. You've only been workin' as Mr. Ingram's assistant a fortnight. God knows if he's even stayin' round here or goin' back to New York. God knows I'd be on the first train back to New York already if I'ze him."

"I'm makin' good money, and honest money too." Garnet retorted as though offended.

"Maybe so," she said, "but your position is as perpetually precarious as mine. So what difference in the goddamn world does it make whether the work is 'honest' or not?"

"That's beside the point," Garnet said while standing abruptly. He glared at Goldie.

"What exactly is the fuckin' point then?" she condescendingly wondered.

"The point is," he stammered a bit unnerved, "you... you don't gotta do this. Just hang in there a while; I can take care of you."

"You can take care of me?" she was disgusted. "Please, the last thing I need is another man to 'take care of me.' For God's sake, I've had men wantin' to 'take care of me' since I was yay high." She flattened the palm of her hand and placed it next to her knee. She then resumed struggling to button the back of the vibrantly colored gown. "Besides," she, who genuinely cared deeply for Garnet, tried to soften her delivery a bit by saying, "I thought you was savin' up for one of those fancy motorcycles so that gettin' to the construction site and back wouldn't take you half the damn day. What, you don't need that motorcycle no more or to keep that job, I reckon?"

"I'd rather be broke than have all those other men, white men no less, havin' their way with you."

"God damn it," she gutturally grunted. "Can we please just drop the fuckin' subject? Can't you see I'm already tied in knots? Why can't you just love and support me. Can't you see I'm hurtin' and you're just makin' it worse?"

A long and tense silence filled the inside of the tiny and humid candle-lit shack. Goldie continued to struggle to button the outfit. Though she had hoped to make Garnet endure a long stretch of the silent treatment to give him a chance to ruminate over her predicament, she needed assistance getting the gown buttoned. He intuitively knew she needed his help, but that she was far too proud to ask for it. He thus inched over to the other side of the shack to help her finish readying to do something he did not at all want her to do. She took a deep breath in as her lover buttoned the gown from her tailbone to the nape of her neck, which he gently kissed. Her sweat was salty but sweet on his lips. She turned around and gently kissed him then gazed deep and soulfully into his dark brown eyes.

"I need this job," she said matter-of-factly. "You know goddamn well I don't want to live like this a minute longer than you do," her somewhat manic eyes darted around the shabby interior of the dimly lit shack erected atop the dirt floor. "You know as well as I do that there ain't no other way for me to make money here until the locomotive comes regularly."

"Please," his heart ached as he lit his joint and passed it to her, "I just don't want you to go; not tonight. I need you. The thought of all those sacks of assholes touchin' your body makes me crazy, makes me sick. Please, Goldie," he pleaded with all his soul as she exhaled a lungful of smoke, "just bear with me a while longer. Now that the railroad is here, jobs will surely follow. It's just a matter a time before I can get us both out of this godforsaken mess. It's just goin' to require some time and patience."

"We've been over this," she huffed while passing the joint to him, then putting on the red lipstick she stole from Mrs. Tuttle's bathroom during the occupation the previous month. "You can't let yourself think about other men havin' their way with me. Whenever those thoughts come into your mind, you need to remind yourself that I hate this nightmare even more than you, but I'm doin' it for us. The sooner we can save enough money, the sooner we can buy that farm and leave this place for good, once and for all."

Garnet desperately wanted to believe that Goldie actually loathed prostituting herself to transient white men from around the world who had descended on their homeland to build the FEC rail lines between Palm Beach and Miami, but deep down in him a heavy, palpable and persistent fear that she secretly gained a measure of pleasure and satisfaction from being considered sexually attractive to white men haunted his more private waking moments. The only reason he got any sleep at all was due to the crate of gin he found buried in an underground bunker at the perimeter of Fort Dallas a few years earlier.

Call it a lover's intuition, but Garnet's fears that particularly dark and moonless evening of Goldie coming to some kind of heinous ignominy proved horribly prescient. By midnight, she was exhausted to the point of nausea. She had by then also lost count of the number of johns she had serviced since her shift began. By 12:30 a.m., she was desperate to get home, take a bath, say her prayers, curl up next to Garnet, and sleep until judgment day came. But she had yet to make the amount of money she had set as a goal for the night, so she agreed to give three seemingly affable chums a foursome in order to conclude her travail as expediently as possible.

Each of the trio was, however, beyond plastered thanks to a bottle of absinth they had shared, of which the youngest of the three – a lad from Belgium – had been saving to indulge until after the golden spike had been laid at Biscayne Bay. Two of the trio gladly and quickly agreed to the terms of the bargain. But the third, the youngest amongst them, who was but eighteen, demanded that she produce stereotypical Native American noises and phrases during coitus as though she were a caricature in a pornographic rendition of *Buffalo Bill's Wild West Spectacular*. Goldie, however, whose body and soul ached, refused to agree to be demeaned any further. The boy, who was particularly excited to watch the other two have their way with her, reluctantly relented and finally agreed to the original terms of Goldie's initial offer.

Goldie, who had been smoking opium and drinking laudanum for most of the night since leaving Garnet's shack, hardly noticed the first two of the men have their way with her at all, nor was she entirely conscious of the fact that the youngest of the three was masturbating whilst watching the two other, who he actually wanted to fuck more than her. Goldie was even more dazed and out of sorts by the time the youngest of the three found his way to penetrating her anus, which she had not agreed to. She stared at a log in the ceiling of the cabin over the bed.

She smiled slightly serene while imagining she and Garnet tending to llamas and alpacas near their quaint little stone farmhouse nestled in the shadow of a gloriously green Costa Rican mountain. Her fantasy was, however, suddenly interrupted by a hard smack across her mouth landed by the boy anally raping her. "Make Injun sounds, you stupid bitch," he demanded while the other two sweat-soaked men, both of whom came inside of her, nonchalantly dressed and laughed merrily, which further inspired the sadism of Goldie's assailant, who laughed manically as he gripped his hands tight around her throat. "I said make Injun noises, dummy," he grunted as he thrust his penis violently into her bloody rectum. She, however, stayed perfectly mum. He thus gripped tighter and wrung her neck as if trying to pop her head from off her shoulders. "Goddamn you, make Injun sounds, or so help me God I'll send you to Injun hell!"

"There ain't no Injun heaven or hell," the eldest of the three chuckled. "These redskins ain't got no souls, everybody knows that."

"Yeah well, let's say we find out, eh?" the boy said as he choked and thrust with all the power his sweaty, sloppy, and inebriated young body could muster. His friends laughed harder and harder. Then, a horrendously loud pop that seemed to echo inside the small, humid and steamy room that reeked of sweat, blood, semen and sex. The three men froze. An eerie silence lingered between them for an extended moment. Goldie's toned and sweat soaked body went completely limp. "Holy shit, man," the second eldest of the trio screeched. "What the hell did you do?"

"I didn't do a damn thing," the youngest said nervously while taking his semi-erect penis out of Goldie's bleeding anus. "You saw it, she was having a good time. She smiled."

The other two rail workers glanced nervously at each other.

"I think you broke her goddamn neck," the eldest of the three terrified men whispered.

"You think she's dead?" the youngest whispered, fearful of the answer. The eldest of the three slowly nodded while looking side-eyed at Goldie's lifeless body draped atop the sweat, blood, and semen-soaked mattress.

"Get dressed quick as you can," the eldest demanded in a low but powerful tone while looking deep into the eyes of the youngest. "Let's get our story straight; not one of us ever laid a goddamn finger on this whore," his callused hand cast accusatorily down at Goldie's listless body. "No matter what, you tell the law, if they even ever bother ask, that we had a whisky with the Injun, but decided we could not sin against our lord and savior, so we went straight back to camp in order to get up early to vote in the election. No matter what the law might throw at us, as long as we stick to the goddamn story, we will get through this." He nodded forcefully, trying to transfer some grit and determination into the other two, who seemed as though they were fast approaching panic. The younger two, however, nodded compliantly, but also quite sheepishly, as though two kids who had just been asked if they understood that Santa Claus had been crucified because of sins they had committed.

As the eldest of the three had predicted, there was little inquiry made as to who actually murdered Goldie. Garnet did his best to investigate, but the murderer and his accessories to the crime had fled the county by dawn, and were in Georgia before her murder was even reported to the newly elected Sheriff of the newly created county of Dade. The first Sheriff of Miami was an FEC employee who had no experience or interest in law enforcement anyway. He was certainly not about to open an investigation that might create bad headlines for the FEC's newest venture. *The Miami Metropolis*, the only paper that existed in Miami in those very early days in the city's existence was owned by the FEC and thus was also never going to print a story about some Miccosukee girl who had been murdered by an FEC employee. Both *The Metropolis* and the Dade County Sheriff, which might as well be considered employees of the same corporation, both, in short, had deeply vested interests in ensuring that news of Goldie's murder did not find its way into the public record. Goldie was gone. But Garnet, who buried her himself near the creek where she took his virginity, never forgot.

CHAPTER ELEVEN

Tuesday, February 15, 1896, Biscayne Bay, Florida

The morning after the Ingram-rigged election, Mrs. Tuttle walked out onto the front porch of her newly finished Spanish villa, which was far nicer, more comfortable, and further removed from the Miccosukee, who she had grown to resent and loathe ever since they became bedfellows with Flagler and the FEC. She and her children had planted a modest orange grove behind the villa, but it had yet to bear any fruit. Though she was pleased with the majesty of her glorious new piece of property and architectural masterpiece, she harbored a great deal of qualms each time she cast her eyes towards the north end of Biscayne Bay, where Flagler's resort was being built by an interracial workforce to resemble Versailles, which she believed to be a terribly gaudy eyesore. She also feared that it was but a matter of time before the entire landscape that stretched out in front of her bespectacled eyes would be scattered with pastel bungalows and shabby enterprises of every stripe.

She pushed the screen door of the porch open in order to go down to check her crab traps in the shallows of the bay. A manila sheet of paper that a trespasser had left pinned into the screen door fluttered across the cool and soggy green earth underneath her bare feet. She plucked the paper up. The very top of the paper read: "*Miami Metropolis*: The Most Southern Paper in All the USA." Her heart sank. "Metropolis?" she muttered frustratedly. Her greatest fears of what Miami was to become seemed to be confirmed by that one word. Her eyes then scanned further down the sheet. "Congratulations," she read in a whisper, "you are fortunate enough to be holding the very first edition of the very first newspaper in the history of Miami, 'The Magic City' under the Florida Sun." Calling the first edition of *The Metropolis* was hyperbolic, if not delusional. The newspaper, as it were, was but one sheet and was comprised mostly of ads for city services and parcels of land that could be purchased, interspersed with a few notices that workers were needed to build the Royal Palm Hotel.

There were only two stories that Tuttle could detect to actually be considered newsworthy on the front page of *The Metropolis* as she stood out on her bayfront lawn the morning after Miami's inaugural election. The first headline that caught her eye was not gladly received. It read, "FEC's Slate of Candidates Sweeps First Municipal Election in City's History." The second and biggest headline was received by Tuttle rather indifferently. It read, "It's a Boy: Emory Ingram, First Baby Born in Miami." There was no mention of anything having had happened to Goldie, Sigrid, or Penelope – as though none of them had ever existed, never mind died the day Miami officially came into existence.

The widow Tuttle, convinced that she had been hoodwinked by Mrs. Applebee and the Polish sorcerer in her time of woe and despair, angrily tore up *The Metropolis* and then tossed it into the wind. She trudged down the rather steep embankment towards the water and waded into the shallows towards a trap full of crawling blue crabs, each stepping on the other in the hopes of escaping their predicament. She planned to boil them all and serve them with butter and parsnip to Charlie, who she feared was neurasthenic, and Margaret, who had grown even more melancholy than normal since her father had passed.

CHAPTER TWELVE

Wednesday, October 29, 1919

There is a tiny two-mule town called Pahokee halfway between Miami and Palm Beach, which, due to high poverty and low employment rates, many of the more superstitious locals believed to be cursed. There was a legend as old as the town itself that when the Spanish first arrived in the sixteenth century in search of Calusa slaves, gold, and the mythic Fountain of Youth, that many conquistadors that had vanished and were never seen again were taken by some mystical force that lurked deep in the thick pinewoods. Some also believed that the Spaniards that had gone missing were lost down one of Florida's many sinkholes. Legend has it that these massive craters that spontaneously open and swallow the earth and anything standing atop it were portals to other dimensions. Still others believed that the legends of the disappeared conquistadors were actually the result of rapacious alligators or pernicious vipers, rather than sinkholes or evil spirits. A third school of thought by which some locals explained the legend of the lost conquistadors suggested that the Spanish were actually woefully clueless as to how big Florida actually was and thus conquistadors' scouts would often set out thinking they could walk a short while from the Atlantic coast to the Gulf of Mexico, but instead would become irretrievably lost in a swamp within two hours. The Spanish thus began to bring ponies by the boatload and set them free all across the peninsula in the hope that if a lost scout were to get stranded, he could, hopefully, find one of these wild horses and ride it back to the nearest fort. But to the Spaniard's great dismay, many horses disappeared too.

Centuries later, these kinds of legends and superstitions had not lost their cultural force in either Pahokee or Miami, especially considering that in 1919 Pahokee had one of the highest rates of poverty, joblessness, and violent crimes per capita in the country. Part of this could be explained by the fact that Pahokee attracted transient workers from all over the American South and the Caribbean, which led to bitter conflicts for what sparse job opportunities existed in the backwater to Miami, which was still in many ways a backwater of the Deep South, which was a backwater of the rest of the nation. Outside of seasonal agricultural work, there were few options for making a living in South Florida, so rates of unemployment, alcoholism, and church attendance were also especially high in Pahokee. Disposing of a corpse was also exceedingly easy in these rural climes, which served as a kind of macabre incentive to murdering anyone who was owed money, could testify against you, and the like. Las Vegas is notorious for the already dug holes surrounding the city waiting to conceal evidence, such as a corpse. But in South Florida, especially parts as removed from urbanity as Pahokee, no hole was ever even necessary; you just drag the body to the closest swamp and let the gators do as nature intended.

Pahokee also attracted the likes of Edmund Flowers, a stern but attractive man who found his calling as a Southern Baptist preacher around the time he reached puberty. His mother, who worked from sunup to sundown at the Winston-Salem cigarette processing plant in North Carolina, was mute due to a beating she received by her mother when she was eleven. She was, as might be expected, also very abusive to Edmund when he was a boy. But she was a devout Southern Baptist. Once the boy began preaching the gospel, he quickly became the favorite of his mother's twelve children, three of whom were bastards, including Edmund.

Before marrying his wife, Michelle, and before their daughter, Scarlet, was born, Edmund rode the rails as far south as the railroad could go, stopping in each Podunk town and delivering sermons to anyone who would be so kind as to listen and drop something – anything – into his collection plate. Edmund was an incredibly charismatic orator and had a fire and brimstone style of preaching that attracted the most fervid evangelicals to his tent. Best of all, he honestly believed the bullshit he was peddling, which is the basis for any great con. He soon became a kind of celebrity amongst the townsfolk who peopled the new cardboard towns that popped up along the new rail lines being built across the Deep South in the decades after the fight over Reconstruction had been settled decidedly by the wealthiest white men in the region.

Edmund's only real vice back in those salad days of his preaching career was a MoonPie every now and again, which he ate with a knife and fork and a tall glass of milk after his Sunday evening sermons. He scrimped and saved for many years like he was a paragon of Max Weber's notions of the Protestant work ethic. Soon after the American Expeditionary Force's "doughboys" had been shipped to France in 1917, he finally had finally saved and borrowed enough money to put out his own shingle and started his own Southern Baptist Ministry in Pahokee.

By war's end, a steep economic downturn that had dovetailed with the sudden lack of manufacturing jobs in war industries, sparked even more of the vitriolic racism, misogyny, and vigilante violence that was already endemic in the decades before the war. Church attendance had likewise spiked all across the Deep South. It was as if this brave new age of secularized consumer capitalism that had fast created wider gaps between rich and poor had had the unintended consequence of renewing the significance in the totally desperate and wholly human search for meaning that might transcend the harsh realities of modern American politics and economics. Darwin's theory of evolution being popularized in public schools all across the nation also stoked greater evangelical fervency, which led to greater attendance at Baptist churches all across the Deep South. Edmund's ministry, in short, benefited mightily by the spike in attendance and especially by the extra tithe paid to him by people increasingly desperate for God to hear their prayers in times of such economic turmoil and social upheaval and despair. He was also the closest thing in town to a charismatic celebrity, which made him more popular than the mayor. Edmund thus began holding services twice a week – on Sunday mornings, then again on Wednesday evenings.

Edmund's personality was somewhat manic whilst in the pulpit. He would come across as a very stoic and stern man when sitting still and while engaged in silent prayer, but he seemed to be possessed by manic forces beyond his control when preaching the gospel with the *Bible* held tight in his right hand like a brick that he might like to hurl at anyone who dare nod off during his bombastic sermons. His slick black hair flapped back and forth atop his long and narrow head while he orated. He also often convulsed and shouted about damnation this and hellfire that, or spoke in a gibberish that he described as "tongues," which he insisted was God speaking directly through him. He would sometimes whip his congregation into such a fervid state that elderly ladies jumped from their pews waving their arthritic hands while vehemently hailing "amen!" and "blessed be the name of the Lord!"

Edmund's intense eyes peered down at the fervid worshipers from the perched point of view provided by the elevated pulpit. "I'm tellin' y'all right now," he banged his fist into the wooden podium in front of him, "that infernal engine made of iron is pullin' that Yankee and mongrel evil from New York City down to our blessed communities more and more each day, infecting us as virulently as the Spanish Flu infected so many millions around the world. Each day more and more sinners of every diabolical stripe are peoplin' our communities, brethren and sistren. Is it any wonder that poor little girls end up dead along these godforsaken rail lines?"

Scarlet, his eighteen-year-old daughter who grew up too fast and forgave too slow, was bored as she gazed at the streaks of multihued sunlight streaming in through the stained-glass window that depicted Christ hanging on the cross behind her father's manically animated mien. But Edmund's ominous insinuation that the railroad was a source of evil piqued her interest. "It is," Edmund added as Scarlet paid greater mind to the sermon, "not merely our civic duty, but our righteous calling to prevent the evil from spreading any more than it has by any means and methods available to us. God has ordained us, especially the young men amongst us, as protectors of our way of life, which is imperiled more and more each day by Yankee Darwinists who coddle the darkies, these shaved apes. I say, if these black beasts insist on coming down to our peaceful and Godfearin' communities to outrage white womanhood whenever they get the urge, then it is our ordained duty to give these niggras a good old-fashioned necktie party as a requisite deterrent to other niggras or Yankees who might have the same kind of mind." An obese woman a few rows behind the front pew, which was occupied by Edmund's wife and daughter, blubbered "amen" while waving a white hanky and her hand high above her head.

Scarlet had finished high school the previous June and was becoming acutely and painfully aware of the charlatan that her father, who was once her hero, was at the core of his being. She thus slightly rolled her eyes as she shifted uneasily in her seat. There was no public school within forty miles, so her momma did the best she could to tutor her in the core academic disciplines. But her mother had never made it past the eighth grade herself, so Scarlet's tutelage had not prepared her to do much of anything but be at some man's beck-and-call, which was a fate Scarlet had no interest in.

"Mark my words, dearly beloved," Edmund bemoaned apocalyptically. "We are being invaded more and more each day by hordes of mongrels due to that infernal railroad and radio. It is not just our right," he said while smashing his fist into the podium, "but our duty as white Christian men to defend our most precious asset on God's good earth – white womanhood." The audience erupted wildly. Many people hollered "amen" and "praise Jesus!"

Edmund then cast a long glance down at his rather distracted daughter. "On that note," he feigned pride as he hollered over the crackling hum of the frenzied and bloodthirsty congregants "I'd like to invite my lovely and precious daughter up front here to sing us all a hymn. Y'all know she sings like an angel!"

The crowd simmered somewhat as Scarlet situated herself in front of the altar. Her father loomed over her from his pulpit. Scarlet, who was wearing a pristine white dress that went all the way to her ankles, smiled nervously and tugged subconsciously at a platinum blond curl tucked behind her ear. Her emerald eyes settled nervously on the stained-glass window toward the back of the apse, which depicted Mother Mary holding a bloody and dead Jesus Christ in her arms. Scarlet's rendition of "There'll be Peace in The Valley" was very moving indeed. Her voice was so pure, clear, calming and angelic that it brought even the most hard-hearted of congregants to a state of momentary, though fleeting, peace of mind, body and spirit. Edmund then concluded the service by offering communion before sending around the collection plates that paid his mortgage. The congregants, almost all of whom were poor, gladly paid their tithe in the hopes that it bettered their chances of one day living in God's kingdom, which was, so many of them believed, the antithesis of the misery that defined their lives in Pahokee.

That evening, Scarlet was sure to lock her bedroom door after bathing and putting on her pink pinstriped pajamas. She cloistered herself inside her room with the newest edition of *The Saturday Evening Post*, which her father had forbidden her from reading. But the taboo of reading it only made her want to do it more. She sat Indian style at the very center of her bed longingly gazing at the vibrant advertisements and pictures in the magazine, receiving some kind of narcotic sense of satisfaction, as if the ads were portals for entering a more exotic, but safer, locale and headspace than could be achieved in her small, dimly lit pink bedroom. A somewhat muffled and quiet rendition of Nick LaRocca and the Original Dixieland Band's "Tiger Rag" blared from the small speaker of the transistor radio atop her dresser that she had shoplifted from Woolworth's two weeks earlier. Her toe tapped manically to the fiery beat, but the rest of her being seemed quietly entranced by the sensual and seductive ads in the magazine. She flipped each page of the *Post* like she were opening a new gift. Her enticed eyes sparkled as she absorbed an advert that read, "Miss Orange Blossom Pageant: Be the Magic City's Most Beautiful Belle and Win $100!" Below the headline was a cartoon crafted by Mr. Sewell, who had organized the pageant, which depicted several white women wearing tiny, tattered and torn dresses of various shades of pastel soaked in seawater frolicking in the shallows with a bright and multihued beach ball. Scarlet caressed the ad gently, almost lovingly, with the tip of her index finger and then held the magazine against her chest as she gazed at the full moon ascending outside her bedroom window.

She imagined herself on stage winning the pageant as her parents and, more importantly, hundreds of strangers cheered wildly and blew her kisses from the raucous crowd cheering her name, "Scarlet! Scarlet! Scarlet!" Though Miami was only thirty-five miles from her father's modest bungalow in Pahokee, it seemed a world away from the majestic Magic City depicted in Sewell's ads.

The sudden jarring of the locked handle, immediately followed by an angered banging on the door, startled Scarlet and derailed her fantasy of being Miss Orange Blossom. Her spine stiffened as she sat up in a fright. Her worried face was suddenly perspiring as she shoved the magazine under her pillow. "Open the door, Scarlet," the preacher demanded. "You know I don't like locked doors in my house." He smashed his fist into the door with the same vitriol he did with the podium in the pulpit at his service that morning while advocating vigilante violence as a proper means of pursuing what he perceived to be God's brand of justice. "Open the door this instant or you're gonna get it again," he threatened.

The previous six times her father had railed during sermon about "black beast rapists" he had later sexually violated his daughter the very same night. It was as if he had grown so titillated by the twisted and hysterical fantasy of the rape of white women by black men that he could not resist imposing that perfidious anxiety and energy onto his own daughter, who he genuinely believed himself to be a protector of.

Scarlet had, as she raced across the field towards the orange groves that provided a shortcut home after Wednesday evening service ended, anticipated her father's desire to outrage her. She thus ran straight home from church and retrieved Edmund's Colt .32 revolver from underneath the mattress of her his bed, which was separated from his wife's bed by a modest end table with a dim and perpetually flickering lamp atop it.

"Open the damn door, young lady," Edmund demanded once more, "or I'll rip it off its hinges."

Michelle, his anguished, frightened, despairing, and unloved wife, momentarily ceased drying the dishes used to serve meatloaf during supper and draped her damp dishtowel over the edge of the sink. She then cautiously crept towards the dining room, then into the living room, and peaked down the darkened hallway leading towards the back of the bungalow, where the two bedrooms were. "This is your final warnin'," Edmund ominously promised. His face was as shiny and red as the Coca-Cola cap atop the dining table next to Edmund's pack of Chesterfields.

Inside the bedroom, Scarlet retrieved her father's pistol from under her pillow, cocked it, and aimed it squarely at the door. Her hands trembled and bulbs of sweat formed on her smooth, sweaty, and tanned forehead. Her breath was heavy. Her eyes widened.

"I'm giving you to the count of three," Edmund snarled as he smashed his now throbbing hand into the door once more. Scarlet lowered the pistol suddenly and then hurriedly grabbed a few items of clothes, but panicked, forgot to put on shoes. She then slid her bedroom window open and crawled through, but fell clumsily into the hedgerow and tore the pant leg of her pajamas. "One," she heard her father holler. She struggled to free herself from the hedge, but finally managed to, and then ran from the side of the house and around to the street lined with modest two-bedroom pastel bungalows and elm trees that provided the sidewalks a modicum of shade during the midday. She looked in both directions, but her bare feet stayed firmly planted in the soft and dewy grass, as if she was paralyzed by fear of the unknown more than the devil pounding on her bedroom door inside his house.

Scarlet had previously, after the third time her father raped her, considered the possibility of killing him. After the fourth time, she decided it might make more sense to kill herself so that her mother would at least have a breadwinner. She took a knife into the bath one night, but feared eternity in hell too deeply to permit herself to cut her wrists open and bleed her insides down the drain. She had, however, never considered running away for the simple fact that she had nowhere else to go. Michelle's grandparents had succumbed to typhus when Scarlet was a small child. Edmund had never said a kind word about his mother, who had been so abusive to him when he was a boy, so Scarlet never even knew her father's side of the family. Now that Scarlet had fled her father's house, she did not know where to go, never mind how to get there.

"Two!" Scarlet heard her father's voice boom through the screen door at the front of the house. She raced over to the front porch and peaked through the screen. She could see her father down the darkened hallway facing her bedroom door with his back to her. Scarlet sneaked into the living room. The screen door creaked. She was terrified her father would hear it. But the sound of his pounding on the bedroom door and his voice bellowing "three" muffled the sound of the squeaking door's hinges. Scarlet's mother, however, anxiously noticed her daughter deftly slide into the house. Michelle took the keys to Edmund's truck from atop the dish-hutch separating the kitchen and dining room and stealthily handed them to Scarlet. "Go as far away as you can," Michelle whispered pleadingly to her only begotten child. Scarlet snatched the keys from her mother's hand and then darted towards the front door of the bungalow.

Edmund smashed the door to Scarlet's bedroom off its hinges with his shoulder and plowed his way inside. He darted over to the pink bed, dropped to his haunches and scanned under the box spring and bedframe, but she was not there. He then ran over to the closet, tore it open and searched it as fast as he could. But she was not there either. He froze a moment, perplexed, pondering hard where she might be. He then darted to the window and poked his head outside just as Scarlet hopped into the driver's seat of his truck.

Edmund sprinted down the hallway and into the living room. Michelle courageously obstructed her husband's path to the porch, so he smashed her in the face with a closed fist. The sudden and violent blow made Michelle swoon. She fell sideways into the hallway wall and slid down to the hardwood floor in a heap. She held her hands over her throbbing and bloody face. Her eyes stared straight ahead as though she had been knocked into another dimension.

Scarlet twisted the keys in the ignition and fired up the engine. Black soot spewed from the tailpipe. Edmund ran out of the house hollering that he'd kill her if she dared defy him further. Scarlet, who took her father's death threat seriously, fired a round from the pistol through the passenger-side window, which barely missed hitting Edmund, and lodged in a pine tree in the front yard. Edmund dropped to the warm and dewy grass and covered his head with his hands. Scarlet plowed over the mailbox next to the curb as she hurriedly put the truck in reverse. She then slammed the gearshift into drive and mashed down on the gas pedal with her bare foot. The truck barreled down the street heading south as fast as it could go, which was not very fast at all.

Edmund chased the truck little more than a tenth of a mile demanding, "you get back here Scarlet, or so help me God!" By then, some of the unnerved neighbors had trickled onto their porches or neatly manicured lawns wondering what all the fuss was about. "Go back in your houses," Edmund demanded as kindly as the charlatan preacher could muster under such trying circumstances, "this don't concern none of y'all. This is a family matter."

He then rushed frantically back into the house where Michelle had just staggered up onto her wavering legs. She clumsily hurried towards the kitchen and successfully arrived just in time to beat her wild-eyed husband to the telephone. She defiantly yanked the cord from the wall so that Edmund could not call the Sheriff, who would thus not be able to pursue Scarlet. Edmund then pried the receiver from his wife's blood-soaked hands and beat her savagely in her face and head with it until she was finally an unconscious collection of bloodied and battered nucleic cells. "You are my wife," he fumed while standing over her and straightening his waistcoat. "The *Bible* says the punishment of defying your husband is death," he huffed gruffly while casting his accusatory finger down at his unconscious, bloodied, and battered wife as he desperately tried to catch his breath. "You're lucky I'm so Christ-like in my ability to forgive others' sins," he huffed. "Now you sit there a while and ask the lord for forgiveness for defyin' your husband."

He then washed his hands in the kitchen sink and dried them off with the towel his wife had used to dry the dishes, then walked calmly into the living room, sat in his favorite reclining chair, lit a Chesterfield, and then opened the *Bible* to the book of *Corinthians* and bellowed so loud that the sound of his voice might soak into his wife's unconscious mind. "Let the husband render unto the wife due benevolence," he recited, "and likewise, also the wife unto the husband. The wife hath not power of her own body, but the husband."

He glared down at Michelle. Blood from a wound on her head seeped into her hardly opened eyes. Her lashes fluttered like butterfly wings soaked in oil.

CHAPTER THIRTEEN

Thursday, October 30, 1919, Miami, Florida

Henry Flagler appeared so oddly pristine and peaceful laying in his coffin during his funeral, which was held in the grand ballroom of the palatial Royal Palm Hotel on Biscayne Bay. The room was packed with some of American high society's most notable socialites, including Cornelius Vanderbilt, H.R. Repogle, and Margaret Singer.

Most of Miami's Brahmins, as it were, were also in attendance, including the boisterous and effusive William Jennings Bryan, the popular yet defeated Populist presidential candidate from Nebraska who Flagler shrewdly hired to deliver sunrise Sunday sermons on the back lawn of the Royal Palm. Bryan's oratorical powers helped attract *Bible*-thumping salvation seekers from all across the American heartland to Miami in the first two decades of the twentieth century. Bryan often shrewdly, although rather dastardly, conflated the will of the Almighty with the will of Miami's city fathers, encouraging vacationers to consider snatching up parcels of land and building themselves beautiful bungalows because, as he routinely reminded parishioners, Miami was overflowing with "God's sunshine." That was, he often declared during sermons, part of the reason South Florida, comparatively speaking, lacked the labor and racial strife of northern cities, which he deemed evidence of the Almighty's sanctioning of Miami as a haven from the "evils" suffered by so many other cities north of the Mason-Dixon Line, especially New York, Chicago, Detroit, and Cleveland.

The Mizner brothers, blue-blooded society types who were heavily invested in land schemes just north of Miami, most notably Fort Lauderdale and Boca Raton and as far west as Monroe County, were also in attendance at Mr. Flagler's wake.

Addison Mizner, the younger of the brothers, was an acclaimed architect and purveyor of casino capitalism. He was especially adept at using mass media, particularly *The Palm Beach Post*, of which he owned a large share of, as a convenient vehicle with which to imbue certain real estate developments that he had a vested interest in with value, no matter how far under water the parcels of land might have been. This tactic he, of course, learned from watching Mr. Flagler, rest his soul, who employed the same shrewd, albeit amoral and underhanded methods, in the preceding decades.

Carl Fisher, the owner of the gaudy and pink Flamingo Hotel on Miami Beach, which was, despite its name and for some odd reason built to look like a huge pink elephant, was also in attendance. His hotel was as hideous as all the sin in Hades, but certainly caught the eye and imagination of the yokels who stayed there. Miami Beach had only recently been made accessible to automobiles as a result of the finishing of the Collins Causeway. The completion of the causeway caused a tremendous spike in the property values on the barrier island, as did the headlines that trumpeted Miami Beach as a soon-to-be "secluded" and "exclusive" resort paradise for the world's elite.

Despite how hideous it was and how gauche Fisher was wont to be, the completion of the causeway was also a boon to the Flamingo Hotel. Fisher had retired from Prest-o-Lite at the tender age of thirty-five after having industrialized and scaled the automobile headlight for mass production and sale. This invention was shrewd and timely in that it was soon purchased by Ford Motors. The sale made Fisher one of the richest men under the age of forty in the country. He had already made a name for himself in Miami by the time he bought the land to build the Flamingo back in 1916. But by the summer of 1919, the Collins Causeway was complete, the Great War had ended, and Mr. Fisher had already doubled his investment, which made him somewhat of a legend in Miami, a city where casino capitalism was peculiarly respected. Other, some might say 'more distinguished' old-money and thus more respected men of Puritan stock, came to see past his gruff and guffawing exterior to respect this young albeit obnoxious millionaire.

After the completion of the causeway, the Flamingo soon came to be the hottest night spot on the Gold Coast, especially Saturday nights. By the end of fall, Fisher's raucous and raunchy parties were infamous and legendary for the tawdry hedonism they had become synonymous with. There's an old saying in Miami: The Roaring Twenties began in 1919 at Carl Fisher's Hotel. The parties he hosted also garnered headlines in lifestyle sections of newspapers around the world because they lured celebrities such as Rudolph Valentino, Clara Bow, Babe Ruth, Al Jolson, Charles Bayha, Al Capone and countless other names that routinely made headlines. And although the notoriety earned him as many enemies as admirers, Fisher was an ardent believer in the newly popularized, some might say delusional, notion that there was no such thing as bad publicity. And while Fisher was still relatively new money in Miami, he shrewdly knew the importance of making an appearance at Flagler's wake in the interest of articulating himself as one of the city's undisputed Brahmin now that Flagler, the "Father of Miami," was finally being laid to rest.

James Ingram and Everett Sewell were also in attendance at the wake, although neither would even look at the other, let alone share words. Neither noticed Fisher either, let alone considered him to be among their ilk. Mutual friends often lamented the rift that had gradually widened between Ingram, Flagler's heir apparent, and Sewell, who thought himself more responsible than Ingram for Miami's meteoric ascendance in a mere generation from a scrappy frontier outpost at the edge of an empire to a sprawling suburban resort metropolis and harbinger for what America was about to become – a consumerist emporium. Ingram and Sewell had shared a rather cordial working relationship in the earliest years of Miami's existence, but relations between them quickly soured and grew increasingly fractured over the years, to the point that by the fall of 1919 neither had spoken to each other in more than a decade. The primary wedge driven between Sewell and Ingram was of a philosophical nature. Although they parted ways on many topics, the particular point of contention was over the identity, future, and fate of the city that both men had had such a heavy hand in building. Ingram envisioned Miami being much as it always had been; a small seasonal resort utopia that catered specifically to the world's richest, whitest, and most famous. "Get the big snobs and the little snobs will follow," Ingram often reminded Garnet, his righthand man, and Emory, his beloved son and only surviving relative. Mr. Sewell, the ad man, conversely, understood the key role technology could and should play in fueling the urbanization of South Florida. Sewell had, like the Mizners, quietly purchased land all across the region since the panic of 1911 and aimed to carve out a place for himself as an American aristocrat comparable to Flagler, the Vanderbilts, Singers, and the Astors. Sewell also shrewdly knew that the invention of the home air conditioning system had the potential to transform Miami from a winter resort backwater that specifically catered to the rich, into a global city and cultural epicenter comparable to London, New York, and Paris, which is why he bought so much stock in Culligan. He was also adamant that the most expedient means with which to quell the pernicious racial violence that had spiked since the end of World War I was to export all of the African Americans residing in Florida back to Africa, which he deemed to be a progressive remedy to solve America's, as he put it, "negro problem." Ingram, conversely, was at his core, a free market capitalist who only cared about one color, the color of money.

Sewell, who was in the final week of an exceedingly long and acrimonious race against Ingram for the mayor of Miami, a contest *The Miami Herald* apocalyptically referred to as "the battle for the soul of the city," never missed an opportunity to build his brand and get his name in print. It thus came as no great surprise to Ingram or anyone else in attendance at Flagler's wake who knew him personally that Mr. Sewell would inevitably put himself at the center of attention at some point during the proceedings. True to form, Sewell climbed atop a wooden chair and clanked his bulky gold wedding ring against the half-empty mason jar of Mint Julep in his hand in the hope of hushing the room to order so that he could say a few words about Mr. Flagler that would ultimately aggrandize Mr. Sewell. "I'd like so very much to thank y'all for comin' to pay your respects to the esteemed father of this great city of ours, the lion of Miami, Mr. Flagler," Sewell's southern drawl filled the room as the last whispers of private conversation faded to a hush. "Now, as y'all know," Sewell continued, "Mr. Flagler was a titan of industry and an uncompromising visionary, not to mention a wizard of Wall Street. But we all in some way also deserve to be commended," Sewell said. "We all share some part in making his magnificent dream – Miami – the glorious reality it is today." He preened, posing for a picture a moment while casting a smug glance at Mr. Ingram. "But now it is up to all of us to take up the mantle of Mr. Flagler's dream and to shoulder the great responsibility of turning Miami, this truly wonderful and Magic City, into all she can be – something far more monumental and memorable than some seasonal resort city backwater at the end of the FEC rail line. With the advent of commercial air flight, it is but a matter of time before Miami will be the capital city of both Dixie and Latin America. I, fine friends of Mr. Flagler and Miami, am just the man to take up that mantle and carry this great city into an even grander future than even the great Mr. Flagler might have imagined when he first planted his flag in our fertile soil. Just a fine and friendly reminder: have one hell of a Happy Halloween and don't y'all forget to vote Tuesday. Now," he concluded while waving the palms of his hands excitedly at the now applauding audience, "if y'all will kindly raise your glass for a toast to Mr. Flagler, and a toast to making Miami into all she can be." Anyone holding a glass in the room raised it.

Garnet, however, raced into the ballroom and pushed his way through the crowd to Mr. Ingram and whispered excitedly into his employer's ear. Mr. Ingram's contorted face that expressed impatience suddenly softened. His tentative and measured smile was steeped in relief. His entire aura changed from stiff and burdened to languid and relaxed by the time Garnet's words, "Emory is almost here," could be fully processed by the father, who was wholly desperate to see his son.

Mr. Ingram and Garnet hurriedly pushed through the funeral attendees towards the egress of the ballroom. "I suppose my opponent has more important matters to attend to than to toast the man who provided his livelihood lo these many years," Mr. Sewell said while smirking haughtily and glaring down at his adversary. Some of the wake's attendees chortled or chuckled at Sewell's haphazard attempt at lobbing an insult veiled as a joke. A reporter from *The Herald*, meanwhile, delightedly scrawled notes with a pencil across a small and worn out notepad. Neither Ingram nor Garnet, however, paid Sewell's desperate attempt at a slight any mind.

The sun was only just beginning to set over Biscayne Bay. It was magic hour in the Magic City. The blue, green, gold, and orange of the bay appeared even more pregnant with color and texture than usual. The lavender, orange, pink, and purple streaks high in the twilight sky overhead seemed like an inspiration for a modern masterpiece that could hang in the Louvre. A tall and lovely bride with a head full of amber waves of hair dressed in a flowing white gown and veil blushed and grinned as her father, who was wearing a crisp black tuxedo and wingtips, proudly and tearfully led the bride down a red velvet aisle flanked on either side by excited wedding attendees sitting in white wooden chairs. An incredible cascade of colors reflected off the bride's crown, which was made of crystal, and rested neatly and gently atop her veil. Her wide blue eyes soaked in the splendor of the scene, wanting the memory to exist forever in her heart.

Up ahead of the bride at the end of a long red and velvet carpet that intersected the rows of seats filled with excited wedding attendees was a studious and distinguished Presbyterian minister; the bridesmaids, all of whom were wearing identical gowns that matched the lavender in the twilight sky overhead, stood to the minister's right; Emory was standing tall and strong next to the minister and gazing over at Quinn, his high school sweetheart, as she walked down the aisle arm-in-arm with her father, whose hair was mostly white with a smattering of black strands in it.

Emory, who was not yet aware he was dreaming, could not understand why he was watching his own wedding from the back of the gathering, but was glad that at least one of him had full use of their legs. Both Emorys in attendance – the one in the wheelchair at the back of the proceeding and also the one waiting anxiously for his bride to arrive at the altar – had not seen Quinn since he had departed for France many months earlier. He was thus understandably awed and somewhat confused and scared at what was transpiring (twice) simultaneously.

Quinn finally made her way to the altar and smiled warmly at Emory (the one with legs). He cautiously returned the smile, but only for a fleeting and confused moment. His face suddenly contorted as his legs dropped out from under him. Panic set in amongst the attendees as Emory began to drag himself on his belly towards his other self, who was at the edge of the bay. Garnet and Mr. Ingram rushed over to aid Emory (the one with legs), but a massive alligator longer than twelve feet in length and one thousand pounds in girth scurried from the shallows of the bay and snatched him by the torso and dragged him into the water. Quinn, her bridesmaids, and many of the other attendees at the wedding-turned-tragedy, rushed to the shoreline as the alligator began its death roll with Emory firmly in its razor-sharp grasp. The Emory still in his wheelchair watched in horrified dismay as the alligator disappeared to the bottom of the bay. He felt as though he himself were suffocating as he watched air bubbles rise to the otherwise calm and glassy surface of the bay.

Forsaken and pinned to the bottom of the bay, Emory quickly resigned himself to his fate and did not even bother to put up a fight. He stared straight up at the twinkling lights and early evening moonlight that seemed suspended on the surface of the water. He stroked the alligator's head lovingly for a time until all the air had fled his body.

Meanwhile, the Emory in his wheelchair back on shore, struggled to roll across the grass towards Quinn, who was standing ankle deep in the bay tearfully observing the last gasp of the other Emory's air bubbles pop at the surface.

"Quinn?" Emory's voice seemed to plead as he rolled nearer. She did not hear him. "Quinn?" he said a bit louder as he struggled to wheel nearer. "Quinn?" he hollered. But again, she could not hear him.

The locomotive screeched and clanked to a sudden halt at a modest open-air train station in the shadow of the Miami News Tower, a magnificent and glittering Mediterranean-style structure that loomed over Biscayne Bay. Emory, whose forehead and upper lip were soaked in beads of sweat, woke suddenly and somewhat dazed and afraid. For a fleeting moment, he was relieved that he had only been dreaming. But then his tired and manic eyes fixated on his amputated limbs pulsating with phantom pangs. He was suddenly very aware of how shockingly hollow, empty and alone he felt in the deepest recesses of his soul. His weary oceans for eyes spotted his father and Garnet anxiously waiting for him at the other end of the platform outside the window of the first-class train car.

Orit, who had not slept a minute of the more than forty-four-hour odyssey from Penn Station to Miami, was especially disheveled. Jasper – who had been high on heroin since the scheduled stop in Charleston many hours earlier, where he had gladly retrieved his kitbag from a much-obliged Emory – seemed to languidly float by as he passed Mr. Ingram and Garnet with his horn case tucked snugly under his arm and his suitcase in his other hand. Neither Garnet nor Mr. Ingram paid Jasper any mind; both were too anxious glancing in windows hoping to catch their first glimpse of Emory, whose malnourished and sickly mien and scraggly beard made him especially difficult to detect as the clean-cut All-American boy who had left for France.

Emory was already aching for another fix of heroin by the time the #7 screeched to a halt in Miami. His hands were trembling like an overheated engine, and not just because he was nervous for his father to see his only begotten son in such a desolate state. His hands shook mostly due to the fact that he was already deep in the sticky-sick thicket of opiate withdrawal.

His angst, anger, and despair were further piqued by the extreme humiliation he endured by being unceremoniously hauled off the train and plopped into his wheelchair by the racist attendant of Irish origin, while his father and Garnet tried desperately to mask their awkward discomfort at the site of Emory's incapacitation. Mr. Ingram and Garnet were kind to pretend nothing was amiss, but both instantly understood that things would never quite be the same for Emory, who had once been a star athlete.

Emory's return from the war was, in short, hardly the homecoming Mr. Ingram had fantasized about since the minute he read Emory's first letter from France. Emory had left home two years earlier a strapping and gorgeous twenty-year-old kid, "the Adonis," was his father's nickname for the boy. With luck, Emory could have been a matinee idol. But he was instead, perhaps naïvely, determined to prove he was as masculine as his hero Theodore Roosevelt and, like Teddy, something far grander than merely the softened son of a rich man. Emory knew when volunteering for the Expeditionary Force that there was a grave possibility that he could end up dead or wounded. But neither he nor his father had ever imagined that the lad might return home a junkie that could not even stand for the National Anthem if he wanted to.

Mr. Ingram and Garnet rushed over to Emory the second the attendant plopped him gruffly into the wheelchair. "It's so grand to have you back," Garnet smiled genuinely as he heartily shook Emory's clammy and trembling hand. Mr. Ingram embraced his son, but the bulky design of the wheelchair made the hug cumbersome and awkward for both men. Mr. Ingram then suddenly burst into tears and sobbed disconsolately, which enhanced the sense of unnerved despair that hung heavy in the early evening air. Emory and Garnet, both of whom were terribly unaccustomed to seeing the elder Ingram exhibit any unsolicited emotion, were taken aback by the father's unvarnished effusiveness.

"I'm," Mr. Ingram stammered while trying to force his thoughts into words between deep blubbering breaths, "I'm... I'm so very glad to have you home, son. I died a bit each day you were away. But," his voice quaked and quivered, "but now that you are home, we can both begin to live again." He ran his finely manicured fingers gently through his son's course and unkempt sandy-blond hair. Mr. Ingram then gently rubbed the stubble on the boy's gaunt and pale cheek. "I have such a wonderful present for you," Mr. Ingram added as his sorrow and relief at having his son home melted into a proud smile. "Come on," he gushed, "I can't wait to show you." He led the way from the platform towards the carpark with Garnet, who had taken the liberty of guiding Emory's wheelchair, following close behind.

Garnet drives Mr. Ingram's new and pristine Ford Model-T convertible about ten miles beyond the city line. Emory, who felt more nauseated with each bump along the dirt road, gazed listlessly at the verdant horizon dissolving into darkness as the Ford kicked up dust behind it. Mr. Ingram sat in the backseat of the car soaking in the bucolic splendor of the marshy hinterland sprawling all around him and his beloved son sitting safely and soundly, or so it seemed, in the front seat of the car. Garnet finally eased the Ford to a gentle idle adjacent to a sprawling orange grove in full bloom that extended as far as Emory could see. "Well," Mr. Ingram's voice seeped with excitement. "What d'ya think, Em?"

Emory's weary eyes slowly scanned the brilliant emerald and orange masterpiece stretching all the way to the horizon. "Just another wasteland in the middle of nowhere," he grunted while shrugging his shoulders.

"It might not look like much now," Mr. Ingram announced proudly as he leaned forward to the edge of his seat and placed his hand lovingly on his son's shoulder. "But soon this land will be one of the most productive orange groves in all of Florida. Consider it a thank you for all you did saving us from those goddamn Huns." Mr. Ingram waited anxiously for his son's excited reply, but Emory simply sneered at the grove as if the oranges were made of feces. "Well," Mr. Ingram finally interrupted the long and tense silence, "what do you think, Em? You officially own one of the largest citrus groves south of Lake Okeechobee."

"What the fuck am I supposed to with all this?" Emory aggrievedly grunted. "I can't even fucking walk. How in God's ass am I supposed to pick citrus?"

Mr. Ingram, gobstruck and hurt, sat back in his seat and rubbed his furrowed brow as he cast a somewhat befuddled gaze upon the land. He was visibly pained as he scrambled to properly and adequately process his son's anger, which had caught him completely off-guard. "Well," Mr. Ingram huffed, "I suppose we'd hire some Bahamians to pick the fruit and bring it to market for you, like the other plantation owners around these parts do. I also thought we could build a nice little cottage house out here for you and your family."

"What goddamn family?" Emory chortled sarcastically as he glared back at his suddenly dejected and downtrodden father. "You think some woman worth a good goddamn is going to want this mess?" Emory smashed the palms of his hands against his withered thighs. He stared back deeply and coldly into his father's nervous and anguished eyes. Mr. Ingram could not bear the weight of his son's menacing stare and finally looked away. He cast his teary eyes upon the orange grove as sweat formed on his forehead. "Let's get the fuck out of here," Emory demanded. "I'm going to be sick."

Garnet's worried eyes meet with Mr. Ingram's in the reflection of the rearview mirror. Mr. Ingram slightly nodded his head and motioned his hand forward. Garnet put the car in drive and floored the gas pedal to the floorboard. A cloud of yellow dirt kicked up behind the Ford as it sped away from the grove. Emory, meanwhile, placed his forehead down on the windowsill in order to get a chest full of fresh air into his lungs. His face and limbs were sweat soaked. Mr. Ingram's tear-filled and confused eyes stared at Emory for a long while. The father wondered who this monstrosity that had replaced his son was and if any semblance of the old Emory even existed anymore.

Despite the tension at the orange grove gifted to Emory by his father, Mr. Ingram was still relieved, overjoyed, and very glad to have his son back from the Western Front. The father proudly boasted as Garnet steered Emory into the lobby of the Royal Palm Hotel, "Hey everyone, my war hero son is back from France! He stuck it to the Kaiser!" Everyone in the lobby cheered and clapped Emory, who was terribly ill. The effete middle-aged concierge with a pencil moustache standing behind the reception desk hollered, "Emory, it's so wonderful to finally have you home safe and sound where you belong. Thank you for your service."

Mr. Ingram, despite the horrendous condition his son was in, was pleased with the adulation. But Garnet and especially Emory were made terribly uneasy by the attention. Neither of them seemed to breathe from the time they had entered the lobby until the three of them were finally cloistered on the closed elevator. Garnet repeatedly pressed the 3-button until the elevator finally began to ascend. He sighed and slightly shook his head while gently massaging Emory's sore neck.

"What are we doing here?" Emory, who seemed to grow more ill and disheveled with each passing second, squirmed uncomfortably in his wheelchair.

"This is ours." Mr. Ingram beamed. "We live here now."

"What about the house in Coconut Grove?" Emory was confounded.

"Sold it," Mr. Ingram happily explained. "Got a nice price too," he added.

"Mr. Flagler bequeathed the resort to your father," Garnet explained.

"Isn't it just grand?" Mr. Ingram gushed. "And all this time I thought Mr. Flagler did not properly appreciate all I had done for his blessed endeavor." The elevator came to a sudden halt at the third floor, the top floor of the mostly wooden hotel. Garnet guided Emory down a long and majestic hallway covered in priceless red and royal blue Persian rugs gifted to Flagler's estate by Queen Victoria. Mr. Ingram stopped at the end of the hall and excitedly unlocked the door and swung it open, revealing a glorious penthouse apartment with an extraordinary view of Biscayne Bay. "Well," Mr. Ingram asked excitedly, "what do you think?"

"It's very nice," Emory unenthusiastically conceded.

"Very nice?" Mr. Ingram was somewhat offended by his son's tepid reaction. "Would you please just look out this window. The view alone is worth the price of admission," Mr. Ingram gushed while pointing his finger towards the bay. "This was Mr. Flagler's very own suite when he stayed here during the winter. Only the finest people on the planet have ever had the honor of staying in this suite. It's fit for a king. Now," he smiled proudly, "it's all yours."

"Gee," Emory said softly, feeling some kind of tender human emotion that he thought had been lost in a trench back in France. "I really don't know what to say, except thanks, I guess."

"You don't need to say anything just now," Mr. Ingram explained while pouring a bit of forty-seven-year-old bourbon into three glasses made of Swarovski crystal; the bottle of which he originally purchased upon learning that Sigrid was pregnant with Emory nearly a quarter-century earlier, but due to unforeseen complications that culminated in tragedy, he had never been provided an adequate chance to taste. His son's deliverance, as it were, from France finally provided the opportunity for Mr. Ingram to savor the spirit. "Don't thank me just yet," Mr. Ingram said to his son, none of this kindness or largesse comes for free. There are strings attached."

"Aren't there always?" Emory rolled his eyes slightly. He felt sicker.

"I need your help rebranding the place," Mr. Ingram explained. "As beautiful and majestic as the Royal Palm is, it is a vast wooden and marble fossil modeled on Versailles. If we hope to compete with places like the Flamingo and Halcyon, we need to be more modern. We need to attract the New Woman and Modern Man, rather than the old fuddy-duddy set that Flagler and his ilk attracted like flies on rotting corpses. We've already hired some of the hottest jazz musicians from New York, New Orleans, and Saint Louis. But I need you to overhaul the look of the hotel; hell, rename it if you want. The most important thing is that we transform this fossil into Miami's most modern marvel." He then handed a glass of bourbon to his son and Garnet, and then raised his own glass. "I propose a toast to my war hero of a son returning to the empire a conquering hero – a veritable conquistador," Mr. Ingram smiled proudly and sipped a bit of bourbon. Both Garnet and Emory downed their glasses. It was the first time Mr. Ingram had tasted liquor since he had left Cardiff. "Now gentleman," he said while moving towards the egress of the suite, "if you'll excuse me, I have an important meeting to attend. There is a welcome back party in your honor at 9 p.m. in the main ballroom," he said to his son. "Garnet has a residence in the suite right next door. If you need anything at all, just give him a call, day or night." Mr. Ingram kissed his son's gruff cheek. Garnet began to exit the room with his employer.

"In case it does not seem like it," Emory said somewhat nauseated and sheepishly, "I am glad to be back home. I missed both of you very much and thought of you all the time. Please forgive me if I need a bit of time to readjust; it's just that," he searched for the right words, "I'm very tired and dispirited. War really is the worst hell you can imagine."

"We missed you terribly too, m'boy," Mr. Ingram said solemnly as Garnet slightly but compliantly nodded his head. "You're home now," Mr. Ingram added. "You can finally put the war behind you. Now, get some rest. We've got great things to accomplish in the weeks ahead."

Garnet swung the door to the hall open and permitted Mr. Ingram to exit first. Garnet then glanced back at Emory and flashed a warm and friendly grin and nod, then exited the room and shut the door behind him. He then entered the suite right next door to Emory's as Mr. Ingram hurried down the hall towards the elevator with his glass of bourbon in hand.

Emory rolled slowly and disconsolately over to the bay window, which he gazed out of a while, before his attention was consumed by staring down at his listless legs. He found himself wondering, as he had countless times before, how in the hell he was ever going to be able to figure out a way to put the war behind him, especially from his wheelchair.

Just as Mr. Ingram was exiting the lobby of the hotel, the notorious "Black Banshees," as they were pejoratively referred to in the local press, arrived like a swarm of locust. The Black

Banshees were a group of rapidly aging and fervidly teetotaling white women who were every bit as much a vigilante group as was the Ku Klux Klan. The Banshees were labeled "black" due to the fact that the mob wore all black Victorian-era dresses, bustles, and veils while tearing local taverns and bars to bits with hatchets and axes. They were led by Carrie Hatchet, who was a personal friend of the late-Mrs. Tuttle. Hatchet and the other fifteen Black Banshees stormed into the Aristocrat, the bar at the other end of the lobby from the elevator. They tore the place apart. "We have come in the name of God's ever righteous law," Hatchet's thunderous Scottish brogue echoed atop the shiny marble in the lobby, which startled the middle-aged concierge manning the front desk, who then rushed into the bar to witness the calamity.

"Call the law, God damn it," Ingram demanded of the confused and petrified concierge, who complied by racing back to the reception desk in the lobby, and frantically dialing the rotary phone as fast as his pudgy little fingers could manage, which was not very fast at all.

"This is private property, you witches!" Mr. Ingram seethed, "You ever hear of the Fourteenth Amendment of the United States Constitution? Private property is sacrosanct!"

He made a quick move for Carrie Hatchet, but she flashed her shiny chrome blade in his face, missing his bulbous pink nose by an inch, which caused him to spill nearly all of the savory bourbon in his glass.

"You, Mr. Ingram," Carrie Hatchet snarled while waving her blade in the hotelier's steely face, "are the one who does not have the right. You have no legal right serve alcoholic beverages in Dade County. This county was voted dry in 1911 and every election since. If the lawmen whose pockets you gild will not enforce local ordinances, well then, it is up to the righteous and

Godfearing Christians of this sin seduced county to enforce the law, come hell or high water."

Garnet raced across the lobby and into the bar. It seemed that every bottle of booze that had been behind the now shattered mirrored bar had been destroyed by the Banshees. Thousands of dollars' worth of product was lost in a matter of minutes. "How the hell are we supposed to throw Emory's party with no booze?" Garnet hollered above the sound of the fracas.

"Find that Negro boy – the cabbie," Ingram demanded while reaching into the breast pocket of his twill blazer. He shoved a wad full of cash into Garnet's hand. "Get whatever we need and get your ass back here as soon as you can."

Garnet hurried past Sheriff Adolf Beauregard, who was a massive man that darkened the doorway of the bar. Garnet then ran past the fretful concierge, and then tried to feverishly flag down a cab in the sun-soaked carpark. Back inside, Beauregard removed his dark and rounded sunglasses from his round and sweaty face and watched a while as the Banshees trashed the bar, which provided some of his deputies in the parking lot time to file into the lobby. Once his reinforcements had arrived, the Sheriff finally approached Carrie Hatchet, who defiantly said, "It's about bloody time you boys arrived. Our real bone to pick is with you for neglecting to enforce the laws that the citizens of this county rightly demand. We, Sheriff Beauregard," she snarled, "have come to tear this fiefdom of sin asunder."

Beauregard then smashed Carrie Hatchet square in her face with the business end of his baton. She dropped down to her knees and stared at some broken glass as if in a drug-induced trance. Beauregard then quickly kicked the handle of the blade from her hand and shoved her face into the hardwood floor and slapped handcuffs on her. The other dozen or so Banshees who were part of the protest ceased defacing the bar and looked at their now woozy leader with grave concern. Sheriff Beauregard waved his pistol towards them, daring them to intervene in their leader's arrest. "Now," the Sheriff said in thick Alabamian accent, "I done warned y'all many times before about this kind of vigilantism. Y'all might not agree with how the laws are enforced in this here county. But the fact of the matter is," he said while jerking Carrie Hatchet, whose face was bloodied, up onto her feet, "this is the Empire of the United States of America. Private Property supersedes all local ordinances. So while you might not like the fact that the visitors to this city demand to have a nice cocktail now-n-again while enjoying their vacations, the hard fact that y'all seem most troubled to comprehend is that this city don't exist without these fine folks and their cocktails with their fancy dinners. As such, your vigilantism is not just an attack on respected business proprietors such as Mr. Ingram here, it is an attack on the entire population of this fair city and the county that surrounds it. Your attack on Mr. Ingram's private property is an attack on all us that work and live here in this fine city. Why can't y'all understand that?"

None of the women dared respond, so he cocked his weapon and planted it firmly against Carrie Hatchet's temple. "I assume your silence is an indication that you do understand the grave danger of this kind of reckless vigilantism, then?" he prodded.

All the women sans Carrie Hatchet, who was suffering from a terrible concussion and only just regaining her wits, nodded as if their leader's life depended on their compliance. "Good," Beauregard sighed as he began to shove Carrie Hatchet from the ravaged bar and towards the lobby of the hotel. "Now y'all get home, or I'm gonna call each and every last one of your husbands and tell them you've been gettin' into trouble again."

"You're not arresting them?" Mr. Ingram was incredulous.

"Nah," Beauregard said, "you are, technically speakin', breakin' the law by servin' booze in a dry county."

Mr. Ingram was startled slightly when the bartender, who he did not realize was cowering behind the bar, suddenly popped up from behind it. "You all right?" Mr. Ingram asked. The barkeep brushed some shards of glass from his dusty white hair and moustache as his wide and terrified eyes scanned over his body in order to make a quick assessment of the damage, or lack thereof. "I think so," he said finally while exuding surprised relief.

Rhett was an especially handsome, dark-skinned, precocious and ambitious sixteen-year-old cabbie. He was flirting with a young African-American maid on her way into her shift when Garnet located him loitering in the carpark. Rhett had access to any number of contraband items that could be very quickly and easily imported into South Florida from the Bahamas, including heroin, cocaine, and marijuana by the bale, and booze by the crate.

Garnet was beyond impatient and annoyed by the time he was finally able to fully explain to the young cabbie the nature of the predicament Mr. Ingram was in, and how Rhett's services were desperately needed to solve the sudden problem created by the black-clad band of teetotalers.

Night was already descending as Garnet and Rhett arrived at a non-descript bungalow just beyond the city limit, not far from the Miccosukee land that was used as a storehouse for booze smuggled in by rumrunners from the Bahamas. The proprietor of the establishment was Rhett's mother, Ruby, who had moved from Bimini to South Florida in 1903 to work on a lemon plantation owned by Flagler.

Under the pale moonlight, Rhett and Garnet quickly loaded a flatbed truck with crates full of rum, gin, whisky, and bourbon. "Whatever you do," Garnet warned while tossing the keys of the truck to Rhett, "don't speed or give the law any reason to stop you. Emory's party begins in less than two hours. This stuff needs to be unloaded and ready to serve by then."

"No sweat," Rhett said coolly while flashing a charming grin, "I got this. Emory'll be too drunk to spell France by midnight." He then fired up the truck and blasted down on the gas pedal. The truck whipped up dust as it sped along a dirt road towards Miami's fledgling and hazy skyline.

Garnet exhaled a deep and nervous sigh, seemingly annoyed that Rhett had already defied his order to not speed. Garnet then hurried into the bungalow a couple more times in order to retrieve a few more crates of gin, and to stuff the wad of cash provided to him by Mr. Ingram into Ruby's callused hand. "You just bought half my inventory for the winter season," she grinned gladly while enthusiastically counting the cash. "There's a special place in heaven for men of vision and enterprise like you and Mr. Ingram," she said while kissing Garnet gently on the cheek. "You sure you don't want to stay a while and have a drink?" she hoped.

"I wish I could," he said while gently caressing her cheek with his thumb," but it's going to be a busy night. I need to get back."

"Next time then, sugar," she said, smiling warmly. She then lifted the last crate of gin from atop the dining table and plopped it into his arms. "Send Emory my love," she said. "I prayed for him every night he was away."

Garnet smiled and nodded appreciatively as he lugged the crate towards the front porch, then hurried from the bungalow. He plopped the crate into the front passenger seat, and then hopped into Mr. Ingram's Model-T, the backseat of which was packed with crates of gin.

Just past the city line, a young Deputy who had been on the force less than a year noticed a young black man powering a flatbed truck full of crates. The Deputy convinced himself that the black boy must have been up to some kind of mischief, if not something totally illicit. He thus flashed his lights and turned on the siren as he fast pursued the truck.

Rhett's initial thought was to pull over and run for it. He knew that no white boy in a blue suit and heavy belt with a holstered pistol could ever catch him if he made a break into the pinewoods nearby. But his fear of letting Garnet and Mr. Ingram down caused him to naively believe that he could somehow miraculously navigate the ordeal and complete the task he had been assigned.

It was fortuitous that Rhett did not follow his initial instinct to run because the Deputy's pistol was already cocked, aimed, and ready for a firefight by the time the precocious cabbie turned off the engine of the idled truck. All of that swaggering charm of adolescence that seemed so deeply embedded in his DNA back at Ruby's place while conversing with Garnet had been suddenly replaced by a palpable and uneasy dread. "Please officer," he pleaded, "I'm sure I was not speeding. I'm a very careful driver."

"Whose truck is this, boy?" the young Deputy demanded in a thick southern accent. "What's in them crates?"

"The truck belongs to the Ingram family," Rhett said nervously, "it's full of supplies for Mr. Ingram's hotel. His boy just got back from the war."

"Mr. Ingram?" the Deputy sneered as if he had caught a pungent whiff of shit. "You mean that carpetbagger that worked for that damned Yankee, Flagler?" Rhett, perhaps wisely, did not respond. "Is that booze in them there boxes there, boy?" the Deputy demanded.

"Can't say, suh," Rhett said softly, "they ain't my boxes."

"You know booze is illegal in this county, boy?" the Deputy grinned like he had cornered his prey.

"Can't say I was aware of it, suh," Rhett lied, "the law don't let us niggas have no say in what is or is not the law, ya see."

"You bein' smart, nigger?" the Deputy demanded.

"No suh," Rhett smirked, "the law don't let niggas do that neither."

"Get out of the truck, nigger," the Deputy ordered. Rhett did not comply. The Deputy then cocked and aimed his pistol of Rhett's sweat-soaked forehead; his eyes stared down at the street. "Ain't askin' you twice," the Deputy declared.

Rhett slowly complied with the order and climbed from the cab of the truck.

"Lay down on your nigger face," the Deputy snarled.

Rhett slowly nodded his head and pretended as though he were about to comply with the order by slowly leaning towards the ground. He then darted around to the other side of the truck. The Deputy fired a shot, which lodged in a crate of rum, which spewed brown liquid. The Deputy then ran after Rhett, who was making a break across an open field for a stand of pinewoods. The Deputy fired another round. The bullet grazed Rhett's right calf-muscle, which sent him tumbling to the grass. Fearing he'd be killed if he stood back up, Rhett tried to drag his body on his belly the rest of the way to the stand of pinewoods. The Deputy, however, quickly caught up and pounced on him like a jungle cat pursuing a titmouse. The seemingly insulted Deputy quickly slapped handcuffs onto Rhett's blistered and worn wrists and dragged him towards the police car idling behind the truck.

Garnet drove by just in time to see the Deputy shoving a blood splattered and battered Rhett into the back of the police car. The Deputy then sped off as fast as his patrol car could travel. Garnet circled back around after the Deputy and Rhett had rounded the corner and were no longer in sight of the truck, the back bed of which was full of booze. He then parked the Model-T in front of a nearby general store and jumped into the cab of the truck, relieved to see that Rhett had left the keys in the ignition.

Garnet made it back to the hotel without further incident. He ordered the kitchen staff to unload the truck and get the crates to the bar and grand ballroom as fast as they could. He then raced into the lobby and up the staircase, then ran as fast as he could to Emory's penthouse apartment and banged on the door.

Inside Flagler's former penthouse, Emory was deep inside a debilitating nightmare in which he was hunkered inside a mud, blood, and rat-infested trench full of mangled corpses and dead bodies. He was having an out-of-body experience of sorts as he watched himself climb out from a trench and charge across no man's land as machinegun fire and exploding bombs blasted all around him. There was so much Mustard Gas and smoke in the air that Emory could barely breathe or even see the moment when he stepped onto the landmine that blew the bottom half of his legs to bits. "No!" both Emorys, the one asleep in a pool of sweat and also the one inside the dream lying in a pool of blood, wailed and screamed.

The Emory in the sweat soaked bed at the Royal Palm woke suddenly inside his suite, panting and red in the face. The walls and ceiling seemed to close in on him. He noticed knocking emanating from the door leading out to the hallway. He gazed a moment out the bay window while admiring something about a moonbeam shining into the suite before finally dragging himself from the king-size bed and into his wheelchair, which was pinned against the nightstand. He then slowly made his way to the door and opened it to find Garnet, who was disheveled.

"Sorry to disturb you, Em," Garnet huffed and puffed between breaths, "it's the law; they got Rhett. I'm sorry to do this to you, but I need your help downtown."

Emory exhaled a deep sigh and rubbed some crust from his eyes. "You can't accomplish the task without me?" he asked.

"Afraid not," Garnet said dejectedly.

"What the hell am I supposed to do?" Emory groggily asked while glancing down at his lower extremities.

"Put on the tuxedo your father sent up this afternoon, comb your hair," Garnet urged while unlocking the door to his own suite," I'll meet you in the hall in ten minutes."

Garnet and Emory were both dressed in tuxedos personally furnished to them earlier in the day by the affable concierge who manned the front desk in the lobby. Though dressed sleekly and elegantly, Emory and Garnet cut a somewhat odd figure when they arrived at the registration desk of the local sheriff department precinct dressed to the nines. A slack jawed, overweight, and sweaty oaf named Barney, who was of a proximate age to Emory, hunched over the front desk aimlessly smoking a Lucky Strike and sipping a warm Coca-Cola. He did not upon first glance recognize Emory, who had left for France such a dashing and strapping lad, now reduced to a sullen paraplegic junkie who was tired, ill and morose.

"Well hey there, Honcho," Barney slurred from somewhere inside a cloud of tobacco smoke, "ain't seen you round in a while. Stayin' out of trouble, I reckon, huh?"

"I've told you a hundred times," Emory growled, "his name's not Honcho, you fucking inbred."

Barney's initial reaction was a recoiled sense of defense. But he quickly softened when he realized the scraggly and jaded voice belonged to Emory, his former signal caller on the Miami Senior High football team. "Well I'll be goddamned," Barney guffawed, "I wondered when the hell you was gettin' back from France, if ever."

"Where the hell is Rhett?" Garnet demanded.

"Rhett?" Barney was a tad more confused than he normally did. "Y'all mean that nigger that was dragged in here with a gunshot wound? He was booked for speedin' and resistin' arrest. That coon's destined for the chain gang, if the doc can fix his leg up, anyway."

"Resisting arrest?" Emory demanded. "What the hell did he do? Why was he shot?"

"Reckon I'm not quite sure," Barney admitted while shrugging his mammoth shoulders. "All'z I know is that the coon was shot in the leg and the doctor was dispatched to patch him up. Doc dun left ten, maybe fifteen, minutes ago."

"Go fucking get Rhett," Garnet demanded.

"Afraid I can't do it," Barney said, "he's been arrested, ya see. The coon still needs to be processed into the system and then confront a jury of his peers, unless of course he has the good sense to plead guilty to whatever charges are brought against him."

"Here's what is going to happen if Rhett is not out here in sixty seconds," Emory glared into Barney's sloppy soul. "First, whoever was dumb enough to shoot my associate is never going to be able to find a job in this city again. Second, your parents' house is going to mysteriously cease to exist within twenty-four hours. That dire scenario will soon be a matter of fact unless my associate is out here in the next sixty seconds."

"You know I'd like to help you and especially your daddy in any way I can," Barney said somewhat sheepishly as his vacant eyes darted towards the floor, "if only for old times' sake, if nothin' else. But my hands are tied here," he said while pressing his wrists together. "I could lose my job. I'm sure you're sympathetic to my predicament."

"You don't understand, the only way for you to keep your job and for your parents to keep their house is to go back there and get Rhett out here in next forty-five seconds," Emory, whose patience was fast waning, assured. "Losing your job will be the least of your concerns. Now hurry on back there and get him, or so help me God."

"You have access to the keys to the holding pens downstairs," Garnet said matter-of-factly while plucking a wad of mint green billfolds from the pocket of his trousers. "Take the keys, get our associate. When he gets here there will be a hundred dollars waiting for you. That's ten times the amount you won for in your stupid fucking pool."

Garnet peeled five Andrew Jackson's from the wad of cash set it atop the reception desk. Barney stared at the cash a moment, calculating the risk versus the rewards of his next set of actions.

"I suppose I could leave the back door open and blame the escape on the custodial staff," Barney said. "He's a darkie too. Everyone knows they'z all thick and thieves."

Barney finally and smartly, which was unexpected, plucked the cash from atop the counter and stuffed it into the pocket of his tight and undersized trousers, which seemed as though they might burst at the seams. He then waddled as fast as he could, which was not very fast at all due to a pesky rash on the inside of his chafing thighs, into the inner sanctum of the precinct. Nearly a minute passed before he, who was now out of breath, returned with Rhett, who was blood-splattered and limping terribly, but not in too much pain due to a most gracious shot of morphine provided by the kindhearted doctor who stitched up the gunshot graze on his leg.

Garnet, Rhett and Emory piled into Mr. Ingram's Model-T and raced back towards the hotel in the hopes of making it to the party before any of the more distinguished guests arrived. Garnet brought the car to an impatient pause at a stop sign from which Emory could see Quinn's parents' house warmly lit up, beckoning him from a distance. "You know who lives on this street?" Emory, who was in the front passenger seat, asked Garnet.

"Who?" Garnet, who cared only of getting back to the hotel as expediently as possible, asked while slightly shrugging his shoulders.

"Quinn's parents," Emory said while casting his index finger at the fifth house from the northwest corner. "It's that one right there."

"You think we ought to stop by?" Rhett, who was somewhat inebriated sitting in the backseat of the car, said. "I'm sure she's dyin' to see you."

"I'm sorry," Garnet said impatiently, "we don't have time to lollygag. I promised your father to have you at the party by nine. I can bring you over to see Quinn tomorrow, if you want."

"Fuck that," Rhett declared, "we're already right here. We might as well drop by."

Garnet cast a long, heavy, menacing and icy look upon Rhett from his vantage in the rearview mirror.

"Just drive by really quick," Emory urged. "We don't need to stop. I just want to see if she's inside. Maybe I could catch a glimpse. It'd be nice to know what she looks like now."

Garnet then made a sharp left onto Merrick Avenue.

"Pull in right there," Rhett said. "Look, right there. There's a spot."

"Might as well," Emory urged Garnet. "Maybe we'll catch a glimpse of her."

"You know if we're late, your daddy is going to have my hide," Garnet said as if both frustrated and impatient as he reluctantly complied with the order and parallel parked the car between two others lining the street. Emory could see right into the living room through the lit up plate-glass window of Quinn's parents' house.

Garnet began to exit the car in order to assist Emory, but the latter stopped him. "Hang on a minute," Emory said. "Let's just sit tight. We don't need to knock. I'm not ready for her to see me like this."

Garnet nodded compliantly as he plopped back into the driver's seat and hunkered down behind the steering wheel. His bright and eager brown eyes stared at the plate-glass window. A carved pumpkin sits on the windowsill. The trio staking out the house tried to look somewhat inconspicuous, but actually looked as though they were casing the joint. This was especially so when another car suddenly rounded the corner and stopped across the street from them.

"Ah shit," Emory tried hunkering down deeper into his seat while whispering. "It's Quinn."

"Who in the hell is the fella she's with?" Rhett sneered while peering accusatorily over at the man dressed very nicely in a white linen suit in the driver's seat of the sedan driven by Quinn's companion. Quinn kissed the man sweetly on his cheek, and then confidently sauntered from the car wearing a one-piece bathing suit, her lower half wrapped in a sarong. "Ta ta, honey bunny," the smarmy man in the linen suit said not quite so suavely as he fiddled his fingers flirtatiously at her, rather than simply waving goodbye. Quinn smiled and waved as she hurried across the street towards the front porch of her parent's house. Emory slunk down even further in his seat and put his hand to his forehead in the hopes that he might obscure his appearance and go unnoticed. No such luck.

Truth be told, Quinn had seen Emory all over the city the entire time he was in France – sometimes entering a bank, the post office, or getting onto a bus. She was always, however, forlorn to find that it was not actually Emory she had seen. Again, she noticed who she initially believed to be her ex-boyfriend, but reconciled herself to it being yet another fleeting mirage of him. She, however, could not resist the urge to make sure, and thus turned around again as she reached the first of three steps leading up onto the porch. She gazed long and hard at the slinking tuxedoed man in the passenger seat of the car. She then began to be lured to the car, drawn by a magnetic force. "Ah shit, she comin' over here,," Rhett whispered.

"Emory?" Quinn's nervous voice queried. "Is it really you?"

"What's the matter, honey?" the man in the car across the street hollered.

"It's nothing," Quinn replied to her beau. "It's just an old friend from high school back from the war. Go on ahead; I'll call you in a while." Her date reluctantly complied and motored around the corner as Quinn approached the passenger side door. "I was wondering if you were ever gonna come back," she said somewhat timidly, nervous but trying to act as calm as she could. "You never returned my letters."

"I'm sorry about that," Emory shamefacedly admitted. "I wanted to. I tried to write you so many times. I just couldn't. I guess it was easier to try and just amputate me from your life than it was to constantly think about what you were doing and who you might be doing it with. Being over there and being in love with you, it was like being paralyzed. You just can't be paralyzed when fighting a war. I really am very sorry if it seemed I was ignoring you or did not care to communicate with you. It really was not like that at all."

Garnet felt terribly uncomfortable listening in on what he believed ought to be a private exchange.

"I understand," she confessed. "For what it's worth, the war, you being over there, was really hard on me too. I just figured you did not really love me, or you'd have never gone over there in the first place."

Rhett, dining on the drama, was completely at ease, thanks in part to the morphine he had been shot up with. "Fuck it," Rhett interjected. "All that jazz is just a little bit of water under the bridge now. Our boy is back a war hero. Hop in. His welcome back party is tonight. Y'all can get reacquainted."

"I wish I could," she said squeamishly, "but I just got done playing at the beach all day. I'm just here to get washed up. My fiancé and I are having dinner at the Halcyon. Perhaps we can have lunch and catch up sometime this week or next? I'm dying to hear all about your adventures overseas." Emory forced a pained but cordial grin and nodded his head politely as if he was unfazed by the declined invitation. But she could tell he was hurt. "Please do call me," she added while making her way towards the porch.

 Garnet hurriedly put the car in drive. Quinn flashed a warm smile and quick wave goodbye, and then disappeared into the house.

"We're so late," Garnet huffed, "your dad is going to have my ass." He gunned the car through a stop sign.

"She still loves you," Rhett slurred while leaning forward in his seat and wincing a bit while he patted Emory on the shoulder. "I can tell."

"Her love for me is as gone as my ability to run and jump," Emory confided, "another casualty of war."

"Nah," Rhett insisted. "She's still in love with you. I can see it in her eyes. The eyes never lie."

Emory's anguished eyes fixated on his lower extremities.

It seemed like the whole city and then some made an appearance at Emory's welcome home soiree. A seven-piece brass band, including Jasper, the horn player who had aided and befriended Emory at Penn Station, wailed away on stage. Babe Ruth, who had only arrived in Miami that day due to the recent conclusion of his first baseball season with the New York Yankees, was also in attendance. The slugger had proven the Red Sox terribly wrong for selling him by smashing a record number of homeruns in his first season in the Bronx. At the party, the Babe gladly smoked Cuban cigars and slurped whisky from a crystal chalice at a large round table covered in crisp white linen surrounded by a cadre of attractive young women. Each woman at the Babe's table had pouting red lips and bobbed hair, and all sported short and vibrantly colored flapper dresses and silk knee-high hosiery that shined in the light. Al Capone, who had only recently turned nineteen, sipped an Old Fashioned across from the table from the slugger. The gangster, who had been tipped off by Meyer Lansky that the fix was in, was in Miami celebrating for the winter after having made a mint betting on the Cincinnati Reds to beat the seemingly indomitable Chicago White Sox.

Carl Fisher, the owner of the gaudy, ugly and pink Flamingo Hotel (which looked like an elephant), who was notorious for throwing parties that could stoke qualms in Caligula, made an appearance with his young fiancé, Mirabel, the reigning Miss Orange Blossom Queen. The soon-to-be Mrs. Fisher's toned and tan legs were longer than a bad day; she, in her high heels, stood nearly a foot taller than her man. Her bright orange flapper dress sparkled like diamonds under the lights inside the ballroom, which made her standout even more than she normally did. Capone and Ruth both gawked at her the moment she entered the room. But despite her incredible natural beauty and charisma, she was a bit skittish while latched tightly onto Fisher's hand, as if there was an underlying and unresolved tension that existed between them, as he paraded her around the soiree displaying the canary diamond ring he had given her as a wedding gift. He also informed anyone that would bother to listen to him for longer than ten seconds that the Flamingo was "going to be the place to be" after midnight. He urged people to make their way from Biscayne Bay and across the Collins Causeway to Miami Beach, where, he assured, "the real action is."

The man of the hour and guest of honor, Emory, was nowhere to be found at the party. He was cloistered in his penthouse suite shivering and shaking as he entered a serious bout of teeth clattering opiate withdrawal. The heroin given to him at Penn Station by Jasper was a kind of lifeline that got him as far south as Savannah before he started feeling violently ill. Emory also appropriated close to a gram for himself before he gave the kitbag full of contraband back to Jasper in Charleston, which he gladly paid fifty dollars for, which was much higher than the market price for such a small quantity. But the reserve pilfered away by Emory had been exhausted earlier in the day, and now he was being sucked down into a spasm-inducing agony, paranoia, and terror that only junkies in need of a fix know the abyss of. He sweated and convulsed profusely in his wheelchair parked next to the window overlooking the twinkling lights of stars and nearby buildings reflecting off the glassy surface of Biscayne Bay.

The constant banging outside the penthouse door seemed to reverberate as though an earthquake were happening, making Emory feel even more nauseous. Garnet, who had been banging for more than a minute without reply, finally managed to open the door with a key hooked onto a ring replete with dozens of others that had been furnished to him the previous day by Mr. Ingram.

"Didn't you hear me?" Garnet asked somewhat frustrated upon seeing Emory shivering next to the open window. Emory did not respond. "You cold?" Garnet, whose body temperature was heightened due to immense stress, added.

"I'm sick," Emory grunted. "I can't go to the party."

"Come on, Em, your dad went to so much trouble," Garnet said. "Shit, Rhett got shot in the goddamn leg so this party could happen. You gotta at least make an appearance, if only for a couple minutes. There are a lot of folks excited to see you down there."

"Seriously," Emory grunted, "I just can't. I feel like I'm going to die." Garnet dug his hand deep into the right pocket of his tuxedo trousers and revealed a small paper baggie with a tiny whitish-yellow brick that appeared to be composed of shiny fish scale. He set the small brick on the windowsill and crushed it with the butt of the revolver he had holstered around his midsection under his tuxedo jacket. "You ever done this before?" Garnet asked while rolling a bill with Andrew Jackson's scowl on it into a sleek tube readymade for snorting.

"Cocaine?" Emory's weary eyes closely observed the substance on the windowsill. "Some of the men in my unit's minds were made of mush by it in France, so I never touched the stuff."

"It's not something you want to get in the habit of doing every day," Garnet admitted while handing the rolled bill to Emory. "But it'll help you make it through the party."

Emory's trembling hand snatched the bill from Garnet. He then tried to lean as far towards the sill as possible, but, due to the wheelchair, could not reach the line of crushed cocaine. Garnet managed to inch the wheelchair a tad closer to the window and lean it forwards a tad, just close enough for Emory to reach his goal without keeling over onto the floor. Emory took a hard snort of the granules, then exhaled a deep and assuaged sigh as he leaned back in his chair and gazed a moment up at the crown molding in the ceiling as the cocaine seemed to cool the hot blood coursing through his aching veins.

"Oh Jesus," Emory grinned languidly. "That's the ticket." His voice suddenly flowed confidently and composed as he offered the bill back to Garnet, who snatched it, then eagerly snorted of slug of cocaine from off the windowsill.

"Keep the rest," Garnet said while handing the bill back to his friend. "Consider it a welcome home gift."

"What about you," Emory asked while leaning towards the sill for another taste, "don't you need it?"

"Ruby's got plenty," Garnet explained. "I can get more whenever I want. I just needed a toot to navigate this damned party."

"What about heroin?" Emory asked somewhat reservedly, letting Garnet in on a secret he had desperately hoped to keep, especially from his father.

"Heroin?" Garnet appeared disgusted and somewhat disappointed at the query. "Yeah, Ruby comes across it sometimes. But you ought to steer clear of that shit. You won't believe the desolation that junk has caused amongst the Miccosukee. That voodoo is pure evil. Besides, your father would feed me to the gators if he knew I was setting you up with heroin. A small bag of cocaine as a welcome home gift to tide you over through this damned party is one thing, but getting you hooked on heroin is another animal entirely. No," he added matter-of-factly, "I can't help you with that. You're on your own if you want to ruin your life with that shit."

"Look at me, man," Emory chuckled numbly, "my life is already fucking ruined."

"Bullshit," Garnet adamantly disputed as he began to guide the wheelchair towards the penthouse exit, "you got your whole life ahead of you, You're lucky. A lot of those boys did not make it home."

"Come on, please," Emory pleaded at the egress of the suite, "let's just you and me stay here and catch up a while."

"Wish I could, but can't do it," Garnet said as he pushed Emory's chair into the hall and swung the door to the suite shut behind him, "just put in a quick appearance so your dad doesn't get egg on his face so close to the election, then you can call it a night. Alright?" Emory wiped a bit of coke-laced snot from his nostril with the back of his hand and licked it, but did not say a word as Garnet pressed the L-button to retrieve the elevator from the lobby. The doors slid shut.

Orit had checked into the hotel earlier in the day and had hoped to get a good night rest before launching her investigation into inveterate corruption in the city's real estate industry the following day. But the throbbing and up-tempo music emanating from the ballroom all through the walls of the wooden hotel was so raucous that getting sleep was, unfortunately, a dream deferred. She thus put on her nicest dress, which was still quite demure compared to the New Women and Flappers shimmying, shaking, and sashaying on the parquet dance floor adjacent to the stage in the ballroom where the Dixieland Band that starred Jasper wailed away.

Orit ordered herself a stiff gimlet from the bar, an ordeal that took nearly a quarter-hour due to the mass of people in the grand ballroom, especially the horde huddled around the back bar, which was wedged next to the dance floor. She stood rather awkwardly in the corner sipping her drink a few moments whilst watching the band play, but felt very much out of place. She thus made her way out onto a sprawling moonlit terrace overlooking Biscayne Bay. The serenity of the terrace felt like a warm bath on a very cold day compared to the tense uneasiness she felt inside the smoke and sound filled ballroom. She gazed calmly at the reflection of the stars and lights emanating from nearby buildings shimmering vividly atop the glassy surface of the bay.

"It is small bit of heaven, isn't it?" a husky and smooth female voice with a thick Cuban accent soaked into Orit from behind. Orit was somewhat startled as she turned around to see a gorgeous thirty-five-year-old woman standing nearly six-fee-tall in heels wearing a velvety red gown seemingly gliding her way like a sailboat through smooth water.

"Indeed, it is," Orit admitted somewhat diffidently. "It seems so peaceful out here compared to inside. The loud music and crowds, I don't know, I guess they just grate my nerves a bit."

"If these kinds of gatherings are not your cup of tea, why have you come?" the sultry Latina asked while lighting a pungent smelling marijuana cigarette.

"I suppose I figured that coming down and observing the scene made more sense than holding my pillow over my head and cursing the party until it ended," Orit said, making little effort to mask her frustration. "If you can't beat em, join em, I guess."

"Your accent is charming," Azure said. "Where are you from?"

"I grew up mostly in Flatbush, which is in Brooklyn, New York. But I'm originally from a small village near Odessa, which is in Ukraine. My mother and I came to America when I was a little girl. I like your accent too. Where are you from, Argentina?"

"I'm Cuban," Azure smiled warmly while offering her hand to Orit. "My name is Azure. I sing here at the hotel. I apologize for being part of the reason you might not get much sleep tonight; my set is next," she said while exhaling a lungful of smoke before offering the joint to Orit, who politely declined. "You are Jewish, yes?" The Latina asked.

"Is it that obvious?" Orit was embarrassed. "My mother is devout," Orit admitted. "But I don't believe in tooth fairies or Santa Claus."

"You can always tell the Jews when they first come," Azure smiled kindly. "They tend to be wound tight when they first arrive."

"But not so tightly wound when they leave?" Orit's journalistic curiosity was suddenly piqued.

"It depends," Azure shrugged rather nonchalantly while exhaling, "I suppose."

"What do you suppose it Depends on?" Orit wondered.

"On whether they had lost their shirt at the Casino or because of some other scheme that had separated them from their money," Azure chortled.

"And how do people lose their shirts down here exactly?" Orit asked, wishing she had brought her pencil and notepad to the party.

"Let me count the ways," Azure laughed as she exhaled another lungful of smoke. Just then the Dixieland band ceased playing. William Jennings Bryan's muffled baritone could be heard announcing, "Give a warm round of applause, folks. Next up is Azure Del Mar direct from Havana!" The raucous crowd cheered wildly.

"They're playing my tune," Azure winked charmingly at Orit. She then took another long drag from her joint and handed the rest of it to the reporter, who, not wanting to offend, awkwardly took the joint from the Latina but did not smoke any of it. "It was very nice chatting a while," Azure smiled politely. "I do hope to see you around the hotel sometime soon."

"I'm here researching corruption in the city," Orit explained. "Do you mind if I talk to you a bit about some of your experiences?"

"Corruption?" Azure smiled as if Orit had gotten herself lost. "You can walk in any direction and trip over it here. You don't need me to help you find it."

"Maybe so," Orit smiled timidly, "but maybe you could help me save some time by letting me know how exactly to see it when I find it?"

Azure, who towered over Orit by nearly a foot, smiled and gently caressed her new friend's soft cheek with the finely manicured nail of her index finger, which was polished a bright shade of red. "You're darling, you know that? What's your name?"

"Orit."

"Well Orit," Azure said, "my room number is 323. Stop by sometime if you ever get the urge to chat."

"I'm just down the hall," Orit said, "room 303."

Orit studied Azure as she strode powerfully and confidently back into the ballroom and stormed the stage as if she owned it. Orit then took a small exploratory hit from the joint, but coughed hard, so flicked the rest over the side of the balcony. She then excitedly hurried inside to finish her gimlet and watch the sultry and seductive songstress perform her tune, which proved to be magnificent. Orit was entranced while watching watched Azure sing, as if spell had been placed upon her. She grew calmer and more lucid.

As Orit was being mesmerized by Azure, Emory had finally found an opportunity to abscond the party he resented having to attend. He navigated his way through the horde and rolled out onto the terrace and stared listlessly over the edge at the lights from the nearby houses and businesses that had been rapidly erected along the shore of the bay while he was away at war. He wondered which, if any, of the lights might lead into Quinn's bedroom.

"I was wondering if I'd ever see you again after Charleston," Jasper, whose lips were swollen and chapped as a result of the fevered set he'd just concluded.

"Hell" Emory, who was somewhat relieved, blurted, "I sure as hell hoped I'd see you again. Please tell me you've got enough of that product and that I can buy some."

"I can break you off a taste to tide you ever until I find a good source down here," Jasper said.

"I could really use a fix," Emory ached impatiently.

"Well shit, boss, I can sell you another gram for fifty to tide you over, if you are desperate."

"Can you meet me in the Flagler Penthouse at the end of the hall on the third-floor in ten minutes?" Emory hoped.

"Sure can," Jasper's affirmation was music to Emory's ears. "But my next set begins in less an hour, so I can't stay too long."

Emory turned his wheelchair away from the bay and back towards the grand ballroom. "You're a goddamn angel," he said as his hand feverishly rotated the tires on his chair. Jasper watched Emory disappear inside the mass of people in the ballroom.

Emory did not even bother to say goodnight to a single party attendee, the vast majority of which were there to be seen, rather than to wish Emory well anyway. Mr. Ingram, however, was somewhat peeved as he saw Emory wheel his way from the packed ballroom and into the lobby leading towards the elevator. Mr. Ingram began to fast pursue his son, but Garnet intercepted him at the exit separating the lobby and ballroom. Garnet graciously explained to Mr. Ingram that Emory was very tired and sickly and wanted to get a full night's rest so that he could accompany his father on the golf links early the next morning, which quelled father Ingram's annoyed anger a bit. "Make sure he is at the first tee by sunrise," Mr. Ingram demanded. Garnet sullenly nodded his head.

CHAPTER FOURTEEN

Friday, October 31, 1919

Garnet was still half-asleep by the time he slinked out of his room and into the hall sometime around dawn. He banged on the door of the Flagler suite. All of the lights were on. Emory was sprawled stark naked atop the Persian rug on the hardwood floor; an empty syringe, corroded spoon laced with heroin residue, and a half-used baggie of heroin was lined neatly on the floor by his side. Atop the bureau was a quasi-shrine that he had forlornly crafted soon after Jasper left the suite the previous night. Quinn's senior was picture flanked by long and slender white candles burning. Wax collected at the base of the sterling candelabras.

After banging on the door for nearly five minutes, Garnet began to worry that the noise he was creating would surely disturb the other guests staying on the third floor of the hotel. He then reluctantly tried to twist the door handle, but the door leading into the Flagler suite was locked and thus did not budge. Garnet thus huffed and reluctantly banged some more. A woman in her late-fifties finally eased the door of her suite open just a crack and glared sullenly down the hall at Garnet, who did not notice that he was being observed. The woman, however, was terribly frightened to see what she deemed to be "a savage" banging on the door and thus quietly closed and locked it and then barricaded herself inside by dragging a small dining table in front of the door. "What's all that racket?" her half-asleep and groggy husband wondered.

"It's some surly redskin trying to break his way into the Flagler suite," her wide eyes stared frightfully at the light seeping into her suite from the doorframe.

Garnet finally hurried into his suite and dug into the drawer of the nightstand next to the bed. He pulled the ring of keys given to him two days earlier by Mr. Ingram from the drawer and then hurried back into the hall. After scouring the key ring for nearly a minute, he came upon the one that could open Emory's door.

Garnet was upon entering the penthouse dismayed to find Emory sprawled naked on the floor and clearly high beyond the point of consciousness. The nubs that had replaced his formerly long, lean, toned, and athletic legs seemed to give Garnet a moment of contemplated pause. Garnet was equally bewildered to see the somewhat odd and disturbing shrine to Quinn that had been haphazardly erected atop the bureau.

He plucked a tall room-temperature glass of water from atop the nightstand table next to the bed and dumped it on Emory's face. There was a strange delayed reaction before Emory finally opened his eyes and glared dazedly up at Garnet. "You need to get up," Garnet demanded while standing over Emory so that their faces were very near. "Your dad is waiting for you at the course."

"The course?" Emory slurred confusedly while wiping water from his nose and eyes.

"You're running late for your tee time," Garnet explained.

"Tee time?" Emory seemed no less confused.

"You know as well as I do," Garnet qualified, "your father's adamant stance on punctuality and lateness."

"Look at me," Emory grunted. "How the fuck am I supposed to play golf?"

"To be honest," Garnet, fast approaching frustration, admitted while shrugging his shoulders, "your guess is as good as mine. All I know is that your dad said to get you to the first tee by 7 a.m. You know goddamn well it's my ass if I don't accomplish the task he demanded. So please, be a pal, get dressed as quick as you can."

"Fuck that," Emory grunted. "My father has officially gone all the way around the bend if he thinks I'm going golfing, especially at this godforsaken hour of the day."

"Fine," Garnet said while kneeling down next to Emory. He snatched the half-used baggie of heroin from off the floor and shoved it into the pocket of his trousers, then stood back up and scowled down as his ailing friend. "If you're not dressed and in the lobby in ten minutes, I'm telling your dad about this disgusting fucking habit you developed while away."

He then turned on the heel of his loafer and hurried from the room, barely resisting the urge to slam the door shut behind him. He stormed down the hall, past Azure, who had just arrived outside of the door to Orit's suite. They shared a polite glance and smile as they passed. She then rapped gently on the door of suite 303.

The inside of Orit's suite had gone from pitch black to that gray glow of dawn in a matter of seconds. Nicholas, her editor, had warned her to beware, so the reporter was slightly startled when she heard a sudden knock at her door so early in the morning. She momentarily wondered if someone with malicious intent waited on the hallway side of the door to do her some kind of harm. She thus cautiously slid out from under the thousand-thread white Egyptian cotton covers atop her queen-sized bed as quiet as could be, and then wrapped the complimentary fluffy white bathrobe furnished during check-in around the worn baby-blue housedress that went all the way to her ankles, then crept slowly towards the door. "Who is it?" her nervous voice meekly demanded.

"Azure. I do hope it is not too early in the morning for a visit. It's just that you said you were not expectant of sleep, so I wondered if you might like to see the sunrise over the Atlantic Ocean with me."

Orit brushed bangs from her eyes while momentarily contemplating, then finally unlocked the door and cracked it open ever so slightly, somewhat nervous that she might look like a mangled mess. She squinted as her eyes tried to adjust to the light illuminating the hallway. Azure donned blue jeans and an oversized red and white gingham button-up shirt she had inherited from a former lover, and a red bandanna tied to her head. She was also wearing sandals on her long and slender feet. The shade of the polish on her toes perfectly matched the red gingham in her ex-boyfriend's shirt. She was also not wearing any makeup. Her clean face further accentuated her natural beauty and pensiveness, which had been somewhat obscured by the mounds of makeup plastered to her face during her performance the night prior. Her black hair was tied back in a French braid. "She looks like a summertime picnic in McCarren Park," Orit silently observed, suddenly conscious of the fact that she was quite smitten in ways she had never been smitten before.

"What do you say?" Azure seduced. "Have you ever seen the sunrise before?"

"I don't remember ever seeing one, not over the ocean, anyway."

"Come on," Azure said invitingly while holding her hand out for Orit to latch onto.

"Well," Orit said while glancing down somewhat embarrassedly at her modest and demure baby blue housedress, "let me put something presentable on first." Orit then rushed over to the suitcase atop the dresser. Azure concomitantly slinked into the room, gently squeezed the door shut behind her, and leaned against the wall and watched Orit hurriedly and nervously slip off the bathrobe and housedress. Orit was a bit uneasy being so starkly naked in front of a woman she had only just met, especially since Azure was so cool, calm, comfortable, poised and powerful on and off stage, as if she owned whatever room she was in, and most especially seemed comfortable in her own skin.

Azure's sensual and intense dark eyes stayed fixated on Orit's diminutive frame as the latter scrambled to pull on a pair of khaki trousers, purple blouse and scuffed white Ked sneakers. She was also taken a bit back on the elevator ride down to the lobby when Azure suddenly pushed a bit of stray bangs from Orit's forehead and tucked the lock firmly behind her ear and said ever so sweetly, "Your face is such a splendor to behold."

Azure's hand continued to envelope Orit's diminutive hand all the way down the elevator, through the lobby, and all the way to the beach. The concierge who never seemed to have a shift off was awed by Azure, who he had always sensed was, as he put it, "queer," leading another woman by the hand in the Deep South. "She must think she's back in Cuba, or something," she thought.

The pair strolled north along the shore hand-in-hand as the fluorescent orange sun began to rise phoenix-like from the dark green horizon of the Atlantic stretching as far as the eye could see. Azure asked Orit some probing questions about her dreams, fears, hopes, wishes, desires, and key moments that had shaped who she was at the core of her being. Orit, who had never been asked such intimate questions before, was subconsciously seduced and drawn into Azure's séance. But Orit did not immediately dare to broach the most harrowing memories she had harbored since a child. The morning was so lovely, Orit thus did not dare ruin the bucolic and flirtatious splendor by mentioning her and her mother's terribly harrowing life and near-death experience in Imperial Russia, lest she ruin the day blubbering her eyes out.

But as the bottom semi-circle of the resplendent sun finally freed itself from the tyranny of the flat plane of the horizon the sky turned myriad shades of lavender, pink and purple, which set a mood that had a power over Orit, who found herself somewhat shocked to find herself divulging to Azure of some of the most intimate details of her life, things she had never dared to tell anyone before, including her reasons for the recent breakup with Moses, as he was proposing, no less. Orit knew it was strange in the moment as she was confessing what she felt to be something akin to sins to Azure, who seemed to be her newfound de facto high priest. But unburdening herself to this lovely and intelligent woman who she might likely never see again after leaving Miami felt so natural and right, so despite her qualms, she just kept talking because Azure seemed to be happy to listen.

Orit was so deep in her own thoughts that she at first did not notice when Azure stopped suddenly and warmly embraced her, enveloping her into her arms. Orit was a bit startled by the abrupt affection cast upon her; her body immediately tensed up as result of the embrace. Azure, however, continued to hold tight to her new companion and swayed Orit ever so gently as the warm early morning sun soaked into their skin. The gentle lapping of tiny waves fizzing up onto the sand created a natural soundtrack that seemed to match the splendor of cascading colors that comprised sunrise and sky.

Orit's tension gradually dissipated and she leaned deeper into Azure's gentle rocking and caress. Azure, who savored the embrace, slowly opened her eyes. Her lean body suddenly grew very tense and she let loose of Orit, who looked nervously up at Azure's concerned face wondering if she had done something wrong. "What is it?" Orit, who was unnerved, asked.

"Is that what I think it is?" Azure fretted. Orit then cautiously turned around. Her disbelieving gaze fixated where Azure's fright filled stare had settled. Orit's curious and worried eyes went suddenly wide; her jaw fell open as if made of heavy metal. "It can't be," she gasped as she cupped her hand over her mouth and slowly approached what appeared to be a corpse situated in the sawgrass up on a nearby dune leading up to the back of the hotel, "can it?"

Mr. Ingram donned crisp and pleated khaki trousers, newsboy cap, argyle sweater vest, and wingtip spikes. The lush green golf course looked lovely in the dim early morning light under a dewy mist. He was, however, visibly distressed as he anxiously awaited the arrival of his son at the first tee. For one, Garnet and Emory had yet to arrive. Worse still, Al Capone and Babe Ruth, who were on the third tee, were making a terrible mockery of golf etiquette. Both "buffoons," as Mr. Ingram gruffly referred to them, were still donning the mussed tuxedos they had worn the previous night at the soiree in the grand ballroom. Both were also very drunk and boisterous, which created divots in the grass that they did not have the courtesy to replace. Mr. Ingram sullenly watched the spectacle with hardly concealed contempt as Garnet, who was struggling to pull Emory up a rather steep incline towards the first tee in a rickshaw, slowly approached from behind. Garnet looked as though he might vomit or pass out when he finally managed to park the bulky and cumbersome rickshaw on steady ground next to the first tee. Emory looked even more put out, sickly and humiliated. Mr. Ingram did not immediately notice either's distress.

"Look at these fools," Mr. Ingram griped while continuing to glare at Capone and Ruth. "Some people have no respect for the game, never mind another man's property." He then cast his ire at Garnet and Emory. "What in the bloody hell took you lot so damned long to get here? Had you gotten here on time we could have been four holes ahead of these clowns."

"Sorry sir," Garnet panted in deep breaths while leaning forward with his hands planted firmly in his knees. "It was too difficult to push Emory's chair up the hill, so I had to go back to the hotel, get a rickshaw from one of the Bahamians, put it in the truck, and then come back. It was admittedly poor planning on my part, sir. But Emory, I assure you, did not have anything to do with our tardiness."

Emory, who was terribly hardened by anger and self-despair, softened ever so slightly as a result of Garnet's unexpected kindness.

"Well," Mr. Ingram huffed. "Just be sure to remember to consider these things the next time we schedule an outing."

"Yes sir," Garnet retorted as a bead of sweat slipped from his nose and fell to the dewy grass between his loafers as he forced a cordial and comprehending grin and nod of the head, ultimately displaying a patient lack of ego comparable to a Tibetan monk meditating on the side of a mountain.

Mr. Ingram then plucked a white golf ball from his trouser pocket and tossed it to Garnet. "Tee me up," Mr. Ingram demanded. Garnet calmly complied.

"Wind slightly from the southeast," Garnet said politely as he gently set the ball atop the first tee.

"You think this is my first time ever golfing, do you lad?" Mr. Ingram said snidely as he planted his spikes firmly in turf while slightly wiggling his hips and shoulders. He cast his gaze firmly towards the ball atop the tee. He took a long and composed breath, trying to block out the noise pollution emanating from Capone and Ruth on the third fairway. Mr.

Ingram finally slid his bulky wooden driver way back behind his head as he readied to whack the ball as crisp and smoothly as he could.

"Excuse me, Mr. Ingram!" A deep and brusque Alabamian accent interrupted the backswing, causing Mr. Ingram's shot to spin wildly off into a thicket of nearby pine trees.

"Consarn it!" Mr. Ingram seethed while slamming the curved end of his club into the green. He did not bother to replace his divot.

"Sorry to interrupt you, sir," hurly burly Sheriff Beauregard bellowed as his bulky legs dragged the rest of his body up the incline to the first tee. "There's been a murder at the Royal Palm. Your immediate presence has been requested by the local press in order to make an official statement on the matter."

"A murder?" Mr. Ingram's voice crackled with consternation as his face contorted to look like someone had shoved smelling salts into his nose. "Is this some kind of sick joke?"

"Wish it were," Beauregard regretted through shallow panting. "It's a real ugly scene over at your hotel. Mr. Fisher's fiancé was found in the dunes nearly buck naked and dead as the dodo. That pretty orange dress of hers was hiked up to her neck and that canary diamond ring she was all too glad to show off to anyone who'd pay her mind was took too along with her ring finger. Cut clean off."

"How do you know she was killed and didn't just die somehow?" Emory wondered. "Was she raped?"

"We're assuming that she was strangled," Beauregard explained. "She had marks all on her neck and a mangled coat hanger we think the killer used. We're not sure if the perpetrator had sexual intercourse with her or not at this juncture in the investigation. The corpse is on its way to the coroner now."

"Who found the body?" Mr. Ingram demanded.

"You boys pick up Carl yet?" Mr. Ingram asked.

"Afraid not," Beauregard lamented. "His lawyer ran an end around us already and convinced the honorable Mayor Merrick to let him turn himself in at some not yet determined point in the future. Merrick is a lame duck, so I reckon he took one nice little last payday from Mr. Fisher before vacating his esteemed position."

"Do you actually plan to stand idly by as your primary suspect walks free?" Emory, who was equal parts disturbed and amazed, asked.

"You know how things work in this city," Beauregard said while smiling a bit uneasily. "Hell, if your daddy wins the election next week, you might have a different perspective on the pressures facing Mayor Merrick at a moment like this."

"I sure as hell wouldn't let some killer loose," Mr. Ingram scoffed.

"I'm quite sure that Mr. Fisher is not at all our man," Beauregard declared rather haughtily and defensively, as if he were a far greater judge and authority on such matters than Mr. Ingram, who had the audacity to question the Sheriff's compliance with the arbitrary wishes of a lame duck mayor more concerned with lining his pockets than with finding a killer on the loose, which anyone with any sense at all knew was bad for a city as dependent on image, tourism, utopianism, and spectacle as Miami was. "A crime like this?" Beauregard added. "If you ask me, that limp-wristed carpetbagger couldn't do nothin' like this, not even if the trollop was two-timin' him with the biggest dicked nigger in the county. Besides, Carl seems pretty shook up and out of sorts by all this. Just between you, me, and the trees, I ain't ever seen a grown man blubber like he did when we told him Mirabel was dead. He was just like a little bitty baby. If ya ask me, it don't make no sense at all for Carl to kill the girl after having struck it so rich. Why would the fella do somethin' as dumb as killin' the girl? Think of the bad headlines for the Flamingo; it'd ruin his hotel. No sir," Beauregard concluded, "it ain't Carl who dun this; mark my words. I reckon somebody killed her to get that diamond and maybe to grift him somehow."

"Think of the headlines for my hotel," Mr. Ingram was aghast. "Miss Orange Blossom was found dead on my fucking property!" He splayed his hands out like he was splashing a headline across the sky. "It's my business that'll suffer most because of this goddamn mess. And how's this going to affect my campaign so close the election? You know, I wouldn't be a bit surprised if that damned scoundrel Sewell didn't dump the girl's body on my property to swing the poll numbers his way."

"We'll get it all sorted out sooner or later," the Sheriff, who was exhausted, sighed. "For now, you'd be wise to come on back and make an official statement to the press; get out in front of this thing as quick as you can. It sure as hell ain't gonna do you no wonders if you'z out here playin' golf while a murder mystery is unfoldin' back at your hotel."

"Goddamn it!" Mr. Ingram smashed the head of his wooden driver into the green and then threw the club into a nearby water hazard.

Mr. Capone, who was staggering drunkenly towards the tee at the fourth hole stopped suddenly to glare back at Mr. Ingram. "Some people just don't got any respect for the game," he slurred to Ruth as the latter slurped back a warm Pabst Blue Ribbon.

"Tell me about it," Ruth belched while watching Ingram, Beauregard, Garnet, and Emory make their way down the incline towards the carpark near the first tee.

Orit sat somewhat anxiously in the lobby of the hotel, which was packed with law enforcement agents and reporters eager to get a statement from Mr. Ingram. Her eyes widened suddenly as Mr. Ingram, Garnet, and Emory entered the lobby. She shrewdly made her way towards the elevator in the hope of intercepting Mr. Ingram.

Garnet did his very best to clear a path through the horde of law enforcement agents, photographers, reporters, gawkers, and sundry hotel guests that had gathered so that his employer could try and make his way as fast as possible towards the elevator. Emory was, meanwhile, subsumed by the horde and separated from Garnet and his father. Nobody, especially the reporters desperate to get near Mr. Ingram, noticed Emory's distress.

Orit's small physical stature was quite advantageous in that it enabled her to wind her way through the scrum that had formed a nearly perfect circle of clamoring reporters all around Mr. Ingram, as if he were at the eye of a hurricane of flashbulbs. Orit pressed the up-button on the elevator and waited impatiently for the doors to slide open.

The elevator finally arrived at the lobby. She smartly slid into the opening doors and positioned herself in the front corner, by the buttons. Garnet finally ushered Mr. Ingram onto the waiting elevator and blocked the entrance so that nobody else could get aboard.

Neither he nor Mr. Ingram noticed Orit in the front corner of the elevator, next to the keypad, until the doors had already shut and the three of them were secluded inside. "Third floor?" her clear, cool and calm voice starkly contrasted the manic yelling of the horde of reporters and photographers in the lobby. Garnet, who was peeved and suspicious, reluctantly nodded his head. Orit smiled cordially and jabbed the glowing round button with the 3 on it.

"I am sorry to ambush you like this, sir," Orit said with a distinct determination and poise. "My Name is Orit Abrahams. I have come to Miami to investigate the endemic corruption in the real estate industry and local politics. I understand you are running against Mr. Sewell as a 'reform candidate.' You strike me as one of the few honest businessmen left in this city, and I'd very much appreciate an opportunity to speak with you about your plans for addressing corruption in Miami."

"Now is not the best time," Garnet interjected. "I don't know if you have heard, but there has been a murder."

"I did hear," she said. "I discovered the body this morning. Do you, Mr. Ingram, think there might be any correlation at all between the murder on your property last night and your agenda for reform?"

"Please," Garnet pleaded. "Mr. Ingram will provide the press with an official statement later."

"Why can't Mr. Ingram say what is on his mind now?" Orit demanded, "unless, of course, he has committed some kind of crime, such as murder? If Mr. Ingram is as honest a man as the local newspapers portray him to be, then why not set the record straight right here and now by simply going on record with what you think?"

"This is terribly gauche of you, young lady," Mr. Ingram snapped, his patience had finally waned. "A beautiful young woman was murdered, and all you care about is writing your goddamn story. There are things bigger than a fucking election. Show some goddamn human decency."

"The decent thing to do, sir," Orit rejoined, "is the expose the endemic corruption in this city and figure out just how deep it really goes so that we can protect other people from being victimized. The fraud in this city does no favors to honest businessmen. As such, your unwillingness to honestly speak your mind makes me a tad suspicious. I can't help but wonder if you do have something you'd like to hide."

"Look," Mr. Ingram grunted defiantly as the elevator came to a sudden stop on the third floor of the hotel. "You think I don't know all about the corruption in this city? You think I don't know how bad it is for business if Miami is widely perceived to a boondoggle, or some kind pyramid scheme concocted by the likes of Sewell, Fisher, and the Mizner brothers? There are lots of corrupt men you can talk to if you are looking for a scoop, young lady, but I assure you that I am not one of them. Now," he added as the elevator doors slid open, "if you'd be so kind to as excuse me." He then set his sights on Garnet; "Escort this woman off my property," he demanded.

"I'm sorry, sir," Orit said while pointing at the door to suite 303. "My suite is right there. I'm paid up through the week."

"Funny," Mr. Ingram glowered, "And here I thought you were just another of those cancerous parasites polluting the lobby." He then set his glare on Garnet once more and said, "Get your ass back down there and bring Emory up immediately."

"Yes sir," Garnet said somewhat sheepishly while mashing his index finger frantically into the round 'L' button.

"And don't utter one word to those parasites," Mr. Ingram seethed. Garnet raised his eyebrows as though his intelligence had been assailed.

Orit did not bother to exit the elevator. The short ride back down to the lobby with Garnet was silent, tense and awkward for both passengers. The lobby was still packed with a ravenous horde of newspapermen when they arrived. Garnet pushed his way into the crowd searching for Emory, who was pressed against the plate-glass window overlooking the front lawn of the hotel. Orit, meanwhile, scrawled "Mizner, Fisher + Sewell" into her worn notepad with her half-used yellow pencil, then pushed her way through the mob of newsmen towards the exit of the lobby.

Babe Ruth was half-asleep while a wide-eyed Al Capone sped back from the golf course to the hotel in the gangster's supped up electric-blue Ford roadster. Both men had yet to properly rest since the soiree at the Royal Palm the night prior. They had been up all-night snorting cocaine and dumping booze into their bloated bodies. Ruth, however, began to crash fast on the seventh hole. He then shot sixteen over par on the eighth. He refused to continue the farce any further after that. Capone, rather miraculously, was still wired up and ready to rage the day away. He thus pulled a long swig of ripple from his chrome and engraved flask and tried to hand it to Ruth, who sullenly refused.

Capone's beady and bloodshot eyes suddenly fixated on an idled truck at the side of a dirt road leading into town. A barefooted young woman wearing pink pinstriped pajamas was curled in a ball and sleeping in the bed of the truck. The bottoms of her feet were completely black due to the layer of dirt she had collected upon them since she had run away from home. Capone began to slow his roadster down. "No Al, come on," Ruth gutturally pleaded. "Big boy gotta sleep now."

"Shut your big trap, ya mamaluke," Capone slurred. "The dame might need a bit of gentlemanly assistance."

He then slid the roadster to a halt next to the truck, which caused a bit of dust to whirl up into her sleeping face. She woke and sat up suddenly as if escaping from some horrid nightmare. The young woman, who Capone would later learn was named Scarlet, was somewhat awed by the vibrantly colored roadster, the shade of which she had never seen before. "Hey there, Little Red Riding Hood," Capone grinned semi-suavely; his gold tooth flashed and seemed to twinkle in the resplendence of the sun high in the morning sky, "I'm the Big Bad Wolf."

"Huh?" Scarlet, who was befuddled by Capone's very existence, wondered.

"What's a tasty young dame like you doin' out here all by yourself?" Capone insisted.

"I was on my way to enter the Miss Orange Blossom Pageant, but the truck stopped workin'," she explained. "Damned if I know why."

"Probably because it's a huge hunk of shit," Capone cackled and slapped the back of his fingers into Ruth's chest. The Babe was not amused.

"Yeah," Scarlet said snidely while slightly shrugging her dainty shoulders, "you're obviously a world class mechanic."

Capone's giddy mien suddenly changed drastically. His quasi-charming mood grew very dark as he glared at Scarlet. "You watch that lip there, hon," he warned. "You never know who is out here on these roads. One of em might be a killer."

"You gonna kill me then, mister?" Scarlet sneered fearlessly, daring him. "Ain't nothin' under God's golden sun you can do to me that's any worse than what's already been dun to me."

"That right?" Capone's mood shifted drastically once more back to the giddied, kindhearted, and gregarious polarity. He laughed heartily. "You got some real sand there, kiddo," he gushed. "What's your name?"

"Scarlet."

"Where ya from, hon?" Capone asked. "More importantly, where you headed?"

"I'm from nowhere worth wastin' breath mentionin'," Scarlet confessed. "I reckon I'm headed wherever the hell you want to take me."

A predatory glint flashed in Capone's beady and sociopathic eyes. "You can't win no Miss Orange Blossom crown dressed like that," he grinned. "Hop in the back," he said while pointing into the back cab of the roadster. "We'll drop this bag of bones back at the hotel," he said while motioning towards the nearly catatonic mound of a man in the front passenger seat. "Then we'll get you some new duds and shoes so that you can knock those Orange Blossom judges' tongues right out of their heads."

"That all sounds like a real nice plan," Scarlet said, "but I'm afraid I don't even have enough money just now to even enter the pageant, let alone go shoppin'. I was hopin' the pageant organizers might consider floatin' me a loan until after I win the contest and the hundred-dollar prize money."

"I got plenty of cash to burn, hon," he smiled wide. "You can thank the Blacksocks for that."

"Who?" Scarlet was confused.

"Ain't a baseball fan, eh?" Capone smiled. "Jump in," he added while reaching back into the cab and popping the back-door handle so that the door could swing open.

Scarlet hopped excitedly from the back bed of her father's broken down truck and into the roadster next to two sets of golf clubs.

"You like to go fast, hon?" Capone hollered back while staring lustfully at her reflection in the rearview mirror.

"Hell yeah, I like to go fast," she enthused.

The force of gravity forced her body to be pushed back in the seat as Capone gassed the roadster.

"Everyone calls me Al," Capone hollered over the sound of the roaring engine; the roadster swerved and shimmied a bit as it kicked up a huge plume of khaki sand behind it as the Ford sped along the narrow dirt road leading towards Miami's fledgling skyline. "This big lug here," he added, "is Babe Ruth." Scarlet looked closely at the passed-out slugger hunched over in the front passenger seat.

"Well, I'll be," she amazed, "I heard of him. He's famous, huh?"

"I guess so," Capone was a tad jealous, "if you can consider a baseball player famous. He's not as famous as I am anyway."

"You're famous too?" somewhat incredulous. "I never seen you before in any picture in the paper or magazines."

"They must not have the right pictures down in Palookaville, or whatever Podunk backwater you're from, darlin'," he tried to remain calm as he hung a hard right, aiming the roadster onto Flagler Avenue.

Downtown, Capone and Scarlet had arrived at the new Sears department store that had just finished being built on Flagler Avenue. It was the "Grand Opening," a stark white banner with red script hanging over the double doors leading into the store alerted consumers. A tuxedoed and bowling-pin shaped doorman covered in a thick film of perspiration caused by high humidity, seemed to guard the entrance more than welcome consumers. He also spoke with an odd faux English accent and mimicked the mannerisms of an especially uptight butler as he greeted visitors to the store. He was especially aghast that Scarlet, whose feet were black on the bottom, would have the effrontery to enter the department store sans shoes. Capone, however, had expected such reticence, if not resistance, and thus already had a crisp ten-dollar bill waiting to shove into the doorman's pudgy and sweaty hand. "Came to get the little lady here a new pair of shoes, pally," Capone grinned in an effort to let the doorman know that he was the alpha male between them. The money and subconscious fear bought the doorman's reluctant compliance, but not his grace or good tidings. He took the cash but looked upon Capone and Scarlet with hardly concealed contempt as they raced boisterously up the escalator towards the women's floor of the department store.

"Get whatever the fuck you want," Capone hollered after Scarlet as she raced ahead excitedly. Capone opened a small bag of cocaine and snorted a bump from the tip of his car key. Scarlet then ransacked armfuls of dresses from the racks. Azure, who was wearing a bright blue sundress while shopping for a new gown on the second-story, watched the spectacle unfold between Scarlet and Capone with some amusement and dismay. Capone, meanwhile, rode the escalator up to the menswear and outdoorsman section of the store on the third floor.

Scarlet finally hurried back towards the rack Azure was casually perusing. "Got anything good over there?" Scarlet giddily asked as if high.

"Not really," Azure lamented while shrugging her shoulders nonchalantly. "It is so difficult to find anything truly beautiful in such a gaudy town. This place will never be Paris, I'm afraid."

"Really?" surprised Scarlet surmised. "I want to get everything in here; it's all so magnificent."

"I see your taste in clothes is not too terribly dissimilar from your taste in men," Azure smirked slightly condescendingly, and then began to glide towards the perfume counter.

"Yeah," Scarlet said diffidently while whishing fast past dresses hung on the rack. She then suddenly stopped whishing and cast an accusatory glare at Azure, who sprayed a mist of perfume into the air to explore its bouquet. "Hey there," Scarlet snarled, "you wait just one goddamn minute. What'd ya mean by that comment? Is that some kind of a slight against me and Al?"

"I'm simply stating that his personality and energy is gaudy and unsophisticated – nouveau riche – much like Miami is," Azure stated. "If you like Miami, it is not surprising that you'd be drawn to a man like Al Capone. I meant it as an observation more so than as an insult."

"What the hell is that – 'new vo reesh'?" Scarlet was confounded.

"It means that he is like a little boy who has just learned to ride a bicycle, but he mistakenly thinks he has wings to fly,"

Azure smiled wryly while twirling her fingers to emulate something smallish flying away.

"So you're sayin' he looks foolish?" Scarlet's giddiness began to sour quickly into bitterness. "And you mean to say I look foolish too, then. Is that it?" she added while walking around to the rack and towards the perfume counter. Azure actually gained a modicum of respect for Scarlet's burst of intelligence, which she had previously underestimated. Azure had assumed Scarlet was but a bumpkin, but suddenly saw some commendable tenacity in her that caused Azure to soften slightly.

"I suppose I do not know you well enough to make such broad denunciations," Azure said as her eyes trained on Scarlet's bare feet. "I do, however, wonder if you don't quite know exactly the kind of man you are involved with."

"What about Al?" Scarlet defiantly demanded. "What could possibly be the matter with him? He's young, rich, sweet, and sort of cute too, in a weird Guinea sort of way. What else is there to know?"

"It's really none of my business, I'm quite sure," Azure said in an effort to diffuse the tension as she started to make her way towards another rack of gowns near the descending escalator.

"Then why the hell did you make it your business?" Scarlet's voice deepened suddenly as she glared squarely at Azure, who was unfazed by the youngster's acrimonious demeanor.

"Mr. Capone has quite the reputation, that's all I'm saying," Azure explained. "Don't you ever read the papers?"

"Hell no, I don't read no dumb newspapers." Scarlet, who was offended by the insinuation, contorted her face. "Newspapers are boring, except for the advertisements with pretty girls from faraway places, like Hollywood."

"Well, your beau, though just a teenager, is one of the most notorious gangsters in the country," Azure said in a tone just above a whisper while glancing over at the escalator to ensure Capone was not on his way back down from the menswear and outdoorsman section of the store. "He's rumored to be a murderer many times over," Azure whispered, "what Dr. Freud in Vienna would refer to as a psychopath."

"Who the hell said what, now?" Scarlet reveled in her ignorance as she attempted to educate Azure. "Besides," she added. "I know Al real good. He'd never hurt a fly. Plus, if he was a murderer, he'd be in jail. I don't know where you're from, lady. But this here is America. We got us law and order here."

"Look, little girl," Azure's voice dripped with frustrated impatience as she ached to conclude the tedious conversation, "all I'm saying is to be careful. That's all. He is a very dangerous man. I was drawn to men of his kind when I was your age. It won't end well for you. I'm trying to help you. You can take the advice or leave it. But one way or the other, you'll have to live with the consequences of your decisions and actions."

Azure then hurried with the stern determination of a runway model towards the escalator leading to the appliances and sweaty doorman with the fake British accent below. Her warning, however, did not deter Scarlet, who discovered that Azure's advice had made her even more attracted to Capone than she had previously been.

"How do you know he shouldn't be careful of me?" Scarlet haughtily hollered after Azure, who disappeared from her line of sight just as Capone hopped onto the elevator leading from the third to second story of the store. "Hey," he yelled while grinning dopily, "look at what I found!" He displayed a double-barrel shotgun over his head as if it were a trophy as the escalator descended. "Ain't it grand?" he added. She giggled while slightly wiggling her toes. Worried Azure hurried past the doorman and onto the sidewalk.

Across town, the coroner, who was an elderly white man with a slightly humped back, was finally concluding his report on what exactly he believed had happened to the reigning Miss Orange Blossom. The old man had been a coroner for more than fifty years. He had witnessed every manner of death imaginable, including dozens of brutal murders and victims of the lynch mob. But he had never seen any killing as brutal as the murder of Mr. Fisher's fiancé.

"What kind of mad dog could do somethin' like this?" his brusque and terrified Tennessean accent quivered. "What kind of sickened mind shoves an orange rind into the poor girl's body? I mean hells bells, Sheriff," the coroner winced as if life had lost most of its meaning, "there were flies, ants, and maggots five inches deep in the poor girl's vaginal cavity. Truth be told," the geriatric coroner confessed, "I nearly lost my lunch."

"So," Beauregard said, hoping to clarify as his sullen and tense dark eyes skimmed the official coroner's report, "she was killed by battery acid and then strangled after she was already dead?"

The coroner, who seemed spooked, nodded his head forlornly.

"And," Beauregard proceeded, "she was sexually assaulted with citrus, but you don't think the perpetrator had sex with her?"

"There was no evidence of any kind of semen inside her vaginal cavity or what was left of her dress," the coroner said as he gently placed the blue medical sheet over the woman's ice-blue face.

An intense exasperation caused Beauregard's sun spotted brow to furrow and crease. "That don't make no goddamn sense, doc."

"You ready for the worst part?" the coroner's nervous and weary eyes looked hard at Beauregard.

"How in the hell can this shit possibly get worse?" Beauregard, who was horribly exacerbated, sighed, while running his fat fingers through the thinning black hair atop his head.

"A week ago, the homecoming queen at Central High School up in Brunswick, Georgia, was found dead," the coroner whispered as if telling a secret. They found a peach between her thighs and a *Bible* by her head, which was nothin' but mush.

"A *Bible*?" Beauregard asked?

"She was on her way home from Church," the coroner explained.

"Battery acid was the cause of death?" Beauregard wondered.

"Can't say for certain," the coroner was baffled. "Unlike our girl, who was strangled after she was already dead and was not, I don't think, raped by the perpetrator, the girl in Brunswick was actually strangled to death and semen was found inside of her. But there was also a trace of battery acid in her mouth."

"Well goddamn it," Beauregard was both excited and frightened. "You know what this means?"

"Bet your ass I know what it means," the impatient old man, whose intelligence had been insulted, grunted, "we got us a goddamn serial killer loose somewhere along the FEC line."

"No," Beauregard huffed fretfully. "Well, yeah," he amended, "I guess that's true too. But worse yet, we're about to be invaded by the goddamn Federal Government. Murder in Georgia, now our girl here, both killed in a similar manner; both murders involvin' some kind of heinous ritual. Shoot, the goddamn FBI'll be here faster than flies on a dead mule, mark my words."

"I reckon you're right," the coroner said sullenly as his tired and old eyes gazed out the window, remembering the horrors of the past, "God help us all."

One thousand miles north of Miami, in the neighborhood of Astoria in the borough of Queens, New York, an Italian-American man named Giuseppe Gallo stood on the rain-slicked cobblestoned street observing many white men under his command raze a tenement building that harbored illegal immigrants from Russia, Poland, Sweden, and the Balkans whom Gallo was convinced harbored sympathies for Bolsheviks. His callous disregard for human rights when raiding tenements for Bolsheviks earned him the affectionate nickname of "The Red's Menace" by his boss, William J. Flynn.

When asked by an ambitious, bold, and young reporter named Orit Abrahams months earlier when his barbaric raids first began why he felt so ruthlessly inclined to employ such draconian measures, he replied, "because illegal immigrants have no rights that an American man such as me, who had to wait in line and work his way up tooth and nail, is obliged to respect. If these people want to come here and infect this great nation with radical ideas that threaten the republic, then they are a cancer or a demon and thus should be extirpated by any means necessary, be it by exorcism or the razing of a rat, filth, and Bolshevik-infested building that is but a festering blight on the soul and spirit of this, God's great nation." The FBI office in lower Manhattan was barraged with angry letters for weeks after Gallo's quote appeared in print. But Mr. Flynn did not mind a stern threat being sent to what he considered to be the leftist parasites who read publications such as *The New York Call*.

The smoldering building finally collapsed, which looked oddly artistic as reflected in the black frames of Gallo's dark sunglasses. He exhaled a relieved lung full of smoke and gazed emotionlessly upon the burning building as scores of hungry, tired, scared, and overworked people were being loaded onto paddy wagons. Another federal agent, a disheveled man cupping a white handkerchief over his mouth in order to avoid inhaling smoke, approached Gallo, who at first appeared annoyed by his presence. Gallo's annoyance, however, quickly morphed into an excitement that bordered on glee. He raced past the paddy wagons towards a black Model-T, which he eagerly hopped into the driver's seat of and then sped away.

Flynn's secretary, an octogenarian with hair so gray it had a bluish tint in the dim light of the office, which due to its position on the inside of Wall Street's narrow canyons, was in perpetual shade. Though the curtains inside the office were wide open, it was still very dark inside. That was fine by Flynn, who had always felt safer and more empowered in the dark and far more vulnerable in the pristine light of day.

Flynn heartily shook Gallo's hand as his excited subordinate entered his office. "By God, Gio," Flynn said matter-of-factly. "You reek of petrol."

"Yes sir," Gallo was embarrassed. "I was in the middle of a raid in Astoria when word came that you wanted to see me at once."

"Yes," Flynn said as he slinked into the leather chair behind his massive wooden desk, which was directly in front of a plate-glass window overlooking the grayish facades of Wall Street. "Please do have a seat. First off," Flynn stared hard across the desk at Gallo, "let me begin by thanking you for your telegram. Your wordplay, 'moving up in the world by moving down to the swamps of Washington' was very clever indeed and thusly very greatly appreciated. Your English has progressed so well so fast, too," Flynn enthused. "Why, I can hardly even detect an accent anymore."

"Thank you, sir," Gallo gushed, "I have been taking elocution classes at night in the hopes of assimilating as quickly as possible."

"You keep Americanizing at the rate you are and why, someday, you may just be sitting where I am now," Flynn grinned disingenuously.

"No sir, that is impossible," Gallo smiled warmly and sincerely. All the men in the field understand as well as I do that your leadership is exactly what this country needs at this fragile stage in human history. I could never imagine anyone but you at the helm of this outfit."

"Well, thank you for your vote of confidence, Gio," Flynn said softly. "That is certainly very kind to you to say. And you know how much your support matters to me in this transitional and very tenuous stage in the evolution of the Bureau. There are powerful forces in this nation that would like to see us disbanded. And, as you know, if it were up to me, I would stay here and continue to supervise the raids, in which you have done such incredibly vital work in order to keep this country safe. But as you also know, the more politicized the Bureau has become since the end of the war, the more imperative it is that I be in Washington fulltime. These are very dangerous times we are living in, Gio, and the Bolsheviks have no respect or honor for our values or traditions. Our politicians, with their vices and their mistresses, they are sitting ducks for Bolshevik agents to blackmail in order to gain influence in our government."

"I understand completely, sir," Gallo said. "What you are doing is nothing less than the will of God almighty, I have no doubt."

"I'm glad you so boldly invoked the will of the almighty," Flynn leaned forward in his chair, "because I feel very strongly that it is God's very will that you be sent to Miami, Florida, at once. I assume you're a Catholic, is that right?"

"Yes sir," Gallo replied a bit reluctantly.

"Well, I do suppose you'll have to answer for that when you die," Flynn, a Protestant, said coldly. "But the important thing for now is that we both essentially believe in the same God of Abraham. As such, your God and my God agree that the Bureau needs you in Miami."

"Miami, sir?" Gallo was confused. "I didn't realize the Bolsheviks had a heavy presence in Miami?"

"Don't be daft, Gio," Flynn was disturbed by his underling's naiveté. "The Bolsheviks, God help us, are nowhere and everywhere all at once," Flynn warned, "especially the places you least and most expect."

"I see, sir." Gallo was slightly ashamed to have been educated by his superior.

"But God does not want you in Miami just now to exterminate vermin," Flynn explained. "I need you to zip on down to South Florida on the next train available and then Brunswick, Georgia, on your way back home. It seems we've got us a serial killer on the loose down in Dixieland."

"But sir," Gallo appeared heartbroken and bewildered, "have I done something wrong? Is it my methods you do not approve of?"

"No, of course not, Gio, no, no," Flynn insisted while standing up to walk around to the front of the desk where he could gaze confidingly down into his underling's nervous and desperate eyes. "I'm not one of those namby-pamby liberals in the press who worries about trifles such as 'human rights.'" Flynn chortled haughtily. "Your methods are effective. That is all that matters to me. As far as Miami is concerned, you ought to think of this particular assignment as a promotion, albeit without an official change in pay or rank. This is the way one moves up in this industry," Flynn educated Gallo. "We all know you are 'The Red's Menace.' You have made a great name for yourself in this business, to be sure. But now it is imperative that you solve a murder to show the powers that be that you are not just a one-trick pony. This is your shot to prove that you are management material."

"But sir, I have no experience investigating murders," Gallo, who felt as though he was being set up for failure, fretted.

"There's only one way to pop your proverbial cherry, lad," Flynn grinned as he patted Gallo gently on his underling's suddenly slumped shoulders. "I need you on a train to Miami twenty-three skidoo. Have Mrs. Barber provide you with the pertinent details and train ticket on your way out." Gallo stood and began to traipse towards the office exit. "Oh, and Gio," Flynn added while smiling teasingly, "I do hope for the sake of the other passengers that you have time to make it home to get a quick bath; the petrol stinks something awful. It's quite nauseating."

"Yes sir," Gallo said while shaking Mr. Flynn's reluctant hand. "Thank you, sir."

"Never mind that," Flynn said graciously, "you earned it. I expect nothing but positive results. In fact, I expect you to have this solved by the time my tenure here ends."

A deep and unnerved sigh escaped Gallo as he compliantly nodded. Flynn, meanwhile, tried desperately to wipe clean the stench of petrol residue left on his hand with his handkerchief.

Dusk had settled over Miami by the time Capone and Scarlet had made their way back to the Royal Palm lobby with several white and blue paper Sears shopping bags in hand. The gangster had rented out the penthouse down the hall from Emory's suite through the end of the season. Once the door had been locked behind them, Capone had but one thing in mind – bedding Scarlet. Scarlet was, however, in no mood. She was terribly nervous and tended to gravitate towards the window overlooking the twilight sky and city lights reflecting off the glassy surface of Biscayne Bay.

"Come on over here, doll face," Capone urged the adolescent as he plopped atop the king-size bed. She did not seem to hear him. "Hey," he grunted a bit more forcefully as he slapped the finely crafted bedspread made of Egyptian cotton he laid atop of. "Don't make me ask a second time." She was taken back a bit by his sudden and aggressive change in demeanor.

"I don't much feel like layin' down just now, Al," she said. "I'm too nervous and excited."

"Don't tell me this is your first time alone with a man," he sneered rather lecherously, "pretty young thing like you?"

"No," she confided, "I'm nervous about the pageant tomorrow. Did you see the other girls who had entered? Some of them are real beauties."

"Ah, come on," Capone said mellifluously as he made his way from the bed to the window. He wrapped his arms around Scarlet's dainty waist and gently rocked her from side to side. She could sense the bulging erection in his pants poking into her buttocks. Her gaze, however, fixated on her own ghostly reflection in the windowpane. "You're gonna knock em dead tomorrow," Capone assured. "The judges' fuckin' tongues are gonna fall out of their goddamn heads when they see those gams in that sultry orange swimsuit we got you."

"Gee Al," she ached for his adoration while turning around and gazing deep into his beady and sociopathic eyes. "Do you really think so? Honest, you're not just sayin' that?"

"I know so," he said matter-of-factly. "You're destined to be the next Miss Orange Blossom."

"I don't know how I'll ever be able to get any sleep tonight, I'm so nervous," her voice was uncommonly timid as she slumped over at the edge of the bed. "If I don't get any sleep, I'm afraid I won't look pretty or remember the words to the song and bungle the talent portion of the pageant. God, I'd just kill myself if I don't win Miss Orange Blossom."

"I've got just the thing to fix you up," he said while rummaging through the bottom drawer of the dresser adjacent to the king-size bed. He soon revealed a paper bag stuffed with coarse brown powder.

"What is it?" she asked suspiciously.

"You see," he grinned, "this is I why I love you so much. You're so goddamn pure and innocent. You're like a babe in the woods."

"I'm not as innocent as everybody seems to think," she pouted, offended by the pejorative slight.

Capone, who was spreading paraphernalia atop the bedspread, including a spoon caked with brownish-yellow residue, silver butane lighter, a few cotton swabs, a plastic bottle of rubbing alcohol, and one syringe, ignored her. He did not notice she had responded to his previous comment, which she felt was a bit condescending.

"This here is the finest Afghan heroin on the planet," he finally broke the silence that lingered, "very powerful stuff, so you gotta be extra careful with it. You just need a taste. Too much of this shit, and it's finito. Capeesh?"

"Finito?" she did not understand. "Capeesh?" she said while shrugging her shoulders as if she does not understand.

"Just sprawl out on the bed, why don't cha?" he urged. "Now, all you gotta do is rest, relax and take deep breaths. I'll get you fixed right up. Tomorrow you'll kill those other girls in that fuckin' pageant."

He then hurried into the bathroom to dab the cotton and heroin with a bit of water from the faucet. He then loaded the syringe with a full dose. Scarlet, who was lying on the bed and staring up at the ceiling, was too nervous and excited to take deep breaths. Capone finally came back into the room and sat at the edge of the bed next to her.

"This may prick for just an itty bitty second," he sweetly said while tightening a rubber chord tight around her toned bicep in order to better expose her vein for plunging needles into, "but then," he added while flicking the side of the syringe with his finely manicured yet somewhat greasy middle finger, "you ain't gonna feel no kind of pain at all. Okay," he asked while exhaling a tense breath, "you ready?"

"I sure as hell hope so," she grimaced a bit. He had already plunged the needle into the throbbing vein protruding from her forearm before the sentence was even completely out of her mouth. He emptied a third of the contents in the syringe into her vein. A hot subterranean breath that had been harboring years of fear, angst, anxiety, heartache, and tension fled from her being as if she were exorcised of demons. Her eyes fluttered and then rolled back deep in her head. She moaned gutturally, soothed to a point far beyond the effable. "There's no pain, no pain, no pain," the words escaped from her trembling lips as a slight grin formed and a solitary tear streamed from her pasty white face and collected on the thousand-count bedspread.

Capone set the syringe gently atop the nightstand and began to slowly unbutton Scarlet's sundress. He then plucked the leather sandals he had bought her at Sears off her feet; the bottoms of which were still filthy, but Capone did not notice or care.

Scarlet also did not notice that she was being undressed. She was too busy envisioning herself in a purple sequence ballgown that seemed to create a kaleidoscopic spectrum of color under the reflection of the stage lights; her hair was in a bob; too much rouge was piled onto her lips and cheeks as camera flashbulbs momentarily blinded her as she posed for pictures on a red carpet outside the Chinese Theater at the premier screening of *The Married Virgin* starring Rudolph Valentino. "Really, you're too kind" and "thank you so very much," she said to the reporters and photographers while smiling and waving her hand as flashbulbs crackled all around her.

Capone, who had just slid his syphilitic penis inside Scarlet's vagina, assumed she was thanking him. "Don't mention it," he salivated while slithering his blistered and calloused penis inside her. He winced slightly from the pain, which gave him a masochistic rush of pure pleasure.

The sun had only just set over Ditmas Avenue in Brooklyn by the time Gallo had arrived in his Model-T at the red brick two-story Victorian house that was home to his family, which included his increasingly bitter wife, his rapidly ageing and angry mother, and his two dimwitted sons, both of whom he prohibited from speaking Italian, which was odd because neither his wife or mother, who only recently arrived in New York from Napoli, could speak much English at all.

Gallo had not even realized it was Halloween until he got home to see his boys donning their silly costumes: the middle schooler was covered in a white sheet with two small holes he could hardly see through, and the younger boy was dressed as an American football player in leather pads and helmet. "Red Grange," his son explained. His father had, however, never heard of the gridiron star.

Gallo privately believed this new holiday was designed to stimulate the economy and thus a rather foolish spectacle, if not also heretical due to what he perceived to be the unabashed celebration of evil tidings as manifested in rituals such as trick-or-treating. But he encouraged his sons to participate in the ritual because it was a new and quintessentially American spectacle that he hoped would help his rather unpopular sons better assimilate into the mainstream of American society, which was increasingly indistinguishable from these kinds of consumerist holidays.

The boys' mother, Mona, was particularly distressed as Gallo hurried past her and then up the stairs without saying a word. She was acutely unnerved that he had arrived home so late in the day. Not only had her husband forgotten that he had promised to take his sons trick-or-treating, thus promising her a much needed night to herself; but she also could tell he was planning to stay out another night, which meant she would have to take the boys trick-or-treating herself after a day full of doing backbreaking housework. She thus rushed up the steps and into the bedroom to confront her husband.

Her ire was stoked even more acutely as he stripped off clothes that reeked of petrol and burnt wood and left them atop of an ornate and handmade yellow and burgundy colored Moroccan rug bequeathed to her by her grandmother many years prior. Worse yet, he had the temerity to ask what she had made for dinner, which prompted her to demand a divorce, for the umpteenth time since they had arrived from Italy. He, however, ignored her while retrieving a suitcase from under the canopy bed. He then angrily yanked clothes out from the dresser and closet and shoved them inside the suitcase.

"I told you," he seethed while glowering at her, "I don't want any Italian spoken in this house. We are American now."

"I," she said aggrievedly in English as she planted her finger firmly in her breastplate and tried to picture the phonetics she wanted to convey in her head, "divorce now."

His trim and naked body darted over to her like he aimed to inflict harm. She flinched, but did not take a step back. He stopped himself just before his fist was about to smash into her cheekbone. He pressed his knuckles threateningly into her jaw. "I'd kill you before I'd ever let you shame my family with a sin such as divorce," he whispered in seething tone. He then calmed and grew suddenly more sympathetic to her plight than he was angry with her. He smiled oddly condescendingly, feeling sorry for this crazed woman losing her bearings in this strange new land she did not understand. "You'll see," he added ever so sweetly, softening under the weight of her fear and despair, "once I prove my worth to Mr. Flynn, you'll love being an American. I'll be home much more often." The domineering husband then tried to kiss his wife's cheek on the way into the bathroom. But she would not permit it. "I suspect you and the boys will be out trick-or-treating by the time I get out of the shower," he hoped, unfazed by her refusal to allow him to kiss her. "Tell the boys I love them and will bring them a present from Miami. I'll give my love to mother on my way out."

"Mi-am-a?" she asked phonetically while shrugging her shoulders as though she did not comprehend what he was referring to.

"It's a city in Florida," he unenthusiastically explained. "I've got an assignment there. I'll be back as soon as I can."

She shrugged her shoulders and shook her head as if to communicate, 'I don't understand?'

"Be sure to study your English while I am away," he, who was slightly annoyed, demanded while rolling his eyes. He then shut the door in her face and locked the door so she could not invade his space. She, who was beyond infuriated, kicked the door, cursed his soul to hell in Italian, and then angrily trudged back downstairs to retrieve her overcoat and scarf from the foyer closet. Her sons, meanwhile, were in the midst of a bitter battle over who would be permitted to take the last sip of Coca-Cola that their grandmother had, despite her daughter-in-law's insistence on not giving the sugary drink to her children, let them split.

CHAPTER FIFTEEN

Saturday, November 1, 1919

Beauregard's tired eyes, which had rings of fleshy, mushy, and heavy blue bags underneath, glared sullenly down at the morning edition of *The Miami Herald* at bold headlines such as "FEC Killer Still Not Caught," below an article with a headline that read, "Can Sewell or Ingram Be Trusted?" To say Beauregard was less than enthused as he waited rather impatiently atop the hood of his patrol car in the parking lot next to the Biscayne Bay train station would be a gross understatement. His massive body seemed withered, as though he had shrunk as a result of an incessant worry that had begun to prevail the previous night after having received a dreaded call from Director Flynn's secretary asking if anyone would be so kind as to fetch Special Agent Gallo from the train station and take him to his hotel, The Royal Palm, and provide any timely assistance with the investigation that might be needed. The downtrodden local lawman reluctantly agreed, but feared the worst – that this federal agency would interfere with the sweet honeypot of corruption that he benefited from hand over fist.

Beauregard, whose ancestors owned a small rice plantation outside of Gump, Alabama, during the antebellum era, also portrayed the common penchant amongst white southerners in the sense that he bitterly resented agents of the Federal Government, which he blamed for the Civil War and the death of what he believed was a far more grand, glorious, and utopian Old South.

Gallo finally exited the station with suitcase in hand looking somewhat disheveled as a result of the long train ride through the night. He walked directly across the lot towards Beauregard, who slinked down from atop the hood of the patrol car and took a deep breath in the hopes of bottling his anxiety and somewhat composing himself. Beauregard was somewhat relieved to find that Gallo was Italian, and not a full-fledged Yankee, when they were first introduced outside the station. He was also a bit self-conscious that his hand was unusually clammy as he offered it to the Special Agent. Gallo kindly tried to express his appreciation for Beauregard having had waited to fetch him from the station.

Gallo was also not terribly inclined to mince words or to beat around the bush. As such, by the time the patrol car had rounded the corner onto Flagler Avenue, Gallo was already shrewdly making an ally of the local police force. "Look, Sheriff," Gallo explained, "Miami's reputation for graft and corruption is, as I'm sure you know far better than I, not merely infamous, it is legendary. Perhaps you are a little involved in the endemic corruption that has sullied this city's good name, perhaps your involvement is a requisite component of this city's corruption." A bead of sweat formed just above Beauregard's right eyebrow. He swallowed hard. "But to be perfectly frank, Sheriff," Gallo continued, "I have no interest in the corruption that does or does not exist in this city or who might or might not be involved in it. Corruption in Miami is, as far as I am concerned, a local matter that the Bureau has no real business getting involved in. Hell," he smiled, "if some yahoo from Minnesota is dumb enough to buy a plot of land ten feet underwater without having the good sense to inspect it first to ensure that the land is on the level, that is that yahoo's own damn fault for being stupid. Understand?" Gallo looked hard at Beauregard, who very slightly but compliantly nodded his head. "I've worked for the FBI three years now," Gallo continued. "In that time, all I ever cared about was catching socialists and communists and bringing them to justice in the interest of protecting and defending this great nation of ours. But as of now, all I care about is catching this killer before he does any more harm. If you can help me catch communists or this killer, Sheriff, then you are an ally of mine, regardless of whether you are on the take in regard to the corruption this city has become synonymous with. Do we understand each other, Sheriff?"

Beauregard nodded once more and exhaled slightly, somewhat relieved. "Yeah, well," Beauregard grunted, "I'm not sure if the killer is still in town. But we sure as hell got us a commie on the loose."

"Oh," the sleepiness exhibited by Gallo transformed into keen alarm, "who is the communist?"

"Some kike that came to town a coiuple days ago," Beauregard sneered. "She sure is puttin' a bug up some folks' asses by askin' lots of questions she ought not be askin'. She's from up near your neck of the woods."

"Oh?" Gallo asked determinedly and with great interest, "what's this Red's name?"

"Abrahams, Orit," Beauregard said as if he had tasted something sour. "She's some kind of writer for some pinko rag in Manhattan."

"Ah, yes, I've had the great misfortune of meeting her on several occasions," Gallo huffed. "It seems like any time the Bureau raids a tenement, that lousy bitch shows up asking questions that do not concern her. It'd be a dream come true if she were to get lost down here and never find her way back to the city, if you catch my drift, Sheriff." Both men smirked slightly while sharing a side-eyed glance.

"I reckon that could be arranged," Beauregard said, "if push comes to shove, that is."

"That falls under the heading of local law enforcement agency business, Sheriff," Gallo said cordially, "which I am determined to steer clear of, unless it directly relates to catching this killer. The sooner we catch this killer, the sooner I can go back to catching commies. The communists are far more pernicious than some lunatic on a kill spree." Beauregard glanced surreptitiously over at Gallo, wondering if the Special Agent had just sanctioned the dispatching of the prying journalist who had come to investigate corruption. "I understand a syringe was found at the scene of the crime?" Gallo continued.

"That's right," Beauregard conceded. "The coroner ruled that Mrs. Fisher died from acute toxicity."

"Hang on" Gallo said while retrieving a pad with notes already scrawled on it from the breast pocket of his blazer. "Let me see if I have my facts straight," he said as his eyes scanned his notes. "Please do correct me, Sheriff, if I have any of the details wrong. I was not, you see, able to get much rest on the train, so my brain is running on cinders a bit at this point. Now, the coroner's report states that the victim here was poisoned, and then strangled after she was already dead; and then sexually assaulted by citrus, but not actually raped?"

"That's right," Beauregard said, somewhat perplexed while slightly nodding his head and shrugging his massive shoulders.

"That does not make any logical sense at all," Gallo sighed, "does it, Sheriff? The murder in Brunswick and here both involve fruit and poison and are too similar to be mere coincidence, but the girl in Georgia had been brutally raped while being strangled to death. Her rape and murder coincided. But the murder down here is at once very similar but oddly different too. I can't quite make sense of it." He slightly rubbed his right temple due to a slight headache caused by sleeplessness, acute frustration, and the stench of coal soot in his clothes as a result of the train ride to Miami from New York. "Is there anything at all you can you tell me about the syringe found at the scene of the crime here?"

"There's still some kind of contents inside the syringe, but I'm sorry to say that we do not have the technology here to figure out what exactly is inside of it, or even if what's in the syringe was what killed Mirabel," Beauregard said.

"I need that syringe as soon as possible," Beauregard demanded. "I'll send it to the FBI lab in Atlanta for analysis."

Beauregard then hung a sharp left and entered the glorious lawn, gardens, and driveway leading up to the front entrance of the Royal Palm Hotel, which was packed with cars and pedestrians eagerly making their way towards the parade route on Flagler Avenue. "What's going on here?" Gallo's curiosity was piqued.

"The Orange Blossom Festival is happening today," Beauregard smiled brightly. "It's one of the biggest days in the year in Miami. People come from all over the place to enjoy the festivities. It's all hands-on deck for us local lawmen. We could sure use us another set of hands, eyes and ears, if you're so inclined."

"I'm afraid I'm going to do my best to get a few hours of rest," Gallo said while fetching his suitcase from the backseat of the patrol car idling under the awning outside of the lobby. "I'd like to hit the ground running in the morning full bore," he added as a young bellhop fetched the suitcase from his hand. "Please prepare the syringe so that I can submit it to the lab."

"Of course," Beauregard said while smiling politely. "I'll have it packaged and ready to send by morning."

"Thank you kindly, Sheriff," Gallo grinned cordially, "your assistance and hospitality in this matter is greatly appreciated." He then shut the car door and made his way towards the lobby entrance with the eager bellhop in tow. Al Capone and Scarlet were stoned as they strolled out of the hotel, just as Gallo entered. Gallo was gobstruck to find one of the world's most notorious gangsters staying at the same hotel. Capone's eyes locked on Gallo's for a brief instant. Gallo watched rather awed a moment as Capone and his date strolled languidly towards the carpark. "Holy hell," the Special Agent muttered under his breath, "what in God's name is this place?"

"Miami," the bellhop chortled, "ain't no place in the world like it, sir."

It seemed that everyone in the city with the exception of Gallo had jammed along Flagler Avenue in order to enjoy the parade, face painting, and sundry other festivities taking place the first Saturday in November. The festival, which was begun by Mr. Sewell himself a decade earlier as a means to attract tourists to Miami, was comprised of a grand parade that begun on the mainland and ended on Miami Beach, near the Flamingo Hotel. The homecoming King and Queen at Miami Senior High were also traditionally crowned after the football game between the local rival high schools and just prior to the pageant. The Miss Orange Blossom contest was ceremoniously held at twilight and drew the biggest crowds of the day.

The 1919 Orange Blossom Festival was, however, somewhat unique; not only because of the tension in the city due to the brutal murder of the reigning queen, Mirabel, Mr. Fisher's fiancé, but because of the bitterly contested election scheduled for Tuesday. As such, a debate between Sewell and Ingram in the bandshell was scheduled between the parade and beauty pageant. The same judges that decided the winner of best parade float likewise judged the beauty pageant.

As was expected and, considering they had won the contest four years running, the John B. Gordan chapter of the Ku Klux Klan won best float at the conclusion of the parade. Their papier-mâché depiction of a fire-breathing dragon protecting little white children from integrationist black children as the white kids entered a red schoolhouse had swept parade honors every year since D.W. Griffith's *Birth of a Nation* premiered in 1915. Many white children in attendance at the parade were thrilled to have their picture taken on the float with the Grand Wizard, who, what with his shiny red suit, cherubic cheeks, and white hair, actually looked somewhat like Santa Claus.

The jovial energy and pageantry of the parade endured only so long as the bitter debate between Sewell and Ingram ensued. The acrimony unleashed during the mostly contentious debate was received with great regret by many of their former colleagues and mutual friends, especially those who had known the two men decades earlier, before their friendship had turned into a bitter rivalry. But those who did not personally know the candidates were enthralled by the palpable and crackling tension that existed during the debate.

Sewell had become incredibly rich in Miami. It was his fiefdom and he came to see himself as a kind of aristocratic figure, a baron of South Florida. Ingram saw himself along similar lines, especially now that Flagler had passed away. Ingram had, in his mind, inherited the mantle of "Father of Miami" and was thus entitled to the mayorship now that Mr. Merrick was finally retiring.

The stickiest wicket that existed between the two candidates was somewhat complex and complicated and extended beyond the fact that the two men were in a heated contest for the supposed soul of the city. Sewell was a southern segregationist who feared that a man who had only exhibited ambivalence towards white supremacy and who had recently styled himself as a reformer could potentially destroy everything he had spent the previous generation concocting from whole cloth with glitzy advertisements that portrayed Miami as a white man's utopia and escape from the filth, grime, crime, and social degradation commonly associated with northern cities in the early decades of the twentieth century.

Ingram, who did not actually advocate anything but free market capitalism, was by no means a leftist, or even liberal for that matter. But his vision for Miami's future was askew from Sewell's vision in some very important ways. For one, Sewell was a southern populist who envisioned South Florida as a white Yeoman's paradise and Miami as a metropole with exceedingly high real estate values. He shrewdly knew that the recent invention of the home air conditioning system was a miracle of modern technology that had the potential to completely revolutionize South Florida, which he envisioned would soon become a megapolis on par with New York, Chicago, London and Paris. He, like his rival, wanted Miami to be a winter retreat for the world's wealthiest and whitest families. But he also, contrary to Ingram, dreamed of making the southern end of the peninsula into the world's richest agricultural market. He thus imagined that South Florida would be America's breadbasket and that Miami would be the country's pleasure palace peopled by an urban aristocracy that would hold the lion's share of the state's political power. He also, unlike his adversary, openly advocated the complete removal of all black people from the state which, he believed was the most expedient way to truly address the endemic racism and lynch terror, which he fretfully believed would dissuade many leisure seekers and investors from the region. Sewell, in short, feared that black inhabitants would diminish property values all across the region and openly advocated their forced return to Africa.

Ingram, whose racial views were ambivalent at worst and benign at best, did not care if Martians bought his parcels of land. He had spent the previous decade quietly buying up parcels of land, grading them, and designing neighborhoods. He, like Sewell, knew that once the air conditioner was commercially available, that the value of the land he had invested in was sure to spike drastically. Miami, he had convinced himself, was a far better place to live than anywhere north of the Mason-Dixon Line. But he wanted the region to be more on par with Newport, Rhode Island, the elite resort city that Flagler had built long before Miami was incorporated. He also did not believe that it was ever going to be possible to ship all of Florida's black inhabitants back to Africa. Class, in short, mattered far more to Ingram than race. He also did not believe that the swamps surrounding the city could or would ever be drained and thus resented Sewell and the Mizner brothers for selling land to working class Yeoman who had been hoodwinked by ads that promised that once the swamps were drained the land would be black gold for anyone enterprising enough to grab the opportunity to buy it. The more Yeoman that had been hoodwinked by empty assurances that could never be kept was yet, in Ingram's mind, one more threat to the value of the actually inhabitable land he had so dutifully graded and cleared in previous years. Sewell, in short, was helping to create a real estate bubble that could ultimately destroy the actual value of the land Ingram owned.

Sewell used the debate after the parade and before the pageant to inflame the heightened sense of vitriolic racism that had spiked since the premier of *The Birth of a Nation* four years earlier, and even more so after the war ended and fierce competition for jobs triggered race riots all across the nation, including Miami, where numerous black men had taken jobs so many of the working white men had been forced to abandon when they were drafted.

"No one here, I'm certain, questions Mr. Ingram's business acumen," Mr. Sewell declared in front of a packed amphitheater overlooking Biscayne Bay at twilight. "What makes this man unfit to be mayor of this grand city of ours," Sewell said while wagging an accusatory finger at Mr. Ingram, who waited rather impatiently to speak behind his podium, "is that he does not discern between who has the proper qualities to be a Miamian and who does not. Why, Mr. Ingram," Sewell added, "hires Injuns, immigrants and Negroes alike. Every colored he hires is one less job available for a white Miamian. Now, anyone who knows me knows I got nothin' against any colored man or woman just because he or she is colored. There is a place for the coloreds – the reservation for the red man and Africa for the black man. But Miami is a white man's town and always will be, so help me God!" The all-white crowd crammed into the amphitheater cheered wildly a while before he finally calmed them. "If this man is elected," Sewell continued while wagging his finger at Ingram, "Miami won't be a white man's town much longer. Y'all mark my words. We'll be just another city of mongrels and miscegenation like New York or Chicago. Why," Mr. Sewell's eyes grew wide with terrible fright, "this man here is not even 100% American. He was born in a land that my forefathers waged a glorious revolution against, a revolution that gave birth to America." Many people in the crowd booed and hissed the idea of a Welshman being mayor of Miami, an American city. A few chanted "USA! USA! USA!" Sewell, however, calmed the crowd down by showing them the palms of his hands and preening a bit. The pause provided the moderator, a retired librarian in his early nineties, to give Mr. Ingram a chance at rebuttal.

"I never have shied away from my heritage," Ingram said forcefully. "I, like every other American excluding the natives, am an immigrant, and proud of it, dagnammit. Immigrants built this great nation into the glorious empire it is today. I am also not shy at all at the fact that I have been known to hire the best men available, regardless of race, class or creed. Why? Because that is what capitalism dictates!" He banged his fist into the podium. "Racial segregation has been proven to have merit in terms of quelling vigilante violence and to dictate the price real estate, but the bottom line is this: Jim Crow is ultimately bad for business and its ignominious end is but an inevitable matter of fact."

Mr. Sewell adamantly interjected. "Racial segregation is the very foundation of our tourism and real estate market. Now," he addressed the audience, "anyone who tries to convince you otherwise is either a cotton-pickin' fool or hopes to make a fool of you. If Mr. Ingram is elected mayor of Miami, why, it'd be but a matter of time before Biscayne Bay and the beaches were overrun with factories, Negroes, and immigrants of every stripe. The Miami we call home would soon cease to be the city we know and love if Mr. Ingram is elected mayor."

"Mr. Sewell is," Ingram raised his voiced over Sewell's, "a fear monger. What is even more unfortunate is that he stands firmly on the wrong side of history and means to sell you all a bill of goods in the process. Perhaps he might like to make Miami into a great plantation reminiscent of his grand pappy's before General Sherman and the Bluecoats came to Georgia. But I, for one, refuse to look back and commit the sin of forgetting history. Miami is on the move into a more glorious future and can never turn back; that is, unless you elect this charlatan. A vote for Ingram is a vote for the glorious future of this magnificent city. If you, brethren, are on the right side of history you shall vote Ingram for mayor this Tuesday!"

Many in the crowd in the cramped amphitheater cheered, including some white women in the audience. But they were barred from voting anyway, so Ingram drew little solace from their support. Straw polls conducted soon after the contentious debate indicated that Sewell had emerged from the contest on more solid footing than his opponent. Some who were polled cited the recent murder at the Royal Palm and Ingram's ambiguity towards race as providing many of them particular pause and also stoked more questions than answers about the seemingly less conservative of the two candidates. The fact that neither African Americans nor women could vote also seemed a great disadvantage to Ingram's chances of winning the election. But as Mr. Ingram knew as well as Mr. Sewell, in spite of their theatrics during the debate, that in Dade County the voters would not ultimately decide the outcome of the election; the vote counters would.

The timing of the crowning of the homecoming king and queen was not planned out well, especially considering the heavy stench of acrimony that lingered in the amphitheater air long after the cantankerous debate between Sewell and Ingram had mercifully concluded. Emory, who was on the steep and savage backside of a heroin high, found that he was getting weepily nostalgic and emotional during the crowning of the king and queen, as the proud parents and blandishing daughters and sons on stage seemed so gloriously innocent and happy to be alive.

Emory's memory drifted back to his own senior year of high school four years earlier. He fondly reminisced about scoring the game winning touchdown under resplendent sunshine as Quinn and the rest of the spirit squad squealed and cheered him on. His memory then flashed to Quinn and he being crowned homecoming king and queen; then flashed to a bonfire on the beach attended by drunkenly rowdy teens. Quinn led Emory by the hand as they strolled along the shoreline, which reflected thousands of multi-hued lights off the black and glassy surface of the ocean. "I love you," she confessed to him for the first time. "I'll always love you." He seconded the emotion and gave her a passionate kiss. Many of the revelers in attendance at the bonfire hooted, hollered, and cheered them on, which terribly embarrassed Emory.

A sudden cheering inside the raucous amphitheater brought Emory's mind back to present. He gazed sullenly down at his lifeless limbs atop his wheelchair. His weary and heavy eyes sparkled slightly as Quinn, who was wearing a midnight-blue flapper dress and a flower crown made of daisies braided into her stark blond locks, suddenly appear from the dark shadows of stage-right to place a glittering and golden crown made of cheap plastic on the blushing homecoming queen's head as the teenager's father gave his daughter a gentle kiss on her cheek.

Emory found himself suddenly nauseated by nostalgia and thus shoved his way towards the back exit of the amphitheater, which was no easy task considering the horde crammed between the stage, he, and the exits. It was obvious that many in the crowd were put out by having to rearrange their vantage point of the proceedings in order to move out of the way of a man in a wheelchair slowly navigating his way through the crowd just as the festivities were heating up.

It took nearly ten minutes for Emory to push his way out of the amphitheater. The sun was by then was setting to the point where only a sliver of it could be seen peaking above the horizon; a brilliant cascade of pastels streamed gloriously across the twilight sky over his head. Emory, however, did not notice the bucolic splendor of the bay that seemed to warmly envelope him.

He lit a cigarette and reminisced about the awkwardness of the night prior to him joining the AEF, which was the first time he had first tried to consummate his love with Quinn. He, however, did not last six seconds inside her before climaxing.

She was very sweet and, due to the pain of losing her virginity, somewhat relieved it had ended so abruptly, though she was quietly terrified she might get pregnant. Emory had always been so popular, poised, empowered and in control ever since they had started going steady at the start of their sophomore year. He was always so solid, especially times when she was at her most stressed out. Her sudden sexual power over him, however, gave her a new sense of herself and the dynamic between the two young adults, which made her love him at a level she had not been able to previously imagine. She adored being able to comfort him and aid him in enduring his emasculated embarrassment. He, however, felt as though he were in need of proving his masculinity to himself.

A thunderous applause from inside the amphitheater brought Emory suddenly back to present. He maneuvered his chair around so that the bay was directly behind him in an effort to shield the cigarette wedged between his lips from the wind. His heart ached deeply the moment he spotted Quinn and her fiancé hand-in-hand as they made their way towards the beau's car parked in the cement lot next to the amphitheater. Quinn did not notice Emory, which was just as well, because he stared at her like she was perhaps the last hope of oasis in an endless desert of self-despair.

"Emory?" Garnet hollered as he exited the amphitheater. Quinn looked over quickly to see Emory staring at her. Her sudden glance forced his awkward gaze away and towards the sound of Garnet's voice, which had carried across the lawn outside the amphitheater. "You want to stay for the crowing of the Miss Orange Blossom Pageant, or head back to the hotel?"

"Take me the fuck home." Emory's voice dripped morosely. "I've had about all the godforsaken pageantry I can stand."

Quinn politely smiled and waved. Emory pretended he did not notice. But Quinn, who felt a sudden sting of rejection, knew better.

The sun had sunk beyond the horizon, which soaked the amphitheater in glowing lavender twilight. Mr. Sewell had a stiff Mint Julep while the homecoming kids were being crowned in preparation for his final speaking event of the day, which was the Miss Orange Blossom Pageant, which he had shrewdly founded a decade prior because he knew the spectacle was sure to win free publicity for him simultaneous to helping to associate Miami with beautiful women, which would, he rightly predicted, attract free spending bachelors from all across the nation's backwaters.

The bitter election battle with his former friend and business partner, Mr. Ingram, was wearing Sewell thin in ways only his mistress – a twenty-year-old black girl from Bimini who worked as a maid at the Royal Palm and who was a month pregnant with his only child – knew the full extent of. As stress inducing as the election was, Sewell was even more consumed with grief over whether to tell his wife of twenty-five years that he had sired a child with another woman, a black woman, no less. He deeply loved his wife, but she was barren. He also knew his wife would surely resent and perhaps never forgive his betrayal and thus requite it with a divorce he feared would cost him half his fortune. But Sewell had the spirit of a riverboat gambler and thus dared to dream that his wife might be willing to raise the child as her own. He, however, wore thinner emotionally and mentally each day leading up to the election, which was exacerbated terribly by the anxiety associated with whether to tell his wife of his unborn child. Many nights he woke covered in sweat with a corrosive pain deep in his belly. Many mornings he wanted to simply quit. But his pride would not permit him set the election loose. Truth be told, he did not even believe half the bullshit he professed during the campaign. He was, however, shrewd enough to understand that race was at the core of both local and national politics and aimed to be the baron of South Florida by any means necessary, even if it meant a few African Americans were lynched in the process. Losing his election bid would also, he was certain, be disastrous to his larger goal of running for state senator in 1922. He had already secured the backing of a northern Democrat named James Cox, a newspaper baron from Ohio who was heavily invested in a number of undisclosed land schemes in Boca Raton and Fort Lauderdale that Sewell and the Mizner's had concocted. Cox's and the Democratic Nationals Committee's support for Sewell in the 1922 election cycle could thus prove to be crucial to putting the ad man over the top with voters all across the peninsula, most of whom resented the Republican Party for waging the Civil War. But Sewell's official backing from Cox and the DNC was incumbent on him not losing his election bid as mayor of Miami.

As disheveled and ulcerous as Sewell was backstage while slurping back his Mint Julep, he appeared cool, calm, confident, and powerful under the bright lights of center stage. He not so coyly reminded the packed amphitheater, less than half of whom could actually vote, that the stakes of Tuesday's election were "for the very soul of the city." He then welcomed Williams Jennings Bryan to the stage and then quickly vacated it and made his way straight for another Julep. The charm and poise he had displayed on stage evaporated the second he stepped into the dark and shadowy wing of stage left.

The energy in the amphitheater was buzzing by the time Jennings Bryan took the microphone from Sewell's clammy and trembling hands. People traveled from as far as Branson, Missouri, to watch the annual Miss Orange Blossom Pageant. Despite the ignominious end to last years' pageant winner, winning the contest had often, it seemed to some, led to bigger and better things for the mostly forgotten women crowned in previous years. Two years earlier, for example, the winner married Charles B. Forbes, a wealthy playboy who regularly wintered in Miami. They were, however, divorced less than six weeks later. She ended up waitressing at a crab shack in Vero Beach. Rumor has it that tips were good – during the winter season anyway – especially if the customer happened to recognize her as the former Miss Orange Blossom. She had also earned a free trip to Paris, where Mr. Forbes took her on their honeymoon, which was grand while it lasted. But she missed it all the days of her life and never returned, which she regretted each day until the fateful night she slit her wrists with a straight razor in a warm tub soon after she had been sexually assaulted by a customer she had waited on many times before.

Miss Orange Blossom 1915 actually made it all the way to Hollywood and even played a member of a harem in a talkie set in Calcutta. Her part, however, ended up being a lost bit of celluloid left on the cutting-room floor and swept up and dumped into a trash bin by a janitor. But her name was still added to the credits at the conclusion of the film, which was never actually shown in the state of Florida, which prohibited any of her family and friends from ever seeing it.

Back in those days the Miss Orange Blossom Pageant was the most exciting spectacle Miami had going for it, except for perhaps having your picture taken with the little Miccosukee kids decked out in their faux native dress as they were posed with live man-eating alligators. A tourist who had returned home to whatever part of the country he had visited from could then showoff these incredible photos of the spectacle to his or her amazed yokel friends in Branson, or wherever, on some long and steamy summer night in the Ozarks, which might inspire even more yokels to venture to Miami during the winter.

The crowd was buzzing in anticipation of the pageant. Jennings Bryan, the great orator, could whip the most pious crowd into a fevered frenzy, be it during his sunrise sermons Sunday mornings on the back lawn of the Royal Palm, which were rather odd events in which he would pitch the attendees on the glory of Jesus's salvation and then conflate "God's love" with the weather and real estate market in the region. "Miami has what man must have," he often reminded revelers, "God's sunshine!" He was also, like most everyone of his social class in South Florida, invested in numerous land schemes and owned parcels of property he was desperate to sell to unsuspecting yokels. He provided the same boisterous bombast while emceeing the pageant as he did during his sermons/sales pitches, which whipped the crowd into a mob.

Orit, who stood at the furthest recesses of the amphitheater from the stage, watched the pageant with equal parts curiosity, dismay and disgust. She could not quite understand why such otherwise lovely and talented young women would debase themselves by engaging in such a disheartening and undignified spectacle in which they openly put themselves on a kind of auction block to be judged upon by a panel of ugly and old but very rich white men. "Must be for the money," which was a grand prize of $100, she mumbled during the opening song and dance routine.

The hokey song was an ode to what a sensual city of splendor and social mobility Miami was meant to be for visitors. "In Hawaii," the contestants squealed and squawked not-quite in unison as they flailed their arms and legs about, "the girls wicky-wacky woo, but on the beaches of Miami, that is not half of what they do. I'd rather be in Miami." Orit, who was offended by the internalized misogyny being exhibited by the gussied-up contestants, smiled and laughed slightly as if she were trying to insulate her psyche from the underlying symbolic violence being celebrated by the audience.

The contest finally concluded with a local girl, the youngest granddaughter of a prominent land developer, judge, and retiring mayor of Miami, George Merrick, being crowded the winner. She barely edged out Scarlet on total points. Although Scarlet actually won the talent portion of the contest due to her jovial rendition of, "Away in Dixie," which the crowd, excluding Orit, merrily clapped and sang along to, Merrick's granddaughter had edged the preacher's daughter out in the question-answer and also the swimsuit portions of the contest. Scarlet, who wore a bright orange swimsuit that seemed three sizes too small for her, had actually won the swimsuit contest after the first tabulation of votes. The pageant was, however, rigged by Mr. Merrick, who promised each judge in the contest a prime parcel of prime land on Star Island, his newest and boldest venture yet on Miami Beach, if they were to fudge their votes so that his girl would, when all was said and done, be crowned. Only one of the five judges had any qualms at all about screwing Scarlet out of the victory, but he was not nearly daft enough to forfeit land so that some girl could win $100 and a gaudy crown made of tin and plastic. Besides, he would have been outvoted anyway. Merrick's granddaughter thus emerged the unanimous winner of the 1919 Miss Orange Blossom Pageant.

Scarlet, still wearing her bright orange swimsuit, knew she had done her very best, which she believed was more than adequate to win the contest, and was thus gutted that she had been cheated out of what she believed was rightfully hers. Tears streaked down her cheeks as her long and slender legs ran as fast as possible in high heels from the stage as Jennings Bryan placed the tin crown atop Miss Merrick's wavy red locks. Capone then shoved his way from the middle of the crowd and pushed against the stage to the front. He threatened the judges with castration if he ever saw them again, and told them they were, "a bunch of lousy sons of motherless whores," which seemed to baffle as much as frighten the panel of rapidly ageing white men. He then climbed up onto the stage and chased after Scarlet. She had by then kicked off her heals and was barefoot, which permitted her to run full speed from the dark and shadowy wings backstage out into the glowing lavender of twilight, which was fast becoming a dark and foreboding sky pregnant with menacing storm clouds pushing ashore from the Atlantic.

  The night of the pageant, Mr. Sewell threw his annual post-Miss Orange Blossom Pageant Party at Mr. Fisher's Flamingo Hotel on Miami Beach, which, due to the association with the death of his fiancé, was an especially odd and insensitive choice of venue. Sewell was a tad fretful of being associated with a man who was under suspicion for murder so close to the election and thus nearly balked on throwing his annual post-pageant soiree at the Flamingo; he even briefly considered hosting it at his own mansion and gardens at Vizcaya, which he had recently bought from the late James Deering's daughter, who had inherited a most magnificent piece property from her father, who had died the year prior. But there were simply too many moving parts related to a gathering of this magnitude to move the venue to his mansion last minute. Sewell had also made the arrangements long before the 1918 winner of the pageant had been slain and was not willing to squander the thousands of dollars that he had already spent provisioning the party. He also very much doubted that he would get his deposit back from Mr. Fisher, especially considering that the latter's cash might be tied up in his legal defense if he were to be charged with murder. Besides, there was perhaps no better place in the region sans the Royal Palm to throw such an elaborate and well-attended party. Numerous visitors to the grounds had previously remarked that its beachfront views, palatial gardens, and sprawling orange grove wedged against the Intercoastal Waterway, "must be what heaven is like." Sewell thus reluctantly decided to keep the original arrangement in place and to host the party at the Flamingo and hope all this nasty business related to the murder of Mr. Fisher's fiancé would be yesterday's news by Tuesday's election.

Sewell, perhaps naively, feared that the murder of Mr. Fisher's fiancé and the fact that there seemed to be a killer on the loose would diminish the merriment of the festivities. But that proved to not be the case, not in Miami. If anything, the specter of death and danger piqued the excitement of the city's revelers that fateful first weekend in November of 1919, which was especially expressed in a greater sense of the "eat, drink, and be merry, for tomorrow we die," ethos and consumerist mentality that has made Miami into the consumerist spectacle it was designed to be by Mr. Flagler and Mr. Sewell.

The revelers at the party dumped drinks into their mouths at the bar and shimmied, swayed, and sashayed away on the dance floor as if the world might end at any moment. Every attendee at the party, except Scarlet, seemed to be living their best life. Capone, who was at first sympathetic to Scarlet's anguish, had by the time the party was in full swing, grown impatient with her sulking and had ventured off to the other side of the ballroom to chase tail with Babe Ruth.

Even Azure, who had convinced Orit to attend the party as her companion, had kicked off her shoes and seemed as though she was having a great time. Orit especially, who had never been to a jazz club or danced like the flappers she had seen in pictures, let loose completely, as if she had been seduced by the city's rhythms and had experienced some kind of cathartic exorcism on the dance floor with Azure, who towered over her. A glowing grin washed across Orit's face and she was soaked in perspiration that made her feel more spiritually clean than ever before.

It was dawn by the time the party at the Flamingo began to wind down. The sense of joy and merriment that existed inside the ballroom was quickly diminished outside of the hotel, where several police officers and Special Agent Gallo were seen racing towards the sprawling orange grove on the riverside of the hotel. Curiosity compelled Orit to follow after the frantic lawmen. "Please come home with me," Azure pleaded as she tried to grab Orit by the hand. But Orit wriggled free and instinctively chased after the lawmen. "I've got to find out what's happening," she said apologetically to Azure while sliding off her shoes and leaving them in the dewy grass behind. Azure sighed, disappointed while watching Orit disappear into the gardens. Azure then made her way towards a cab idling under the awning of the hotel.

Orit's chase of the lawmen led her through a massive labyrinth of vegetation and exotic wildlife, including a gaggle of brightly colored peacocks and pink flamingos. The sun was edging up above the horizon by the time the lawmen made it to the deepest recesses of the orange grove, which opened to a long wooden dock that extended one hundred yards out above the Intercoastal Waterway. The shade of the hut at the end of the dock made for a popular spot to fish for guests staying at the hotel. It was, however, a fisherman in a dilapidated dinghy in the middle of the river who lived on the other side of the causeway who had first discovered the body.

The reigning Miss Orange Blossom, Mr. Merrick's granddaughter, was sprawled naked and face down atop the dock. Her lifeless hand dangled slightly in the water. Her dress was nowhere to be found. Flies and mosquitoes buzzed around her unkempt vagina like a plague of locust. Orit was stunned and disgusted by the site and stench of the corpse, which made her want to vomit. Her knees buckled and her legs plopped atop the dewy grass. Her eyes stared hard at the fast bluing and bloated body as if it might somehow possess some mysterious and mystical clue to the meaning of life and death. Gallo, having suddenly noticed Orit observing the proceedings, demanded that Beauregard and some of his men escort her from the grounds and then cordon off the grove into a sealed crime scene so that nobody else could contaminate it. Orit, however, citing the First Amendment to the United States Constitution, refused to be moved.

"Why won't anyone murder that bitch?" Gallo thought as Beauregard sulked back to the dock full of frustration at Orit's obdurate refusal to allow her rights to be violated.

CHAPTER SIXTEEN

Sunday, November 2, 1919

Mr. Sewell was furious and disheveled upon entering the lobby of the Royal Palm Hotel. He demanded that the concierge manning the front desk furnish an immediate audience with Mr. Ingram. The effete concierge's manicured and trembling hands frantically dialed the rotary phone as fast as he could, which was not very fast at all. He then spoke in short and garbled tones and phrases as Sewell slumped begrudgingly into one of the couches in the lobby and lit a cigar.

Garnet arrived in the lobby from off the elevator in less than two minutes. His cool and calm demeanor starkly contrasted with Sewell's hardly concealed ire. "I asked for the king," Sewell grunted while exhaling a plume of tobacco smoke as he noticed Garnet approaching him from across the lobby. "I have no goddamn interest at all in conversing with a jester."

"Mr. Ingram is," Garnet was unflappable, "indisposed at the moment. How might I be of assistance, Mr. Sewell?"

"You tell that him we need to have a talk and I ain't leavin' until I give him a hunk of my mind."

"I'm very sorry, Mr. Sewell," Garnet said politely while motioning towards the exit of the lobby, "but Mr. Ingram is not taking meetings with anyone not already listed in his calendar today. Now, if you'll please."

Sewell stood up quickly and put his nose less than three inches from Garnet's. Sewell's breath reeked of bourbon and Panamanian tobacco. But Garnet did not blink. "You listen here, you goddamned diabolical Injun," Sewell seethed while japing the tip of his index finger into Garnet's chest, "you're treading on quicksand, boy. You know how much dirt I got on you and the old man and his son? I could ruin the whole lot of you with one quick call to *The Herald*.."

"Mr. Sewell," Garnet grinned while glancing over at the unnerved concierge who was eavesdropping, "the stress of the election is clearly wearing you thin. Perhaps you should just concede and save yourself some semblance of sanity and respectability. Besides, your outlandish and idle threats just make you seem like a damned fool." He leaned in a bit closer towards Sewell and stared menacingly into his eyes and whispered, "you ain't gonna call *The Herald*."

"Oh no?" Sewell blubbered as though he were being dared, "and what in God's name is gonna stop me?" He chuckled. "You, little man?"

"We got all the goods we need on you, Mr. Sewell," Garnet smirked while whispering into his adversary's ear.

"Is that right?" Mr. Sewell sneered.

"You leave this lobby in the next ten seconds," Garnet's patience was wearing thin.

"Or what?" Sewell smirked haughtily, welcoming confrontation while jabbing the moist end of his cigar into Garnet's chest. "You gonna scalp me, boy? Is that it?"

"No," Garnet resisted the urge to laugh, "but the newspapers and then soon after that your poor wife will surely find out about that pregnant mistress you've been fucking since the girl was thirteen." Garnet gazed past Sewell as if a reckoning were approaching. "Why," he added, "just think of what news of you being kin with a Negro would do to your poll numbers this close to the election. Hell," Garnet laughed slightly, "I'm quite certain you could not recover from such a public relations fiasco."

"If goddamn girls keep showing up dead," Sewell's paranoia was peaking, "there ain't gonna be nothin' left for any of us anyhow. Now," he sneered while inching even closer to Garnet, "I got a good mind that the old man has something to do with all this."

"I assure you, Mr. Sewell," Garnet, who was growing weary of debating, said, "there is clearly a dark power that has descended over the land. It has been here ever since the railroad came. But I assure you, the tragedies that have occurred this week don't have a goddamn thing to do with anyone employed by this establishment." His dark and almond shaped eyes stared unwaveringly into Sewell's tense and sleep deprived peepers.

Sewell glared as deep into Garnet's soul as he could for a moment before finally growing satisfied that he was not being conned. "You tell the old man that we need to talk," he demanded, then made his way toward the lobby exit.

"I'll pass your message along," Garnet said, "but I wouldn't hold my breath for a meeting any time before the election if I was you."

"This nonsense has to stop," Sewell said while straightening out his pinstriped waistcoat and smoothing a stray strand of hair falling across his forehead. "This carnage and mayhem is bad for business, which is bad for the whole lot of us, the old man included. You tell him that." He then shoved open the doors leading from the lobby into the resplendent morning sun cascading across the lawn.

Up in Pahokee, Reverend Edmund Flowers had just concluded his Sunday sermon. He had spent nearly an hour railing against the evils of science and reason, citing the theory of evolution being taught in public schools as "evidence" that there was a grand conspiracy to, as he put it, "murder Jesus Christ," which was odd, considering he provided a ritual to congregants in which he and his followers ate the flesh and drank the blood of their messiah.

The once white t-shirt underneath his black suit was by the end of the sermon yellowed and drenched with his piquant sweat. Edmund sipped a chalice full of communion wine and dabbed the perspiration from his tensely lined forehead with his handkerchief while reviewing the notes he had scrawled into a notepad behind the podium in the pulpit as most of the parishioners filed out of the sanctuary and into the bright Sunday morning light outside the chapel. An elderly woman with the morning edition of *The Miami Herald* wedged between her arthritic hands did not seem to mind the acerbic and vinegary smell emanating from the preacher. She was too excited by the contents on the front-page of the paper to even notice her spiritual leader's stench. "Excuse me, Reverend," her high-toned and gravelly voice creaked.

"Yes, Mrs. Jefferson," Edmund smiled as sweetly as could be. "What did you think of the sermon this week?"

"It was certainly very spirited," she conceded.

"What can I say?" His huckster smile contorted instantly into a seemingly earnest scowl. "I just get so tired of these immoral eggheads with the audacity to declare that God is dead."

"Well," Mrs. Jefferson was nervous and impatient, "nobody can't never say you ain't doin' the Lord's work, that's for sure. Say, where's Mrs. Flowers this mornin'?"

"Oh," he forced a toothless and awkward smile to conceal his discomfort over the fact that his wife had stayed home because her face was bruised and battered. "Scarlet," he lied, "seems to have caught a case of that flu bug that's been going around lately. We thought it best that she stayed home to mend so as to not miss anymore sermons. Her momma is lookin' after her this mornin'. I expect they will be in attendance next Sunday. I'm sure both would greatly appreciate your prayers."

"Of course," she said.

Edmund then suddenly noticed Mrs. Jefferson appeared to be distressed, so he came down from behind the pulpit to get a closer look at her. "Is there anything the matter?" he asked in earnest while placing his hand gently on her shoulder. "You look as though you've seen a ghost. Is Mr. Jefferson feelin' alright?"

"He's the same ornery old scoundrel he ever was," she sighed slightly.

"Then, whatever is the matter, Mrs. Jefferson?" he prodded. "You seem awfully upset."

"It's just that," she paused a moment while trying to find the right words to say, "I just don't know how to tell you."

"I reckon it's best to just tell me," his voice sunk an octave as he peered into her fearful squinting eyes. "What is it, Mrs. Jefferson? Please, you are safe here. I am your shepherd. You can tell me anything with complete confidence in my discretion."

She then sighed deeply while flipping over the newspaper to reveal the front-page. His fretful eyes frantically examined the headlines. His attention was first commandeered by the headline that alerted readers to the horrid fact that the newly crowned Miss Orange Blossom Queen had been heinously murdered. "By God," he looked up at Mrs. Jefferson with genuine lamentation in his eyes. "A serial killer is on the loose?"

"A girl was killed in Georgia, now two in Miami within the past week," Mrs. Jefferson seemed spooked.

"This is truly terrifying," Edmund said. "But how exactly can I help? Are you afraid? Do you need counseling of some kind? Would you like to pray with you?"

"No," she pleaded while jabbing her arthritic and wavy finger into a picture towards the bottom of the page, "look here."

His worried eyes soaked in the image. Miss Merrick was smiling gleefully as William Jennings Bryan placed a tin crown atop her wavy locks. "She's very lovely," Edmund forced compassion as a kind of special effect. "It is such an abomination when God's beauty is snuffed out in its prime. Her death is a terrible tragedy. I will pray for this dearly departed beauty's soul and her family as well with you, if you like." He held his hands out for her to clasp onto.

"No," Mrs. Jefferson's frustration was fast approaching anger, "look here," she said while jabbing her crooked index finger into the background of the picture; Scarlet was wearing a shiny sash that read, "Runner Up" on it. Her scowling face and tear-filled eyes glowered directly from the page at her father. He snatched the paper from Mrs. Jefferson's hands and held it inches from his face. She winced due to a terrible paper cut; the preacher did not notice. He was entranced by his daughter's glare.

"Well I'll be a monkey's uncle," he, who was beyond flabbergasted, muttered. His kneejerk reaction was embarrassment that he had been caught lying by saying that Scarlet was not in attendance at church that day due to illness. His second and most palpable and profound emotion was, however, excitement that he now had some idea of how to track down his wayward daughter.

Orit was steel eyed and focused on the dossier of research stuffed into a manila folder plopped atop her lap as she sat in the back of a cab chauffeured by a sixteen-year-old black dwarf who would not have been able to see over the steering wheel if not for the cigar tin he sat atop of. He'd also not have been able to drive if not for the wooden blocks affixed to the accelerator and decelerator pedals. Orit, who was engrossed in her research, did not seem to even notice the boy was disabled nor did she exhibit any kind of concern for her safety. She furiously jotted notes in her pad and circled key points and ideas in the documents, preparing herself for inevitable confrontation, which she fully expected at her destination – the headquarters of Addison Mizner Real Estate Corporation, LLC, which was a nondescript office out past the railroad tracks in Hialeah.

Orit took a deep and composing breath upon arrival. She then tipped the cabbie handsomely, paying him an extra ten dollars to keep the meter running and to wait for her. "If I'm not out in two hours," she kind of kidded, "send for help." He, who was happy to be paid for napping, gladly complied.

She composed herself once more with an even longer and deeper breath before charging towards Mizner's office. Orit peered into the window. There did not seem to be much action happening inside, which was to be expected so early on a Sunday morning, even during a wild speculative period such as the one that currently existed in Miami during her investigation. But she noticed what appeared to be a shadow pass in front of an open light in the back office and thus ventured in.

Her nervous hand reached for the door, then paused a moment. She took one more quick breath in the effort to steady her nerves, and then finally turned the handle, which she was glad twisted and jarred the door open. She stealthily eased inside and cautiously poked her head down a short, narrow, and dimly lit hallway. "Hello?" her determined voice filled the space. She sensed tense energy from the back office where light was emanating from. "Is anyone back there?" she asked rather nervously while creeping towards the source of light.

Addison Mizner, a fifty-two-year-old renowned society architect and the son a prominent lawyer and American diplomat, was sitting somewhat awkwardly at his desk. His personal assistant, a rather attractive man with a head full of sandy blond hair and a slight build who was no older than the tender age of twenty-two, was on his knees crouched down under Mizner's desk. Both Mizner and his lover were somewhat frightened by the unexpected intruder who had found her way into the sanctum. Mizner slid his now semi-erect penis from his assistant's mouth and quietly zipped up his fly and buttoned his black tuxedo trousers just as Orit poked her head into the office.

Both she and Mizner were somewhat unnerved and taken aback by the other's presence. Mizner plopped down in his finely crafted leather chair and scooted it closer to his desk, which pinned his assistant, who was wearing the black tuxedo he had worn to the soiree at the Flamingo Hotel the previous night, painfully underneath. He did his best not to make a sound or even to breathe, which was no easy feat. He winced agonizingly as the blood stopped circulating to his lower legs.

Orit did not at first notice the secretary, but did notice two half-empty glasses of whisky atop Mizner's desk next to a framed portrait of his wife and children.

"Mr. Mizner, I presume?" Though nervous, Orit's voice was suddenly steeped in a fearlessness she had mastered over the years.

"Who the hell are you?" Mizner demanded.

"My name is Orit Abrahams. I am an investigative reporter for *The New York Call*."

"You mean, *The New York Times*?" he wondered if he had misheard her.

"No," she said while resisting the urge to roll her eyes. "I've been assigned to investigate corruption in the real estate market here in South Florida and I wonder if you might be willing to chat on the record for a while."

"There's no corruption here," he said while smirking disingenuously. "You're wasting your time, young lady."

"Mr. Ingram over at the Royal Palm indicated that you might be a valuable source," she said while quite presumably sitting down in the chair across the desk from Mizner.

"Oh, he did, did he?" Mizner scowled. "This is really very gauche of you, young lady, coming in here on a Sunday like this. We're not even open for business just now. I've just come in to pick up some papers on my way to brunch at the Halcyon."

"Yes, well," she said, "I do appreciate you taking the time to talk with me then. The sooner I get to the bottom of things, the sooner I can get back to New York and we can all get on with our lives."

"It seems to me as though you've come to ruin lives," he chuckled while taking a quick sip of whisky. He then slid the top drawer of his desk open. Orit's chest tightened and her breath shortened as Mizner reached inside. She was somewhat relieved that he merely pulled a cigarette from a sleek silver case with his name engraved on it. He wedged the cigarette into his mouth, lit it, and exhaled deeply, making no effort to avoid directing his exhale across the desk from his newfound adversary.

"I've come to find out the truth," she said matter-of-factly, "nothing more or less."

"And what exactly is truth?" he chortled quite arrogantly.

"From what I can tell," she elaborated, "a lot of working men and women have come to Miami because they've been sold on the American Dream of owning a home. But from numerous reports I've read in newspaper clipping from all over the country, many of these working men and women lost their entire life savings on land three feet under swamp water."

"Even if it were true that some folks purchased parcels of land under water," Mizner conceded, "that land will surely be drained soon enough, mark my words, young lady. Even the governor, who is hardly the most astute man, has made draining the swamps part of his reelection platform. Once the Everglades are drained, the land will be some of the richest and most fertile soil in the world – black gold for those brave and bold working men and women of vision and courage smart enough to snatch it while they can. They won't be peasants after the state of Florida drains the swamp, I assure you. They'll have far more than the American Dream, too. They'll be rich beyond their wildest dreams."

"Real estate developers seem convinced of that, to be sure. But you see," Orit said determinedly while digging into her briefcase, "you speak of draining the swamp as if it is a simple inevitability. But draining the swamp does not actually make any sense at all."

"It makes perfect sense," a shit-eating grin formed across Mizner's disingenuous face. "The canals designed to drain the swamp and deposit that water into the Gulf of Mexico on the one side and the Atlantic Ocean on the other are already being built right as we speak, young lady. You can go out and inspect them for yourself if you are so inclined. But I suspect you are not at all inclined to go see glorious progress being made because you are too damned determined to find corruption that does not actually exist."

"From what I understand," she rejoined while plopping an official report published in a respected academic journal the previous month, "these drainage canals you seem so proud of are one of the biggest boondoggles in human history, and paid for by the taxpayers of this state no less."

"Maybe that is the problem," Mizner haughtily interjected while smiling condescendingly. "You are clearly not at all an expert on the matter." He reached down into the lower drawer of his desk. He noticed his assistant's face was contorted as though the young man was in terrible agony, which, considering the lack of blood flow to his legs scrunched under him, was an accurate portrayal of the physical pain he was enduring in an effort to remain unnoticed by this fiercely determined muckraker. Mizner reached further into the drawer and snatched a book-bound research study in a respected academic journal devoted to publishing cutting-edge scholarship related to ecological research and dropped it on the desk in front of Orit. "Have you by chance read Professor E.O. Wilson's study? You see, Dr. Wilson, who holds a PhD in biology, has determined that draining the Everglades is a simple feat that will make South Florida into the most fertile farmland in the world."

"You went to prep school with Mr. Wilson in New Hampshire and then were later fraternity brothers at Harvard, isn't that correct, Mr. Mizner?" Orit asked as if she already knew the answer but was eager to put the tycoon into a corner. Mizner was wise to stay mum. His scowl, however, spoke volumes. "Would you care to comment on this very obvious conflict of interest?" Orit glowered back.

"I fail to see your point," Mizner, who was fed up, grunted. "I do not see any real connection or relevance to Dr.

Wilson's keen expertise regarding such matters and whether we know each other."

"You see," Orit elaborated, "I can't help but wonder if Professor Wilson's very faulty, some might say fraudulent, analysis has been bought, either with actual money or by his loyalty to you, or perhaps some combination of the two."

"You're making some very wild and serious allegations now about two men with impeccable professional records," he fumed.

"Maybe so," Orit was unbowed. "But I know something rotten is happening here."

"Is that right?" he smiled arrogantly while exhaling a lungful of tobacco smoke towards her. "You really strike me as woefully incompetent and out of your depth."

"Funny," Orit smirked, "I was thinking the same thing about you. You're either completely clueless or completely corrupt. Either way, I'm going to get to the bottom of it."

"You seem very sure of yourself, little girl," Mizner smirked while exhaling a lungful of smoke.

"I guess you could say that," she said flatly. "That's because I know you are either completely incompetent or just a fucking liar who has no qualms about destroying people's lives so that you can get just a bit richer."

"Since you're so certain, how about you educate me?" he sneered.

She pushed the report he furnished aside and moved her document across the desk and closer to him. "I've read this report by Professor Cronon at the University of Chicago in which he directly refutes Dr. Wilson's erroneous findings. Cronon's study clearly elaborates that the swamps can never be drained. You see, Mr. Mizner, the water is constantly bubbling up to the surface from natural springs several meters under the earth's surface, which means even when you build those pointless drainage canals that the taxpayers of this sad state have been bilked out of via their property taxes, the land will always be under water. Always," she reiterated for effect. "That means the working men and women who wasted their lifesavings buying a dream sold to them by hucksters and robber barons like you will never recoup their investments. But as long as these folks keep being duped, you keep getting richer and richer. Now, Mr. Mizner, you are either criminally incompetent, or, worse yet, you are not all incompetent and you know full well the hard fact of the matter that those lands will never be drained and you simply don't care because caring does not jive with your economic interests. Either way, you are helping to craft the obscenest real estate bubble the world has ever seen. Whether you are incompetent or just plain greedy and evil is neither here nor there; I aim to make as many people aware of what an incredible boondoggle the city of Miami is."

Mizner scooped Cronon's veracious report from off the desk and dumped it into the waste-bin. "You have your version of the truth," he said smugly. "I have mine. You have your sad little no name rag a thousand miles away from here that nobody gives a good goddamn about. I have an ownership stake in six newspapers along the east coast of this state alone. I get free advertising, including news stories, in every newspaper I have a stake in all across this great nation. On top of that, I can afford to buy articles and other ad space in any newspaper I want on the planet. I can buy the entire front-page of *The New York Times*, if I want, little girl. So go right ahead and print whatever version of the truth you want. My version of the truth is always going to be bigger and better than your sad little version could ever be. I'm selling the American Dream. I'm selling people who detest their backbreaking and soul crushing jobs the very tangible promise of social mobility. Whose version of the truth do you think the American workingman is more apt to buy, the version they want to believe or the version they don't want to believe? And on the subject of truth, young lady, the fact of the matter is, you don't realize what you are up against. You are a road apple about to be steamrolled by a reality you can't even begin to comprehend. Now," he snarled, "I suggest you pack your little briefcase and go back to your godforsaken cesspool of city. The draining of the Everglades is inevitable, whether you choose to believe that version of the truth or not. But as of now, they are home to countless kike eating alligators, if you catch my drift."

"That sounds an awful lot like a threat, Mr. Mizner." Orit stood up from the desk and stared fearlessly down at her adversary.

"It is simply a fact that you'd be wise to be more aware of," he glared, "it's my version of the truth, as it were."

"Thank you for your time and candor," Orit said as she began to make her way into the dim and narrow hall leading towards the front of the office.

"One last thing," he added as she departed. "Nothing said here today was on the record. If my name is ever quoted in any story by you, so help me God, I will sue you and your pathetic little paper into oblivion."

"Go ahead and sue us," she defied. "We've got nothing to lose but our morality anyway."

The assistant under Mizner's desk slightly groaned due to the incredible aches and pangs in his legs, which had lost all flow of blood to them and tingled as though he were being stabbed at once by thousands of little needles. Orit glanced back fast at Mizner one last time and added, "Don't you even care at least a little bit about the lives you're ruining? I've read reports in many newspapers in which you profess your unabashed love for America, but you seem to have no qualms at all about ruining the lives of working Americans," she lamented.

"Haven't you ever heard of the theory of evolution?" he peered intensely while exhaling a billow of smoke. "It's a dog eat dog world. Every man for himself. Survival of the fittest."

Orit did not bother to respond. The assistant crouched under Mizner's desk finally crawled out from underneath and was equally agonized and soothed as the blood rushed back into his lower extremities. "Say, Addie," he timidly asked with a high and annoyingly squeaky voice as his big and doughy brown eyes glared up at his lover, "that piece of property you sold me for such a nice price last month, that's not underwater like the reporter said, is it?" he glared down at his assistant as if he aimed to punch him in the jaw.

Scarlet was tanning atop a blue towel by the palatial Royal Palm pool and grotto in the late-morning sun in a skimpy red polka-dot one-piece bathing suit bought for her by Al Capone at Sears during their shopping spree. Her tired eyes were shaded by dark sunglasses with plastic red frames. A solitary shadow befell only her. At first, she assumed it was a stray cloud impeding the sun's rays. But the shadow loomed. She squinted quizzically up at the shadowy figure that seemed to eclipse the sun, then gasped and sat up abruptly. She snatched the sunglasses from her face. Her fearful eyes widened.

"Fancy meetin' you here," her father said while glowering down at Scarlet. He then smacked her hard across her kisser with a rolled-up version of the morning edition of *The Herald,* which stung and stunned her. Only a few people scattered around the pool seemed to notice the assault. They, however, did not involve themselves in the incident.

A bit of crimson blood formed at the base of Scarlet's bottom lip. Angry and anguished tears welled in her frightened eyes. "Don't you dare make a scene," he seethed. "It'll only make things worse for ya. Where in God's name is my truck?"

She slightly shrugged her shoulders and shook her head, expecting another slap in the face no matter the answer she provided. "It broke down," her voice quivered, "I left it."

His wiry fingers wrapped suddenly around her wrist. He yanked her up out of the lounge chair and dragged her to her feet. "Let's get you home," he snarled, "your mother is out of her mind with worry."

Scarlet was terrified by the man forcefully leading her across the pool deck and into the lobby. The affable concierge working the reception desk finally asked, "Is everything alight?" She, however, did not respond as Edmund dragged his daughter from the elevator to the lobby doors overlooking the front lawn of the hotel. Scarlet glanced back at the concierge. Her frightened emerald eyes pleaded for help. But the concierge at the reception desk did not call for help as Edmund escorted Scarlet from the lobby and into the resplendent sunshine soaking the front lawn outside the hotel.

In the carpark, Capone and Babe Ruth were dressed in their golf skivvies and piling out of his electric blue roadster with golf bags slung over their shoulders. Both men were rather inebriated from the beer and cocaine they had imbibed while on the links. Capone, who was eager for a Sunday morning swim, was especially ebullient as he hurried across the lawn towards the hotel entrance. His smiling face, however, contorted to confusion the moment he noticed a man manhandling Scarlet.

"Hey," Capone, who was suddenly spiteful, hollered, "Scarlet! Where you headin' with this big palooka?"

"Mind your own business little man," Edmund demanded while shoving Scarlet into the backseat a cab idling in the carpark. Capone stopped dead in his tracks and dropped his golf bag. He then reached down into his golf bag and revealed a chrome Colt-45 revolver, which he aims at Edmund.

The cabbie in the front seat of the sedan cowered down and put his hands over his head. "Scarlet is my business, pallie," Capone snarled at Edmund, who notices the cowering cabbie and thus turned quizzically around to see Capone aiming the pistol at his head, which caused him to flinch and fall atop of Scarlet in the backseat of the car. Scarlet was both relieved and proud that Capone aimed to save her.

"Looks like you've got things covered here, Al," Babe Ruth slurred somewhat unnerved, "I'm going to catch some zs under the cabaña out by the grotto." Ruth then picked up Capone's golf bag from the lawn and pulled it over his other shoulder and lugged both towards the doors leading into the lobby. "I'll have the concierge take your bag up to your suite," he smiled timidly while hurrying away from the scene of the conflict.

"Get off of the girl," Capone demanded of Edmund, who slowly crept out of the backseat of the sedan and put his hands helplessly over his head hoping he might avoid being shot. "See that beautiful electric-blue Ford over yonder?" Capone motioned with the business end of the pistol at the supped-up roadster across the carpark. Edmund nervously nodded his head to admit that he could see the car in question. "Good," Capone smirked slightly, "walk over to it as cool, calm and collected as you can. Don't make any wacky moves or I'll shoot you dead right here and now. Capeesh?" Edmund was somewhat confused by the prepositional phrase that had tumbled so clumsily from the gangster's mouth.

"Capeesh means, 'you understand?'" Scarlet explained. Edmund then frantically nodded his head.

"Good," Capone added. "Come on Scarlet. Get you shoppin' bags. Let's all go for a little ride out to the country."

Capone then cautiously glanced over his shoulder at the terrified cabbie cowering behind the steering wheel. He then kept his pistol trained squarely on Edmund's back as the trio conspicuously tried to appear nonchalant while making their way fast across the lawn and carpark towards Capone's Ford.

The canvas top of Capone's convertible was already down. He ordered Scarlet to drive and her father to sit in the front-passenger seat. Capone, meanwhile, crawled into the backseat of the car, where he could keep a watchful eye on Edmund.

"Who the hell is this guy, Scarlet?" Capone demanded.

"He's my father," she was terribly embarrassed to concede.

"So this is the pervert preacher that likes to touch little girls, eh?" Capone grinned rather sinisterly. Edmund glanced side-eyed at his daughter, mortified that she had told this smarmy stranger about their deepest and darkest secret.

Scarlet was likewise ashamed and thus had some difficulty nodding her head in an effort to answer Capone's query. "What are you goin' to do to him, Al?" she asked Capone while glancing at him in the reflection of the rearview mirror.

"Nothin' at all," Capone said while grinning and placing his pistol atop his lap. "What are you goin' to do to him? That's the question."

Scarlet's frightened mind seemed to be quickly processing a number of ideas for revenge she might like to exact on the father who had tormented her since before she had reached puberty.

Nicholas, the managing editor of *The New York Call*, the newspaper where Orit was modestly employed, was somewhat inured to the commotion transpiring outside his office. His mind at the moment was far more focused on the ringing telephone in his office than on the band of marauders donning blue or gray suits tearing documents out of file cabinets and desks, kicking over furniture, and the sundry other activities the FBI was fast becoming infamous for in cities like New York during the Red Scare.

Nicholas cloistered himself in his office, locked the door, closed the blinds and picked up the phone. "Hello?" he hollered into the receiver in an effort to drown out the sound of ransacking transpiring outside his office.

"The Feds are back at again, eh?" Orit, who could hear the racket in the background, said frustrated from the phone booth in the bar next to the lobby at the Royal Palm Hotel.

"Afraid so," Nicholas huffed while slightly rolling his eyes.

"What are they after this time?" Orit wondered.

"Same as usual," Nicholas explained. "I don't think they actually plan to find any kind of evidence of illegal activity. I imagine they just aim to slow production again. They think if they can put us out of business for a few days, then they can put us under for good."

"But last time you said that the next raid really could put us under for good," Orit's voice was laced with an emotion beyond concern. "Should I even bother staying in this godforsaken city? Will I even have a paper to publish this piece in by the time I get back?"

"Don't you worry about this mess?" Nicholas said. He seemed defiant as he attempted to offer solace. "I'll figure something out. I'll take out a second mortgage on the apartment, if I have to. You're already down there. You might as well stay and see what you can dig up. If you were to crack something big, we might be able to sell enough copies to buy us another six months of operation."

"Well then, it might be wise to call Bank of America for that second mortgage now because I don't think I'm going to be able to get much of a story together. The code of silence amongst the corrupt is pervasive, as if they have all colluded."

"How do you mean?"

"It's as though there is some unwritten agreement that nobody, not even the working-class folks, will even acknowledge that there is a rotten stench."

"Surely somebody must want their story to be heard?" Nicholas hoped.

"Not this time, I'm afraid," she lamented. "Everyone is so invested in this game of hot potato that nobody wants to talk for fear of the bubble bursting."

"Hot potato?"

"That's what the real estate industry is here. One guy buys a plot of land, and then rolls it over to another man for a little more money. But then he figures out how worthless the land actually is. So he rolls it over again but tells the buyer he is sure to double his money in no time. The speculative bubble continues to expand and inflate until, all of a sudden, too many people figure out that the exorbitant real estate prices are just that – exorbitant – then the whole deck of cards comes tumbling down atop of the man holding the hot potato – the deed to the property that has just suddenly become worthless again."

"Why do people keep buying the potato?"

"Because every time they open *The Herald, Times, McClure's*, or *Saturday Evening Post*, they are assured by this add or that supposedly reputable 'news' story paid for by the Miami Chamber of Commerce, Everett Sewell, or Addison Mizner, that investing in Miami is a gilded path to social mobility sans the drudgery of hard work."

"Can't anyone see what the hoax for what it is?"

"Even if they could, they wouldn't want to believe it," Orit sighed. "Ever since the war ended, credit has been easy to get. The banks usually don't even bother to check a borrower's references or bona fides because the banks win either way. The deck is always stacked in their favor and stacked against the borrower. The banks can't possibly lose. The borrower either pays them back with interest, or doesn't and the bank takes the property and keeps rolling it over and over. Workingmen show up to Miami drunk on the idea of not being wage-slaves and of owning a little slice of paradise for a low down-payment and small interest loan and somehow getting rich by going into debt. On top of that, there are binders waiting like wolves at the train and bus stations to exploit these workers' fantasies, fears and desires. Before they know it, the workers are in so deep over their heads, they don't know which way is up or down. Most don't even have fare to make it back to wherever the hell they came in the first place by the time the binders are through with them."

"What about the murders down there?" Nicholas hollered into the receiver in an effort to drown out the sound of the marauding agents ransacking the place. "Any chance they are connected to the real estate corruption?"

"Maybe," Orit shrugged her shoulders a bit and squinted into the distance. "But it's hard to say. There are some people down here, most especially Mr. Ingram, who want to keep Miami a small seasonal resort town that caters mostly to the rich and famous, rather than a year-round urban-industrial center. It's conceivable that someone could have slaughtered these girls to make bad headlines for the city in an effort to dissuade people from coming."

"You don't sound like you buy it?" Nicholas said while plugging his finger into his other ear in an effort to hear Orit better.

"It's a bit overelaborate, don't you think?" she rhetorically asked. "I think the smart money bets on the killer being a psychopath, a Jack The Ripper kind of character."

A federal agent then smashed the door to Nicholas's office open with a battering ram. "I'd better let you get back to things then," Nicholas's voice cracked and quivered as the agent separated him from the phone. Another agent manhandled him and led him from the office.

Orit nervously asked, "Hello, Nicholas? Are you there?" her muffled voice could be heard at the other end of the line. A federal agent hung up the receiver while the other forcefully escorted the fearful editor down a long and dimly lit hallway where a half-dozen other employees at the publication were lying flat on their faces with their arms and legs spread wide.

Feeling especially stressed and adrift, Orit decided the best course of action in such a precarious stage in the investigation would be to take the rest of the day off. She had yet to get more than three hours of uninterrupted sleep since arriving in Miami, so opted to take a desperately needed but ultimately fateful nap by the lazy lagoon out back of the hotel.

A nearby cadre of nannies tended to children building a sandcastle. Orit, wearing a modestly designed black swimsuit, took a dip in the warm ocean, the surface of which was glassy. She then sprawled out atop her yellow beach towel and fell fast asleep as the gentle and ambient sound of small waves lapping against the shore, birds chirping, and children playing seemed to create a kind of natural and soothing symphony with which to doze off to. But almost the exact moment she fell asleep Orit's mind was invaded by a harrowing memory her subconscious had been desperate to navigate since she was a small child and thus especially vulnerable to trauma.

In the dream, which was as much a childhood memory as it was some fanciful concoction in her mind's eye, snow fell in thick white piles, which made it especially difficult to flee from her father's assailants. Mayhem ensued all around Orit as a frantic little girl, her at the age of five, ran as hard as her fierce, determined, but tiny body could manage through knee-high snow. The little girl, wearing little more than a shabby red wooler coat draped over tattered rags, ran raggedly past a small boy being clubbed to death by a grown man. A terrified scream escaped the little girl as she ran past two Imperial Guards decapitate her dad. "Papa!" The words lurched from her body, but terror and courage compelled her to keep running towards the forest as her hillside village burned behind her. Her legs finally abandoned her. She fell and curled into the fetal position. Trembling, she waited to be slain. A malnourished and disheveled woman, Orit's mother, however, dragged the little girl away from the village turned caldron and into the dark and menacing woods a few hundred meters up the ridge from what was once their home. The terrified mother and her nearly catatonic and frostbitten daughter huddled and cowered inside a small cave all through the harrowing night and late into the next day while the world outside seemed to burn and collapse around them. "It's just us now," her mother said over and over again manically while cradling the terrified child in her quivering arms.

Orit woke suddenly. Her body was soaked in a film of sweat. She sat up panting and tried to wipe the grogginess from her sleep-deprived and worried eyes, which then scanned the beach to the north; the idyll expanded as far as her squinting eyes could see. Sunbathers lounged in the shallows and children played in the shore-pound. Orit then glanced down at herself. A pool of perspiration had soaked into her yellow beach towel. Her pale skin was beginning to pink.

She then detected a very pungent but pleasant smoky odor, a combination of hashish and tobacco, which lured her attention to the south, the direction of the stench. She flinched slightly as Azure, wearing a one-piece baby-blue bathing suit and matching sunglasses, sat down into the sand next to Orit.

"I watched you for a time while you were sleeping," Azure said while exhaling a lungful of smoke. "But I didn't want to wake you." She offered the joint to Orit, who politely smiled and waved her hand to decline. Azure took another long and methodical drag from the joint. "You were having a nightmare?" she asked concernedly.

"More of a memory than a nightmare, I suppose," Orit said as her squinting eyes watched intently as a frantic blue crab disappeared underneath the surface of the shore-pound.

"Anything you care to share?" Azure exuded genuine curiosity.

"I'd really rather just forget it, to be honest," Orit confided while wiping some sand-laced sweat from her weary eyes.

"If you aim to forget, then perhaps you might reconsider a hit of this," A mellow giggle escaped from Azure's full red lips. She then offered the slim white joint wedged between her slender thumb and index finger to Orit. "It'll fix you right up."

"What is it?" Orit asked.

"Just a bit of hash and tobacco," Azure said as a relaxed grin washed across her gorgeous face.

"I've never really gotten high before," Orit said while clumsily taking the joint from Azure's finely manicured hand, the nails of which were polished a deep shade of red. Orit then took a small nip from the joint and then coughed deeply for nearly fifteen seconds while handing it back to her new friend. Azure gently rubbed and caressed the top of Orit's back in an effort to assuage the slight burning in the journalist's lungs.

"How is your article coming along?" Azure, who hoped to distract Orit from the pain she could sense her friend was harboring due to her bad dream and burning in her lungs, asked after taking another quick hit from the joint.

"Not great," Orit, who was sighed frustratedly. "There is almost too much corruption to be able to report on it at all. I can't get my head, arms, or legs around it." Orit noticed that the words seemed to suddenly flow up from her with greater ease than she was accustomed to. "The corruption in this city is as endemic as anywhere I've ever known."

"But that seems like it'd be a good thing for an ambitious investigative reporter, no?" Azure asked while passing the joint back to Orit, who reluctantly took it and indulged in another, though far more cautious, nip. "You could make a career of covering corruption down here," Azure added. "Maybe you could write a book?"

"Maybe," Orit said, somewhat dejected and only humoring Azure, "but I need sources either way. The problem is, everyone here worth talking to as a source is so deeply invested in corruption that nobody wants to talk for fear of being the one to knock over the house of cards.

"How do you mean?" Azure asked.

Well, "Orit tries to find the right words, "take Brooklyn. It has Domino Sugar. Detroit has Ford. Chicago has Armor. Atlanta has textile factories. North Carolina has tobacco. But from what I can tell, Miami does not actually make or sell anything but the idea that Miami is somehow better than any other place, so graft here is not just endemic, but inevitable. The whole place is a con." She then took a long and methodical hit from the joint, and then passed it back to Azure.

"You know what your problem is?" Azure asked while holding the joint inches from her lips.

"What's that?" Orit wondered while gazing at a small and frothy wave lap against the smooth and sandy surface of the earth.

"You came here determined to find what was wrong with Miami," Azure smiled wryly then inhaled a quick hit and held it in for a few seconds. "Perhaps it never occurred to you that though there is plenty of wrong to find in Miami, to be sure, there is also plenty of right too." She exhaled as she spoke and handed the joint back to her friend.

"You think?" Orit grinned.

"Perhaps that is because you have not had a proper guide," Azure said while standing, which cast a shadow over Orit. The Cubana appeared to be a skyscraper next to diminutive Orit hunched over with her sun kissed hands between her pink legs. Azure dangled her hand down by Orit's sweat soaked head. "I can show you some of my favorite places to escape to," Azure urged. "Come with me, I'll show you that there is real balance in the universe, even in Miami."

"I don't know," Orit sighed frustratedly. "I really need to make some headway on this feature. The paper I work for is in financial peril, so I have a bit of a gun to my head in terms of a deadline that needs to be met. The paper's existence might well depend on me getting something great written. I've already wasted so much of the day idling."

"Come on," Azure cajoled. "Take the rest of the day to explore an adventure. Take a step back to get a clearer picture. Everything you are so worried about now will be still waiting right where you left it." Orit reluctantly clasped onto Azure's hand. "I have something very special I want to show you," Azure said excitedly while helping Orit up onto her wavering legs.

Capone's electric-blue roadster careened a bit as Scarlet, who was driving, hung a hard right down a dirt road leading into a thick patch of pine forest that finally led into a majestic orange grove that seemed to stretch far beyond the horizon. Capone, who was in the back seat of the car, stared disconsolately at Edmund, who stared over at his daughter, pleading for reprieve.

"Stop up in the clear!" Capone hollered to Scarlet, who mashed her bare foot into the break-pedal as hard as she could. The Ford finally skidded to a halt between two glorious orange trees that provided ample shade from the midday sun. "Please, Scarlet," Edmund blubbered as Capone stuck the gun into the back of his cranium. "I'm beggin' ya; set me free. I know we've had our issues from time to time, but I can forgive you runnin' away and for all the strife and strain it's caused your momma and me. With time, I'll even find a way to forgive this abomination," he said while glancing back at the Gangster. "That's what Jesus would want, for us to forgive."

"Shut your trap, preacher," Capone snarled, "God's sick and tired of hearing all your bullshit. It's time for God to exact a little justice in the form of this little lady's spite here. Now get out of the goddamn car!" Edmund reluctantly complied with Capone's order as the gangster handed his pistol to Scarlet. Her dainty hand trembled. Even with the adrenaline pumping through her veins and boosting her sense of physical strength and mental clarity, the gun seemed heavy as a pillowcase full of nails. "So here's the moment of truth," Capone's whispering voice slithered into Scarlet's ear as she stared down at her father from behind. Edmund began to blubber and pray for forgiveness, which he was not convinced Jesus would provide. Edmund, the charlatan, was not even sure if the fantastical notions of salvation and redemption that he had sold for most of his life were at all rooted in veracity, and was thus very frightened of dying now that he was forced to directly confront the prospect of being killed.

"What are ya goin' to do to this slimy *Bible*-thumpin' shit for brains that robbed you of your innocence?" Capone seethed into Scarlet's ear. In that moment, Scarlet felt great peer pressure to kill her father because she assumed Capone really cared for her. In truth, the gangster's animus towards Edmund's incestuous pedophilia was deeply rooted in his own deep seeded and dark hearted resentment towards the priest who had molested him when he was seven, which had sundered the formerly devout Catholic's belief and faith in God.

Scarlet felt a surge of embarrassment and shame well from the deepest recesses of her soul, which piqued her sense of bitterness towards her father. She took a long and hard breath and then cocked and aimed the pistol at her father's sweat and tear-soaked face.

"Shoot this piece of shit and exorcise yourself of this demon," Capone urged. Scarlet used the gunsight that extended the length of the chrome barrel to measure her shot. But her hands quaked and quivered far too much for her to keep a solid beat on her father's head. She thus lowered the barrel of the pistol and concomitantly ceased measuring her shot in the site and squared the gun towards her father's chest. She took a deep and composed breath, closed her eyes tight, gritted her teeth, and turned her head to the side.

"That's it," Capone encouraged, "now just breathe and squeeze nice and easy."

A subterranean breath lurched from her incredibly tense chest. The gun in her hand then dropped heavily to her side. "I just can't do it," she was ashamed.

Edmund exhaled a deep and assuaged breath, as though he had received a miracle granted aby the almighty, who had heard his prayers. Edmund vowed to his daughter right then and there to be the man God designed him to be. "I won't let the devil in no more," he assured his dejected daughter.

"Shut the fuck up, you!" Capone barked at Edmund as he angrily snatched the pistol from Scarlet's hand. "You gotta kill this evil prick or else what he did to you will haunt you the rest of your days in ways you can't even imagine. Believe me, I know. He might also do what he did to you to some other little girl. How can you abide by that?"

"Please Scarlet," Edmund pleaded. "Remember the Decalogue? Number five on God's list of Commandments is to honor your father. Number six is thou shall not kill. Maybe you hate me. Maybe your head has been filled up with all kinds of lies by this awful man here. You might have even convinced yourself that I've wronged you in some terrible way. But if you pull that there trigger, Scarlet, there ain't no comin' back from eternal hellfire. Now, darlin' you need to think long and hard about whether or not you are willing to pay the cost for what you might be a thinkin' a doin.'"

"Don't call me 'darlin,'" Scarlet snarled while taking the pistol back from Capone.

"Show this cocksucker who's boss," Capone seethed while casting an accusatory hand at Edmund's frightened face. Scarlet stared down the gunsight of the pistol and took aim at her father's chest. Her hands were steady. She exhaled a deep and soothing sigh. Complete clarity washed over her and fill the space between her ears. Her finger, however, was unable to pull the trigger. "Nice and easy," Capone cajoled.

The gun's white-hot blast sent birds flying frantically from the trees. What seemed like a million leaves and dozens of oranges fell to the verdant earth. Scarlet then lowered the pistol to her side. Grey smoke spewed from the chrome barrel.

"He's right," she sighed. "I can't kill my daddy, no matter what he did or did not do. There's no forgivin' patricide. It's like killin' God his self."

Capone huffed bemusedly as he angrily snatched the gun out of Scarlet's hand. He glared at her a moment, disgusted by her cowardice. "I'll show you what almighty looks like," Capone said while cocking and aiming the pistol down at Edmund, who had fallen flat on his face and was groveling in the grass.

"Please don't kill me, mister," he wailed. "We can pretend this never even happened." A brown spot from the human waste excreted from Edmund's anus collected at the backside of his trousers. Capone, who was delighted by the spectacle, cackled. But the humiliation of her father softened Scarlet somewhat. She lunged in front of the pistol Capone had trained on her father.

"Don't shoot my daddy," Scarlet began to weep. "Please, Al, I'll do anything you ask. He might not be the best father in the world, but he's the only daddy I'll ever have."

"Get out of the way, Scarlet," Capone demanded. "I'm your daddy for now on."

"You are?" her entire mien glowed. Her tense eyes suddenly seemed to turn to dough as she gazed up at Capone's fierce and furious scowl.

"That's right, doll," Capone said matter-of-factly, "now get out of the way."

Scarlet stepped out of the line of fire and placed her arms around Capone's sweaty neck. "Please daddy," she whispered ever so seductively into his ear. "He's better off dead. It'd be far crueler to let him live. Look at him. He pooped his pants, for God's sake. Hasn't he been through enough? Please, daddy, let this pathetic nobody live and I'll be your little princess forever and ever. You'll be my king."

"I'm gonna hold you to that," his voice slithered from off his tongue, "or else I'm gonna kill you, then drive out to that Podunk one-cow town you came from and kill this cocksucker and your mother, too. Capeesh?" Capone negotiated.

"Whatever you say, lover," she consented with a warm smile and nod of her round and symmetrical face. Capone took a long and steady breath as he stared into the gunsight, carefully weighing his options a while. For a time, he contemplated killing them both and dragging them into the nearest marsh where, he was certain, an alligator would soon dispose of the evidence. But he, who fancied himself as a benevolent tyrant, finally decided that he could make a good living by pimping Scarlet for a time, at least long enough to pay for his winter in Miami. He thus reluctantly opted to let them both live. If worse came to worse, he surmised, he could always send her back to her father's home if she were to ever prove to be to be too huge a burden to carry.

Capone then smashed Edmund over the head with the butt of the pistol, which knocked the preacher unconscious. Capone then trudged back to the roadster and climbed into the driver's seat. "Alright," Capone hollered as he fired up the supped-up roadster's engine, "let's get the hell out of here before someone wonders what the gunshot was all about." Scarlet hurried into the passenger seat but kept her sympathetic eyes trained on her father, who was motionless. She feared he might have died. Capone then floored the gas pedal and hung a hard U-turn, which caused a plume of yellow dirt to swirl up towards the clear blue sky above the lush orange grove.

Azure led Orit by her unmanicured hand through sprawling and palatial gardens and mazes behind the Royal Palm Hotel. They then cut through a thick orange grove that seemed to sparkle under the midday sun. Grey clouds, however, quickly moved in. A slight mist was falling as Azure led Orit, who was a bit nervous, into a thick patch of pinewoods. The mist and rays of sun cascading through the trees, coupled with the rainbow overhead made it appear as though the forest were enchanted. Then, about one-hundred yards deeper into the trees, the ground suddenly opened dramatically. A sinkhole more than forty feet in circumference and two-hundred feet deep seemed to stretch all the way to the earth's core. "What in the hell is it?" Orit was in awe, curious and frightened all at once.

"This part of the peninsula sits atop porous rock," Azure explained as she leaned forward and planted the palms of her hands on her knees in order to rest and get a better vantage of the deepest recesses of the sinkhole. "When the Spanish conquistadors first came to la Florida in search of gold and the Fountain of Youth, many of them were lost forever down these sinkholes. The Calusa, the native people who originally inhabited the peninsula, believed the holes were portals to other dimensions. The Miccosukee and Seminole later used them as traps for the American army in the 1830s."

"It is magnificent." Orit confessed as her intense brown eyes gazed over at her new friend, "but also very scary."

Azure stood up straight and latched onto Orit's hand again and led her carefully around the edge of the sinkhole and deeper into the forest. "Aren't they wonderful?" Azure asked excitedly as she knelt in the grass next to what seemed to be a desiccated pond full of mushrooms sprouting up from the mud.

"Mushrooms?" Orit wondered why Azure was enamored.

"Not just any mushrooms," Azure's excited eyes sparkled, "Purple mystics." She gently separated the base of the pristinely white mycelium from the soggy brown soil and tossed the mushroom into her mouth and swallowed it whole. "They have been growing wild here since the Spanish brought cattle over from Africa in the fifteenth century."

"What is so special about them?" Orit was intrigued.

"They have powerful alkaloids. People that eat them see into new dimensions," Azure smiled while plucking a few more from the ground. "They can help to heal your soul and make you know thyself more intensely and intimately."

"Mushrooms can do all that?" Orit was unconvinced.

"These one's can," Azure assured. "Just you wait. I'm going to make you a very special tea and then take you dancing at the hottest juke joint in the city. You'll feel as though you had never actually heard music before. By morning you will be a new woman." Azure's warm grin, however, contorted into a concerned scowl as she suddenly sensed a nearby presence in the dark vastness of the forest. She then placed her index finger softly to her pursed lips in order to urge Orit to listen intently concomitant to being silent. Heavy and seemingly methodical steps slowly approached. The closer the presence came, the more concerned both Azure and Orit became. "Who's there?" Azure finally demanded. The mysterious steps paused momentarily, and then took a few heavy steps closer. Orit noticed she had stopped breathing due to the palpable tension.

Finally, a beautiful white mare with black and brown variegation all over its body poked its head around a pine tree and stared directly at Orit, who stared intently and lovingly back at the animal. A relieved exhale escaped her suddenly relieved and more relaxed body. Azure gently approached the mare and caressed its course mane.

"It's the most beautiful horse I've ever seen," Orit grew uncommonly emotional, fighting the urge to cry. "It reminds me of a horse a man in my village had when I was a child. I always wanted to ride it, but never had the chance."

"Why not?" Azure wondered while lovingly pushing a stray strand of hair that had draped down over Orit's eyebrow and obscured the songstress's ability to peer into her friend's eyes.

"The Czar's men shot it when they burned our village," Orit explained. "The horse was shot for no reason at all. I once visited a psychologist in Midtown who asked me when, if ever, I felt my childhood ended. All I could think to tell him was that it happened the moment that beautiful horse was shot dead for no good reason. I can understand killing other humans. There's so much darkness and evil in humans, even the best amongst us. So you gotta figure that one less human is a whole hell of a lot less darkness in the world. But why did they have to kill the horse? That question haunts me still. They could have just kept it, ridden it, loved it. But they just killed it for no good reason. I'd have given those men anything they wanted – anything – had they only let that horse live.

"I'm very sorry," Azure said as she grasped onto Orit's hand and squeezed it tight.

"Maybe this is that horse reincarnated," Orit said while slightly smiling and shrugging her shoulders. "What do you suspect such a beautiful horse is doing out here on its own?" she wondered.

"I think it is wild," Azure explained. "When the Spanish first arrived, they did not realize what a vast expanse of land la Florida actually was. The Spaniards early maps depicted the peninsula to be as a very narrow isthmus and vast chain of islands. That, coupled with the sinkholes, meant that Spanish scouts often got lost, never to be found again. The Spanish thus decided to have priests bless entire boatloads of this beauty's descendants and set them free all across the peninsula in the hopes that if a scout were to get lost, he could hopefully come across one of these mares and ride it to the nearest fort in order to survive the ordeal. There was far more of these horses and cows than people south of Lake Okeechobee for hundreds of years, but that all changed when the railroad came." She lamented.

A sudden gunshot close by frightened the mare, which ran frantically away in the opposite direction of the blast. Orit and Azure dropped instinctively to the ground in reaction to the violent sound that shattered their soulful bonding experience. They stayed perfectly still and quiet for an extended and tense moment as the horse vanished into the vastness of the fast darkening forest.

"What should we do?" Orit finally whispered; her voice full of fright.

"We should go see where the shot came from and if anyone needs our help," Azure whispered matter-of-factly.

"Shouldn't we just get back to the hotel?" Orit pleaded. "It could be a hunter. If they mistake us for a deer, we could wind up dead."

"We're too close to town for anyone to be hunting deer out here," Azure was certain. She plucked a few more mushrooms from the ground and cautiously made her way back towards the orange grove adjacent to the hotel's gardens. Orit reluctantly followed. Her head seemed to be on a swivel. They sneaked along the perimeter of the orange grove for a few minutes.

They then noticed the electric-blue roadster kick up dust as it sped away. Once the sound of the car's engine could no longer be heard, Azure entered the grove in order to investigate. She finally came upon Edmund, who was concussed but unconscious due to the bloody gash opened on his head by the butt of Capone's pistol. His breathing was heavy. "Hey mister," Azure said nervously while jabbing the man with her big toe, "I think you had some kind of accident." A guttural groan seeped from Edmund's body.

"Are you okay?" Orit's nervous voice was just above a whisper. "Who did this to you?"

"No police," Edmund groaned as he gathered his sorts just enough to climb up from being flat-faced in the grass up onto his haunches. Beads of sweat rolled from off his face. Orit reluctantly helped Edmund up onto his feet and steadied his woozy and wavering body. "Just leave me be." The words tumbled clumsily from his mouth as he made his way slowly to the front of the grove. A particularly cloudy, moonless, and dark night was beginning to descend over Miami.

"Come on darling," Azure said to Orit while extending the hand not cradling a bushel of Purple Mystics. "Let's get back to the hotel before dark." Orit watches Edmund stagger slowly away, and then finally latched onto Azure's hand, which comforted her, but only a bit. Azure then led Orit back into the enchanted but suddenly very dark forest as an intended shortcut back to the Royal Palm.

Capone and Scarlet had only just arrived back at the hotel. Scarlet was especially disheveled and lost in her thoughts. Capone hurried from the parking lot towards the hotel lobby, then onto the elevator leading up to the third floor of the hotel. Scarlet lags behind. "Hurry the fuck up!" Capone growled at Scarlet while keeping the elevator door from closing with his straight arm as she walked sullenly towards him. Neither spoke a word on the way up to the third story of the hotel. The doors slide open.

Gallo, wearing his standard black suit, stepped out of his suite, which was across the hall from Capone's, and nearly collided with the gangster. "Excuse me, Mr. Capone," Gallo smirked as if he were privy to a secret.

Capone glared at Gallo and nodded somewhat suspiciously. Gallo ignored Scarlet entirely, which was just fine by her. Capone played it cool. His calm façade, however, disintegrated suddenly the moment he and Scarlet were secluded inside his suite.

"Did you see that fuckin' guy?" Capone was unnerved.

"Who," Scarlet was somewhat dismayed, "the palooka with the shiny shoes who said hello?"

"They'z wasn't just shiny shoes," Capone said while glancing out the window suspiciously. "They'z gumshoes!"

"Gum shoes?" Scarlet was perplexed while looking down at her soiled and bare feet.

"He's a G-man," Capone explained as if growing tired with Scarlet's questions as he planted his hands on the sill and peered outside the window in both directions, "a federal agent."

"You mean the man is in the FBI?" Scarlet gazed hard over Capone's shoulder out the window hoping to spot the man and take a closer look. "How do ya know, Al?"

"Didn't you see how he was dressed, the smug way he carried himself?" Capone squinted while looking hard at Scarlet. "Didn't you hear him call me 'Mr. Capone'?"

"I just figured that since you was in the papers sometimes that he might have recognized you, or somethin'," she shrugged nonchalantly, which stoked his ire.

"You think it's just some fuckin' coin-ki-dink a G-man just happens to be stayin' on the same floor in the same hotel as me?"

"Well yeah," she was indifferent, "lots of people come to Miami in the winter, probably even some G-men."

"Yeah," Capone ran his greasy pug fingers concernedly through his thinning black hair, "maybe," he huffed. "But we need to figure out why the hell he's here exactly. If he's here for me, we're gonna have to either get out of here, or take care of him." He then saw Gallo get into Sheriff Beauregard's prowler. The car sped away from the hotel grounds.

He then snatched Scarlet by her wrist and led her forcibly into the hallway. "Gimme that bobbi-pin in your hair," he demanded. She quickly plucked one from her musty and unwashed hair. He snatched it and fast fashioned it into a pick. "Stand right here," he ordered of her while positioning her against the doorframe so as to serve as a shield to any prying eyes that might happen to be coming suddenly off the elevator. Her nervous eyes scanned up and down the hallway, then seemed to closely study Capone's technique as he scrambled to jimmy the lock, which he managed to do is less than thirty seconds. "Get the fuck in there and see if you can find anything about me," he demanded of Scarlet.

"Like what?" she asked unnerved.

"I don't fucking know," he grunted, "paperwork, newspapers – something – anything with my name or face on it!" He then grabbed her hard around the back of the neck and forced her inside Gallo's suite. "I'll keep a look out," he explained. "If I cough, it means get the hell out of there quick. Capeesh?"

She did not even bother to respond to his demand because, really, what choice did she have? Scarlet quickly flicked on the light inside the suite. Her frantic eyes scanned the top of the bed, dresser, bureau, and windowsill. She then hurried over to the dresser, dropped to her knees, and searched quickly through the garments neatly folded in the dresser. She, however, found nothing that even remotely referenced Alphonse Capone.

She then hurriedly popped open the suitcase that had been slid under the bed, but it too was empty.

The hum and bell that signaled the elevator had come to a halt on the floor pinged, which alerted Capone, who forced a granular and flemmy cough, which sent Scarlet running from Gallo's suite like a scared rabbit running from a starving greyhound. Capone locks the door to Gallo's suite.

Capone then closed himself and Scarlet in his own suite just as the elevator door was sliding open. Garnet hurries from the elevator into the hall en route to his own quarters.

"What did you find?" Capone demanded of Scarlet.

"I didn't see nothin' about you," she conceded in quick and halting verses, short on breath.

"I need you to make nice with him to figure out what he's doin' here," Capone ordered.

"Make nice?" Scarlet was confused and annoyed at the demand.

"You need to get close to him," Capone qualified. "Hell, suck his cock if you have to. But whatever you do, you gotta find out if he has any goods on me."

"Don't you think if he had goods on you," Scarlet huffed, "he'd have arrested you already instead of renting a suite across the hall?"

"You never know with these goddamn G-men," Capone was genuinely scared, which Scarlet found to be terribly unattractive. "Hell," Capone continued, "this could be some kind of twisted long-game to catch me in some kind of honey hole or something. Flynn's boys are very wily. You never know what angle they're coming from."

"Please Al," she pleaded, "I don't want to seduce any G-man. Can't I get into big trouble for somethin' like that?"

"Get in trouble? What the hell for?" he sneered. "Flirtin' with some mameluke? That's not illegal. Not yet anyway. Is it?"

"But you said you loved me?" she plopped sullenly at the edge of the bed.

"I did?" he seemed to have trouble remembering ever having said those words to anyone.

"If you really loved me," she persisted, "you would not want to even think of me flirtin' with another man, let alone suckin' his cock. Would you?" Her longing eyes ached for some kind of sweet retort that the gangster was not willing or able to provide. Capone, however, suddenly realized that lying to Scarlet and telling her he loved her would make manipulating her far easier.

"I do love you," he huffed frustratedly as he sat at the edge of the bed next to her and draped his arm lovingly around her slumping shoulders. "I'm gonna marry you someday, baby," he lied. "But we ain't gonna have too great a life together if I'm an inmate at a federal penitentiary now, are we?"

"But I thought you said you were a legitimate businessman?" Scarlet, who was scared of his answer, asked somewhat timidly. "Why would a G-man even want to arrest you?"

Capone's already fading patience shifted suddenly from forced charm to bitter anger. He stood up suddenly from the edge of bed and stood directly over Scarlet with his fists clenched. He scowled down at her as if he had an urge to punch her in the face. "Don't be so goddamn naïve," he seethed. "I am a legitimate businessman, as legitimate as Rockefeller or Carnegie is. But I'm Italian. They hate our kind here and want to send all us Guineas back where we came from just like we're a bunch of niggers from Africa."

"But that man looked as Italian as you, Al," Scarlet said defiantly. Capone then slapped her hard across the face. She swooned. The sound of a siren seemed to fill her concussed head. She fell back atop the bed and cupped her mouth with her hand. For just a fleeting moment, she mistook the gangster for her father through the bulbous tears that had welled in her weary and frightened eyes.

"After all I done for you," he bemoaned, "you can't even bother to do me this small favor?" He dragged her from the bed by her hair and then across the wooden floor towards the egress of the suite. He pinned her face against the pastel palm tree-print wallpaper. "If you can't do this small favor after all I done for you, then you can get the hell out of here and never come back."

"Please Al," she sobbed. Her tears streamed down the multi-hued wallpaper and collected at the wooden baseboard next to her soiled bare feet. "I got nowhere else to go."

He then ceased pinning her face to the wall. She dropped to her knees and hyperventilated while sobbing. Her tired and disheveled shoulders slumped forward. He then shoved her face into the floor, crawled on top of her, and pinned her wrists next to her ears. Her face was pink, swollen, and throbbing.

"Now, what'd you say?" he demanded she revise her response.

"I'll do it," she said after realizing for the first time in her life that she was truly alone in the world, agreed to Capone's sinister yet rather jejune plot. "I'll do whatever you say," she sobbed disconsolately.

"There," he said sweetly while kissing her stinging and pink face and neck, "that wasn't so hard, was it?"

She wailed as he climbed off and stood over her. He then straightened his waistcoat and resumed his paranoid gazing out the window. Scarlet, meanwhile, crawled into the bathroom, shut the door, and cried silently while contemplating the quickest and most painless way she might end her own life.

Azure looked ravishing in the sleeveless orange sequin dress that reflected the bright moonlight from above, the hem of which rose just above her knees. She stood under a palm tree outside of the hotel smoking a cigarette rolled with hash and tobacco as she calmly waited for Orit to show. She winced slightly as she sipped a viscous, reddish and pungent substance from a large crystal chalice. She then became delighted by the sight of a young black man parking his car at the curbside near her. "Howdy do, darlin'?" the driver said while flashing a warm and charming smile. "Fancy seein' you here."

"Rhett, what a lovely surprise," Azure smiled and leaned into the open passenger side window. "You're a feast for starving eyes, as always. I haven't seen you around in a while. What's been occupying so much of your time?"

"Mostly same old same old, you know how it goes," he huffed. "Fuckin' cop damn near shot my leg off last week, so I been laid up a while."

"You Negro men are an endangered species down here, it seems, especially since the war ended."

"Don't I know it," he sighed sullenly. "I been attending some really important meetings lately, too. They been openin' my mind to the black man's history in this empire."

"You don't say?" Azure's eyes widened with curiosity.

"You heard of the United Negro International Association?" Rhett asked.

"That's Marcus Garvey, yes?" she said while squinting off into the distance as if to picture the flamboyant leader. "He's the Jamaican who dresses like Napoleon, right?"

"Yeah," Rhett conceded somewhat embarrassedly. "We don't pay much mind to his clothes. But me and some of the other black cabbies really understand brother Garvey's ideas of a universal brotherhood of Negroes and the desire to start fresh in Africa. Me and some of the other cabbies been thinkin' about movin' on up to Harlem in New York City. I hear it's a whole different world up there."

"Different how?" Azure's curiosity piqued.

"For one," he explained while suddenly whispering and glancing around to ensure privacy, "Negro cabbies in Harlem don't get lynched for drivin' white folks around like they do down here. There's also all kinds of black uplift and self-improvement, arts, music, food – you name it. In Harlem, Negroes is free to be free as we want to be. I just don't know how much longer I can stand all this goddamn terrorism down here; it's killin' me more each day."

"Harlem sounds wonderful," she admitted. "When's the soonest you can go?"

"Don't know just now," his enthusiasm was damped by Azure's question. "I gotta save up enough cash to make the move first. Problem is, it's gettin' harder and harder to make a livin' drivin' this damned car ever since the white drivers got back from the war. They demand a closed shop and ain't afraid to doll out necktie parties to keep niggers from pickin' up anyone but other niggers. Can't nobody make no damn livin' under this white tyranny. That's what Brother Garvey done so well to make us understand; this country ain't for us. What I'm supposed to do, just stay in Colored Town all the live long day? Can't nobody make a livin' doin' that. Niggers can't even afford taxis."

"I'm terribly sorry about your predicament, Rhett," she sighed a plume of smoke and then passed her joint to Rhett, who gladly indulged in it as if it contained some kind of antidote to his despair. Orit, wearing a demure blue dress that went to her ankles and were replete with sleeves that went to her wrists, exited the building seeming somewhat unsure and uncomfortable in her own skin.

"She with you?" Rhett asked Azure while passing the joint back to his friend.

Azure turned around and warmly greeted the diminutive and shy journalist with a gentle caress of her cheek. "There you are," Azure shined with excitement, "I was beginning to wonder if you had changed your mind."

"I'm very sorry," Orit said slightly embarrassedly. "All the sun and excitement earlier wore me out. I dozed off a while; lost track of time, I suppose."

"Es nada," Azure graciously assured her new friend while opening the backseat to Rhett's rugged and worn Model-T.

Rhett, meanwhile, glanced nervously around to ensure that nobody was observing him picking up a white woman from the Royal Palm, which the white cabbie's trade union, which was affiliated with the American Federation of Labor, had prohibited under threat of death and castration for any Negro who dared to defy the edict.

The ride from the Royal Palm to "Colored Town," as the section of the city was described in local maps back then, was not too terribly far. The ride, however, provided enough time for the journalist to ask a few questions of the singer and cabbie about the nature of the city's identity and existence. Orit asked Rhett specifically why he believed the murders had happened. He then informed her of a rumor that had long existed in the city's lore that proffered the notion that Miami had been cursed.

"You mean that old wives' tale about Miss Tuttle cursing the city as revenge on Mr. Flagler and Mr. Ingram?" Azure asked Rhett while taking a thick sip from the viscous syrup in her crystal chalice. She then handed the chalice to Orit, who, thinking it was sangria, took a long swig from it. She, however, had trouble swallowing the substance and looked quizzically at Azure, who winked and smiled excitedly.

"Nah," Rhett said, "I mean the Miccosukee curse."

"Miccosukee curse?" Azure leaned forward and draped her long, slender, and neatly manicured hands over the back of the front passenger seat. "I've never heard that one."

Orit took a more tentative swig of the shroom tea in the chalice.

"Yeah," Rhett explained, "it's been around ever since I can remember. You know that quiet old Indian that works with Mr. Ingram – the little fella?"

"You mean, Garnet?" Azure said while handing Rhett the joint. "I know him. He's a lovely man." Rhett took a long and methodical drag from the spliff and passed it back to Azure, who passed the joint over to Orit, who took a small and reluctant nip, which suddenly activated the hallucinogenic alkaloids swirling in Azure's chalice.

"Yeah, Garnet, that's the fella," Rhett said while glancing at the women via his vantage in the rearview mirror. "I never asked him about it; but legend has it that he was in love with some incredibly beautiful Miccosukee girl. My momma said the girl was beyond beautiful; a veritable Angel who fell from the stars and ended up in this godforsaken place.

Orit noticed suddenly that Rhett's words became visible once they exited his mouth, as if written by typewriter, which both elated and frightened her in equal measure. "She had a braid of shining raven hair that went all the way down her back," Rhett continued. "Her face was as pleasant as any sunset over Biscayne Bay. She was supposedly the chief's daughter, or some shit like that. So everyone respected and revered her as a princess of sorts."

"So this woman from the legend," Azure asked somewhat confusedly while exhaling, "she cursed the city?"

"Nah," Rhett said, "legend has it that in the early days of the city lots of the rail workers used to go over to the Miccosukee's land. There was some kind of house the white fellas frequented, if you catch my drift."

"A brothel?" Orit asked in an oddly loud tone. The surge of energy and adrenalin caused by Azure's special brew caused Orit's voice to sound like a shout, which startled her somewhat. Azure, however, giggled magnanimously.

"The Noble Savage is the unfortunate name given to the brothel that has been an institution on the Miccosukee reservation ever since the white man built his railroad here," Azure informed Orit. "Many men of means who live in or visit the city regularly patronize it."

"Are Miccosukee prostitutes that big a draw for men in this city?" Orit sneered.

"You have no idea," Azure said while rolling her eyes. "These white men have dreamed of bedding a little native girl ever since they first heard the legend of Pocahontas and Sacagawea. But the Noble Savage has girls from all over the place – Latinas from Cuba, black girls from Atlanta and Bimini, and bumpkins from Palatka. There is a wide variety."

"Have you ever been?" Orit asked Rhett.

"Shit," he quipped, "ain't no black man allowed anywhere near the Noble Savage."

"I've been there several times," Azure said matter-of-factly while exhaling a plume of smoke. She handed the joint up to Rhett, took a steep sip of tea from the chalice, then handed it back to Orit, who took a deep and composed breath before slurping back another sip of the viscous concoction, which she nearly spit back out before finally managing to swallow it. "I dated Charles Forbes for a time before he was married," Azure explained. "He used to get his jollies watching me play with some of the girls there, especially black girls."

Orit seemed as though she had been enlightened as she nodded her head as if desperately trying to process all this new information with a mind that seemed to be disintegrating under the weight of the hallucinogenic alkaloids she had consumed. Rhett, whose eyes darted towards Azure's reflection in the rearview mirror, seemed impressed too.

"From what I heard," Rhett continued, "one of the painted ladies at the Noble Savage was Garnet's first and only love. He supposedly begged her not to make her bones whoring, but she was desperate for a better life. She worked there to save money so that Garnet and she could live happily ever after, as it were. Anyhow, that's how the story was told to me a long time ago. I don't know which parts, if any, are true."

"Garnet is still here and I've never heard of this dame before," Azure said, "so that plan must not quite have worked out."

"Guess not," Rhett added while shrugging nonchalantly. "Word has it that one of the rail workers strangled the poor girl to death while having his way with her. The girl's daddy supposedly cursed the city. But my momma said he was dead long before her, so who knows what the truth is."

"You think the ritual killings this week could have been Garnet?" Azure asked.

"I know Garnet," Rhett said. "He's a fine man. But he's also a man, if you catch my drift."

"What do you mean?" Orit blurted as her bottom crept to the edge of the backseat."

"I mean," Rhett struggled for just the right words, "even a good man has a killer somewhere deep inside. Shit, if somebody killed my girl, I might have a mind to get revenge to."

"But as someone who knows the man," Orit asked, "do you personally think he has it in him to brutally murder girls he likely had never even met before, or hardly knew? From what I read, the brutality of these murders indicates that the murderer likely knows these women."

"I consider Garnet a friend," Rhett said. "I like to think I know him pretty well. But how well can you really know another man, especially a man who keeps to his self as much as Garnet does?"

"I know Garnet pretty well after all these years singing at the hotel," Azure said while assuredly shaking her head. "I do not believe that he has it in him to do something so evil."

"Shit," Rhett retorted, "every man has that level of deep-down darkness in him. It don't take all that much to tap into it. Y'all don't believe me? Just ask those boys that just come back from the war. Betcha none of them boys ever dreamed they could be made into killers, but they was."

"Do you think the murderer might be a veteran?" Orit asked. "Lots of the boys who came back to New York from France were not at all right in the head. Some might never be right again."

"I don't know nothin' bout that," Rhett said. "All I know is I hope they catch the killer soon and that it's a white man, cuz if it ends up bein' a black boy that done this, the Klan might decide to genocide all us."

Rhett brought the car to a sudden stop at a rather dilapidated wooden structure painted bright red. Throbbing and pulsating drumbeats and sounds from brass instruments seeped out from the establishment, which excited Azure, who reached down into the cleavage of her dress and revealed a thick grip of cash. She peeled off a twenty-dollar note and handed it to Rhett. "Keep the change, darling," she said while smiling gladly, then downed the rest of the viscous tea in her chalice. "Have this too," she said while placing the empty glass in his lap. "It's made crystal. Sell it. It'll help you get to Harlem faster."

"Geez," he said as his wide and excited eyes gazed at the twenty-dollar bill in his calloused hand, "this is what I make in a whole month!"

"Get to Harlem as quick as you can, babe," she said while leaning forward and kissing him on his cheek. "Harlem sounds like the kind of place you belong." She then grabbed onto Orit's hand and led her gently from the backseat of the car and hurried towards the front of the building, which had a long line that she strolled confidently past.

The Deputy assigned to watch the juke joint and to harass any patron as he saw fit as they left the establishment was in the driver-side seat of his prowler staking out the joint from a secluded alleyway across the street. The tips of his fingers had a bit or residue from the rind of the orange he was peeling as an after-supper snack. His anger was particularly piqued by seeing Azure kiss Rhett on the cheek. "Son of a bitch," he seethed as he plopped the orange in the passenger seat next to him and wiped juice from his hands onto his trousers.

Scarlet loitered near the elevator at the end of the third-story hallway, as if waiting for someone, which she was. She had been disappointed twelve times in the prior hour by vacationers staying at the hotel leaving their rooms, hoping that each time a door down the hallway opened, it would be Special Agent Gallo, which it had yet to be. Gallo finally did exit his suite donning his standard three-piece black suit. Scarlet took a deep and composed breath as Gallo made his way towards the elevator.

"Is anything wrong with the elevator?" he asked Scarlet, who was somewhat startled by the question. "Oh ah," she stammered, "no, ah, I just I forgot to push the button." He forced a half-cordial but suspicious grin as he pressed the button to retrieve the elevator to the third-floor hallway. An awkward and tense silence hung in the air between them. The elevator door finally slid open.

"After you," Gallo said while deftly motioning with his hand for Scarlet to climb aboard.

The doors slid shut as Gallo pressed the "L" button, which sent the elevator sinking towards the lobby.

"You know, mister," Scarlet said meekly, as if forced, which she was, "I think you're real cute."

"I'm sorry?" Gallo's eyes squinted as he glanced side-eyed at her. He was sure he had misheard her.

"You look dapper in your crisp black suit," she said with a bit more gumption in her voice. "I don't suppose you'd like to buy a girl a drink at the bar?"

He turned his body away from the doors and directly towards her. He invaded her space and stood threateningly near to her, towering over her as he cast his accusatory glare down at her, which frightened her. She backed away into the corner of the elevator. "Never in a million years would I buy a drink for a filthy girl who shares a bed with Alphonse Capone."

The bell signaling that the elevator had arrived at the lobby pinged. Gallo straightened his tie and pocket square slightly as his attention turned back towards the doors, which slide open. He strode determinedly across the lobby. The heels of his wingtip shoes clacked atop the smooth and polished marble floor.

"Have a wonderful day," the affable concierge called out after Gallo as the agent departed the building. Gallo did not bother to requite the salutation.

Scarlet, who had yet to depart the elevator, seemed dazed and embarrassed. But then Jasper Jackson, the handsome horn player, stepped onto the elevator. It felt as though the air pressure and atmosphere moistened and soften. "Howdy there, little one," he said while charmingly smiling. "Goin' up?" he hoped.

She stared blankly at him a moment, then finally nodded her head. He smiled warmly and chuckled affectionately.

"What number?" he gazed into her soul. She flashed three fingers. He, the sensitive artist, sensed her trepidation and thus made a reflexive effort to diminish it. "I saw your picture in the newspaper. You know," he smiled, "I heard you was the real winner of the Miss Orange Blossom Pageant. Word has it that those judges robbed you blind." She giggled and blushed a bit.

"What's your name?" Scarlet asked while extending her hand. "I seen you around too. You've got to be the prettiest Negro I ever did see, that's for sure. That said, that might be cuz you look so close to bein' white."

"Jasper," he chuckled flirtatiously while and clasping onto her outstretched hand. "Well," he gushed, "you might just be the prettiest little white girl I ever seen too, and that includes the girls I seen in the movies."

"That's the nicest thing anyone has ever said to me," She gushed. "You think I could be a star like the girls in pictures, like Clara Bow, even?" Scarlet, who was in desperate need of healing due to Gallo's recent and vitriolic rejection, asked.

"If you ain't pretty enough to be in pictures," Jasper declared, "I don't know who in the hell is."

"Funny you should say so," she explained, "I always dreamed of goin' to Hollywood and of becomin' a big star."

The elevator doors slid open at the third-story hallway. Capone's scowling face greeted Scarlet and Jasper. Fury welled in Capone's eyes the moment he saw Scarlet's diminutive white hand touching Jasper's. "What the fuck took so long?" Capone snarled as Scarlet snatched her hand from Jasper's. "Who's the nigger?"

"Oh, hi Al," Scarlet seemed filled with sudden dread as she lurched her hand from Jasper's, "this boy is stayin' at the hotel. He plays horn in the brass band. You remember, we saw them play at Mr. Ingram's party the other night? I just met him here on the elevator."

Jasper, who did not know of Al Capone, extended his hand to the psychotic gangster, who stared down at Jasper's hand with cold and indifferent eyes. Capone declined to shake Jasper's hand. Jasper thus finally dropped his hand back to his side and appeared equally emasculated and embittered by the slight. "Get your ass inside," Capone demanded of Scarlet. She hurriedly complied without offering Jasper even a polite glance as a substitute for a proper goodbye.

Jasper held the elevator door open with his arm and watched Scarlet hurry down the hall after Capone into his suite. Capone slammed the door behind Scarlet. The sensitive musician worried if Scarlet would soon suffer a beating or some other callous mistreatment due to his interaction with her. He then pressed his index finger into the 2-button, which whisked him to the second story of the hotel, where his suite was.

"He didn't go for it," Scarlet shamefacedly explained once secluded inside Capone's suite. "I tried my best with the gumshoe, but I think he might be a queer, or somethin'."

"Goddamn it!" Capone seethed. "From what I can tell you'z too busy making eyes at niggers to even get close to the fed." A long and tense pause filled the room. "We're gonna have to figure out a way for you to earn your keep," Capone finally broke the silence, "one way or the other."

"How am I supposed to do that? The only skills I have is singin' and bein' pretty," Scarlet's disgust for Capone was growing. "I reckon I could be in the pictures. You know anyone in Hollywood?"

"You got more talent than you know in those loins," Capone smirked lasciviously, "and I'm gonna teach you how to earn your keep and then some."

Rhett navigated the cab out of the juke-joint carpark, which was a dirt lot next to the building. He did not notice the police car concealed by the darkened alleyway across the street. The officer tried to wipe the sticky orange juice from off his hands by rubbing his palms against his trousers, and then frantically fired up the engine to his car with a quick flick of the ignition switch. The patrol car darted across the road and skid to a halt in the parking lot. "Hey," he hollered at Azure and Orit, both of who whom were very high, hallucinatory, and nearly to the entrance of the juke joint. Everyone waiting in line nervously observed the seemingly irate Deputy with grave fear that he might turn his ire towards them. "Hey you," he hollered, "you! The little white girl and spic bitch! Come over here!" He demanded. Those in the line were somewhat relieved to not be targeted by the aggrieved lawmen.

Azure turned around calm and confident, accustomed to dealing with the strange iterations associated with the local police force. Orit, in stark contrast, was very uncomfortable and terribly frightened. Orit, unable to look at the officer directly, stared at the dirt that comprised the lot. "You been warned before not to patronize these goddamn black cabbies," the cop growled at Azure as she approached the car. "I did not lose buddies in the trenches of the Western Front to come home and have niggers take the jobs of the heroes who saved the world for democracy."

"It's a free country," Azure smirked defiantly, "isn't it?" She knew damn well that freedom only extended as far as property-owning white men in Miami.

"You're free to patronize white cabbies, all you like," he explained. "Miami is a closed shop town. It ain't proper for you foreigners and goddamn Yankees to come down here and force us to miscegenate."

"Where is your family from, officer?" Azure asked calmly.

"Buford, South Carolina," he seemed proud.

"Ah, I see." Azure rejoined. "So your family actually hails from a much further distance from Miami than mine, which is from Cuba?"

"But South Carolina is America, darlin'," he educated her. "Miami is America. Y'all Cubans are of Spanish and nigger stock."

"I'm American," Orit, whose patience had waned completely, blurted defiantly as she clasped onto Azure's hand for emotional support. Azure was surprised as she glanced down at Orit's hand in hers. Azure, who liked that Orit had come to her defense, smiled slightly.

"Word around the precinct is that you're a kike," the cop sneered, "so you don't quite qualify as 'American.' Besides, New York City ain't exactly America. It's a godforsaken cesspool of foreigners and miscegenation."

"Oh really?" Orit's anger emboldened her. "When was the last time you've ever been to the city, if ever?"

"Ain't gotta go to know what a shithole it is."

"You might be the most ignorant man I've ever had the great misfortune of conversing with," Orit smirked condescendingly.

"You stupid mongrel whores are too goddamn thick to understand that I'm trying to protect what little womanhood you dikes have from these jigs," the officer seethed. "If these niggers had their way, all you whores would be poppin' out little nigger babies every nine months. Is that really what y'all want?" he sneered disgustedly. "Hell," he added while fixing his gaze on Orit and Azure's hands clasped together, "looks to me like y'all don't fancy men of any kind at all. Ask yourself, 'do I really want to be raped by some jig that drives a cab for a livin'?' The nigger can't even vote; he ain't even a real man."

"If you're the alternative," Azure said snidely as her fierce brown eyes soaked into his, "I'll take any woman or sweet Negro boy into my boudoir every time; twice on Sunday," she smiled confidently as she led Orit by the hand past the secretly amused doorman, who she tipped handsomely. Azure then led Orit into the juke joint, which was packed with revelers dancing to the hottest jazz that could be heard South of New Orleans.

The surly and emasculated officer stared at the juke joint a moment as if he wanted to burn the place down. He then floored the gas pedal, which caused his tires to leave imprints in the dirt lot. He then fast pursued Rhett's cab as the cabbie made his way back uptown towards the Royal Palm. The patrol car blasted through every stop sign it encountered, which nearly caused another motorist to careen off the road.

He had caught up to Rhett, who had stopped for each sign for fear of being pulled over, in less than two minutes. Rhett's big brown eyes glanced up into his rearview mirror. They seemed soaked in sorrow and trepidation as he noticed he was being pursued. He considered skidding the car to a halt and then running from the officer, but his leg was already wounded and knew his ability to get away would be significantly diminished. Rhett also acutely remembered that the same Deputy tailing him and a few of his buddies knew where he lived due to the fact that the lawman had invaded his mother's home two months earlier in order to threaten the cabbie for having the audacity to drive white patrons from the train station to hotels in white sections of the city. Rhett insisted that he had a right to drive anyone willing to pay. He took such a savage beating that night that he could not walk, let alone drive, for more than a month. He was also quite sure he would be shot and killed if he tried to run from the officer.

He thus perhaps wisely pulled the cab along the shoulder of the two-lane road that stretched all the way from Homestead to Hialeah and hoped he could somehow reason with the irascibly racist police officer. No such luck.

The officer hurried from his to Rhett's car, which was idling along the shoulder of the road. The cop's service revolver was in his hand and aimed at the cabbie's head by the time he arrived at Rhett's door, which he slung open. He grabbed Rhett by the back of the neck and collar to drag the cabbie into the street. The Deputy shoved him face-first atop the rugged concrete. He then plopped on top of his victim's back knee-first so that Rhett's arms were pinned to the street, and then pistol whipped the kid in the back of his skull. Deep abrasions soon formed on Rhett's bloody and mangled scalp. A few cars passed by during the assault, but no one stopped to aid the assailed. "It's none of my business," or, "the nigger probably deserved it," were the most prominent thoughts in the minds of those who passed.

That, however, was not at all Garnet's sentiment. He was on his way back from Ruby's with an ounce of pure cocaine in his pocket and bed full of booze in the back of the truck. He parked the truck fifty yards down the road from the assault. He then calmly removed a machete, which was wedged between two crates of rum, from the back bed of the truck and briskly circled back on foot to where the savage beating was occurring. The officer was so consumed with hatred and anger as he assaulted Rhett, who was unconscious, that he did not even notice Garnet fast approaching from behind. The officer raised the bloody butt of his pistol once more to mash it down into Rhett's skull. But Garnet sunk the blade of the machete into the officer's neck.

Quinn's mortified fiancé happened to be driving by as Garnet was hacking the officer. Garnet's instinct was to pursue the witness and dispose of him. But he could tell by looking at Rhett's mangled head that he would very likely die if not immediately taken for medical treatment. Garnet, who was five-feet and five inches tall and weighed less than one-hundred and forty pounds sopping wet, seemed to have superhuman strength as he dragged the cop's body from off of Rhett's. He then dragged Rhett, who was taller than six-feet, up off the dirt and plopped him over his shoulder, and carried him all the way to the truck and somehow managed to put him the passenger side seat. Garnet, now covered in Rhett's crimson blood, sighed bewilderedly and frightened as he climbed into the driver's seat of the truck and mashed the gas pedal underfoot. There was no hospital in the city where either a black man or Native American had the right to receive medical attention. He thus made a hard U-turn and gunned the truck towards the medicine man that lived on Miccosukee land, which was more than a mile beyond Lemon City. Garnet was certain Rhett would die before they arrived at the destination, if they even ever made it before being apprehended by the law.

Capone was beyond annoyed with Scarlet due to her inability to seduce Special Agent Gallo. The gangster had also gotten bored with Scarlet's neurosis, but was not yet ready to cast her aside just yet. He saw value in her. He had thus become particularly determined to recoup the hundred or so dollars he had spent on her entrance fee, as well as her gown, bathing suit, shoes, and the makeup that she wore so spectacularly during the Miss Orange Blossom Pageant. But Scarlet had no real job experience or skills. One thing, however, she was flush with was physical beauty and charisma, which Capone aimed to profitably exploit. He thus took her to the brothel on Miccosukee land in the interest of making her earn. Capone, in short, intended to pimp Scarlet, which he believed could pay for his winter in Miami.

He thus rented her a dingy and disgusting room in the Noble Savage, which set him (her) back ten dollars a night. "Small price to pay for overhead," he thought while peeling a billfold from his herculean wad of cash and handing it to the elderly woman who had owned the place since back when Miami was known as Fort Dallas. There was just one hitch in Capone's scheme: Scarlet had no interest at all in being whored out to men she had never met. "I'm the reigning Miss Orange Blossom Queen," Scarlet declared while sneering as Capone locked the door of the rented room behind them. "You'll see," she added defiantly, "I'm going to be a celebrity."

Capone gave her a hard open-hand smack across the mouth, which spun her backwards and atop the blood and cum stained mattress plopped atop the creaking wooden floor. "You're only the reigning Miss Orange Blossom Queen because that other dame got killed," he grunted, "so get off your high horse."

Scarlet was stunned by the strike and angry, but she did not cry; she would not give Capone the satisfaction of seeing her weep, which was a skill she had honed from enduring years of abuse doled out by her father. "You think you'd have even been allowed in that goddamn pageant if not for me handin' over all that dough for entry fee and to those judges?" he snarled as if her naiveté was a pang of nausea. "You think those judges would have paid you any mind if not for all the swag I bought you? If not for me?" he mashed his thumb haughtily into his pinstripe waistcoat, "you'd be a barefoot bumpkin gettin' fucked by your goddamn father if not for me."

Scarlet sprung suddenly from the mattress with the ferocity of a cornered honey badger who had been poked one too many times. He, however, darted out of the way like a matador leaping from an angry bull's path. He dangled his leg in front of her, which caused her to trip and fall. Her head smashed smack-dab into the wall, which was made of wood. A hollow thud sound filled the room. She did not move for a long moment. He half-hoped she had died. He rolled her onto her back. Her dazed eyes stared up at him beseechingly, "Why is this happenin' to me?" A single tear streaked down her face. He huffed as he lugged her up from the dusty hardwood floor and plopped her listless body in the squeaky and creaky bed. "Why'd this happen?" the helpless and hopeless words slurred from her pink chapped lips. "Why doesn't anybody love me?" she wondered in a defter tone than a whisper.

"Lots of fellas are gonna love you soon enough, sweetheart," Capone snorted while dragging her listless body onto the soiled mattress.

"I love Jasper," Scarlet confessed while Capone fetched a kitbag from a small suitcase sitting on the floor by the door. He laughed manically.

"Look at how much I love you," he said while holding up at least an ounce of golden-brown heroin stuffed into a piece of parchment paper tied at the top with a rubber band in one hand and a syringe in the other.

Scarlet curled into a ball and faced her back towards Capone, who sat at the edge of the bed and then heated a spoon with the kerosene flame emitted by a silver lighter. He then sucked the viscous liquid that filled the spoon up into the syringe. Scarlet covered her hands over the veins in her arms so that Capone could not get a clean shot. But he simply stuck the needle into a vein in Scarlet's foot, the bottoms of which were covered in black soot.

In a matter of seconds, her incredibly tense mien seemed to blossom like a tulip in a hothouse, to the point that her fully flexed body became one continuous flow of smooth energy sprawled atop a tainted mattress. That was in large part due to the fact that Capone had given her twice the dose she had grown accustomed to.

"Oh, Al," the words seeped from Scarlet suddenly soothed lips as she let loose of a deep sigh, "you do love me, don't you?"

"You bet that sweet tuckus, I do," Capone said while gently kissing and caressing the bruise and lump that had formed on her concussed forehead. "You're gonna pay for my vacation, darlin'," he smiled. "And then," he added, "when the season ends, I'm gonna take you to Chicago and turn you all the way out. You could make $200 a night up there with those animals."

"Not Chicago," Scarlet whispered, "Hollywood. I'm gonna be in the pictures. Rudolph Valentino and Al Jolson are gonna fight over who adores me more."

"Sure you are, hon," Capone sneered condescendingly while putting the contraband back into his kitbag, which he then placed into the suitcase next to the door. He then exited the room and made his way down the darkened hallway past a half-dozen other doors; the sounds of coitus emanated from some. Addison Mizner, who waited rather impatiently in a reception area, as a young Miccosukee girl who stood smaller than five-feet tall and looked younger than fourteen years of age sat uneasily in his lap. "She's all yours," Capone announced while ushering the oddly paired couple towards the dark and dank hallway leading to Scarlet.

Mizner then led the Miccosukee girl by the hand towards the dark hallway. He gladly shoved a wad of billfolds into Capone's hand. The sight of the cash in Capone's hand made him feel powerful and virile. "She's all yours until the sun rises," Capone said while smiling and shoving the cash into the finely pleated pocket of his tailored trousers. "She's eagerly waitin' for ya in the last room on the left."

Mizner then led the girl by her slight and trembling hand into the darkened hall, past the sounds of sex emanating from some of the other rooms. He excitedly swung the door open, Scarlet's tear-soaked and glazed eyes gazed up at a wooden beam that extended the length of the ceiling. "Hello Miss Orange Blossom," Mizner said lasciviously while slightly licking his upper lip and mustache, "I'm the King of Miami." Scarlet tried to speak but could not utter but a deep and pained moan.

"I think she's stoned," the Miccosukee girl said meekly, "she seems really out of it."

"Don't you dare say one goddamn word unless I ask you a question first," Mizner snapped, which startled the Miccosukee girl. "Now," Mizner softened while exhaling a deep and soothing breath, "go over there and unbutton her dress very slowly, then wait for further instruction."

The frightened girl crept over to the mattress and quietly complied with Mizner's demand.

The inside of the nightclub had purple velvet walls that seemed to pulsate in the dim light. The stench of tobacco smoke and human sweat filled the air. Azure and Orit, who were a few of the only white revelers patronizing the establishment, danced and swayed to the beats and riffs produced by the highly competent seven-piece brass band. Orit is especially absorbed in the moment, as if there was no past or future – only present. She had never danced with such freedom or careless abandon and lack of self before. She smiled brightly and gleefully as she twisted, shimmied, sashayed and twirled. Azure was overcome with glee that her new friend seemed to be having the time of her life.

"I'm desperate for a cold beer!" Azure hollered into Orit's ear over the throbbing sound of the band wailing away. "Want one?"

"Huh?" Orit answered as she opened her eyes wide, somewhat surprised to find herself dancing. Her pupils were dilated to the point that her entire iris seemed black.

"A beer?" Azure mimed pouring a bottle into the mouth, then pointed at the bar along the back wall of the establishment. Orit eagerly nodded.

Azure led the way in navigating the horde and then leaned against the bar trying to catch her breath while flashing two fingers towards the bartender in order to alert him to her order. "Are you having fun?" she hollered into Orit's ear.

"So much fun," Orit said while smiling warm and wide as if soothed. The bartender slid two cool and perspiring beer bottles down the bar a few yards to Azure. Azure left a dollar atop the bar. "I never get a chance to dance like this," Orit confided. "It feels like it is scrubbing my soul of lots of old crud I did not even know I was harboring."

"Such as?" Azure queried while savoring her first frosty and frothy sip of cold beer.

"I don't know that I want to spoil the evening with my problems," Orit was reluctant.

"Getting anxiety off your chest won't ruin my evening any," Azure assured. "It might be cathartic to talk about it a bit."

"It's the paper where I work," Orit tried explaining, "I really care about working there. I think what we are doing is vital, but the paper does not attract many advertisers; we're perpetually in the red, always running a deficit. I don't even know if I'll have a job by the time I finish this article – if it ever even gets written."

"I see," Azure sympathized while taking another quick sip of beer. Orit, who was dehydrated and deep in anguished thought, took a long swig from her beer.

"I also just broke up with a man I've been in a relationship with since college," Orit continued.

"You have?" Azure's eyes widened with curiosity. "When? Why?"

"To be honest," Orit sighed and shrugged her burdened shoulders, "I'm not quite sure. I suppose it just felt like the right thing to do at the time."

"Why?" Azure wondered.

"He asked me to marry him just as I was leaving for Miami," an odd sense of shame suddenly washed over Orit as she explained to her friend that Moses had proposed to her. "It spooked me," she confided. "I felt like I had conned him or something."

"What do you mean?" Azure seemed suddenly very intent and earnest. "You don't love him?"

"I do," Orit admitted. "I love him very much, but I could never quite make out how to love him as anything more than a friend."

"You don't think he is smart or handsome enough?" Azure wondered.

"It's not that," Orit explained as her eyes pensively wandered past Azure towards the band wailing away on stage. "He is very smart and handsome enough, to be sure." She paused, unable to locate adequate enough words with which to explained.

"Then what is it?" Azure slightly shook her head while shrugging her shoulders.

"I dunno," Orit desperately tried to find the correct collection of words in her mind. But she was lost for words. "No matter how hard I try to really love him passionately – with eros – I just can't seem to manage it. I can't really explain it better than that. I want to feel that eros level of love for him, but it's always more philia or agape than eros. He's such a good guy, such a sweet man. He just deserves so much better than me, than what I am able to provide." Orit's head hung slightly, exhibiting the shame of a sinful Catholic after a particularly revelatory confessional. Azure was her de facto priest.

Azure placed her index finger under Orit's chin and slightly lifted her friend's head in order to make deep eye-contact. She stared into Orit's soul for what, due in part to the psilocybin, seemed like a minute; the rest of the world seemed to slow down and blur all around them. She then leaned in and kissed Orit passionately. Orit at first flinched frightenedly, and then fell deeply and passionately under Azure's seductive spell.

The bartender tried not to stare, but was enthralled at such a novel spectacle. He was somewhat put out when another patron broke his observation of the new lovers' kiss by being asked to fetch a beer. The bartender's annoyance, however, shifted quickly to panic as the front door to the juke joint was battered off its hinges by a marauding cadre of Dade County Sheriff Deputies who bum-rushed the establishment hollering manically and wildly swinging their batons, chopping down revelers as though they were stalks of sugarcane.

The brass band up on stage stopped playing and scrambled towards the back of the establishment in the hopes of escaping with their health and livelihoods intact. Azure latched tightly to Orit's hand and chased after the band, who she assumed knew the most expedient way to escape the building. Outside the juke joint, the band frantically piled into two jalopies and a pickup truck. The majority of them did not even bother to case their instruments, their most prized possessions and source of livelihoods.

"Please," Azure beseeched the trombonist as he jumped into the driver's seats of the truck, "I'd be ever so grateful if you'd be willing to take my friend and me to the Royal Palm Hotel."

"Sorry, ladies," the man, whose lips were puffy, swollen and sore from playing his trombone all night, huffed, "can't do it. It's too dangerous to leave Colored Town after dark, what with these goddamn sundown laws. Ain't too keen on temptin' the devil no more this evenin'."

"Please," Azure pleaded while revealing a sweaty wad of cash from the lining of her bra, "there's a killer on the loose. You're not going to let two ladies walk back uptown in the middle of the goddamn night, are you? I'd be glad to pay you handsomely for your trouble and risk."

"How much?" the trombone player asked nervously while firing the grumbling engine of the truck up. The other members of his band that had piled into the two jalopies had already fled the parking lot.

"All of it," Azure said while plopping the soggy wad of cash in the driver's lap. He looked queryingly at the tuba player in the front-side passenger seat. The tuba player shrugged his shoulders and nodded ever so slightly. "Make up your damn mind," he pleaded.

Two enraged police officers hurried out of the back of the juke joint and raced across the lot towards the truck. "Damn it," the trombone player's voice quavered, "hop in, hurry." Azure and Orit lunged and crawled into the back bed of the truck as fast as they could while it was already rolling away from the fast approaching cops who had drawn and aimed their firearms.

One of the cops demanded that the driver "halt!" But the driver was too wise to heed the command. He floored the gas pedal. The truck fishtailed slightly in the dirt that comprised the carpark. The other Deputy fired a shot from his revolver, but it sailed over the truck and lodged in the stop sign nearby. The trombone player hunkered down in his seat so that he could hardly see over the steering wheel as he sped away from the juke joint as fast as the hunk of metal on wheels could go, which was not very fast at all.

Luckily for the trombone player and his passengers, many other patrons of the juke joint and the barkeep ran out to the parking lot hoping to escape the melee, which diverted the deputies' attention.

Orit was oddly thrilled, frightened and fascinated as the humid wind whipped through her hair. She curled nervously against Azure, who cradled her in the nook of her underarm. They seemed to fit together like pieces of a puzzle. Orit found the sweetness of Azure's perfume mixed with pungent and piquant odor of her pheromones to be intoxicating. Orit suddenly and very consciously realized she was under a spell that she was in no hurry at all to crawl out from under.

It did not take the powers that be too terribly long to figure out that the cab idling behind the patrol car with dead Deputy lying in the street next to it belonged to Rhett, who had seemingly fled the grisly murder scene in which a local lawmen had been hacked into pieces by what one would assume was a madman. Quinn's fiancé, Harold, who had witnessed the assault, made an anonymous telephone call to the downtown precinct to alert them that he had seen what appeared to be a Miccosukee man hacking the lawmen with a machete.

Word of the slain officer spread around town fast and destructive as wildfire. Someone crafted a rumor that a black man, rather than Garnet, had killed the cop. Half-dozen black men were lynched in Dade and Broward that night in an odd spectacle in which many white men seemed to feel that they were restoring some semblance of order by creating even more terror and discord in the community.

By 10:00 p.m., however, the consensus was that Garnet was the actual perpetrator. By 11:00 p.m. a lynch party comprised of two-dozen white men donning white hoods and robes had assembled at Biscayne Bay Park. Their caravan first headed out to Lemon City, a predominately black section of Dade County peopled mostly by migrant agricultural workers from the Bahamas where Rhett lived with his mother, Ruby, and little brother, Bernard, who had only just turned thirteen on Halloween.

By 11:30 p.m., the lynch party that had first assembled at Biscayne Bay Park had invaded Ruby's humble bungalow, thereby making private property into their public domain. Two of the white men who comprised the lynch party, both of whom were also police officers, ripped Rhett's mother and brother from their respective beds and forced their victims to lay face flat in the dew covered grass out front of the porch. But the lynch party did not find Rhett. Some Klansmen smacked Rhett's mother and brother around and manhandled them just for fun as the Wizard of the Klan demanded to know where the cabbie was hiding. Neither Rhett's mother nor brother, however, had a clue as to where he was. Ruby, however, was especially desperate to find out. One of the more enterprising Klansmen crawled up into the attic of the bungalow in the hopes of locating Rhett, but instead found crate upon crate of rum and sundry other spirits stowed away.

By midnight the Klan had cleared all the liquor out of the attic and set a torch to the bungalow. Rhett's mother sobbed and wailed about how her attackers were proof of the absence of God's existence – and not just for the damaged and destroyed booze or her razed house, but out of terror for the fate of her eldest son. Ruby held tight to her youngest boy and stared through eyes swollen with tearful fear and anguish as the bungalow disintegrated into glowing orange and charred cinders.

"What'd ya say boys, let's head on over to Miccosukee land?" The gravelly voiced Wizard of the Klan hollered, "those Injuns and niggers tend to be thick as thieves when it comes to helpin' each other evade justice. I'll betcha dimes to donuts that nigger and Injun are on the reservation."

"We can't," another Klansmen lamented. "That's federal land. Fuckin' with the Feds," he added, "that's a hornet's nest we don't dare poke lest we aim for another invasion by the Union Blues."

"To hell with the federal government and the goddamn Injuns they coddle," the Wizard defied. "If that cotton-pickin' coon and Injun think they can kill a white man, an officer of the law no less, in Dade County and get away with it by hidin' out on federal land, they got themselves another thing comin'. Lettin' these diabolical terrorists get away with murder is the first step towards social anarchy. Now load up," he demanded as if he we Custer intending to lead his Calvary into Lakota lands, "let's ride!"

The other Klansmen piled onto the trucks, which sped away from the burning bungalow and into the dark night. Ruby clung tightly to Bernard, who was quietly sobbing. Her eyes gazed disconsolately at the blaze.

By 12:30 a.m. the lynch party had arrived on Miccosukee land, which was a sprawling property spread out across a vast section of the Everglades. It included the Noble Savage, which many in the posse, including the Wizard, had happily patronized in the past. Many were thus somewhat familiar with the lay of the land. There were also several hutched huts, bungalows and houses that had been haphazardly erected over the years; the nicest of which was owned by Garnet, which he built in 1896 by himself as a means of coping with the devastating mourning he had to endure after Goldie's murder. His home was atop the only hill on the property, and was about a quarter-mile from the brothel, which provided a nice vantage point of the sprawling property.

The trucks transporting the two-dozen Klansmen skid to a halt outside the brothel. The vigilantes hurriedly piled from the cabs and beds of the trucks as if ready for war. Climbing out of the back bed of the truck was, however, no easy task for many who comprised the lynch party considering many of them were overweight and were also donning bed sheets that diminished mobility and the ability to see. One of the fatter Klansmen stumbled while departing the back bed of a truck and fell face first in horse manure; his shotgun inadvertently misfired.

A round of buckshot shattered the window to one of the rooms in the brothel. Inside the room, Mizner, who was stark naked, dropped suddenly to the hardwood floor under foot and cowered on the far side of the mattress, using Scarlet's unconscious body as a kind of makeshift bunker. The frightened Miccosukee girl hid under a sheet covered in odd blotches made of dry sweat and cum strains. Scarlet, who was still high due to the especially potent dose of heroin Capone had injected in her hours earlier, did not notice the clattering gunshot, sound of broken glass, or the commotion it caused in the rest of the house and outside of it.

Capone, however, who had been in a room down the hall having intercourse with a young black girl, hurried into Mizner's room buck naked with his pistol cocked and ready to shoot. He cautiously made his way over to the broken window and peaked outside. A small army of men dressed in bedsheets had assembled. Capone, who had feared the shot was fired by Gallo or some other federal agent, was somewhat relieved that the lynch party was not interested in him.

"We know y'all are here somewhere!" The Wizard hollered. His voice echoed across the swamp and up the hill to Garnet's house. Garnet, white-knuckling a chrome Winchester rifle, peaked out the darkened window in his upstairs bedroom overlooking the brothel. He too seemed ready for war, as though he had been anticipating and even hoping for just such an encounter for years. Behind him, illuminated by the kerosene lamp on the end table, sleeping in Garnet's grand canopied bed, Rhett laid perfectly still, his head was bandaged, he was barely breathing, but miraculously alive. A Miccosukee medicine man dressed in a tattered white t-shirt, well-worn blue jeans, black Stetson, and scuffed brown cowboy boots sat in the armchair in the corner of the room facing the bed, earnestly praying in a language foreign to Rhett's ear.

"The nigger and Injun that done killed a white police officer got themselves one minute and not one second longer to turn their persons over to white justice," The Wizard declared. "You got one minute startin' now or we burn this whole godforsaken village to the ground."

Garnet, with bated breath, peered down the hill as some Klansmen began to light torches and approach the brothel. Two other Klansmen cautiously walked up onto the porch of the brothel and waited for their order to torch the place.

"Your minute has expired!" The Wizard declared his beady and menacing eyes peered from the slit in his hood at the modest watch wrapped tight around his wrist. "Y'all boys left us no choice but to raze this village in the name of universal law."

Capone peaked out the window. He seemed frightened that the building he was in was about to be set ablaze. He thus fired a shot through the broken windowpane. The bullet lodged in one of the trucks in the lynch party's caravan. Exhaust fumes spewed from the engine block. Many Klansmen, thinking they were under attack, fled for cover, including the two on the front porch of the brothel. One of the two inadvertently dropped his torch while fleeing. The porch caught fire.

Small and fast approaching headlights suddenly appeared in the vast darkness that seemed to stretch for eons around the brothel turned inferno. Beauregard and Gallo arrived at the scene. Inside, Capone shoved his clothes and shoes into the suitcase that harbored his heroin. He then pushes the suitcase out of the open window and crawled through. Mizner – who was also stark naked – scurried from a first-floor window at the back end of the house and made a break for a dark thicket of forest. The young Miccosukee girl and Capone pushed Scarlet's listless and naked body through the opened window, which caused cuts and abrasions to form on her breasts, torso and legs.

Luckily, everyone in the domicile managed to escape the fire unharmed by racing out the back windows and doors. The panic that had ensued amongst everyone also provided opportunity for Capone, Mizner and Scarlet, who was draped over Capone's shoulder, to escape into a nearby thicket of woods undetected by any of the Klansmen or lawmen that had arrived at the scene. Mizner, who, unlike Capone, did not think to retrieve his clothes while fleeing the fire, cowered in the woods nearby a while and watched as the conflict up the hill intensified.

By 1:00 a.m. the Noble Savage was a pile of smoldering cinders. Capone hurriedly pulled his trousers on. He then dragged Scarlet and his suitcase through mud and over rocks to his roadster; he plopped her in the back of his car. He regretted that the seat of his beloved roadster was soiled with mud and a bit of Scarlet's blood. But his primary fear and greatest focus at that particular moment was being apprehended by Gallo, who had cautiously made his way up the hill with his pistol drawn towards Garnet's house. Gallo, in short, did not even notice Capone's roadster as it sped away from Miccosukee land. His car passed another car with a reporter and photographer inside en route to the scene.

A terribly disheveled Mr. Ingram, who was still wearing his bathrobe and slippers, arrived with Emory moments after Gallo and Beauregard had arrived on the scene. Gallo warned the Klansmen that they had no jurisdiction on federal land and that they all could be arrested for trespassing and arson. He was, however, far more interested in arresting Garnet, who he believed was the most likely suspect in the recent murders of which the special agent had been sent to Miami to investigate.

"I have a warrant here to search any and every property on this land in order to execute an arrest of Garnet Reynolds," Gallo declared. "This is federal property and I thus have a right to enter any domicile on this land with impunity in order to locate Mr. Reynolds, who is hereby wanted for capital murder. I have an arrest warrant for Mr. Reynolds and I do not plan to leave Miccosukee land until the order has been executed.

Garnet swallowed hard as he peered around the curtain and down the hill at Gallo, who held the warrant aloft as if a preacher holding the Good Book.

"Please Garnet," Mr. Ingram hollered while climbing out of the driver's seat of his car, "I know you did not commit the crimes you have been accused of. If you can hear me, please come out. I know you do not want any more trouble to come here. The sooner you turn yourself in, the sooner we can sort through this goddamn mess." He shielded his eyes when the photographer took his photo.

"Tell him about the lawyer," Emory reminded his father.

"We will get you the finest legal counsel available," Mr. Ingram promised, "you have my word."

"The men assembled at the foot of the hill near the smoldering structure waited anxiously for more than a minute. But Garnet did not reveal himself.

"You leave me no option," Gallo said while starting up the hill with his gun in one hand and the warrant in the other. He was followed closely by Beauregard, who was followed closely by a few Klan members. Those men were followed closely by Mr. Ingram, who was determined to see to it that none of Garnet's human rights were violated as he was taken into custody. Garnet feared that if the lawmen were to enter his home that they would take Rhett into custody too; or worse yet, castrate him and stuff his genitals into his mouth until he suffocated to death. Garnet thus took a deep and steady breath as he readied his shotgun to unleash death on anyone who entered his home. "Don't do it," the medicine man urged, "they'll kill us all." Garnet thus reluctantly handed the shotgun to the medicine man and urged, "Please stay with him until he makes it through the woods." The medicine man nodded compliantly. Garnet then cautiously made his way down the stairs and onto the front porch of the house with his hands held high above his head. "Let's just get this over with," he said.

Capone, who had Scarlet draped over his shoulder and a suitcase in his hand, scurried from the parking lot into the lobby of the Royal Palm. Capone donned only his trousers. But the snoring concierge behind the reception desk was sound asleep, and thus did not notice the half-naked gangster and reigning Miss Orange Blossom, who was completely nude and covered in scrapes and mud, draped over his shoulder.

Capone's aching legs quavered as he hurried onto the elevator. He finally dropped Scarlet like a sack of wet hammers after the elevator door slid shut. He bent and planted the palms of his hands atop his knees in desperate effort to catch his breath. The elevator doors slid open. He then dragged Scarlet's listless body across the Persian rugs lining the third story hallway, but struggled to unlock and open the door, partly due to fear that some other hotel guest might see and report him.

He, however, finally managed to open the door leading into his suite, where he draped Scarlet across the bed, then doused her with a full glass of cold water and slapped her soaked face a bit, which gradually lulled her from her stupor.

"I was startin' to think you was dead," Capone sneered. "I was afraid I was gonna have to dump your body in a swamp.

You might have overdosed. Whatever you do, don't go to sleep. You might never wake up again." He then took off his trousers and closed himself in the bathroom. The sound of running water from the shower sounded through the wall.

Scarlet, whose first thought upon waking was of Jasper, slowly made her way from the bed and wiped a bit of grogginess from her eyes, then wrapped her body in a plush and fluffy white bathrobe provided by the hotel upon check-in. She then went over to the exit of the suite, slowly opened the door, and peaked outside into the hallway. Orit, whose hair was mussed and dress was wrinkled and who had her shoes tucked tightly under her arm, quietly exited Azure's suite and quietly hurried down the hallway in the opposite direction from Scarlet, and then shut and secluded herself in her dimly lit suite. She had not noticed that Scarlet had observed her abscond from Azure's room.

Scarlet then made her way cautiously down the hall to Azure's suite. There, with bated breath she slowly twisted the door handle. Scarlet's tired but curious eyes peered into the shadowy gray light of dawn that seemed to fill the room. She saw Azure, who donned a skimpy black negligée, lying on her side with her faced towards the open window and her back towards the intruder. Azure's face was illuminated by a moon beam coming in from the window. She sat up suddenly and glanced suspiciously around the room, sensing she was being watched. Her dark, quizzical and concerned eyes scanned the seemingly haunted room, and then settled on the closed door, which she stared at a moment. She then laid her head back atop the pillow and gazed out the window a moment before closing her eyes.

CHAPTER SEVENTEEN

Monday, November 3, 1919

Even in the least trying of times Scarlet was insomniac. Her chest was often very tight due to stress, which made it tough for her to breathe. Her mind was also most often full of thoughts that raced by and back around as if on a carousel. Even coming down hard from a heroin high, she could not turn off the tidal wave of emotion inducing thoughts that churned in her heart and mind. Capone snoring loudly in the bed next to her did not help matters. She thus opted to take a long and hot bath in the hopes of quelling the anxiety tying her in knots.

Her hair was still sopping wet as she dressed herself after her bath in one of the new outfits Capone had bought her. She places the rest of her belongings quietly into a paper Sears shopping bag, and then looked upon Capone a moment. She did not exhibit any positive or negative emotion. She just gazed at him with a blank thousand-yard stare. She then exhaled deeply and absconded from the suite. The sound of the door clicking shut behind her did not wake Capone.

Scarlet made her way onto the elevator, which whisked her quickly down to the lobby. The concierge is asleep with his head atop the reception desk. Scarlet jars him awake by ringing the bell next to his head.

"Yes," he huffed, "what is it I can help you with, young lady?"

"That light-skinned Negro horn player," Scarlet broached, "what room is he in?"

"I'm very sorry, Miss," the concierge said while gazing beyond her at the early morning sunlight soaking into the sprawling front lawn of the hotel, "it is hotel policy to not give out room numbers of guests unless previously alerted by said guest."

"Maybe so," Scarlet glared arrogantly, "but the Negro ain't no guest. He's an employee."

"I suppose that's true," the increasingly vexed concierge said while rubbing sleep from his tired eyes, "but I'm not at license to give out his room number either. You're more than welcome to have a seat on one of the sofas next to the elevator and wait for him to come down, if you like." He forced a semi-polite smile.

"Do you know who I am?" she demanded.

"I'm quite sure I do not," the concierge tried not to laugh at her arrogance.

"I'm the reigning Miss Orange Blossom!"

"I was under the impression that the mayor's daughter had won the contest," he smirked antagonistically.

"Yeah," Scarlet continued, "she is dead, so now I'm her majesty, as it were."

"Be that as it may," the concierge sneered, "I am not at liberty to supply room numbers of the hotel's guests or employees."

"Do you have any idea at all who I am stayin' here with?" Scarlet's sudden burst of startled the man.

"I'm quite sure I don't," the concierge admitted while slightly rolling his eyes.

"Al Capone," Scarlet said, "you know, scar face, the gangster. You may have read about him in the papers."

"I see," the concierge's resistance transformed fast into trepidation. "Mr. Capone is an admired businessman and welcomed guest at this hotel."

"He's a goddamn killer," Scarlet blurted impatiently while staring deep into the concierge's nervous and blanching eyes. "He has bought me a trumpet lesson with that Negro boy in the employ of this hotel. You see, I am already runnin' late for my lesson. Mr. Capone is goin' to be none too pleased with you when he learns that you have refused my very simple request and thus have ruined my birthday present due to your unwillingness to be even slightly helpful."

"My goodness," the concierge said sweetly and attentively while flipping through the big and leathery registry book atop the desk, "you're too right, ma'am," he confessed. "I'm very sorry indeed. It's just with all this mayhem going on the past week, I need be very careful. But you seem like a very nice young lady," he added as if unnerved. "Certainly you'd have to be if Mr. Capone has taken a liking to you." He forced a toothy and rather clownish smile. His eyes, however, belied fear.

"I understand completely," Scarlet grinned wryly.

"Mr. Jackson is in room 227," the concierge said while motioning towards the elevator at the other end of the lobby. "You just take one flight up to the second floor. It'll be down the hall on your right. You can't miss it."

Scarlet nodded her head appreciatively, then strode confidently towards the elevator with her shopping bag stuffed full of her belongings in hand. Orit, wearing a bathing suit with a towel draped over her shoulders, passed her. They share a cordial grin. Scarlet pressed the 3-button while watching Orit make her ways towards the pool deck. The concierge's forced saccharin smile transformed into a glowering scowl the moment the elevator doors slid shut.

Orit sipped her black coffee on the shaded veranda by the pool while reading the morning edition of *The Miami Herald*. Some children nearby her chair excitedly splashed about and did jackknifes and cannonballs into the deep-end of the pool. She instead lowered her dark sunglasses and peered up at one of the third-story windows of the hotel, half-hoping she might catch a glimpse of Azure.

Inside the hotel, on the third story, a Japanese woman named Yamoto was navigating a maid's cart through the hallway. She stopped suddenly at a closed suite door and knocked. "Housekeeping," she seemed to labor to make the words legible through her thick accent, and then waited for a response. None came. She thus knocked once more and waited a bit less patiently than she had the first time. But again, no reply came.

She thus unlocked the door to the suite and entered. Her gentle and dark eyes took a moment to adjust to the dimness of the room. Her hand rubbed the wall in search of the light switch. She noticed the bay window was gaping open and wind was causing the curtains to flap and flail. She was somewhat embarrassed as she noticed someone under the blanket in the bed. "I'm so sorry," the words seemed to tumble from her mouth as if made of marbles. "I knocked, but there was no reply. Please excuse me."

She bowed politely and then started to back her cart into the hallway. She froze and peered a bit harder into the darkness at the body in the bed. A sudden sense of dread and peril overloaded her sense of barging embarrassment as she finally properly processed the fact that there was a distinct stream of blood leading from the white bed sheets to the floor, where a pool of blood had soaked into the rug. She took a hard step back towards the suite's exit but smacked into the wall, which dazed her somewhat. She fell to a knee. Fear that someone who aimed to do her harm mixed with curiosity of what had already happened compelled her to glance back up at the bed. She noticed a golden envelope opener jutting out of a woman's neck. She did not immediately recognize the bloated face with eyes bulging from the skull. She was frantic as she pulled back the bedspread a bit.

Yamoto then noticed the woman as the beautiful Cubana singer who had a residence at the hotel. Azure's nude, blue, and bloated body appeared, due to the bruises and markings on her neck, to have the life strangled from it with the wire coat hanger next to the bed sometime in the night. Yamoto then sprinted from the suite hollering, "Satsu! Satsu! Satsu!" which translates to "Murder! Murder! Murder!"

The sounds of the maid's shrill horror sent a chill running up the skin of Orit's sun kissed arms. She dropped her porcelain cup full of black coffee, which shattered atop the pool deck. She then hurried into the hotel, across the lobby, and onto the elevator and nearly collided with Al Capone, who was just exiting the elevator into the lobby.

When the elevator doors finally slid open, Orit sprinted past Yamoto, who was on the floor sobbing and mumbling a Shinto prayer in her native tongue. Orit then stopped at the open doorway leading into the suite. "Azure?" Orit's voice quivered as if she were trying to fight the urge to cry. "Azure?"

The doors to the elevator popped open on the second story of the hotel. Scarlet strolled confidently down the hallway until coming upon room 227. She took a deep and composed breath and then banged on the door. She waited for nearly a minute. But nobody answered. She thus banged on it more loudly and persistently.

After more than another minute, Jasper, who donned nothing but white boxer shorts and black socks, was especially groggy and dazed as he inched the door open and squinted into the brightly lit hallway. He was quite surprised and somewhat delighted to find Scarlet, who was covered in scrapes due to her ordeal the previous night. She could sense his happiness at her surprising him, so she dropped her shopping bag on the Persian rug and draped her arms lovingly around the back of his neck and kissed him passionately. He was, due to the fact that he had never kissed a white girl before, as scared as he was excited and enamored. He thus pried his mouth from hers and nervously poked his head into the hallway to ensure that no one had witnessed the kiss. The coast was clear so he scooped her up and carried her into the room and tossed her atop the bed, and then fast snatched her shopping bag up from the hallway floor and tossed it under the bed. He then locked the door behind him and plopped atop the bed next to Scarlet and ravenously kissed her neck.

Scarlet's eyes had adjusted somewhat to the dimness. She thus noticed the syringe and spoon on the nightstand next to the bed. A soothed sense of relief washed over her. She then kissed Jasper gently on his pursed and swollen lips. "I sure could go for a shower and shot of heroin," she seduced.

"Reckon I could use a hit," Jasper said while inching towards the nightstand.

"We got to go someplace far," Scarlet urged.

"Where to?" Jasper asked while keeping his eyes keenly trained on the flame from his lighter boiling the viscous spoonful of heroin.

"Anywhere but here," Scarlet explained. "It's only a matter of time before Al figures out that I left him. He'll kill us both, unless he can't find us."

"Does he know you're with me?" Jasper asked, unnerved as the needle slurped up the brown liquid into the plastic measuring tube.

"Hell no," she insisted. Her terse words, however, provided Jasper little comfort.

"I don't get paid until Friday," Jasper explained. "Besides, I've been hired as a resident horn player until the end of the season. This is a good gig for me."

"Well," she said, "why don't we go to Hollywood? Men have told me I was pretty enough to be in pictures since I was a little girl. Don't you think I'm pretty enough to be in the pictures?" Her bashful eyes batted slightly flirtatiously, as if she were trying to harness and fully exploit the power deeply embedded in her natural charm, charisma and physical beauty.

"You'z the prettiest white girl I ever seen," Jasper conceded while flicking the side of the syringe with his middle finger. "That's for damn sure."

"Then it's settled," she said excitedly while sitting up abruptly in the bed. "We'll go to Hollywood! That's really where I'm meant to be anyway."

"You got some money I don't know about, or somethin'?" Jasper asked quizzically while tying a soiled black sock tight around Scarlet's upper arm. The vein in her forearm bulged and pulsated. "Cuz," Jasper added, "I don't think we got enough money to make it all the way to Hollywood. I spent my last bit of cash on the train ticket here. I'm broke until Friday."

"We can't wait until Friday," she huffed. "I reckon I can steal Al's gun," she said. "Why don't we just knock over that Bank of America on Flagler Ave? We'll be in Hollywood before you can say 'Action.'"

"We gonna rob us a bank?" Jasper chortled and half-grinned as he scooched a bit closer to Scarlet. "You not just the prettiest white girl I ever seen," he said as he smooched the supple nape of her neck, "you'z also the craziest I ever met."

"Why can't I knock over bank, because I'm not a man?" she blurted offendedly while displaying her index fingers for him to look at. "These here fingers can pull a trigger just like a man's can. Besides, those bankers don't think twice of robbin' everyone else blind. What's to stop us from walkin' in there, wavin' Al's pistol in the teller's face, then hightailin' it for California? You said yourself that I's pretty enough to be in pictures. Hell, maybe you can be in pictures too; not as a leading man like Rudolph Valentino or Al Jolson, of course, but maybe as a savage in the background of somethin'. I seen a nigger playin' an aborigine in *Tarzan* last month."

"You really think so?" Jasper enthused.

"Why not?" she shrugged her shoulders nonchalantly while asking rhetorically.

"Wouldn't that be somethin'?" he gushed excitedly as his big brown eyes gazed at the horizon outside the window. "Jasper Jackson up on the silver screen. Say, you think them boys out in Hollywood would ever let me play my horn on the big screen?"

"I don't see why not," Scarlet said confidently as her new beau rubbed her protruding forearm vein with a cotton swab doused in rubbing alcohol. "I seen Louis Armstrong play his horn in a newsreel before," Scarlet added while anxiously awaiting her next dose of heroin. "I'm sure you can't be any worse at playin' the trumpet than that fella is."

He glanced at her, somewhat offended that she could not decipher Louis Armstrong's virtuosity, but ignored the slight of his hero as best he could. He then plunged the syringe full of heroin into the bulging vein in Scarlet's forearm, emptying half the contents into her bloodstream. A deep breath seeped from her body. Her eyes rolled back in her head as she sunk into the mattress.

"That's the stuff dreams are made of," she mumbled while smiling. Hot tears streamed down her suddenly calm and grateful cheeks. Jasper slowly removed the needle from his lover's arm and carefully licked it. Scarlet stared at him a moment, then everything faded to brown, then the deepest shade of black imaginable.

Jasper then tied the sock around his arm, rubbed and blotted his vein with the acerbic cotton swab, and was just about to plunge the needle into his own arm when he heard "Satsu! Satsu! Satsu!" seep through the wooden ceiling overhead. Jasper was somewhat frightened by what he assumed was some kind of cry for help. He looked over at Scarlet. A soothed, warm and contented grin formed across her round and pale face.

Gallo, donning his black three-piece suit and starched white shirt, sat at the head of a long conference-room table in a second-story room at the Dade County Sheriff's Office. Mid-morning sunlight flooded into the room through the window. Across the table from him sat two apparently learned white men. One of the FBI's coroner and an anthropologist hired by Gallo, both of whom also donned black three-piece suits and starched shirts, carefully examined documents and evidence that had been contained in manila folders stacked one on top of the other atop the table.

"What's the verdict, Dr. Newman?" Gallo asked the coroner.

"Some of it is quite surprising," Newman said while pushing his spectacle from the bridge of his nose. "Cause of death was not the heroin or strangulation."

"You're joking?" Gallo bemused. "What in God's name was the cause of death, then?"

"Poisoning," the coroner said as he slid his official report across the table towards Gallo. "I detected traces of battery acid in both the local victims' bloodstream. My guess is that battery acid was mixed with some substance, perhaps water, and then injected into the victims' bloodstream. Strangulation most likely occurred after the victim was unconscious or dead."

"I'll be damned," Gallo's mind seemed blown. "What do you think, Professor Varon?" he asked the anthropologist who had been summoned from the research agenda he had undertaken at Harvard, in Cambridge, Massachusetts. His scholarship, as it were, was mostly famed for his very precise skull measurements taken from cadavers from some of the furthest recesses of the scientific imperium of which he was a member. The data from said measurements was most often employed to form erroneous conjectures regarding which skulls belonged to the more racially inferior and were thus least fit races for survival.

"After interviewing the red man," the anthropologist explained of Garnet in a thick Bavarian accent, "I am no less convinced that he is the primary suspect in these ritual killings by a savage hellbent on revenge."

"Revenge for what?" Gallo was frustrated. "From what we have gathered, he did not even know these girls."

"Ah, but you see," the anthropologist qualified, "it does not matter whether he knows them or not. The red man admitted that his lover was killed many years ago by a white man or men who built the railroad. He also admitted that he believes that the white man has created more problems than solutions since arriving in the New World in the fifteenth century. He admitted to knowing that Europeans had brought citrus trees with them from the Old World. The citrus employed in these heinous crimes could be a symbol of what the red man believes to be the rape of the natives of this continent by Europeans. The use of citrus in the assaults are, I believe, evidence of the red man's psychotic ritualistic revenge on not these girls, per se, but on our entire race. I'm quite certain your serial killer is the red man sitting in a holding cell in the basement of this building."

"The Ingram's gave the Injun an alibi for the girl murdered in Brunswick," Gallo grunted frustratedly.

"It is entirely possible that they are lying," the anthropologist reminded Gallo. "Or perhaps there are, in fact, two killers. Your savage could have heard of the killing in Georgia, and then copied it in order to have an embedded alibi."

"What do you think, Dr. Newman?" Gallo, who seemed unconvinced, asked the coroner.

"I think it is a plausible explanation," he said. "If you were a savage, wouldn't you want a taste of revenge too?"

Gallo's attention was then lured toward the door of the conference room, which swung open suddenly. Beauregard, who was huffing and puffing, out of breath and covered in sweat, seemed to fill the entire doorway.

"What is it?" Gallo, who was deeply concerned, asked.

"There was another killin' at the Royal Palm," Beauregard wheezed. "We gotta get over there."

Gallo hurried from the room with Beauregard, trying to catch his breath, lumbering behind. Mr. Mizner, who was donning a navy-blue pinstripe suit and matching fedora, intercepted them on the staircase. "Special Agent Gallo," he demanded while extending his hand, "I'd like a word with you."

Gallo quickly shook Mizner's hand on his way out of the building. Beauregard, now covered in a film of perspiration, had made his way down the steps and hurried after Gallo. "I'm sorry, sir," Gallo said as politely as he could under such immense stress, "but," he added, "I need to get to the Royal Palm at once. I'd be very glad to speak with you at a later date if you had an appointment."

"You've heard about the murder at the Royal Palm, then?" Mizner persisted as he followed Gallo out of the building. Dark gray storm clouds that blocked out the sun seemed to form suddenly overhead. Gallo did not answer the question. "I can save you a trip to the hotel," Mizner said. "I know who the killer is, and it's not the Injun."

Gallo stopped in his tracks and glared hard at Mizner. Beauregard finally waddled up. The Sheriff placed his bear-paw-like hands on his knees and bent over as he tried to pull heavy and humid air into his inflamed lungs.

"What are you driving at, sir?" Gallo demanded of Mizner.

"It's that commie kike reporter," Mizner declared. "She's the killer. She's got to be the primary suspect, anyway."

"What in God's name are you talkin' about, Mr. Mizner?" Beauregard wheezed. "She's nearly a foot shorter and twenty-five pounds lighter than Mrs. Fisher. How in the hell is a little girl like that is goin' to be able to kill a person that much bigger?"

"With battery acid," Gallo said matter-of-factly. "The killer poisoned his victims and strangled them after they were already dead."

"All this goddamned gore and mayhem arrived when that Bolshevik arrived," Mizner seethed. "For all we know she is part of some grand communist conspiracy to undermine the future of Miami and American capitalism in one fell swoop. If the bubble bursts here, it'll burst everywhere else across this grand economy, just you wait. She's not content to destroy the real estate industry with her bullshit stories and reports, now she's trying to make our fair city into the murder capital of America. And for what? To sell some goddamn pinko rag! Terrifying tourists and would be homebuyers with these horrendous murders is the quickest way to destroy Miami, which will be the first domino to collapse in on this glorious free market!"

"There's no way a woman could have done all this," Beauregard wheezed. "I just don't see how."

"Don't let one of these goddamn suffragettes hear you say something like that," Mizner scoffed sarcastically. "Besides, rumor has it that the reporter and the singer had gotten a bit too cozy for comfort, if you catch my drift. Maybe the singer said something the kike didn't like, so the kike killed her."

"It is usually a lover that does the killin' in this kind of situation," Beauregard conceded.

"We know the killer is not the red man," Gallo was pained to admit. "He was on ice last night. There's no way he could have killed the singer from inside a holding cell. The reporter is the best suspect we have, hands down. For all we know she was in Georgia last week. We need to at least pick her up until we know for certain."

Gallo and Beauregard hustled to the patrol car parked along Flagler Avenue. Mizner was pleased and somewhat relieved as he walked in the opposite direction. He then noticed a man hunched over atop the sidewalk on the other side of the avenue. The man appeared malnourished, sun stroked and dazed. "You there," Mizner called out to the man, "is everything all right?"

The grizzled man, Scarlet'sd father Edmund, looked up at Mizner with sullen and psychotic eyes. "A reckonin' is comin'," Edmund declared in a booming voice. "Mark my words. A reckonin' is most assuredly comin'."

"Jackson Memorial Hospital is just a few blocks over," Mizner said while smiling wryly as he climbed into the driver's seat of his automobile. "They can fix you right up over there. Do be sure to stay off the streets. We don't want you itinerants eschewing patrons away from our fair city, do we now?" Mizner then lit a cigar and motored away, brimming with gleeful optimism that order would soon be restored before too much more mayhem could be done to the city's already inglorious reputation.

"A reckonin' is most assuredly comin'!" Edmund cried out as a steady rain began to fall. "You mark my words!"

Jasper, who was sitting in the lobby dazedly polishing his horn, was suddenly alerted to Mr. Capone, who donned a pair of canary yellow swimming trunks, a tight white t-shirt, and flip-flops on his unkempt feet, exit the elevator and make his way determinedly across the lobby's marble floor. Capone spoke fast and forcefully to the effete concierge behind the reception desk. But Jasper could not make out what had been said.

Capone had, in fact, ordered the concierge to immediately alert him if the latter were to spot Scarlet anywhere on the hotel grounds. Capone's hands seemed to strangle the lily-white towel he held as he feverishly spoke to the concierge, who, though terrified to make eye contact, hung on every word as though his life depended on it. Capone then pushed his dark wayfarer sunglasses firm against his face and exited the lobby bound for the pool and grotto out back.

Jasper tried to seem inconspicuous as he shoved his horn into its case and then slinked from the couch in the lobby and slid onto the elevator just as the doors were sliding shut. He stopped at the second floor, and then hurried from the elevator into the hallway as soon as the doors opened wide enough to let him out. He sprinted down the hall to suite 227 and burst inside.

"It's time!" he blurted while shoving the horn case under the bed. "We gotta hurry!"

"He's gone?" Scarlet said as she sat up excitedly in the bed. "You're sure he's gone?"

"He's sunbathing out at the pool," Jasper explained. "I just saw him. Now move your ass."

Scarlet hopped out from under the covers and ran from the room and down the hall towards the elevator as fast as her toned legs could carry her. She, however, forgot to put her shoes on. She had already frantically pushed the 3-button several times by the time Jasper had caught up to her inside the elevator. He looked quizzically down at her bare feet, but was so fretful of the time constraints involved in the plot that he did not bother to mention that she had forgot her shoes, never mind return to his suite to retrieve them.

The couple had arrived at the third floor of the hotel in less than a minute. Both Jasper and Scarlet had a bit of difficulty concealing their nervousness as they tried to look nonchalant while briskly walking down the hallway towards Capone's suite. Scarlet's slight and trembling hand twisted the door to Capone's suite in the hopes of entering. But the door was locked. She thus furtively pulled a bobbi pin that pegged a golden lock behind her ear and tried to jimmy the lock, like she had seen Capone do before in order to get into Gallo's suite. But her nervous and trembling hands could not manage the task.

Jasper thus snatched the pin wedged between her thumb and forefinger, then tried to pick the lock, but had no more success than Scarlet had had in her failed attempt. Both were spooked by the ping sound emitted by the elevator arriving at the third floor. Scarlet's frightened and anticipatory eyes stared at the elevator. She, fearing it might be Capone arriving to kill her, momentarily stopped breathing. The elevator doors slid open.

Emory pushed his way from the elevator onto the hallway. He seemed in a fog. Scarlet could breathe again. "Hey Jasper," Emory slurred slightly while smiling somewhat cordially. "I've not seen you around in a few days. I sure could use some more of that medicine. My supply is waning but my tolerance is rising."

"Sure boss," Jasper, though obviously unnerved, tried to play it cool. "I can bring some by later on, if you like."

"Can you drop by before your set tonight?" Emory hoped.

"Sure thing, boss," Jasper said diffidently. His nervous and ashamed eyes stared down at the Persian carpet under foot.

"Is anything the matter?" Emory, suddenly noticing that Jasper and his companion seemed terribly suspicious, asked.

"He's just not feeling very well," Scarlet blurted while grabbing Jasper's hand. "He needs some of that special medicine too, I reckon." She then led Jasper down the hall towards the elevator by his hand.

"See you tonight," Jasper assured Emory while glancing back over his shoulder. Emory watched them with hardly concealed suspicion until the elevator door slid shut behind the teenagers. He then unlocked the door to his suite and rolled inside. His shrine to Quinn still occupied the bureau in the bedroom, though the candles had been blown out. He thus straightened her picture a tad so that it was perfectly upright, then lit a slender white candle, lurched from his chair onto the hardwood floor, and began to undress.

Down in the hotel lobby, Scarlet walked determinedly towards the reception desk. The concierge was full of dread the moment he noticed her approach. Jasper tried to appear nonchalant as he loitered near the sofa next to the elevator, which made him seem particularly conspicuous. "I need a key to Mr. Capone's suite," Scarlet demanded of the concierge, who was somewhat stunned that Scarlet appeared eager to locate a killer who was evidently very angry with her. The concierge opened his mouth to speak, but only illegible stammering trampled out. "Come on, goddamn you," Scarlet snapped impatiently and slapped the desk hard. "Mr. Capone is waiting for me to fetch his cigar case, now quit dawldlin'." The concierge aggrievedly furnished a key to the suite.

Scarlet then hurried back across the lobby and onto the elevator. The concierge was too busy frantically flagging down a bellhop to notice that Jasper had sneaked onto the elevator after Scarlet. The bellhop alerted by the concierge hurried from the lobby towards the pool deck, where Capone was glistening due to dense humidity coupled with the rays of sunshine being soaked into his pudgy and sweaty physique.

By the time the bellhop was delivering the message to the somewhat perturbed gangster, Scarlet had entered Capone's suite. Jasper hung back in the hallway in order to serve as a lookout. Scarlet frantically rifled through Capone's suitcases and drawers, but could not locate what she was hoping to find.

Back at the pool deck, Capone was hurriedly pulling his flip-flops onto his hairy but pedicured feet. He then ran across the sprawling lawn separating the lush lobby from the luxurious pool deck. He paused a moment at the reception desk, where he exchanged a few tense words with the frightened concierge. He then ran as fast as he could across the lobby. He impatiently mashed his chubby index finger into the up-button several times. But the elevator seemed to take an entire season to arrive. He thus opted to take the stairs.

Scarlet, meanwhile, raced into the bathroom of Capone's suite. She frantically searched through the medicine cabinet, but found nothing worth stealing. Jasper could hear the hum of the elevator ascending. "Hurry the fuck up," he pleaded. "Somebody is comin'."

Scarlet was angry and frustrated as she hurried from the bathroom and into the bedroom. She, however, stopped suddenly at the threshold of the bathroom and glanced back at the black leather satchel sitting atop the tank of the toilet bowl. She hurriedly zipped it open. Capone's 32-caliber revolver was stuffed down at the bottom of the bag next to a quarter-ounce of heroin neatly wrapped in parchment paper and tied with a red bow. She tucked the satchel under her arm as if it were precious cargo and sprinted from the suite. Jasper opportunistically snatched Capone's car keys from atop the dresser and chased after her.

Scarlet feverishly pushed the down-button. But it seemed to take forever and a week for the elevator doors to slide open. Jasper frantically mashed the L-button with his calloused index finger the moment he climbed aboard the elevator. The doors to the downward-bound elevator mercifully slid shut just as Capone entered the hallway from the stairwell. He ran as fast as his portly legs could carry him down the hall. He burst into his ransacked suite hoping to trap Scarlet inside. He noticed immediately that his satchel had been stolen. Capone dropped to his knees and glared under the bed in the hopes of finding Scarlet hiding.

He then raced over to the window and scanned the property where he witnessed Scarlet run out of the lobby below hand-in-hand with her new beau. He vowed to cut his betrayer into tiny pieces with the Swiss Army pocketknife he had cherished since he was nine years old if he were to ever see her again.

Though he was enraged to see Scarlet's new beau steal his car, his greater concern was the small army of local and federal lawmen arriving. He assumed they had arrived to apprehend him.

Scarlet and Jasper were also afraid that Gallo and the other lawmen suddenly arriving at the scene might possibly have come to apprehend them. But that was naïve conjecture on their part. Neither Gallo or Beauregard even noticed as Jasper and Scarlet climbed into Capone's electric blue roadster and hightailed from the parking lot.

Jasper, whose attention was fixed to the road ahead, looked very sickly and disheveled. Scarlet, in stark contrast, was elated as she looked back at the hotel grow smaller and smaller in the distance behind them. "Hollywood, USA, here we come," she gushed joyously. Jasper, however, was consumed by heavy dread.

Orit could hear the sounds of sirens fast approaching outside the window of her suite at the Royal Palm. Her mournful eyes were bloodshot and puffy due to spending much of the morning crying. She was dazed as she stuffed her belongings into her suitcase in the hopes of getting out of Miami on the next available train. Curiosity, however, compelled her to pause packing to gaze forlornly out the window at the scene unfolding on the lawn. She saw Mr. Ingram in what seemed to be a fevered debate with Special Agent Gallo and Sheriff Beauregard near the lobby entrance.

Gallo pushed his way past Mr. Ingram and into the lobby of the hotel, at which point Orit lost sight of him. She thus continued to shove clothes and sundry other items into her suitcase. She finally fastened her luggage shut, retrieved the room key from off the top of the dresser, turned out the light, and then hurried into the hallway towards the elevator.

She did not have to wait long for the elevator to arrive at the third floor of the hotel. Gallo, Beauregard, and Mr. Ingram were all crowded together on the car, which prevented her from climbing aboard.

"Orit Abrahams?" Gallo said while showing his shiny silver FBI badge wedged in his brown leather agency issued wallet in her face.

"Yeah," Orit said matter-of-factly. "I'd like to say it was nice to see you again Special Agent Gallo, but I won't insult your intelligence."

"You're under arrest for capital murder." Gallo resisted the urge to smirk.

"Capital murder?" Orit, who was totally nonplussed, muttered. "You're joking."

Beauregard pried the suitcase from Orit's tight grip. Gallo then turned her around, shoved her face hard into the wall, quickly cuffed her, and manhandled her onto the elevator.

Mr. Ingram was consumed by a tense and uneasy feeling as he stared down the hallway at Emory's room. He realized he had not seen or spoken to his neighbor in days. "I'm going to check in on Emory," he said softly to Mr. Ingram, who nodded appreciatively as he followed the lawmen back onto the elevator. Mr. Ingram quietly knocked on the door to Emory's suite while Orit was being briskly escorted through the lobby downstairs.

Inside the suite, Emory's naked body was covered in a film of sweat and sprawled on the hardwood floor next to the shrine he had created to Quinn. Viscous and yellowish foam seeped from his mouth. A syringe emptied of its contents jutted from his arm. His body writhed and convulsed, but he did not regain consciousness. He was way down deep in a dark memory his soul was desperately trying to reconcile and to ultimately transcend for the sake of his sanity.

The harrowing incident that haunted him and fueled his addiction happened September 11, 1918, near the end of the war. The air was musty and heavy inside the tiny candlelit cottage on the outskirts of the village of Saint-Mihiel, in the northwest part of France. Emory was curled into a ball in the corner of the cottage with his army green tunic crumbled under his head like a musty and coarse pillow. A vibrant Valencia orange given to him by a grateful elderly French woman glad that her village had been liberated from the Germans was tucked tightly under his arm like a beloved stuffed animal that provided comfort.

The other men in Emory's unit, which were part of the American Expeditionary Force under the command of General John Pershing, had been in France little more than a year. But in that time, they were driven relentlessly to punch a hole through the line of der Kaiser's Western Wall so that the British and French could bludgeon into the vital nerve center of the German's heavily industrialized fighting force. The Americans suffered terrible and catastrophic losses at the Battle of Saint-Mihiel, but emerged from the fray with their objectives won; the German lines had been forced back a few hundred yards.

Some of the boys in Emory's unit fondly referred to themselves as "Pershing's Cowpokes" due to the fact that they hailed from Texas, as well as New Mexico and Arizona. The soldiers from Arizona and New Mexico were especially gung-ho to prove themselves as true American fighting men, and only partly because of their insecurity over the fact that the states they hailed from were only officially part of the Union for less than five years respectively by the time the AEF had landed in France. Florida was admitted to the Union in 1845, though most Floridians continued to identify more with the values of the Confederacy had fought to preserve, namely the protection of white supremacy. But most members of the AEF, truth be told, no matter where they hailed from, were in France simply because their number had been called during the Draft, which predominately targeted working class men. But Emory, who was by no means working class, had not been drafted; he had volunteered, a fact that haunted him from the moment he left for boot camp.

The sense of emasculated insecurity that had first lured the lad into joining the military was not the sinking of the *Lusitania*, or some desire to heed President Wilson's outlandish call to defend democracy, nor to bat back the Hun, which the propaganda posters along Flagler Avenue urged him to do. None of that mattered to Emory, who was determined to prove to himself that he was a man of merit, and not simply his father's privileged and overprotected protégé. By the time Emory had graduated from high school at the tender age of eighteen, four years prior, his father was a veritable baron of Miami – Mr. Flagler's right-hand man. Not only was Mr. Ingram known for being a widowed teetotaler in a city full of drunkards, he also had the renowned reputation of having hosted some of the Magic City's most memorable parties, many of which were happily attended by some of America's most renowned socialites, including Addison Mizner, Margaret Singer, H.R. Repogle, Cornelius Vanderbilt, as well as several members of the Rockefeller and Astor clan. Andrew Carnegie was the first man to have ever played golf at the new course built adjacent to the Royal Palm Resort, which Emory's father had designed.

Emory had been offered a football scholarship to the University of Florida and also Georgia. His father, however, saw little wisdom in the boy risking the loss of his good sense by smashing his head into other college boys. "The whole thing seems a bit queer, if you ask me," Mr. Ingram sneered when Emory showed interest in playing quarterback for the Blue and Orange. "All those silly boys running into each other and rolling around on the ground," Mr. Ingram scoffed. "It was fine when you in in high school. I was happy for your coach to toughen you up a bit and instill a bit of leadership and discipline in you. But the plan has always been for you to learn business under my direction after you received your diploma. College would simply be a waste of time at this juncture," he explained, "and worse yet, a waste of time in which you could be earning some real money and building long-term wealth, rather than naval gazing and rolling around in the grass with other boys who ought to be earning a living too."

Emory thus followed his father's wishes and reluctantly accepted a business apprenticeship under his father's tutelage. His father was, however, like Mr. Flagler had been to him, quick to heap scorn concomitant to being especially stingy with praise. Mr. Ingram had always felt as though he needed to be extra tough on his boy, since Emory had just the one parent to look after him in a town that due to his last name tended to coddle him. Mr. Ingram was keenly aware that most everyone else in Miami who the lad came in contact with was sure to treat him very preciously indeed. But by the time the U.S. had finally joined the allied cause in Europe, Emory was aching for a reason – any reason – to get the hell out from under his father's long and immense shadow.

He knew his father would surely pull strings to get his son out of the line of fire, and thus did not even tell his dad he had joined the AEF until two months after boot camp, when Emory was already in France. He waited even longer to inform his girlfriend, Quinn, who was his high school sweetheart, until many months after he broke the harrowing news to his father. His father was, as expected, fiercely determined to get Emory out of harm's way, but it was too late. Emory had distinguished himself and been promoted. General Pershing thus refused to let Emory leave until the war was won. Despite Emory's acumen as a soldier, there was not a single day that passed since boot camp began that the lad did not consider killing himself for making such a fatefully stupid decision. But he was stuck and had to manage the mindless misery of war, by any means necessary.

The men in Emory's unit were held over a few days in in Saint-Mihiel, a quaint little village they had pried back from the German invaders whilst the unit awaited orders to prepare for the Meuse-Argonne Offensive. Saint-Mihiel was no larger in sum than the size of five football fields combined, and was comprised of a rapidly decaying Catholic Church with a spire nearly three stories tall, a bombed-out town hall, and a cobblestone market square where the farmers who tended the lands surrounding the village traded their goods and wares on Saturday mornings.

Pershing's cowpokes had been decimated in the months preceding the occupation of the village, but most of the survivors in the unit were beyond inured to confronting the specter of death. Dealing with death was simply part of the job. The men in Emory's unit had different ways of coping with the vacillation between intense boredom and the sheer terror of trench warfare. Emory, for example, made every effort to sleep as much as he could in the hopes that it would make the time melt away faster. But sleep was nearly impossible in trenches infested with rats and rotting corpses. When he was able to find sparse patches of unconsciousness resulting from exhaustion he was often haunted by visions of his own dismemberment or castration.

He writhed as though agonized in the dark and dank corner of the cottage while other men in his unit smoked cigarettes and gambled their rations at a tiny table illuminated by a beam of sunlight cascading into the cottage from a tiny window next to the door, which was closed. Several men from his unit then burst excitedly into the cottage. Emory woke suddenly from a nightmare panting for air. He was soaked in late-summer sweat. Two of the men who had burst into the cottage had their dirt covered hands wrapped tightly around the pale and pudgy arms of a blond-haired milkmaid who was no older than thirteen. "Look what the cat dragged in," one of the Texans at the makeshift poker table crowed lasciviously in a deep southern twang. "You boys know the score. I had the most confirmed killed krauts last time. That means I get first crack at the lass."

"Leave her alone!" Emory grunted. "She's French, goddamn it!"

"I don't give a good god's ass if she's the Queen of England," the suddenly surly Texan said as he stood abruptly from the table. "We're fighting a goddamn war, here. We freed this little girl from the Hun. Least she can do is provide us men with a little bit of tender appreciation."

"She's a little girl, for Christ's sake," Emory rejoined as his exhausted body lurched up from the dusty floor. "She's probably a virgin too."

"Virgin my eye," the Texan snapped back. "This frog hussy probably had every Kraut officer on the Western Front before we liberated her."

"We're supposed to be here to save these people, not rape them." Emory seethed. "They are our allies. Have you no decency, at long last?"

"Believe me, Mi-am-a," the Texan said condescendingly while grinning grossly, "I'm gonna do this little one far better than decent, never you mind that." He then snatched the petrified milkmaid by her wrist and began to drag her towards the exit of the cottage. Emory made a quick move to intercede, but was sucker punched by a former prison guard who hailed from Yuma, Arizona. The sudden and violent blast knocked Emory off balance. He then smashed his head on a jagged piece of stone that protruded from the interior façade of the cottage. The room seemed to spin wildly for several seconds. He then lost consciousness. "I've got second dibs," the Arizonan said to the Texan as the latter dragged the little girl from the cottage and towards the wilderness nearby.

Mr. Ingram grew more desperate to break down the door with each pained second while waiting impatiently in the hallway for what seemed like an arduous lifetime. He banged on the door as hard as he could until he feared his hand might fracture. He could hear a guttural writhing sounds emanating through the door, which concerned him terribly. He thus kicked the door harder, louder, and longer while pleading for Emory to "open up." His blood pressure spiked as he heard a muffled moan and gurgling sound seep through the door. He finally rammed his shoulder into the door until it came off its hinges and he was able to push his way inside the suite.

Mr. Ingram was mortified by the site of Emory's mangled and sweat-soaked body writhing in what seemed to be both agony and ecstasy. He was stunned a moment as he stood over his boss's devastated son, as if not having the foggiest idea of how to even begin to amend the situation. Matters worsened as a thick pea-green colored vomit began to spew from Emory's mouth. He choked violently. Mr. Ingram hurriedly turned Emory's body over onto its side. Puke spewed onto the priceless Egyptian rug underneath Emory's body.

Mr. Ingram then hurried into the bathroom and turned the water in the shower over the claw foot tub on. He then raced back into the bedroom and lugged Emory's listless and naked body across the hardwood floor, into the bathroom, and up into the tub. Mr. Ingram winced due to the water being so icy and frigid. He then rocked Emory back and forth while cradling him in his arms. "Come on, son, come on, please," he pleaded. A deep cough and last bit of viscous vomit spewed from Emory's mouth and splattered on the white tile wall. Emory's dazed, heavy and tired eyes finally opened and stared blankly at the blue bathroom tile next to the tub.

"Where am I?" his voice was soaked in confused fear.

"You're home, son," Mr. Ingram exhaled deeply while pressing his face lovingly against Emory's wet hair and cheek. "You're home now."

"Where are you?" Emory asked confusedly.

"I'm here too," Mr. Ingram panted as a bulbous and solitary tear streaked down his face, "I'm right here."

"Who are you?" Emory asked.

"I don't even know anymore," Mr. Ingram confessed as the icy water washed over him. Tears streamed from his eyes.

Scarlet and Jasper used the gun stolen from Capone in order to rob the Bank of America on Flagler Avenue. The elderly security guard did his best to chase the young couple as they escaped with a bag full of billfolds, even wildly firing a round of ammunition from his .32-Special. But the bullet never really threatened the star-crossed lovers as they fled the scene of the robbery. The fleeing teenagers were hopped up on adrenalin, and the heroin they had injected hours earlier was starting to wane, which made them extra desperate and aggressive. Scarlet wanted to drive straight across the country to Hollywood. "Even if we get caught for the robbery," Scarlet enthused as the electric-blue Ford whipped around a street corner heading back towards the Royal Palm, "we'll come out winners."

"How you figure that?" Jasper asked bemusedly while glancing nervously into the rearview mirror for any pursuers seeking to apprehend them.

"Either way," Scarlet gleefully gushed while happily rifling through the Sears shopping bag stuffed full of cash, "I'm gonna be famous,"

Jasper then glanced side-eyed over at her with deep suspicion in his eyes, realizing suddenly that she was completely and dangerously mad. He then slammed the steering wheel sideways causing the roadster to tightly cut a corner and aimed the car directly for the Royal Palm. "What in the holy hell are you doin', Jaspa?" Scarlet demanded. "We can't go back. Al will kill us both!"

"I gotta get my brass," Jasper explained disconsolately.

"You mean that infernal horn?" Scarlet was dumbstruck. "Why in the hell didn't you bring it with you in the first place?"

"Because I didn't think we was actually gonna rob a fuckin' bank!" He blurted while coming to his senses, "not to mention I was high as a kite."

"Forget that old hunk of tin!" Scarlet urged. "You can buy yourself ten more of them on the way to Hollywood, if you want to."

"You don't understand," Jasper explained somewhat glumly. "The horn was my great granddaddy's. He played it when he was a boy in the Union Army fightin' Johnny Reb at the battle of Yellow Rouge. I can't just leave it. It's more than a horn; it's my heritage; history."

"Well goddamn," Scarlet muttered as the Ford skids to a halt in the hotel carpark. "You stay in the car and keep the engine runnin'," she demanded while exhaling deeply though her nose.

"Ain't you gonna leave the money here?" Jasper asked as Scarlet fast exited the car.

"Leave a black boy sitting in a stolen car with a bag full of cash in Miami?" she asked sarcastically as if he was daft. "Fat chance."

She then hurried into the lobby of the hotel hoping to go undetected. Beauregard followed from a distance, as if surveilling her. The bellboy getting off the elevator as Scarlet was entering the nearby stairwell saw her. Beauregard followed her from a distance. The bellboy alerted the concierge, who was interacting with a guest. Beauregard entered the lobby followed Scarlet. The concierge excused himself to the patron chatting with him and then called up to Capone's suite.

"Is she alone?" Capone demanded.

"I believe so," the sheepish concierge admitted. "I can't be sure, though. Seems she's headed for the second floor."

Beauregard enters the lobby and sees her get on the elevator. Scarlet hurried down the second-floor hallway and then into Jasper's suite. She closed and locked the door behind her. Capone hurried from his suite and down the third-floor hallway. She could not immediately locate the horn, which was tucked safely in its case, which had been shoved under the bed. She had a bit of difficulty prying the horn case, but finally managed the task. She then darted for the door. A stern knock, however, the hollow reverberations of which seemed to fill the room, stopped her in her tracks. She froze stiff and was as careful as she could be to not let herself breathe for fear of being detected by whoever waited for her in the hallway. The reverberating knocking noise filled the room again. "Open up," a brusque voice demanded. She was relieved it was not the sound of Capone's voice.

"Who's there?" Scarlet asked.

"Sheriff Beauregard. Open up the damn door."

She hurriedly shoved the Sears bag full of cash and horn back under the bed. She then took a deep breath in the hopes of composing herself before creaking open the door. Beauregard white knuckled his pistol, which was cocked and ready to fire. His nervous eyes cautiously looked past Scarlet and quickly scanned the interior of the room behind her. "You alone in there?" he asked.

"Yeah," she admitted.

"Don't you dare lie to me now, little girl," he grunted. "Where's the nigger horn player at?"

"Can't say, Sheriff," she said defiantly. "I guess he's somewhere else. Say, what's this all about anyway?"

"You need you to come down to the station," he demanded.

"What in God's name would I ever do that for?" she scoffed.

"We got us a call from your momma up in Pahokee," Beauregard explained as his nervous eyes scanned the interior of the room behind Scarlet. "She says your daddy came down here yesterday to find you and ain't heard from since. We got us an eyewitness that says you, Alphonse Capone, and a man fittin' the description of your daddy were spotted headin' out of town in a bright blue Ford."

"I'm sure I don't have the foggiest idea about none of that, Sheriff," Scarlet assured the lawman. "Honest, I really don't."

"Yeah well," he said as he put his massive hand on her diminutive shoulder in the interest of leading her out of the suite and down the hall, "we'll get it all figured out down at the precinct. Let's go, young lady."

Beauregard presses the down-button but the elevator takes some time to arrive.

"Ah hell," he said as if aggrieved. "Reckon we might have to take the stairs." Beauregard lead Scarlet towards the stairwell.

The elevator coming from the third to second floor of the hotel pinged. The doors slid open. Capone stepped off the elevator into the hallway just after Beauregard and Scarlet had entered the stairwell. He did not see them. Capone then noticed that a door down the hall was agape and inched down the hall.

He was disappointed the room was, for the moment, uninhabited by anything worth shooting. His chance for revenge thus seemed thwarted. Besides that, he was afraid that Scarlet might inform the police of information that might later prove crucial in his prosecution and conviction. His fear was momentarily abated the moment he noticed a few billfolds leaking out of a Sears shopping bag wedged under the bed. Curiosity compelled him to risk vulnerability. He thus dropped to his hands and knees. His beady eyes suddenly grew wide with excitement to find a shopping bag stuffed full of cash

Downstairs and out front of the lobby entrance, Jasper's heart lodged in his throat as he watched Beauregard escort Scarlet from the hotel lobby and place her into the back of his patrol car. He drew some sense of solace that she was not handcuffed and did not have the money with her. His overriding emotion was, however, fear that she would inform the law enforcement agents that he, a black man, was responsible for the bank heist in the interest of saving herself from prosecution.

Back upstairs, Capone rushed from off the third-story elevator and sprinted down the hallway and then into his suite with the bag of money under his arm. He slammed the door shut and locked it behind him, then hurriedly stuffed all his belongings into the suitcase atop the bed. He then stuffed the bag of money into the suitcase, and then ran as fast as he could back towards the elevator, which seemed to take an agonizingly long time to arrive. Anxiety finally compelled him to sprint to the other end of the hallway and run as fast as he could down the service stairwell and into the lobby, next to the bar.

The concierge watched with bated breath as Capone rushed through the lobby and out of the hotel. "Are checking out, Mr. Capone?" the concierge sheepishly asked, trying to mask his sense of hope that the gangster was finally leaving. Capone did not bother to respond.

Capone, upon exiting the hotel, could not believe his luck. Jasper, as if in a sickly stupor, was ducking down behind the driver's seat of the gangster's electric blue roadster. "Get the fuck out my car, nigger," Capone demanded. Jasper frantically complied. He then ran headlong around the back of the car and then into the lobby of the hotel. "I ain't done with you yet," he hollered after Jasper as the latter absconded into the hotel. Capone then stuffed his suitcase and Sears bag full of cash into the backseat of the roadster, hopped into the driver's seat and hightailed north towards the Tamiami Trail in the hopes of making it back to his fiefdom, Chicago, by Friday.

"What's she doin' here?" Scarlet, who was being led by Beauregard to an interview room, asked somewhat spitefully of Orit, who was being escorted by Special Agent Gallo from a holding cell to a bank of telephones. "She's been arrested for murder," Beauregard apprised.

"Y'all think that little lady is the killer?" Scarlet was both surprised and impressed.

"Could be," Beauregard said as he opened the door leading into an interview room and ushering Scarlet inside. "Hard to believe it could be a woman, but she's a Jew so all bets are off, I reckon."

"She's gonna be so goddamn famous," Scarlet was jealous.

"More like infamous," Beauregard corrected. "And watch your tongue. Swearin' is a sin and it ain't ladylike."

"Don't matter none if she is famous or infamous," Scarlet continued, "people are gonna talk about her from one town to the next," she lamented. "That's all that really matters, ain't it, Sheriff? It ain't whether people love you or hate you, but that they care about you at all. Indifference really is the opposite of love, ain't it Sheriff?"

"I'm quite sure I've not got the slightest idea what exactly you're talkin' about, darlin'," Beauregard said, disinterested in the topic as he slung the interview-room door shut behind him.

Down the hall, Orit held tight to a small and crumpled slip of yellowed paper with a phone number scrawled on it. She pleaded with the operator to connect her to the number on the slip of paper. Gallo stood nearby blocking the egress to the cramped room as Orit impatiently waited for a reply at the other end of the line. She finally made contact, but was placed on hold for another moment as someone at the newspaper tracked down Nicholas, the managing editor of the publication. "The bastards arrested me," Orit blurted the moment she heard Nicholas's voice crackle at the other end of the receiver.

"Arrested you? he asked. "What the hell for?"

"They are trying to pin the murders of these girls on me," her voice quivered.

Nicholas tried to calm Orit by promising to find the best defense lawyer in all of Dade County and summon him to her aid the moment he hung up the phone. "I don't care if it bankrupts the paper," he assured, "we'll get you out of there quick as the wheels of justice will permit." He further promised to find a way to post her bond after her bail hearing, which was scheduled for the early evening. Orit was, however, terrified to hang up the phone.

"They're all fascists here," she whispered as Gallo eavesdropped, "they could just dump me in a swamp before the lawyer even gets here. That'd be the end of it."

"They won't do that," Nicholas promised her. "I know exactly where you are. If you disappear, I'll go straight to the FBI."

"The goddamn FBI is standing right here watching me," she whispered as her weary and frightened eyes glanced surreptitiously towards Gallo, who was equally bemused and amused by Orit's fear.

"Now look, Orit," Nicholas urged, "I know you are scared, but I need to hang up in order to get you a lawyer."

No," she pleaded, "don't do that. They won't do anything with you on the phone, I don't think."

I have to hang up," Nicholas's assertion filled Orit with terrible dread. "I can't find you a lawyer until we hang up," he pleaded. Orit finally, albeit very reluctantly, hung up the phone after Nicholas assured her to get a lawyer to her within the hour. Gallo then led the terrified reporter back down the hallway past the interview room occupied by Scarlet and Beauregard, and finally towards the staircase leading down to the holding cells. Scarlet could not take her eyes off the frightened reporter as the latter passed the plate glass window.

Inside the interview room, Beauregard questioned Scarlet about the last time she had seen her father. "Ain't seen him since Sunday last," she said.

"Why'd ya suppose your momma thinks you had somethin' to do with his disappearance?" Beauregard was perplexed.

"I'm quite sure I don't know, Sheriff," Scarlet smirked slightly, which emasculated the lawman just a tad. "Have you ever met my momma? Up in Pahokee, she has gained quite the reputation for spinnin' more yarns than Joel Chandler Harris."

"Okay," Beauregard redoubled, "then why'd ya suppose we had some entirely other fella who don't know you or your daddy from Adam and Eve claim to have seen you, Alphonse Capone, and a man fittin' the description of your daddy high-tailin' out of town a couple days back? Furthermore, why in God's name do ya suppose your daddy ain't been seen since?"

"I'm quite sure I don't know, Sheriff," she promised a bit more forcefully, growing impatient and offended with the line of questioning. Beauregard stood suddenly from the interview table and glared down at Scarlet as though he might like to slap her across her perfectly symmetrical face.

"I don't think you understand what kind of trouble you'z in, little girl," he growled. "I know something happened to your daddy – your own flesh and blood. I understand you got involved with Capone – a goddamn animal. Now, I don't think you'd hurt your pa. But I do think you are protectin' a fella who may have harmed your pa. How'z that make you look, young lady? How's a jury full of father's peers goin' to feel about you protectin' the man who hurt your own daddy?"

"I'm sure I don't have any idea what in God's name you're gettin' at, Sheriff," Scarlet said while smirking slightly. Beauregard ripped Scarlet up from her seat and pinned her against the concrete wall by her throat. Her bright and round pink face expressed grave fear, but only for a fleeting moment. Then a steely calm washed over her.

"Now you listen, and you listen good," he threatened, "you're gonna tell me what in the hell happened to your daddy and where to find him or I will bury you so deep under a cell not even a Chinaman will be able to find you."

A sudden knock at the door startled both of them. A curious young Deputy poked his head inside the room. He was made slightly uncomfortable as he processed the homunculus Sheriff pinning a little girl to the wall by her throat. "Sorry to interrupt, Sheriff," the Deputy said, "but I called the Royal Palm; the concierge over there seemed very pleased to report that Mr. Capone checked out in one helluva hurry this afternoon."

"Did you send out an APV and see about settin' up a roadblock on the Tamiami Trail?" Beauregard hoped. "I betcha he's on his way back north."

"No sir," the Deputy nervously proceeded, "not just yet."

"Well, why in the hell not?" Beauregard bemused.

"Because the missin' person has been located at Jackson Memorial," the Deputy explained. "He was a bit beat up, dehydrated, and out of sorts. But he'll pull through okay. He said that Capone roughed him up pretty good, but that he doesn't want to press any charges. The preacher said he just aims to take his little girl home to her momma, who's been worried sick, and put the entire ordeal behind him as quick as can be."

Scarlet's burning, inflamed, and oxygen deprived lungs pulled life-redeeming air in the second Beauregard eased his python-like grip from around her throat. She fell hard to her knees, which started to bleed. Tears streamed down her cheeks. Though she was relieved to be alive, the news that her father aimed to take her back to Pahokee filled her with an unspeakable dread. She knew all too well that her father would gravely punish her for her sins.

"That's certainly an unexpected bit of good news in an otherwise godawful week," Beauregard said while straightening his shirt and tie. "What's the latest on the commie kike?"

"She's downstairs hollerin' that she has been set up by fascists," the Deputy sneered, chuckled, and slightly shook his head, amused by Orit's desperation and fear.

"Shoot," Beauregard laughed, "that's what they all say, ain't it? Beauregard began to follow the Deputy from the interview room. "Stay put," he ordered Scarlet, who was still on the floor trying to compose herself. Beauregard then hurried down the hallway and staircase after the Deputy towards the holding cells, where the sound of Orit's declaring her innocence wafted.

Scarlet then took a deep and cleansing breath as she pulled herself up from the floor. She wiped some tears from her eyes and then inched cautiously towards the egress of the interview room. She cracked the door open less than an inch and scanned the hallway and staircase leading to the lobby and reception desk. She could faintly hear Orit hollering about being framed emanating from the holding cells below. She then noticed Barney excitedly hurry from his post at the reception desk next to the entrance of the precinct back into the holding cells to take part in the fun of heckling and harassing Orit. Adrenalin permitted Scarlet to sprint as fast as her tired and aching body and now sore and bloody knees would permit down the hall, then staircase, and out of the precinct.

The bright orange sun was setting in the west, which sent a veritable masterpiece of cascading colors across the twilight sky. But Emory, who was sickly and downtrodden hunched forward in his wheelchair next to the window, was too consumed with grief and anguish to notice the splendor of the sky outside his suite.

A soft knock sounded outside his door. He, however, ignored it. There was an extended moment of silence, but it was quickly replaced by a more determined and louder knocking. Emory, sure it was his father, ignored it once more. There was another long silence; so long that Emory believed that whoever the would-be intruder of his solitude might be had mercifully gone away.

Emory's desolate despair transformed into coiled anger as he clumsily navigated his wheelchair away from the window overlooking the bay. He shoved his chair over to the door. He clumsily managed to position his chair in such a way that he was able to finally crack the door open ever so slightly. "What in God's name is the matter?" he demanded.

Emory, however, wished he could pull he words back the moment he saw Quinn nervously gazing down at him. He was a mixture of glad, embarrassed and terrified for her to see him in such a terrible and helpless state.

"Brought you some flowers," she said ever so softly and diffidently as she held up a fresh bouquet of vibrant yellow and black sunflowers.

"What are you doing here?" Emory asked Quinn brusquely and impatiently.

"We've not had a chance to catch up since you got back," she said shamefacedly.

"I've been here the whole time," he said while slightly shrugging his shoulders, somewhat annoyed at her disingenuousness. "Can't really go too many places but here, you know." He added while embarrassedly looking down at the lifeless lower half of his torso and pajamas.

"I figured you'd be busy helping your dad with the campaign," she said. "But I think about you every day. I've wanted nothing more but to just sit and catch up a bit, talk to you about France, and what it was like, and how you are now that you are home. I suppose life has gotten in the way a bit. But I'm here to redress that." She offered the flowers to him. "Brought you these; hope they might brighten up the room a bit," she glanced past him into the dimly lit suite. "Can I come in?"

"It wasn't wine, cheese, and the Eifel Tower, you know," he grunted, "I hate to pop your balloon about France."

"That's okay," she resisted the urge to be offended at his gruff attitude and demeanor. "I'd like to know what the experience was like for you, just the same. Do you mind terribly if I come in and sit a while?" Her bright and bashful eyes darted towards the floor as she braced to be sent away.

"Come in?" he asked exasperatedly. "What for?"

"Just to spend a bit of time together," she said softly while smiling charmingly and slightly shrugging her shoulders. "Can't a girl miss a fella she wants to while away some time with without getting the third degree? I miss you. I want to talk. Isn't that enough?"

"You don't miss me," he blurted flatly. "You miss the memory of who I used to be."

"Maybe so," she conceded while slightly shrugging her shoulders and shaking her head, "but I'm keen to get to know the new and improved version of you, if you'd be so kind as to let me."

"Where's your fella?" Emory said as his weary eyes looked past her and into the hallway. "The old man?"

"God knows?" she was annoyed. "He's most likely at Mizner's casino up in Boca losing his shirt again, or at the track in Hialeah losing his mortgage on some starving greyhound desperate to catch a rabbit. To be honest, I don't think it is going to work out. I gave him his ring back last night."

"He must have been beside himself," Emory feigned sympathy but was actually quite pleased with the unexpected tension between Quinn and her fiancé.

"Come on Emory, let a lady in already," she smiled sweetly while offering her flowers once more. "You don't want your flowers to die, do you?"

He reluctantly eased the wheelchair back away from the door in order to make just enough space for her to enter the suite. "Nice place," she said as her curious eyes scanned the interior of the quarters. Her quizzical eyes then, however, settled on the makeshift shrine Emory had made to her. "Is that my senior photo from the annual?" She asked confusedly. The candles surrounding the photo dripped white wax.

"Yeah," his voice got quieter as he reluctantly and embarrassedly admitted. "I cut it out of the yearbook a while back, before I left for France. It was with me the whole time. I guess I just missed you, is all." His voice shook slightly as if he were trying to prevent himself from crying. He was certain she would run as fast as she could from his suite and would not stop until she was back in the arms of her fiancé. Emory was too ashamed to even look at Quinn. He hoped the floor might open up and swallow him, which, he believed would be a better alternative to the mortification he was suddenly enduring as a result of Quinn seeing how obsessed he was with her.

She, however, set the bouquet of sunflowers atop the unkempt bed, then sat down softly in his lap, draped her arms around the back of his neck, and passionately kissed his lips, which he gladly reciprocated, as though she contained the antidote to all his ills. Both sobbed while kissing for what seemed like ten minutes without pause.

"I've ached to do that for ages," Quinn finally whispered into his ear. Tears streamed down his cheeks.

Mr. Ingram pulled his car in from of the hotel. Garnet, who is exhausted and disheveled, sat in the passenger seat. "Thanks for bailing me out," he said. "I'll figure out a way to pay you back."

"Never you mind all that," Mr. Ingram said. "You may be off the hook for murdering those girls, but they aim to fry you for what you did to that Deputy."

"What was I supposed to do, let him kill Rhett?"

"You know damn well no jury in this state is going to consider the sanctity of a black boy's life when deciding what to do with you." He sighed. "Get whatever you need from your suite, then meet me in my office. I'll get some cash out of the safe so you can go on the lam."

Garnet compliantly nodded his head and exited the car. Mr. Ingram parked the car in his spot and then rested his head on the steering wheel as if deep in contemplation.

Garnet climbed onto the elevator as Scarlet entered the lobby. "Excuse me, young lady," the miffed concierge called out to her as she stormed across the marble floor in the lobby towards the gilded and wooden elevator. "Mr. Capone has left the hotel and has not paid his bill." Scarlet did not even bother to glance back the concierge as climbed aboard the elevator and mashed her finger into the 2-button.

The elevator then whisked her to the second floor of the hotel. She tried to open the door leading into Jasper's suite, but it was locked. Scarlet thus mashed her fist into the wooden frame several times consecutively, trying to smash through it. The sound of the knocking filled the entire hallway. It also reverberated hollow inside Jasper's room.

He was cowering under the bed, fearful that Capone was sure to return and kill him. "Open the goddamn door!" Scarlet finally screeched. Jasper cautiously slid out from under the bed and cracked the door open and peaked into the hallway. Scarlet shoved her way inside the suite. Jasper locked the door behind her.

"Come on," Scarlet demanded, "we gotta get the hell out of here. Grab the money and your horn," she ordered while rushing to gather up what few belongings she had ownership of in the room.

"Where are we supposed to go?" he was flush with trepidation.

"Hollywood, dummy," she was annoyed and bewildered by Jasper's impotent inaction. "We got us enough cash to make it. If we run out along the way, we'll just knock over another bank."

"Ain't got no money left," he heartbrokenly confessed. "Someone done got it while we was out."

"Someone got it?" she said as though dismayed. "Who got it? Where did he go?"

"I'm sure I don't know," he grunted. "Maybe your boyfriend made off with it, took it afta the Sheriff took ya away."

"Don't be daft, Jaspa," Scarlet squinted disgustedly. "I know damn well who it was," she said as she sat at the edge of the bed calculating wild conspiracies in her mind.

"I swear to everything holy that I did not steal it," Jasper said, reflexively expecting the white girl to blame the black man for the crime.

"Shit," she said while slightly rolling her eyes, "I know you'd a never had the inclination nor the balls to take the money and run."

"Then who took it?" Jasper, who felt suddenly even more emasculated, asked.

"That nosy little kike reporter from New York," Scarlet sneered. "My daddy said a Semite would rip your arm off for a nickel. You stay put," she ordered, "I'm gonna go get us our money back." She then grabbed Jasper's kitbag with heroin and syringe inside and bolted for the exit of the suite.

"You takin' my medicine?" He was scared and suddenly even more cowardly than before. "Ain't much left, especially if we gonna need us enough to get to California."

"Don't worry, darlin,'" she offered solace while unlocking and swinging open the door to the suite. "I'm just goin' to use enough to get us our money back." She then cautiously opened the door and peaked into the hall, which was clear of guests. She then furtively exited the suite and made her ways back towards the elevator, and then back down to the lobby.

"I'm so glad to see you, Miss," the concierge was equally relieved and despairing. "You see," he continued, "Mr. Capone has apparently checked out of the hotel without paying his bill. You see, I could be terminated for letting the guest leave without having paid first."

"Oh gosh, Scarlet smiled graciously, "that's right. I nearly forgot. Mr. Capone has asked me to pay the bill before I check out. But the problem is, ya see, sir, I left all my money with my new friend. She has it and I need to get it from her. It's in her suite, but I do not remember what number it is."

"I see," the concierge smiled cordially. "And who is your friend?"

"The little Jewish lady from New York," Scarlet grinned.

"Ah, Miss Abrahams," the concierge said while scanning the registry book atop the desk. "She's in room 303."

"That's right, 303," Scarlet nodded appreciatively while snapping her fingers to indicate that she had just remembered what had been forgotten. "I'm afraid I've never been very good with numbers." She smirked and nodded appreciatively while starting back towards the elevator. He stared at her bare feet glide across the marble floor with a sour puss on his disheveled face.

"I've got to get the hell out of this godforsaken backwater," he said under his breath.

Scarlet, meanwhile, noticed the fruit basket resting atop the coffee table near the couches adjacent to the elevator. She picked a bright and shining orange and then hopped onto the elevator and pushed the 3-button.

She slid from off the elevator the moment it opened on the third floor, and then sprinted to room 303. She cautiously twisted the door handle, which, to her great surprise, popped right open. Scarlet could not believe her luck.

Orit, who had been arrested the last time she had left the suite which prevented her from locking the door behind her, had yet to be bailed out by the lawyer summoned by Nicholas. Her suite was thus momentarily unoccupied by anyone but the intruder. Scarlet flicked the light switch on, and then set the orange down atop the small wooden dining table next to the bay window. She then hurriedly searched the drawers, Orit's suitcase, and then under the bed. But the money was nowhere to be found. She thus turned off the light and sat down at the modest dining table near the bay window. Slowly and with great splendor she peeled the orange as a beam of opaque moonlight washed over her. She then unpackaged the contents in Jasper's kitbag and neatly laid them atop the table.

Orit was somewhat lucky that Nicholas had contacted a lawyer in Miami who knew the legal system in South Florida quite well. The attorney had gone to law school at Stetson University up in Deland with the presiding judge and both were members of the Sigma Chi fraternity. The judge who set bond thus released Orit on her own recognizance thanks to a wire transfer payout footed by Nicholas, which would surely bankrupt the newspaper.

As he dropped Orit at the hotel, the lawyer, who was not entirely reptilian, urged his newest and most begrudging client to not leave town under any circumstances until he had secured payment for himself and his frat brother. Though she promised to stay in the city as long as needed in order to resolve the horrendous frame-up she had been ensnared in, she was actually quite adamant, albeit secretive, about leaving town the first chance she got. She knew that the exorbitant cost Nicholas had paid to free her would bankrupt the paper, and she was thus acutely aware that the story she had come to Miami to research and write would almost surely never even be published anyway.

She was also terrified that dark forces might conspire to make her vanish before she even had a chance to prove her innocence at trial. She was also quite sure that she would not be received well by the all-white and all-male and most likely racist and sexist jury the prosecution would inevitably select to condemn her. Her plan upon arriving back at the hotel was thus to order the stiffest drink available at the hotel bar, cut her hair short as a boy's, and then catch the first train out of South Florida.

The concierge, busy chatting with another patron and bellhop, did not notice Orit enter the lobby and make her way towards the bar.

Orit did not even bother to sit at the bar after ordering a triple-bourbon on the rocks. She slurped back the stiff glass of spirits, and then staggered up to her room. She was, however, so drunk and exhausted by the time she arrived at her suite that she had decided to take a long nap before buying a bottle bleach, scissors, and a train ticket north.

Her hand fumbled clumsily for the light switch inside the suite, which she finally located. The light inside was so bright that she squinted a bit. She then shut and locked the door behind her, locked it, and began unbuttoning her blouse. There was so much on the reporter's mind, including booze, that she did not immediately notice Scarlet sitting at the table, which was topped by a loaded syringe and half-eaten orange. The canary diamond on her ring finger seemed to glow and glitter. Orit flinched at first, but then appeared somewhat relieved, albeit confused to see Scarlet sitting at the table.

"I'm terribly sorry," Orit slurred slightly. "I must have the wrong room." She then began to button the ones she had undone on her blouse and exit the room. But she suddenly grew befuddled by seeing her suitcase open atop the bed. She finally managed to process the syringe atop the table next to the orange.

The embarrassment on Orit's face contorted into delayed terror as she connected the dots in her mind.

"Where's the money, you goddamn kike?" Scarlet barked.

"I'm sorry?" Orit wondered if she had misunderstood the seemingly confused teenager.

"My money!" Scarlet seethed. "Where is it? Daddy always said not to leave money around if there was a kike nearby."

Orit's confusion suddenly melded into an acute understanding and fear. She looked again at the orange and syringe atop the table, piecing together that both were hallmarks of the grisly murders that she had read about in *The Miami Herald*.

"You're the killer?" The words tumbled from Orit's mouth. She then frantically unlocked the door in the hopes of fleeing the suite. Scarlet darted from her seat with the syringe held tight in her hand like a dagger she was eager to stab Orit with. Scarlet clattered into Orit just as the latter was able to unlock and squeeze the door open. The collision, however, caused the door to slam shut. The sound of the door slamming closed reverberated all across the third floor, alerting Emory and Quinn.

Scarlet and Orit struggled fiercely. Scarlet fell atop Orit, who managed to pin Scarlet's wrist so that the younger of the two could not jab the needle into her face. Orit fought as if her life depended on it, which it did. But Scarlet had leverage and the force of gravity on her side. The needle thus inched closer and closer to being gashed into Orit's eye

Garnet was drawn out of his suite into the hallway by the curious sounds of slamming doors and the epic struggle emanating from down the hall and instinctively made his way towards the melee. Emory, whose chair was guided by Quinn, also cautiously exited his room and followed Garnet. Curiosity compelled the three to creep closer and closer to room 303. Garnet finally knocked on the door, but the struggle inside did not abate.

"Open it," Emory frightenedly demanded. Garnet adamantly complied. He swung the door open and paused a moment while surveying the scene. He then tackled Scarlet just in time to save Orit's eye from being skewered by the heroin-laced syringe. Garnet pinned Scarlet flat on her back. Quinn used the rotary phone to call down to the concierge for immediate assistance as Garnet managed to subdue Scarlet, who put up a good fight for more than a minute before resigning herself to her fate.

Orit, meanwhile, tried to compose herself as she pulled her aching and drunken body up from off the wooden floor and tried desperately to catch her breath.

"I'm gonna to be even more famous than you," Scarlet grinned maniacally. "I'm gonna be on the front-page of every newspaper from here to Timbuktu," she gushed and giggled. Orit and Emory shared a long and somewhat sympathetic glance as both came to suddenly understand that Scarlet was as much a victim as a villain. Garnet and Quinn, however, stared down at the girl as if she were evil.

Dénouement

Scarlet was apt in assessing the fact that her picture would be on the front page of a number of periodicals from one coast to the next. She actually smiled proudly for her mug shot in the hopes that some producer or director might somehow see it and cast her in a movie, if a jury were to find her not guilty. The bold headline at the top of the morning edition of *The Miami Herald*, however, read, "Ingram's Injun Catches Killer Cutie." The story took up nearly the entire front page. There was only a small blurb about the impending mayoral election set for the day after Scarlet's arrest.

Ingram's association with Garnet – the depicted hero in the newspaper – seemed to be enough to push the supposed "reform candidate" over the top in his contest against his former friend turned adversary, Mr. Sewell. It was a very narrow victory, but Ingram had won and he was determined to make Miami into one of the most culturally relevant cities in all the world; mentioned in the same breath as London, Paris, and New York, though more exclusive than those places. Ingram also promised his supporters during his victory party speech at the Royal Palm the night of his election triumph that he was determined to make Miami into a "brave and bold new city." And in terms of real estate values, it did not take Miami long at all to rival the western world's most renowned metropolis. By the end of the 1920s, for example, Miami was widely considered to be one of the hottest markets on the planet, despite the fact that a devastating hurricane had helped precipitate a terrible bust all across the region, which triggered a global economic depression the world had not yet witnessed that came to be known as the Great Depression.

Mr. Sewell, who was never one for honest introspection, ultimately abandoned his wife of more than two decades like a thief in the night. He cashed in his Culligan stock and bought a glorious and sprawling piece of property in Rhodesia that he hoped to turn into a winery. He took his young mistress and baby boy with him. His winery, which shipped thousands of bottles to some of the finest restaurants and hotels in the western during the Interwar Era, was a great success until after World War II, when it, due to Sewell's old age and a stark postwar economic downturn, fell into disrepair and ultimately folded.

Rhett spent more than a month recuperating from the head wounds he had received from the Deputy Garnet killed, but eventually recovered, though his vision in his right eyes was never quite right. He never drove a cab in Miami again, but finally made it to Harlem in 1922, which provided him a much nicer life than he imagined could exist in South Florida. Garnet graciously paid to have carpenters erect Rhett's mother and younger brother a nice new house at the edge of the Miccosukee reservation, further from the reach of the Klan vigilantes who continued to terrorize Dade County's black resident's long after Orit went back to New York.

After having been bailed out by Mr. Ingram and awaiting trial for the murder of the Deputy, which he was sure to be convicted of, Garnet cashed out what little of his savings account remained after paying to have Ruby's new house built. Mr. Ingram bribed the officer assigned to detect any would-be bond jumpers at the port to permit Garnet to board a ship bound for Panama. From there, Garnet set sail for Costa Rica on the *SS Columbus*. He never again returned to the Everglades. And though Mr. Ingram and Emory were both decidedly upset to see Garnet off when he departed the hollow and wooden dock at the Port of Miami, both also understood and supported their friend's decisions. Mr. Ingram grew uncommonly emotional as Garnet boarded the ship. He wept a bit as he confessed to Garnet, "you're like a son to me," and "if you ever need anything at all, I'd be honored if I could help." The old man then deeply embraced his longtime employee and kissed him on the cheek, which Mr. Flagler would have never dreamt of doing. Emory did not cry but his voice quaked slightly when he told Garnet how much he "loved and respected" the only man he deemed worthy of being his best friend.

Garnet bought the small farm he and Goldie had dreamt of when they were kids. He had moments of intense and deafening loneliness and deep despair tending to his remote yerba mate plantation in the shadow of a verdant Costa Rican mountain, but all-in-all he was glad to have escaped a nation that seemed to have no value or respect for him as a human being. He never returned to Miami, not even to visit the reservation. Despite the bouts of loneliness and despair he endured from time-to-time in Costa Rica, he felt, for the first time in his life, fully human – a contented Yeoman Farmer whose life had real meaning and purpose. His plantation was also very successful. His second year on the plantation, he met a nice Costa Rican woman selling plantains at the market. She was a widow with a young son. Garnet had coffee with her on Saturdays after market and soon developed a deep and abiding affection for her and her son. They were married within a year of having met. They suffered through the same petty pangs and squabbles any married couple does, but were almost exclusively happy. Garnet and Quinn came to the wedding, which was a beautiful beachside sunrise service. Everyone wore white.

Emory and Quinn were likewise married within six months of his father's electoral triumph over Mr. Sewell. The young lovers were also parents by the general election won by Calvin Coolidge. They adopted a young Miccosukee boy whose mother had died of dysentery and built a quaint cottage out by the sprawling orange grove that Mr. Ingram had gifted to his son soon after the latter had arrived back from France. Emory had taken on the monumental task of running the grove, which he had no experience at all doing. He, however, quickly took to it and discovered he enjoyed cultivating and running a business. He also shrewdly hired a small army of pickers from the Bahamas and American South, which he paid better than any other growers in the region. They thus worked very diligently and with a better attitude than was common amongst workers on many other plantations. Emory's grove soon grew into one of Florida's most prosperous. Most of the produce and juice produced at Ingram Estates made its way to markets as far north as Nova Scotia and as far south as Ciudad de Panama. Emory only rarely ever missed heroin. He was too busy running his farm, investing his money, and raising a family to really ever consider the loss of his limbs, which was the true inner strife that fueled his addiction in the first place. He had, in fact, grown to see losing his limbs as a requisite part of him becoming the complete and contented human he had ultimately become as a result of overcoming the setback.

The New York Call, as was especially expected after Orit was set to be railroaded and thus needed to be bailed out of jail, shuttered its doors before the intrepid reporter could finish the story she had written about her investigation in Miami, which was titled "Seven Days in Magic City of Sin," when it was finally printed in The Saturday Evening Post. The success of her feature in The Post earned her an interview as a stringer with The New York Times, a position she gladly accepted and parlayed into a column within a year. Nicholas lived off his meager savings for two months before finally landing a plum editorial role at The San Francisco Chronicle.

Jasper had managed to escape any suspicion or punishment for his association with Scarlet, or his robbing of the bank. She never mentioned him to investigators. In spite of everything, Jasper still harbored a deep affection, some might say obsession, for Scarlet, especially after she had become so famous and had men all over the country sending her gifts and visiting her at the Federal Women's Prison outside of Ocala, Florida. Jasper's residency at the Royal Palm concluded at the end of the winter season. He already had another gig lined up at a swank new jazz club on Chicago's Southside. But he had a couple of weeks in between gigs, so he gladly snatched the opportunity to travel to Ocala to see Scarlet in the interim, though she had not summoned him nor was she expecting to ever see him again.

The inside walls of Scarlet's prison cell were plastered with news clippings about her. Though she was glad to be famous, prison life did not suit her free-spirited nature. Also, ever since she was convicted of the murders, Scarlet had suffered terrible nightmares in which she relived a terrifying and harrowing experience that helped meld her into the destructive force of nature she had ultimately become. The nightmares grew so haunting and heavy by summertime that she contemplated suicide each morning upon waking. She fantasized about smashing her gorgeous face into the concrete walls over and over again until her head was nothing but bloody mush. Though she was famous and very oddly adored by people she had never met, just as she had always dreamed, the debilitating nightmares that accompanied her infamous notoriety made her rue ever wanting to be so superficially adored in the first place.

The recurring nightmare always started at the same point, like it was a script she was forced to relive and endure nearly every night. The script-like temporality of the dream, which was rooted in an experience she suffered a week before Mr. Fisher's fiancé was killed, alerted her to the fact she was dreaming, but she could never manage to escape the terror by waking, even with the knowledge and understanding that she was dreaming. It was as if she were being punished for her sins.

The nightmare always went something like this: Edmund's truck was stalled on the side of a bucolic road under a late afternoon sun. He looked mightily disheveled as he gazed into the steaming engine block of his truck. Scarlet, who was very bored, climbed out from the cab of the truck and stood next to her father and stared blankly at the engine. She absentmindedly set her hand atop the battery. Edmund slapped her hand and scolded her. "Damn it, child," he scowled, "don't put your damned hand there!"

"Why not?" she asked.

"For one," he explained, "because I said so. Secondly, because you can hurt yourself real bad if you get battery acid in your eyes or mouth. You could even wind up dead. So smarten up."

Her eyes were pregnant with trepidation at the smudge of residue on her hand. She feverishly wiped the smudge onto her pretty white dress, which she had worn to a revival she had attended with her father that morning and early afternoon, which, due to her boredom, seemed a lifetime ago already, though the sun was still more than an hour yet from setting. Edmund was likewise dressed in his Sunday best – a black suit, black tie, white shirt that had yellowed due to sweat.

Scarlet was mortified to see that a bit of crimson – almost black – blood had seeped down her leg somewhat. She was mortified at the very thought of her father noticing. He, however, was too busy fiddling with some loose tube and fidgeting with a cable to notice the blood soaking into Scarlet's white tights. "Think it might be a spark plug," Edmund grunted as Scarlet quickly darted back towards the cab of the truck in the hopes he'd not notice that she were bleeding. Edmund then pushed the sparkplug into what he hoped was its proper place. "Okay," he hollered to Scarlet, who had sat carefully in the driver's seat in the cab of the truck, careful to not let her body sit too flush against the fabric for fear of soiling it with her menstruation.

"Fire her up," Edmund hollered. Scarlet flicked the ignition switch and jiggled the keys. The truck, to Edmund's great relief, sparked right up. "Hot damn!" He celebrated. "Slide over, darlin'. Ah heck," he thought again, "you know what, why don't you drive a while, at least until we make it to the motorist lodge in Jacksonville?"

"Really?" she was uncommonly enthused. "But you're always ramblin' on about how females should not be permitted to vote or drive," she giggled in the hopes of eliciting his affection. "Looks like you're becomin' a veritable Progressive."

"Well, I been preachin' all day," he exhaled a deep sigh, "and need a bit of shuteye, that's all. God knows women have no place votin' or drivin', that is unless I need a bit of shuteye," he smiled.

"Hot dog!" Scarlet cooed as she held manically tight to the steering wheel and hopped up and down a bit in her seat. She was so momentarily excited that she momentarily forgot the streak of crimson blood that had formed across the front of her otherwise white dress.

"What in the hell is this, oil?" Edmund asked just before climbing into the cab of the truck. He glared hard at Scarlet's dress. She was terribly embarrassed and afraid. He then noticed an even deeper blood deposit at the crotch of his daughter's white dress. "Oh," his voice wavered slightly as if he were somewhat sickened by the sight, "I see," he grumbled. "Looks like you are officially a woman, I guess," he forced an awkward and uncomfortable smirk that seemed to comfort neither of them. He removed the hanky from the breast pocket of his worn and soiled blazer and dabbed the blood in her lap a bit. "Careful with the seat now," he said, "or it's comin' out of your allowance. Ya hear?" But by then her blood had already stained the fabric. "Maybe your momma can get the stain in your dress out with somthing back at the house – iodine or something, " he said as graciously as he could in such an imbroglio, but it just made matters worse for Scarlet, who felt six inches tall all of a sudden. "Shame your momma was too sick to make the trip to the revival this time round," Edmund added while dropping the hanky in her lap.

A terribly long and tense silence filled the space between father and daughter as the latter navigated the truck along a vast stretch of two-lane highway that passed mile after mile of peach groves, shotgun shacks, and general stores in southern Georgia, just north of the Florida line.

The sun was beginning to set in the west, which sent an array of pastels streaming across the humid twilight sky above the groves. "Another of God's infinite number of signs and wonders if you look hard enough," Edmund said gladly while gazing up at what Scarlet assumed was the heavens. He, however, was referring to a lovely amber haired young woman wearing a purple dress made of linen with a *Bible* wedged tightly under her arm. The film of perspiration on her dermis made her white skin glisten. "Slow down," Edmund ordered his daughter. "Let's see if our young sistren in the Lord needs a ride to town." Scarlet complied with her father's wishes and brought the truck to a gentle meander near the young woman, who could not have been a day older than eighteen.

"Howdy, little sister," Edmund warmly grinned. "What'd ya doin' way out here on this lonely stretch of road so close to dark on a Sunday?"

"I was at *Bible* study at my cousin's house," the girl explained somewhat tentatively, as if she had been warned by someone she loved and trusted about speaking to strangers. "I gotta get home for Sunday supper. My momma is makin' spaghetti and meatballs."

"That sounds mighty nice," Edmund said. "How far ya from home?"

"Oh, not too far," the girl explained while motioning towards the horizon with her hand. "Just yonder that dirt road that cuts through the peach grove. It's about a mile-and-a-half down there."

"Mile-n-a-half?" Edmund said. "Well shoot, darlin,'" he batted his beady and predatory eyes somewhat flirtatiously, "me and my daughter'd be glad to escort you the rest of the way, if you like."

"Y'all sure it ain't no trouble?" the girl asked as she peered over at Scarlet and hoped the daughter might veto her father's insistence. No such luck.

"No trouble at all," Scarlet said. "We'z in no great rush. Hop on in!"

The girl reluctantly climbed into the back bed of the truck. Scarlet mashed the gas pedal, and then hung a sharp left at the dirt road that cut through the grove. Once in the grove, it became a maze of intersecting and confusing dirt roads. "Stop right up here," Edmund demanded of his daughter as he gently slapped the dashboard. She quickly complied.

Edmund hopped from the front-passenger seat of the truck and went around to the back bed. "You mind if I pluck a few peaches right quick for the road, little darlin'?" he asked ever so sweetly. "Me and my daughter have a long trip ahead of us," he added in the hopes of gaining the girl's sympathy.

"I suppose it'd be alright," the girl said while shrugging her shoulders nonchalantly, masking her anxious impatience. "But this ain't my pa's land," she qualified. "Besides, my momma might be glad to feed y'all, if she has enough spaghetti to go around. I'd be glad to ask her just as soon as I get home."

"Hells bells," Edmund chuckled, "I'd never dream of imposin' on y'all like that, especially Sunday supper. A couple a fine peaches is all we need to see us through to the motorist lodge across the state line. Ain't that right, Scarlet?" Edmund smiled dopily.

"Reckon so," Scarlet said while shrugging her shoulders.

"Alright then," the girl sighed, "take as many peaches as your arms can carry, I reckon."

"Would you mind helping me at all?" Edmund pleaded with the increasingly annoyed girl. "It's so close to dark already, I'd hate to wander off in this labyrinth and get lost."

"Alright," the girl's patience was waning faster. "But we gotta hurry. My momma will be mad as a pit of vipers if I'm late for Sunday supper again."

"We won't be but a minute," Edmund promised. He then offered his hand to the girl in order to help her climb down from the back bed of the truck. She grabbed onto his hand, but held even tighter to her *Bible* tucked under her arm.

"You can leave your *Bible* behind," Edmund smiled charmingly.

"I prefer to hang onto it, if it's all the same to you, mister," she explained. "It's kinda like a security blanket, I guess."

"Suit ya self," he smiled, tickled by her insistence.

He continued to hold onto her hand even after her tan and sandaled feet were flat on terra firma. She thought this a bit odd. Her hand began to perspire nervously. She tried to free it from his grip, but he held her hand even firmer. Scarlet flicked the ignition switch off and climbed from the cab of the truck.

The amber haired girl being led into the wilderness by the preacher immediately felt a deep and sorrowful pang of deep distress and despair the moment she noticed the blood stains on Scarlet's dress, which made both girls even more uneasy. "Get back in the damn truck, Scarlet," Edmund growled; all his charm seemed to disintegrate in an instant. "We won't be but a minute," he softened slightly.

Scarlet was somewhat confused and offended as she watched her father lead the girl back into the groves. She then lost sight of them. But within a minute Scarlet's body was covered in goosebumps from the chilling sounds of the girl screeching for someone – anyone – to help her. Scarlet ran from the cab of the truck towards the ominous shrieks that echoed and reverberated in the pastoral peach grove. She saw her father pinning the girl to the ground with his knees burrowed into her chest simultaneous to bashing her over the head with the *Bible*. The girl finally lost consciousness and stopped fighting. Edmund then tore the girl's pantyhose open at the crotch and thrust his throbbing penis inside her virginal vagina, violently tearing her open. Her blood soaked into his trousers and intermingled with the dirt and grass underneath her listless body. He strangled the life from her but did not climax. He then lurched from atop his victim and slowly fastened his trousers. He then plucked a peach from a nearby tree and bit into it ravenously. Juice spewed down his neatly shaven chin.

"Daddy!" Scarlet pleaded while sobbing disconsolately. "What in God's name are you doin'?"

Edmund spit out a bit of peach into his hand and shoved the fruit into the victim's blood drenched labia and stared down at her bulging eyes staring up at his for an extended moment. He finally chased after his daughter. She sprinted as fast as she could back towards the truck. He chased her round and round it, then finally caught her at the front bumper. He forced her to open the hood of the truck. She was, however, so terrified that her trembling hands had difficulty complying with the demand. He thus finally popped the hood his self and forced her hand to intermingle with some battery acid residue that had collected atop the engine block. He then led his daughter forcefully by her tainted hand quickly towards the young girl's lifeless body.

"Put your hand in her mouth." Edmund demanded. Scarlet, who was nearing panicked hyperventilation due to terrified sobbing, stood stock-still as she gazed down at the victim. "Put your hand in her damn mouth." Edmund seethed impatiently. Scarlet's terrified and wide eyes stared at him, unable to process the information he was transmitting to her. "Put your goddamn hand in the girl's mouth," he threatened, "or you're next." She finally complied and rubbed battery acid into the girl's mouth. "There," Edmund said as he dragged Scarlet away from the victim and back towards the truck, "if you ever tell anyone about this, you're goin' to be in as much trouble as me. This is our secret," he added as he shoved his daughter into the front passenger seat of the truck. "Anybody finds out about this, you're dead. Understand?"

Scarlet was petrified and did not respond. He slapped her hard in the face, which smartened her up a bit. She frantically nodded her head as tears streamed down her cheeks. He slammed the door shut and raced around to the driver's side of the cab.

Scarlet, donning a black and white horizontally-striped nightgown woke suddenly in a pool of sweat in a cramped concrete cell with just one small window that permitted a beam of light to illuminate her. The walls of the cell were adorned with news clippings and pictures detailing her killing spree in Miami and subsequent trial. Jangling steel keys slid into the gray door made of iron, which caused an awful clanking sound. But the prison guard, a fat but reptilian man who had a five o'clock shadow five minutes after shaving, known to Scarlet as Officer Stallworth, did not open the door to the cell. Stallworth, like so many men before him, had sexually assaulted Scarlet many times in the months she had been incarcerated. She, however, often pretended the sex was consensual in order to gain favor or avoid further and more elaborate forms of torture. "You got another letter," he said while peering between bars into the dim and dank cell.

"Who's it from, my momma again?" she asked drowsily while wiping sleep from her morose and exhausted eyes.

"Some fella named Jasper; the return address is New Orleans," Stallworth huffed.

"Jasper?" Her suddenly glimmering eyes gazed out the tiny square window above the cot as if she were resisting the urge to fondly reminisce. "New Orleans?"

"Come on," the surly, obese, and greasy guard barked, "ain't got all day."

Scarlet eased off the cot as if exhausted and sore and then tried to retrieve the letter from the slot in the door made for sliding in trays of food and cuffing inmates' hands. The guard, however, pulled the letter from beyond her reach. "Who in the hell is Jasper fella?" he bluntly demanded.

"Damned if I know," she lied. "You know as well as I do that I get letters from crazy fellas from all over the place at least once a week. Ain't none of them mean nothin' to me at all, not compared to you, darlin'. You know that."

"Bess not be lyin' to me again," he grunted, "you don't want me to take the metal end of my belt to you again like the last time you was caught lyin' do you now, darlin'?" Unbeknownst to Scarlet, Stallworth had already read the letter and was plotting his revenge.

"No sir," she said flatly, as if rehearsed to the point of being reflexive. "Baby girl dun learnt her lesson the last time. You know I'd never lie to you again." She smiled coyly, but her eyes belied her plot to kill him with his own keys the next time his pants were around his ankles inside of her cage. "Can't wait fer ya to stay the night again," she lied. "Say, when's the next time that fat little old wife of yours and her sisters are stayin' a weekend down in Miami?"

"I was wantin' it to be a surprise," Stallworth grinned and slightly licked his lips. "But I rented her a suite for her and the girls at the Royal Palm for her birthday next weekend. She's goin' to be out of town from Friday evenin' to Sunday night."

"So we'z havin' another sleepover Friday?"

"I'm playing cards with the fellas Friday," he said lasciviously, "but if you're daddy's good little girl all week long I might let ya stay over Saturday night."

"Be still my heart, daddy," Scarlet practiced her acting chops by smiling as pretty as could be, though she actually wanted to vomit in her mouth. She then snatched the letter from the guard's greasy sausage-like fingers as he was trying to figure out if she was being authentic or not. She was not.

"Toodle-oo," the guard wheezed as he wobbled away from the cell, his keys jingle-jangling all the way.

Scarlet did not read the letter; she devoured its contents as though it contained an anecdote to all the turmoil in her life.

"Dearest Scarlet," the letter began, "I have devised a plan to prove your innocence of these crimes. I am going to kill a girl in a ritualistic fashion in Miami to make it seem as though the killer is still on the loose and that you are, as you claimed to be all along at your trial, innocent of the murders and were truly only scared the kike journalist from New York to get publicity, and because you had been cheated out of the Miss Orange Blossom Pageant crown and title, which everyone knows you rightfully won fair and square. I know that you are innocent of these heinous crimes and I am determined to free you and take you to Hollywood, where the whole world can see what a shining star you truly are. I'm hoping to find steady work playing my horn in Tinsel Town, too. With Love," the letter concluded, "Jasper."

Scarlet then hurriedly pulled the yellow pad of paper, small envelope, and worn and chewed pencil nub from the tiny shelf next to her cot and feverishly scrawled, "Dear Jasper," the letter began, "I am so overjoyed to have received and read your correspondence, but am also very terrified that you might consider killing some poor and innocent girl for my benefit. The mayhem needs to end, at long last. I do, however, plan to kill a prison guard Saturday night next and leave this godforsaken place and never ever come back again. The lousy bastards that run this penal institution will not permit you or any other Negro to visit, but I'd be so very delighted to see you and a dependable mode of transport waiting for me on the street outside this penal institution when I walk free next Saturday night. Hope to see you soon and forever more. Very Much Yours Truly," the letter concluded, "Scarlet."

She then folded the letter with great care and sense of splendor, slowly sealed the envelope with the tip of her tongue, scrawled Jasper's name and address on the envelope, kissed it, then held it to her chest as she gazed hopefully out the window into the distance.

After dinner the inmates were permitted some time to mill around the prison yard and garden. Scarlet took the opportunity to drop her letter in the slot in the mailroom door. The rat-faced mail clerk, however, knew that Stallworth, the lecherous guard on Scarlet's ward, had won first rights to her in a game of cards her first week incarcerated. The clerk thus associated Scarlet with Stallworth, and thus rightly assumed the minute he noticed that Scarlet was writing to some man named Jasper in New Orleans that his comrade would not just want to know about it, but also be desperate to know the contents of the letter, which was written by a piece of property that Stallworth had, in the mail clerk's mind, rightfully won fair and square.

The clerk thus fast furnished Stallworth with the letter at closing time that evening, just as the latter was making his way from the main wing of the prison towards parking lot. "Scarlet and this Jasper fella figure on pullin' one over on me?" Stallworth seethed as he stuck the letter back in the envelope, and then handed it back to the clerk, who placed it into a new envelope so that Jasper would not be wise to it having been read by anyone other than its author. He then carefully scrawled the prison's mailing address on the outside of the envelope, and then neatly resealed the letter inside. "Go ahead and mail it this Jasper fella," Stallworth urged the clerk. "This dumb cunt's got another thing comin' to her." He grinned like an excited kid expectant of a present her was anxious to open.

Jasper snatched his horn case from atop the small dresser in the corner of the bedroom in his humble French Quarter apartment in New Orleans. He plopped it atop the bed next to the suitcase, which he quickly filled with clothes and his kitbag of heroin.

The window in Jasper's dingy apartment was wide open in order to let a bit of fresh air inside. The curtains fluttered wildly thanks to a stiff breeze whipping up from Lake Pontchartrain. The sound of steps methodically approaching his apartment from the stairwell caused Jasper to pause. He cowered down on the far side of the single-bed in the back room and peered nervously at the wind fluttering the curtain of the window in the living room. Though it had been months since he had the temerity to steal Al Capone's car, he had read with great dismay of the gangster's meteoric rise in gangland Chicago. He had read that Capone was now one of the bosses of the syndicate and had branched out into a number of legitimate enterprises, including movie producing and real estate speculation (if you consider those anymore legitimate than importing guns, booze, murder, and the like). Though he hoped that Capone had grown rich and famous enough to let bygones be bygones, he was not so foolish that he would assume Capone had let him off the hook. Jasper thus tended to keep a close watch over his shoulder at all times for fear of Capone exacting revenge, especially now that he had taken a spring residency at a club on the Southside of Chicago, which made him especially uneasy about Capone's goons being able to track him down, if they were ever so inclined.

Jasper cocked the rusty revolver he had acquired two weeks prior at a Ninth Ward pawn shop and aimed it at the window as he stared at the site atop the barrel. A fuzzy figure entered Jasper's line of site. He placed his index finger on the trigger. He, however, stopped short of firing because he noticed the light blue fatigues and white hat synonymous with the postman, who nonchalantly dropped a letter in the tin box next to the door of Jasper's apartment. A deep and relieved sigh escaped from Jasper as he shoved the weapon into the waistband of his revolver. He then climbed to his feet, straightened his tie, pulled on his black blazer, and then hurried towards the door with his suitcase and horn case. His rent was days overdue, so he did not even bother to close the door behind him to an apartment he never ever intended to return to anyway.

His somewhat jaded heart, however, thawed ever so slightly the moment he noticed the author of the letter left by the postman was Scarlet. His excited eyes absorbed her words as if they soothed his bruised and battered soul.

Jasper hurried gleefully down the steps of the quaint apartment building replete with windswept terraces to ground level. He plopped his luggage on the street next to his feet and waited in the searing sun a short while with his thumb pointed towards the sky. But no driver heading east even noticed him, let alone pump their breaks to offer him assistance. He thus walked rather aimlessly about a block-and-a-half. His excitement soured quick as it dawned on him that he would surely never make it to Scarlet in time to help her to get free. Though he had stopped believing in God's existence in a trench in France, he was desperate enough to offer a meek prayer to the heavens in hope of a miracle, just in case he had miscalculated things.

Whether it was divine intervention or dumb luck, he noticed while passing that the postman had quite unwisely left the keys to the small white mail transport truck in the ignition. Jasper tried to seem nonchalant as could be as he glanced nervously over each shoulder for the mail carrier, who was still making his rounds somewhere in the apartment building.

Jasper hurriedly pulled full bags of mail and boxes full of packages from the inside cab of the mail truck and chucked them on the sidewalk and street. He then shoved his horn case and suitcase into the back of the cab. The mail carrier exited the apartment building and rounded the corner. He was at first stunned to see Jasper shoving his horn case and suitcase into the truck. "Hey," the worried and irate postman hollered. "Get the hell away from there!"

Jasper dove headfirst into the driver's seat, slammed the truck's gearshift into drive, and mashed the gas pedal as hard as he could. He grinned, relieved and guided by a glorious sense of obsessed destiny as he glanced in the rearview mirror to see the furious mailman flailing his hands about as he chased the truck. Jasper then careened around a corner and then steadied the mail truck onto the stark two-lane highway leading towards Mississippi, Alabama, and beyond.

Jasper drove all through the night and most of the next day. He, however, had to get gas and a map in order to find the Florida women's prison outside Ocala. He thus stopped at a black-owned station outside of Gainesville, just an hour north of Ocala, as the sun was sinking beyond the bucolic horizon. He diligently studied a map, but had a great deal of difficulty locating the women's prison, which he did not know the name of. He, however, finally did locate it after asking the kindly and elderly clerk manning the cashier's desk inside where to find it. Jasper then dutifully mapped the route out with a pencil. But just as Jasper was climbing back into the driver's seat, an Alachua County Sheriff Deputy pulled into the station. The Deputy aptly ascertained that something was amiss about this dapperly dressed young light-skinned black man driving a mail truck. "Are niggers even authorized to deliver mail round here?" the Deputy wondered as he set his hand atop the handle of service revolver tightly fastened in his holster. He then cautiously approached Jasper as the latter of the two fired up the engine to the truck.

"Hey there, boy," the surly and suspicious Deputy said as he approached the driver-side door. Jasper rolled the window all the way down with a dopey look on his face meant to be artifice to convince the cop that he was some empty-headed minstrel character. He simultaneously set the barrel of his pistol onto the windowsill while asking, "Hey there officer, why is the sky blue?"

Jasper then blasted three shots right into the Deputy's chest, which sent the lawmen stumbling back and instantly turning his insides to gushing mush. The poor bastard never knew what hit him. He fell flat on his back. His guts and entrails splattered atop the shiny white asphalt next to the bright red, black, and white Texaco gas pump. The Deputy's bulging and empty eyes stared at the early morning sky, which was clear blue but for the white and fluffy clouds. "One of them clouds looks like a vagina," was the final thought the man ever had.

The elderly and overall-clad clerk with cataracts who manned the counter inside the gas station hurried from it as fast as his tired, aching legs could carry him. He took some profound satisfaction in seeing the lawmen that had long harassed him, his family, and his patrons lying dead as the dirt. He spit out a wad of worn chewing tobacco that had long festered behind his bottom lip, and then went back into the store and took a long and fizzy sip from cool Coca-Cola bottle covered in humid condensation. He waited a moment before using the phone to call for help.

It was well after dark by the time Officer Stallworth, the guard who kept Scarlet as his pet, arrived back at the prison. The guard, who had downed a six-pack of Pabst Blue Ribbon in the parking lot in the span of a half-hour, lived just a few streets over from the correctional facility and thus had sauntered over wearing a wrinkled and sweat-stained seersucker suit, rather than his standard blue work-issued uniform. Stallworth cut a quite peculiar figure, especially considering that despite not wearing his uniform, his outfit on this fateful night did include his hostler and gun around his hip, cowboy boots on his feet, and a white Stetson atop his head.

The houses surrounding the prison were modest but nice; the residents tended to keep quiet and to themselves, except for the occasional sound of some resident's radios turned up too loud in this or that house.

Stallworth was tipsy by the time he passed a conspicuous mail truck parked around the corner from the prison with a sharply dressed young black man napping in the back of it.

"Ain't no niggers allowed to deliver mail round here," Stallworth was certain, "this coon must be here for Scarlet."

Stallworth confidently sauntered right into the prison, past a few of the night staff workers, more than half of whom were sleeping. He exuded the energy of a cat setting a trap for a rat. The inside of the prison was nearly completely dark. He wound his way through what seemed to be a labyrinth before finally arriving outside Scarlet's cell. He stared down at her a moment like a hawk watching a bunny. Scarlet sat up suddenly in her bunk out of breath, as if escaping from the nightmare. "It's late," she said somewhat drowsily, "I wasn't sure if you was gonna make it over tonight. I reckon I dozed off."

"Yeah, well," he smirked, burped and slurred, "daddy's home now."

"What time is it?" she asked while gazing out the window at the full moon bright in the North Florida sky.

"Time for you to die," he seethed as he unlocked the cell door, yanked it open, and slithered inside. "But first I'm gonna show you how a real man fucks a filthy little whore."

"A real man?" Scarlet was undaunted and rather amused.

"That nigger you wrote to is outside waitin' on you," Stallworth, who had been emasculated by her lack of fear, seethed. "I knew you was a whore all along, but I didn't know you was low enough to copulate with a nigger."

"I'm quite sure I don't have the slightest idea what you mean," Scarlet said as she scurried from the cot and looked excitedly out the window in the hopes of spotting Jasper on the sidewalk outside. Her wild and desperate eyes scanned up and down the street, but she did not see him. Stallworth, meanwhile, took his holster off and set it on the edge of the cot. He then unfastened his pants and let them drop around his ankles.

"Did you really think I wasn't gonna find out about you writin' a letter to some nigger to come spring you?" Stallworth was peeved to have had his intelligence insulted.

"I'm quite sure you're mistaken, daddy," she pleaded.

"I'm fixin' to kill ya," Stallworth said matter-of-factly while slightly chuckling, "then me and some of the boys are gonna string your nigger up and shove his dick down his throat until he chokes on it. We gonna have us a good ole timey necktie party with that nigger that come to 'save' you." He laughed.

"You don't lay one goddamn finger on him, ya hear!" Scarlet snarled as she turned from the window to stare Stallworth down; his semi-erect beans-n-frank looking penis protruded out from under his potbelly.

"Assume the position," Stallworth seethed.

"Not until I have your word that no harm will come to Jasper," she pleaded.

"This ain't no goddamn negotiation, darlin'," Stallworth sneered. "Here's what's gonna happen. First, you gonna assume the position like I dun taught you. Then, you gonna die. I'm gonna tie your bed sheet up yonder," he said while pointing to a thick metal bar atop the cell doors. "Then I'm gonna tie your neck to the other end. By tomorrow morning all anybody gonna remember about you is that you're the crazy bitch that dun killed all those pretty girls, then killed herself too. I already wrote your suicide note fer ya." He removed the letter from the breat pocket of his jacket, unfolded it, and dropped it atop the cot. "Far as I'm concerned, you'z already dead. So now you gonna assume the position and you may as well enjoy the last time you ever gonna feel any kind of sensual pleasure again in this lifetime. Option two is, I could just kill ya then have my way with ya. Either way, the story ends with you and that nigger hangin' by your goddamn miscegenationist necks, followed by an eternity of hellfire."

Scarlet wanted to cry, but did not dare give Stallworth the satisfaction as she pulled her black and white striped nightgown off her otherwise nude body. She then got down onto both knees, put her hands behind her back, and opened her mouth wide as if about to receive Holy Communion. Stallworth stood over her masturbating a moment. It, however, took him quite a while to become fully erect. The more he concentrated, the more difficult it was to get hard. He finally placed his somewhat erect penis in her mouth. "That's a good girl, now," he said while patting her on the head like she were a golden retriever. "Now squeeze my balls in there too now," he slurred. She compliantly cupped his balls. But then she, as if acting on instinct, bit down as hard as she could and snarled.

He screamed and crowed so loud that the sound of his agony echoed all through the prison and woke a number of inmates and handful of guards. Those inmates that had been likewise assailed by Stallworth gained some measure of satisfaction by the dire sounds of his manhood being removed.

Scarlet then stood suddenly and spit Stallworth's penis from her blood-soaked mouth.

She then jabbed the small pencil she used to write letters up into Stallworth's nostril, and then scrambled to the edge of the cot where she snatched the pistol from his holster. She fired one devastating round into his left eye, which left a bloody crater where his face had once existed. He writhed and gargled on his own blood while lying flat on his back as Scarlet hurried to pull her blood-and-brain splattered gown onto her trembling but exhilarated body. She pried the keyring from off his belt, then hurried past a number of other cells containing inmates who hooted, hollered, and pleaded to be set free.

She cautiously made her way through the maze, then finally towards the front of the prison, where she was confronted by another guard who was white-knuckling a double barrel-shotgun. "Come hell or high water," Scarlet explained to the terribly scared guard, "I'm walking out of here. You can either survive your shift, and then go about livin' a normal albeit pathetic existence," she bargained, "or I can kill you right here and now. It's your choice. But ain't nothin' on God's green earth keepin' me in this goddamn prison one more night, ya hear?"

"Drop the weapon now." The horrified guard pleaded as his finger flicked the safety button off. "I don't wanna kill nobody. But I will if I haft a."

Scarlet was offended that the man had the temerity to threaten her. Besides, she had no qualms about exterminating another human being's life. She thus shot him square in the chest. His shotgun fired. A bit of buckshot tore into Scarlet's thigh.

Jasper woke suddenly as a result of the hollow but jarring sound of the gunfire inside the prison. He sat up quickly, and then nervously scanned out the windows of the mail truck.

He then cautiously clicked the safety on his own rusty revolver into the fire-when-ready position while stealthily climbing from the back of the truck. He rounded the corner on foot and slowly approached the prison with his pistol leading the way.

Inside the prison, Scarlet could hear other guards hollering and approaching from behind. But she focused on finding the right key with which to open the main door to the exterior wall of the prison. Other guards got closer and closer with each key she tried. She fired another haphazard round back behind her in the hopes of pinning the approaching guards down a while and buying a bit more time.

She finally located the magic key that opened the door. Her bare dragged atop the concrete and she stumbled along the sidewalk. "Scarlet!" Jasper hollered as she raced towards him. She was sobbing as they embraced. Time, space, and matter seemed to blur around them as they embraced.

The sound of a gun blast, however, shattered the stillness of the desolation of the rural Florida night. Jasper grabbed onto Scarlet's trembling hand and led her around the corner to the mail truck. He hopped into the driver's seat as she slid into the front-passenger seat. He fired up the ignition, and pulled a very sharp U-turn away from the prison. Two guards gave chase. One of them fired a round, but the bullet missed the truck. Scarlet was wild-eyed but happy as she peered back at the two guards getting smaller and smaller as the truck sped away.

"Hollywood, California, here we come," Jasper hooted and hollered.

"We need to go south before we go west," Scarlet said.

"How come?" Jasper wondered.

"I got a score to settle in Pahokee," she declared determinedly. "Besides, I figure it might be wiser to take a ship from the Port of Miami to Panama, than from Panama to California. It's too risky to drive all the way west. Every cop from here to the Pacific will be looking for us along the road to California."

"You see," he smiled wide, "this is why I love you so much – brains and beauty."

"Can't nothin' stop us now," she declared.

One thousand miles to the north, Special Agent Gallo, his mother and his two sons were huddled around the dining room table. All were singing "happy birthday," except Gallo's wife, who seemed poised to blow out the candles planted in buttercream frosting atop the cake in front of her. The phone blared about halfway through the rendition. Gallo hurried from the room to answer it. His wife secretly wished that her husband would make a better effort to spend more quality time with his family and less time concerning himself with his work. She then blew out the candles. Her affability, however, was significantly diminished by her husband's animated concern. "I'll get down there as soon as I can," she, whose English was improving but still not great, was sure she heard him declare. "Send a team to the Port of Miami," he demanded, "I have a feeling they will go south rather than west. The Port is quickest way out of the country."

He then hurried upstairs and fast shoved clothes and toiletries into a suitcase, then ran back downstairs where he was confronted by his wife at the staircase adjacent the foyer. She impeded his path to the front door of the house. "I'm sorry," he pleaded. "The killer, that little girl from Florida who I told you about, broke out of prison. Mr. Flynn has requested that I get back to Miami at once."

"Well," she said while nodding somewhat disconsolately and in garbled broken English, "why don't you take a piece of cake with you?"

"Really, mi amor," he said, "I can't. I'm already racing the clock as is."

"No," she said flatly while trudging into the dining room, where her mother-in-law and sons were hunched over waiting rather impatiently for their sweet treat. She cut a piece and placed it atop a shiny blue plate, "I insist." Her words were garbled.

She then hurried back into the foyer where her husband was sliding his arm into an overcoat. She smashed the piece of cake into his face as her baffled and somewhat amused children looked on with great interest. Gallo's mother was, however, not even slightly amused. She darted up from the dining room table and slapped her daughter-in-law hard across the face, which sparked a terrible scuffle, that, due to the fact that Gallo was preoccupied wiping buttercream and angel cake from his tear soaked eyes, the eldest boy was forced to break up.

"It's alright, momma," Gallo hollered as he wiped a bit of buttercream from chin and necktie. "My wife simply does not understand all of the incredible sacrifices I have made to keep her safe from the evil in the world, never mind provide for her and her children," his hand lashed frosting onto the finely polished hardwood floor. He then charged into the foyer, snatched his suitcase up from off the rug, departed the house, and hurried down the porch steps as fast as his legs could carry him. The anger in Gallo's wife turned to tearful despair as she cleaned the cake up from the hardwood floor in the foyer.

Edmund had yet to be apprised of the fact that his daughter had escaped from the women's correctional facility outside Ocala as he delivered his Sunday sermon. He, however, ironically urged his congregation to not demonize one member of a family if another member of the same family was evil. He used Cain versus Abel as an example, which seemed to sink into all the congregants save one – his wife, who was sitting in a back pew. She stared disconsolately at the vibrant stained-glass depiction of Mother Mary cradling her son, Christ the Redeemer, as he wept and bled to death in order to save the world from the sins of her husband and daughter. A bulbous tear fell from her cheek. She did not bother to wipe it. But nobody noticed her anymore anyway. Edmund then berated his congregants for their increased parsimony in recent weeks when the collection baskets had been passed. More than a few of the worshippers resisted the urge to roll their eyes. Edmund and his wife had fallen on harder times financially since Scarlet's conviction. Many parishioners had left the congregation; a few had quit God altogether.

Edmund was thus especially keen to keep new parishioners when they did visit the church. So after communion and Edmund's especially verbose final rites had mercifully concluded, the pastor kindly requested that a young family comprised of a husband that was a lawyer, a wife who was his clerk, and a surly sixteen-year-old daughter upset about being forced to change schools, over for Sunday supper in the hopes of keeping what Edmund assumed were big money congregants as part of the fledgling flock.

"Y'all sure you don't want any pie?" Scarlet's mother hollered to Gloria, the daughter, as the latter perused pictures in the living room, bored while her parents, Lisa and Herbert, drank coffee with Edmund in the dining room.

"No ma'am," Gloria, who wore a pretty lemon-yellow sundress, politely hollered back. "Thank y'all anyhow."

"What made you move from Macon to Pahokee?" Edmund, who was sitting at the head of the dining room table, asked while lighting his post-dinner Chesterfield with a matchstick.

"Politically speakin', I'm Progressive," Gloria's father explained while exhaling a plume of smoke, the layers of which seemed to morph and fold under the shabby chandelier hanging over the dining table. "Now," he added, "I know everyone said the war killed Progressivism. But I'm a big believer that activism is needed more than ever just now. I was makin' good money in Macon. But these migrants that work the fields out here, they got nobody lookin' after them, really. I figure it was put up or shut up time, so I closed my practice in Macon and decided to set up a shop round here offerin' to help defend the workers' basic human rights. All the lawyers down here seem to be on the side of management and the the workers needed somebody, anybody, lookin' after their interests."

"They got Herbert," Lisa smiled, "God help em all."

"Truth be told, Gloria hates me and her pa for making her move away from all her friends and teachers," Lisa chimed in. "But in time, I hope she'll see that we did the right thing not just for us, and her, but for all mankind."

Gloria, who was eavesdropping, rolled her eyes and smirked as though her mother was completely daft.

"That all sounds a little red, if you ask me," Edmund sneered.

"You see," Herbert smiled charmingly as he leaned towards Edmund, "this is the problem with the country right now; any time anyone talks about upliftin' the poorest amongst us we are labeled Bolshevik."

"Well," Edmund chortled condescendingly, "if it walks like a duck and talks like a duck."

"Alright now fellas," Michelle said while placing a piece of pecan pie atop her shiniest and whitest China in an effort to ease the mounting tension.

"Who's this?" Gloria hollered in from the next room while gazing down at a picture she held in her soft and delicate hands. Scarlet's mother quickly set two more pieces of pecan pie atop her finest China, then set them down on the table in front of her guests. She then poked her head from the dining room into the living room. There, Gloria stared down, spellbound at Scarlet's portrait. The heart inside Michelle's chest sunk and stopped for just an instant.

"Oh," Michelle's voice dropped an octave due to deeply harbored despair, "That's my little girl, Scarlet."

"Where's she at?" Gloria, as teenagers are wont to do in new places where they are bored, prodded.

"She lives up near Ocala," Michelle reluctantly admitted.

"What's she doing up in Ocala?" Gloria insisted.

"Say," Edmund shrewdly interjected as he stood up abruptly from the table, "I know y'all got lots of peaches and pecans up in Macon," he said, "but I reckon you don't get to see many citrus groves up yonder. We got us a beauty right out back here. What's say we go pick us some winners. Y'all ever had a glass fresh squeezed orange juice before?"

"We're right in the middle of havin' pie and coffee," Michelle said peevishly, "set on down a while."

"To hell with the pie," Edmund defied. "Can't you see the girl is bored nearly half to death? Some fresh South Florida air might perk her up a bit." He looked intently at Michelle and said, "what'd ya say, darlin', ya up for a walk in the orange grove?"

"Why not?" she shrugged, "it's cooled off a bit I reckon now that it's almost twilight."

"We'll bring y'all back some fine oranges," Edmund smiled at Gloria's affable parents, "then make y'all some fresh juice as a house-warmin' present."

Scarlet's momma was sickened and terrified. "Now, I insist, let's finish our coffee and pie. Then we'll all go together."

"Nonsense," Edmund's voice grew stern as he opened the front door leading out onto the porch, "the girl said she don't want any of your damn pie, woman, now let it alone." He forced a cordial smile, but the guests, including Gloria, had clearly gown a bit uneasy by the tense exchange between the hosts. "Don't worry," Edmund added in an attempt to quell the tension. "We'll be back before dark."

Michelle paused ever so slightly and then followed Edmund from the house and out onto the porch. The sun had half set beyond the western horizon. A mail truck with smoke and fumes spewing from the tailpipe fast approached from a hundred yards away. Edmund did not notice. The phone rang.

"Excuse me," Michelle sighed, and then hurried into the kitchen to answer the phone. She listened intently to the receiver placed to her ear. Her face contorted in a complex and concerned way, as if some odd mixture of happy, sad, and scared. She dropped the phone atop the wood floor in the kitchen and then sprinted from the house.

"It's Scarlet!" Michelle blurted the second she stepped onto the porch.

Edmund was nearly to the sidewalk, but turned face his obviously concerned wife. "She's dead?" Edmund asked as though he had long anticipated being told that his daughter's life had ended. Michelle was sure she detected a twinge of hope in his tone.

"She escaped," Michelle's voice shrieked. "The Sheriff said the FBI thinks she might be headed here or Miami."

The mail truck skid to a halt adjacent the sidewalk, less than ten feet from where Edmund seemed to be having trouble processing the information he had just received from his hysterical wife.

"Hi daddy," Scarlet said as she stepped determinedly from the cab of the truck with Stallworth's chrome revolver aimed squarely at Edmund's chest. "Bye, daddy," she said just before unloading a white blast of deadening hot and heavy lead into her father's chest. Bright red innards and blood splattered all over Gloria's face and lemon yellow summer dress. Her horrified parents scurried onto the porch to see Edmund fall straight onto his back. Scarlet's mom wanted to run into the house as her daughter began to approach, but was, like Michelle and her parents, terrified stiff.

Scarlet, due to the buckshot wound in her leg, limped and winced, as though agonized up onto the porch, where she gave her mom a gentle and warm hug and kiss on her cheek. "You're welcome," Scarlet whispered into her mother's ear. She then twirled the gun like she were Annie Oakley performing in *Buffalo Bill Cody's Wild West Show*, and then planted the pistol firmly in Stallworth's holster, which fit very loosely around her waist. "I'll send for you when I'm famous," she promised her momma.

Scarlet then raced down the porch steps toward the idling mail truck. Jasper floored the gas pedal the second Scarlet was back in the cab. Scarlet did not bother to look back. What would be the point?

Michelle hurried back into the house and frantically picked up the receiver to the rotary phone she had left dangling in order to investigate the commotion on the front lawn.

Gloria and her family, meanwhile, hurried into the family sedan as if fleeing a robbery. "Guess Pahokee's gonna need a new pastor," Herbert, who had always been adroit at stating the obvious, said as his right foot smashed down on the gas pedal. He aimed the car in the opposite direction from that which the mail truck had gone. His wife and daughter slowly and disconsolately nodded their heavy heads, oddly entranced by the horror they had seen.

Gallo was bundled in a leather aviator jacket and wore dark goggles. He was hunkered down in the seat in front of the pilot of a small biplane made of little more than cloth and wood. The Expeditionary Force had taken to using these planes as surveillance tools during the war. Dozens of them were sent home afterwards, a few of which were purchased surplus by the FBI. Gallo glared into binoculars a few hundred feet down at the Dixie Highway, which was an engineering marvel that made getting to from Montreal to Miami much cheaper and faster than by rail, at least for auto owners.

Gallo spotted the small white mail truck speeding towards town south of Lake Okeechobee. Peering through his binoculars, he noticed some billfolds flutter from the back of the truck. Gallo's excitement was, however, fast transformed into dismay the moment he noticed a roadblock set up at the Miami city limit that consisted of two Dade County Sheriff's Office patrol cars that comprised a makeshift barricade. The mail truck blasted right into the frontend of both cars, but managed to push them apart, squeeze through, and keep on rolling along into the city of Miami.

It was high-noon when Gallo worriedly demanded that the pilot set the plane down at the newly built Cedar Key Air Station as fast as could be safely managed. The pilot nodded compliantly; the plane then dropped steadily as a stone falling to the bottom of pond.

The air station was a short drive from the newly built port, where Scarlet and Jasper planned to catch the first ship bound for Panama. The fact that the mail truck had been slowed by the collision at the city limit provided Gallo a bit extra time to ready for what he was sure would be an epic confrontation at the port's entrance.

Gallo finally arrived at the entrance gate to the port in a car chauffeured by the man who had been piloting the airplane. Dozens of G-men had been summoned to the location. There was also a submachinegun mounted onto a bulky tripod and a man eagerly gripping onto the handle next to another fully capable man more than eager to feed .44-calber bullets into the same brand of death-making machine that had killed millions during the war.

Gallo was especially pleased that Scarlet was fast approaching the ambush. The mail truck careened around the corner and aimed at the blockade. Gallo's sanguine demeanor diminished greatly as he noticed that the mail truck was being fast pursued by Beauregard.

One of the bullets tore into the back-right tire of the mail truck, which sent it swerving and then smashing into the blockade. The submachinegun behind the barricade fired wildly. Dozens of bullets ripped into the cop car trailing the mail truck, which then crashed into some of the G-men hunkered down behind the barricade at the entrance to the port. Beauregard, whose face was shredded by the windshield, was killed on impact. His head ended up fifteen feet away from the rest of his body.

Gallo had taken cover behind the barricade and barely missed being run over by Beauregard's car. When he finally lifted his head out from under his hands, he noticed that Jasper was nowhere to be seen. Scarlet was, however, hopping on one leg yet dazedly towards a massive black steamship floating in the harbor. The buckshot wound in her leg was unbearable. Blood oozing from a gash on her forehead seeped into her eyes, which obscured her vision. Stallworth's holster and pistol fit so loosely around her hip that she was forced to hold it against her torso, which exacerbated her slow and halting hops.

"Stop right there!" Gallo demanded. Scarlet, who was wincing in agony, ignored the order and began to slowly ascend the gangplank leading up to the ship, dragging her wounded leg behind her all the way. "Young lady," Gallo ordered, "don't you dare take another step or I will shoot you dead." Scarlet finally turned around and stared blankly at him through blood-soaked eyes. "Put the pistol on the deck," he instructed, "then put your hands in the air and walk slowly."

Scarlet winced as she planted both feet firmly in the ground. She then fast snatched the pistol from the holster around her waist and fired a shot, just as she had seen the cowboys do it in the movies. It was, however, not nearly fast enough to beat the speed of Gallo's finely trained trigger finger. The heavy and hot blast knocked Scarlet off her feet and into the harbor. The saltwater washed the blood from her eyes, which stared up at the sky as the sun soaked into her porcelain skin. She then sunk underneath the surface. Air bubbles fluttered to the murky surface. Other agents rushed towards the sound of gunfire. A few congratulated Gallo on a job well done while others jumped into the harbor to retrieve Scarlet's body. Though Gallo cordially thanked the well-wishers for their kind words, he was by no means beaming with a semblance of accomplishment. That was in large part due to the fact that Jasper was still unaccounted for.

When Jasper woke soon after the mail truck crashed into the barricade, his head was pounding as though having been squeezed inside a vice. His weary and dazed eyes gazed confusedly over to see Scarlet covered in blood and trembling like a newborn baby. She was also unconscious. He was certain she would soon be dead. Scarlet then woke suddenly, as if from a nightmare. She had just enough sense to know she needed to catch the ship in the distance. She thus pried open the door and staggered from the car without saying goodbye to Jasper. He was somewhat relieved to see that the lawmen who had survived the crash was all too consumed with following and apprehending her.

Though he was severely concussed, Jasper had just enough of his wits intact to know that if he stayed, he was as good as dead. He thus grabbed his horn case, the bag of billfolds, and his pistol from the backseat of what remained of the mail truck and set off on foot into a nearby thicket of woods leading southwest towards Lemon City, where he hoped he might be able to hide out a while.

He dazedly meandered through thick shrubs, pine trees, mangroves, and dense bogs all through the day. Within an hour, Gallo was back in the plane scouring for the runaway fugitive. But Jasper was wise to stay in forests and groves and avoid the dirt roads as he ran.

Dusk had settled over South Florida by the time he found himself in a vast orange grove that seemed to stretch further than the horizon. Since the shadows were thick and heavy and he could no longer hear the motor of Gallo's plane circling overhead, he momentarily felt secure enough to stop moving a while in order to nourish himself with an orange. As he rested, he spotted a quaint cottage wedged near the southern-most edge of the property. He feared that the residents would report him to the law if they found him. He thus decided to keep running for a short spell, hoping to make it to Lemon City or Miccosukee land by daybreak, where he hoped he could receive help hiding out from the Feds.

But as he ran away from the cottage, the earth suddenly collapsed out from under his feet and swallowed him whole. He fell more than sixty feet into a sinkhole that he stood no chance of ever climbing out of without aid. The violent impact of the collapse and fall caused several of his ribs to shatter. The pain of which caused him to lose consciousness.

He slept through the night. His eyes did not open again until a midday ray of sun had settled on his pained face. When he woke, he noticed a small, dark red, and cherubic-faced Miccosukee boy wearing a big straw hat and blue denim overalls peering over the edge of the cavernous crater down at him. A basket full of freshly picked oranges was tucked tight under the boy's pudgy arm.

"Please, sonny," Jasper grunted and wheezed as though he was suffering terrible agony, "I need help. Is there any Indian or black folk in the vicinity that can get me a rope and help lug me out of this infernal pit?"

The curious boy was all of a sudden frightened. He dropped his basket of oranges and darted away. One of the oranges rolled and then fell into the crater. Jasper, who was dehydrated, was desperate for nourishment and thus snatched the orange and tore into the rind with his teeth. Juice spewed down his chin onto his sweat-soaked, torn, and tattered shirt. He was starving and thus had never tasted anything so sweet in all his life. But all the while he ate, his wide and aggrieved eyes stared helplessly up at the sky. "Little boy," he pleaded, "are you there?" But no reply was returned.

Dark gray and pregnant with rainstorm clouds began to form overhead by late afternoon. Jasper feared that if the frightened boy bothered to return at all, he would surely return with agents of the law or a lynch mob, rather than a black advocate with a rope long and thick enough for him to climb out of the godforsaken hole in the earth that had devoured him.

The rain poured all night long. By morning, Jasper was almost completely underwater. By dawn, only his head could be spotted above the surface of the pond that had mired him. The rain mercifully stopped by mid-morning, which spared the horn player his life. He was desperate to find a way to survive, so tried to climb his way up and out of the cavern. But the slick soil and rocks, coupled with his badly injured ribs and limbs made it impossible for Jasper to make any progress. He thus resigned himself to death.

Then, as if the voice of an angel, the horn player heard a familiar man ask, "Jasper, is that you?" He held his hand over his forehead to block out intense midday sun rays shining down on him. He wondered at first if he was hallucinating seeing Emory, flat on his belly, staring down at him. The little Miccosukee boy stood next to his adopted father, gazing down at Jasper. "What in God's name are you doing in this damn hole in the ground?" Emory queried.

"Dyin', I think," Jasper winced and wheezed. "I'm hurt real bad. I'm wonderin' if this is the grave God made for me for all the heinous sins I committed."

"Shush now," Emory chortled. "You hang in there a while. We gonna get you out of there by nightfall." Emory crawled back to the cottage on his belly and pulled himself up into his wheelchair. "Quinn," he hollered into the window, "call some of the men and get them down here. Tell em to bring the longest rope they can find."

Jasper vowed then and there to serve Jesus for the rest of his days on God's green earth. Then a diamondback rattlesnake fell out of a nearby orange tree and wiggled into the sinkhole.